THE LORMES
OF CASTLE RISING

FANNY CRADOCK

THE LORMES OF CASTLE RISING

Saturday Review Press | E. P. Dutton & Co., Inc.
New York

ISBN: 0-8415-0437-7
Library of Congress Catalog Card Number: 76-358

TO JOHNNIE

because we can both echo Justin
Aynthorp's *'vale'* . . . *'je t'aime et je ne regrette rien.'*

JILL

Acknowledgment

The author wishes to express her very great gratitude to her colleagues in the *Daily Telegraph* Information Offices for their infinite patience in researching information for this book during a period of over three years.

Contents

The Family from 1907 descendin

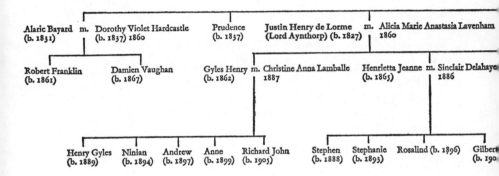

Alaric Bayard m. Dorothy Violet Hardcastle   Prudence   Justin Henry de Lorme   m. Alicia Marie Anastasia Lavenham
(b. 1831)   (b. 1837) 1860   (b. 1837)   (Lord Aynthorp) (b. 1827)   1860

Robert Franklin   Damien Vaughan   Gyles Henry m. Christine Anna Lamballe   Henrietta Jeanne m. Sinclair Delahaye
(b. 1861)   (b. 1867)   (b. 1862)   1887   (b. 1865)   1886

Henry Gyles   Ninian   Andrew   Anne   Richard John   Stephen   Stephanie   Rosalind (b. 1896)   Gilbert
(b. 1889)   (b. 1894) (b. 1897) (b. 1899) (b. 1905)   (b. 1888) (b. 1893)   (b. 190

rom Justin, Lord Aynthorp

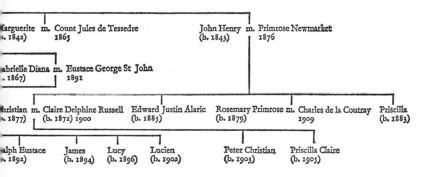

Marguerite m. Count Jules de Tessedre   John Henry m. Primrose Newmarket
(b. 1842)   1865   (b. 1843)   1876

abrielle Diana m. Eustace George St John
(b. 1867)   1891

Christian m. Claire Delphine Russell   Edward Justin Alaric   Rosemary Primrose m. Charles de la Coutray   Priscilla
(b. 1877)   (b. 1872) 1900   (b. 1885)   (b. 1879)   1909   (b. 1883)

alph Eustace   James   Lucy   Lucien   Peter Christian   Priscilla Claire
(b. 1892)   (b. 1894)   (b. 1896)   (b. 1902)   (b. 1903)   (b. 1905)

Author's Foreword

I began this book in 1966. The name I gave to the Lorme castle just walked into my mind. I wrote just over 25,000 words and then set it aside owing to other commitments.

Many months later our friend Miss Alison Leach, who had been our personal assistant for many years, came down to see us and announced, 'I suppose you know there *is* a Castle Rising in Norfolk!' She showed us a little guide book which she had found in which it was mentioned. We subsequently discovered it marked on a modern map, just above North Wootton and a few miles from King's Lynn; but as it is no longer inhabited and is, in fact, a ruin, I decided to retain the name since it had by now become inseparable from my thinking on this book. In the original ms I had sited my Castle Rising on the edge of the Blakeney Marshes because of the Viking Funeral.[1] The original Castle Rising then turned out to be only twenty-six miles from Blakeney!

When I resumed work on this book in the winter of 1972–3 I decided to help myself to my own family history from 1064 in Normandy to the 1800s in England. By then I was in possession of some ancient family data which took me into Essex on numerous explorations which were relevant to records showing that a certain Sir Gilbert de Peche, Bart.—a Norman—settled in this country in the eleventh century. The records stated 'Peche was the name of a considerable family who owned many manors hereabouts.' So I resited my Castle Rising on an eminence above one of these.

I then discovered that the dictionary definition of *péché* is 'sin, trespass, transgression'; if however this is made plural—*les péchés capitaux*—it becomes in translation 'the deadly sins'. Small wonder then that Sir Gilbert de Peche is recorded as 'sometimes called "*Peccatum*" meaning sin in abstract "for he was a verie naughtie fellowe" '!

[1] See p. 17.

This settled for me—as any reader who fights his way through this book will appreciate—that from then onwards I would plagiarise certain aspects of my own family for certain Lorme characteristics. Later I gave the Lormes the Peche crest, an astrolabe,[2] and the arms of our Norman ancestor Sir Gilbert. In fact, the earlier Lorme 'runts' are Peche 'runts'; but those who come after the 1800s are entirely my own creation and bear no relation whatsoever to any person or persons either living or dead.

Des Cotils   FANNY CRADOCK
Jersey, C.I.

[2] An old instrument for taking altitudes.

CHAPTER I

Henri de Lorme

Henri de Lorme was the fourth son of Edouard, Count of Normandy, who was despatched by an arrow in the spleen one year and three months before his master invaded Saxon England.

The family was not hard put to reconcile itself to its bereavement, for Edouard's had been an overworked spleen. Indeed, as his Relict confided to her ladies when they resumed work upon yet another tapestry, 'It was always a trifle more restful when my lord was abroad upon the Duke's lawful fighting occasions.'

Having thus pronounced her late husband's requiem, the Lady Mathilde called her seven sons to council. She began by addressing her first-born, who was likewise named Edouard, as 'My Lord' thus establishing her willingness to approve, as well as accept, his seigneury of their small castle. After which she confided to his safe-keeping the truss of keys which her irreverent progeny had dared swear her ladyship lodged upon her chastity belt when her spouse was away at the wars.

She then gave the rest of the brood the benefit of her opinions. Gervais, her second son, she was soon done with, dismissing him as a 'frippet', a 'missish thing tangled, like a chittering starling, with a brood of shrill-voiced, scented demoiselles in breeches'.

Number three then received a warm and courteous dismissal. 'As the sworn property of the Mother Church and our good Bishop, you, Bayard, are honourably bespoke.'

Whereupon she gave a heave to her small, portly person and petticoats which plainly declared she was now embarking upon her *moutons*.

Launching herself, with a sharp glance at the rest, she then gave number four her attention and his marching orders saying, 'Thus it falls upon you, Henri, to replace your father's sword in the service of His Grace', a title she uttered as though her mouth were rinsed with alum, for, like all her equals and contemporaries, the earthy combination of tannery and bastardy were not calculated to please, and both she and they still privately considered William of Normandy to be an 'upstart'.

Henri—sprawled at ease beside the embrasure, the scent from his Mama's apricocks gratifying his nostrils—remained silent until the general audience was concluded. Then, with ritual honoured and his three younger brothers despatched about their home-based affairs (Gyles to his books and tutor, Alain and Geoffroy to their affianced), he asked quietly 'I would know, madam, if His Grace is appraised of our intention?'

'This twelve month,' snapped Lady Mathilde. 'Knowing your father's predilection for *mêlées* we planned according when His Grace last visited.'

Henri's mouth twitched slightly as he rose and stretched. 'I see, I should have comprehended,' he said wryly. 'And therefore there is nought else to be said?'

Her ladyship looked up sharply. 'Pray what else should be said in the line of lawful conduct and duty to your House?' she said tartly and was repayed by the brief reply, 'Naught, Mama. I thank you.'

Seven days later Henri's horse trotted him across the draw-bridge in the van of an adequate, if not lavish, retinue and there-after only a handful of ill-writ, misspelled missives gave news of him until the traditional fanfare proclaimed his return.

As the Castle's châtelaine confided later to her confidante, the Comte de Valaise's widow, 'Henri has become obsessed by That Man in one short year and all his talk is of his bastard-achievings. It is all Duke William's archers and this flaxen-haired Saxon called Harold Godwineson, of whose mishaps I am a-wearied.'

On being pressed by her news-avid crony she further vouch-safed: 'It seems this Saxon was shipwrecked off our coast at Ponthieu and held by Count Guy for ransom, chained and under the threat of torture should the English not meet his demands. So far as I can ascertain the Duke, being Guy of Ponthieu's *suzerain*, then exercised his right—as ever he does—and bade Count Guy render up the Earl to him forthwith "*sur peine de cors et d'avoir*".'

The Lady Mathilde paused, frowned a little and said more slowly, in the throes of what her descendants might one day describe as 'putting two and two together', 'Indeed, Judith, now that I come to reflect, I am of the mind that some great thing is afoot which somewhat nearly comes to fruition.'

'What thing?' her companion pressed.

Lady Mathilde shook her head. 'I cannot name it yet but it stirs in my mind with growing conviction.' She took up her tapestry once more and began to ply the needle to and fro. 'It seems,' she resumed, 'that when Guy surrendered up his hostage Duke William housed him nobly and supplied him with many amusing diversions. Side by side they hunted deer with those leaping greyhounds of his, fleeting them out to bring down the wounded deer . . . He commanded joustings at which this Harold acquitted himself somewhat nobly and there was talk of his having instructed the Duke's knights in the outlandish Saxon method of fighting with great axes—his own too heavy for our kith and kin to wield! There was talk also of the Saxon's mighty strength . . . of how Duke William invited him to accompany him in suppressing those wretched Bretons—such an idea! He even gave him a company to command and Henri babbles of how the Saxon saved some bowman's wretched life at mighty risk to his own and is come to be thought a hero by our soldiery. Yet, although Henri said not so, the Saxon has but exchanged a prison cell for another prison-in-luxury and goes not abroad on any of these ploys save followed by the spies of his Grace of Normandy. I asked Henri, oh yes I did! I said, "What means the Duke for this Saxon lion? Is it for England to cede rule to him?" Henri just closed up his lips and looked away; but England *is* the heart of the matter I am assured, aie! That upstart tanner's son burns with vaunting ambition.'

While the women gossiped and conjectured, Henri busied himself about the estate and visited his wedded brothers. During this same period Harold Godwineson went with Duke William to Rouen and swore the fatal oath across the dead saint's bones. He then departed for his own shores, wed to Adela, William's child and forsworn of the English crown. Then for a spell William was quiet and few rumours drifted to the small castle on the hill.

'I will send word,' the Duke had assured Henri, 'so take this rare chance and go home awhile, *Sir* Henri.' Henri had looked up in astonishment at his black-haired master. William just nodded. The next day he dubbed him and sent him about his private occasions.

Of this too the Lady Mathilde had expressed her views. 'Alack!' she cried out when Henri acquainted her of his knight-hood, 'what pity that you were not gentilhomme-dubbed, my poor knightling!'

During Henri's sojourn and despite his mama's well-nigh un-ladylike manoeuvring to get him wed, he rode off again un-trammelled, when the Duke's summons came at last and, turning his bay's head in the direction of the Normandy beaches, dined off *Tripe à la Mode de Caen*[1] at William's eve-of-invasion banquet.

Though of French birth, this was to be his last night upon his native soil. He was destined to become the first of the English de Lormes.

When the Archbishop held the golden Crown of England above Duke William's head in the Abbey of St Peter's, Westminster, Henri was still in attendance. He was within a pace or two of his lord—as he had been throughout that grim voyage—when the *Mora* ground on to the shingle at Pevensea; when the Duke leapt, stumbled and fell, but, instantly recovering, seized a handful of those same pebbles and holding them aloft claimed in a ringing voice *seisin*, for all to hear, of the England he had yet to conquer. Henri was likewise present, standing within Duke William's tent at Hastings when Harold's arrow-pierced body was borne in at the Duke's express command and Henri also rode within call throughout the long march on London.

During that march he met many Saxons and witnessed them come to the Duke to pay their homage before the Crown of England was held above that black head. Henri was indeed in such company as was far greater than he and older too, for almost every man among them could give him several years; but the Duke had desired his presence and thus had seen to it that such was brought about. This was when Henri came to know well such great Normans as were also companions to the Duke throughout; among them the Lord of St Cler and Gualecheline de Ferriers.

[1] The great Norman classic made with six kinds of tripe and with Calvados, cooked in what looks remarkably like a lidded earthenware flying saucer called a *Tripière*. The author had the honour of being installed *Grande Dame de la Tripière d'Or et de la Gastronomie Normande* at the annual Tripe Festival in Caen in 1957.

It was in the company of such chivalry that the young Norman came upon his destiny.

Their march had brought them to Essex. They had encamped for the night. The Duke's tent was raised and he ensconced with, for a marching man, a certain sumptuousness. His scouts, having gone before him, had found provender, slain a deer, and indeed the board was set and he about to take his place centrally when a truncated fanfare sounded without, and after it some scuffling. Then, handfasted by two Normans, a herald appeared, struggling, in the tent aperture.

'And pray what brings about this unseemly scrabbling?' enquired the Duke a-sprawl, goblet in hand, swirling the golden thing between his fingers, relaxed and seeming only idly interested. The youthful herald gasped out between his captors: 'I am but come to announce a nobleman who would render his allegiance, and thus was I roughly set upon.'

'Loose him,' the Duke commanded, 'advance, boy, and name thy lord.' But before the lad could speak the tent flap parted once again and a vast, fair man strode in. One sight of him and the Duke spoke, marvelling, 'How thou art like Harold in stature *messire*, pray how art called?' Ere the man could make reply Henri's sword flashed out and swung between the Duke and the intruder. 'Nay, Henri,' rebuked William, without turning his gaze from the incomer, 'what would an unarmed gentleman need of violence who offers none himself?' and Henri, flushing, put up his sword and in parlous English stammered his apologies while the rest of the assembled company watched in a silence jarred only by the herald's panting breath.

'I am called Cnut the Dane,' spake the giant. 'I am descendant of that most mighty Cnut who built the stronghold y'clept Danbury when my forbears ruled these parts under the late Saxon monarchs and in time rose to rule as Master of this whole kingdom.' The speaker bent his knee. 'And now I, the present Lord of Danbury, am come to render my homage to the future King of England.'

William stretched out his hand. Danbury touched brow to it then rose and spake again, unsheathing his sword and proffering it, hilt forward. 'If you, my lord, accept the Sword of Danbury then pray accept the hospitality of Danbury also. My castle is at your disposal. My men would rally to your cause. I and my lady would like to have you and your attendant gentlemen feast at our board this night.' For the first time Danbury's grim countenance relaxed and a faint smile flickered at the corners of his mouth. 'Indeed, Sire, we can also couch you in a manner somewhat more fitting, if such be your wish.'

The Duke rose smilingly. 'Right gladly, my Lord Danbury, will we sup with you this night and drink at the board of so *puissant* a new associate,' he accepted with some grace, 'but it is ever my way in battle to sleep amongst my archers and my chivalry. For this I crave your pardon, yet so am I sworn. For the rest,' he whipped his cloak up and swung it across his shoulders, *'en avant, messires.'* He glanced about him, paused, then threw back the command, *'et sieve qui puet!'*[2]

Then flinging back the further command, 'Henri, accompany me,' William himself drew back the tent flap and signalled to Danbury to pass him out. Striding alongside, the fair head and the dark moved down the slope and thence to Danbury Castle, St Cler and de Ferriers at their heels and Henri among the further gentlemen who followed.

For so long as Henri lived he was ever able to close his eyes and see the re-enactment of that night ... the lowered portcullis illumined by the high-held, flaming brands ... Duke William bending graciously above the extended fingers of the Castle's châtelaine, the Lady Gyda ... the Great Hall into which the company swept, the fresh-laid rushes rustling under their tread ... and finally a small face, framed in a *couvre-chef*, lifted to his as he heard William's voice saying formally, 'By your leave my Lady, may I now present Sir Henri de Lorme to your daughter?'

---

[2] Colloquially, 'let's go gentlemen ... and follow those who can.'

CHAPTER 2

The Heirloom

Within a month of this encounter Henri had word from Normandy, brought to him by no less a messenger than his eldest brother Edouard who was in foul humour upon arrival. He made this manifest by his chilling courtesies to all who were presented to him and endured the formal preliminaries with such ill-concealed impatience and mutterings beneath his breath to Henri concerning his dislike of all things English—and of the land herself—that Henri withdrew him as soon as possible. It was not until Edouard had flung himself down upon a stool in Henri's chamber, reached to the table for a flagon and poured himself a generous quencher that he disclosed the reasons for his coming. Only when even Henri's patience was at cracking point and Edouard had replenished his goblet for the second time, did he consent to speak, beginning: 'I must say, Henri, without further preamble, that I am come with much reluctance to this land. Never did I care for these Saxon barbarians. Meeting with them and journeying, seemingly interminably, upon their land, has only served to heighten my dislike.'

'Knowing this,' said Henri calmly, 'you can appreciate I am eager to learn what brings you on a journey which causes you so much displeasure. For my part of course I am rejoiced to see you.'

Edouard looked up from his glowering. 'Our Mother is dead,' he said curtly. 'Upon her death bed she gave charge to me which I was thus compelled to honour speedily; though why,' he added with seeming irrelevance, 'you should be the recipient and not I beats all imagining.'

So saying, he withdrew a casket from his cloak folds and set it upon the table. Henri ignored it. He had turned towards the embrasure to stand with his back to his brother. 'What was the manner of her passing?' he asked harshly. 'Did she suffer much? Pray tell me *something* of this most sad event.'

Edouard gulped from his goblet yet again but kept silence. He seemed to be making a genuine endeavour to revisualise the happening. Finally he attempted a description. He said, 'She set aside her tapestries one day, some seven weeks agone—remember I had this from her ladies with whom she sat at work—then she said to them with a great sigh, "It will be your charge now *mesdames* to complete this narrative embroidery. I have done with it," and so saying she laid down her stitchery and tinkled on that bell of hers. When the answering page came running she bade him go summon her chaplain and ask that he wait upon her in her bedchamber. Then without more ado she walked from the room and such was the atmosphere she had engendered that none spake but just watched her go in silence.'

Henri's head moved slightly and the setting sun darkened his hair into the likeness of a copper beech tree. 'And then . . .' he prompted.

Edouard drank yet again and then resumed. 'When Père Ansèlme's ministrations were ended she said in that most stately way of hers, which none of us has ever dared gainsay, "Thank you most humbly for your blessings, and now pray do me the office of informing my bedwomen I desire their presence and also our young Lord for I would see him on the instant."

'I had just returned from hunting, had but dismounted and was handing my mare's bridle to a groom when Père Ansèlme appeared and bent his head before me. He bade me make all speed to accompany him. He urged me, imagine, Henri, he urged me *not to inform my spouse nor take her with me to our Mother's bedchamber*, so somewhat angered I went with him, never, as you well know, having cared to gainsay the Church. We discovered our Mother, already laid to bed, her hands composed before her, her bedwomen gone—indeed I now recall we passed them in a huddle on the stairway, weeping.'

Here Henri broke in, 'But what ailed her? What brought the matter about? Had she complained or given any indication?'

'None,' said Edouard flatly. 'And you ask me, I'd say naught came upon her save a determination to have done with living, and God knows you are informed enough of Maman's determination.' Despite his sense of dignity Edouard slipped back into their childhood name for the Lady Mathilde.

Henri nodded, 'So then?' he prompted.

'She withdrew a great casket from beneath the furs which

covered her. Then she held it out to me saying, "Bear this to Henri, for I tell you, Edouard, I have the gift to see forward at this time. The thing within this casket is of no value so I take naught from your inheritance; but, as I do see most clearly, it is not you but Henri who will carry the name forward for many a century. Gervaise has ever displayed that distaste for females which gives good ground for the supposition he will not wed; Bayard being prelate plays no part; and the line, though in Normandy it will descend through Geoffroy, *his* issue, with *his* predilections, will mostly be in bastardy; whiles Gyles, I do maintain, will not wed until very late in life and thus Alain be the only other one who breeds apace." She paused awhile, and I had begun to suspect she slept, when she spoke again. She said that though I would have issue and my sons' sons also, my strain would not continue very long.' Edouard then laughed. A humourless sound, not unlike a bark, and appended, 'I remain unconvinced by a dying woman's fancies.'

Henri commented, ' 'Tis remarkable that she should speak thus since I was about to ask the hand in marriage of a maid when you did come among us. I shall in due course do so. Moreover, I have a hankering for a brood about me. . . .' He broke off once more and fell to musing.

'Maman said more,' Edouard resumed. 'She said, "Charge Henri that he treat the contents of this casket as an heirloom to his descendants and that he pass the word on thus to his firstborn and so down the line, *for whiles he does so there will be Lormes who put down good roots, bear fruit and seed themselves beyond the limits of my vision.*" Then it appeared she began to weaken. She fell into a doze whiles I thought about the words that she had spoken. After a time she seemed to rally again. She murmured, as it were to herself, "Soldiers, courtiers, family men, and missish things like Gervaise too, all will weave themselves into the pattern of the English land and hold fast to what they represent, not gaining mighty stature, but strong in convictions they hold to staunchly and above all . . ." and here her voice became faint and distant, but I will swear upon the bones of saints if necessary, her last words were "*sor tote rien seroit Edouard proz chevalers et corters*"[1] and that is almost all there was to it. She seemed to drowse again. I summoned the family, Père Ansèlme, her ladies,

---

[1] 'Above all Edward, they will be courtly and gentle knights,' i.e. in modern French—'*Chevaliers de la Courtoisie.*'

and when all were come about her she opened her eyes once more and they were suddenly very bright and sparkling. She looked us over. She studied us all very slowly and carefully and I dare vow I saw her twinkle... and then she *laughed*! ... a birdlike sound, intense in pleasurable amusement, like a maid who has just played some mischievous jest... and so laughing... she died.'

It seemed that once his tale was told and the casket had passed from his possession Edouard shed something of his ungraciousness and looked with a more kindly eye upon his cousins by conquest. He bent his knee with grave and due deference to King William when Henri asked leave to present his eldest brother and he left behind him a far different assessment of his character than that which he had evoked upon his arrival. It was as if the casket and his errand had been like goads about his shoulders and, with these lifted, he became a different man. When finally, after staying far longer than he had intended at the onset, he took his leave of the court, he accompanied his brother upon his journey to Castle Danbury. Once arrived he accepted with some grace and show, at least, of pleasure, the Lord of Danbury's invitation to stay awhile before embarking on his journey homeward into Normandy. He also made himself exceeding pleasant to his brother's future wife.

Henri swiftly pled his cause to Thyra's father and, obtaining permission to address his suit did so with such precipitation that the maid was startled. She begged his leave to wait awhile, to spend some more time in his company and learn to know him more nearly. Thus it was that she and the two brothers passed some weeks of that hot summer in each other's company. It took a carping message from Edouard's Céleste, filled with bewailings at his neglect of her, to make him exclaim ruefully, 'Aye, certes indeed I give her cause for I have wholly turned my coat and let the days slip by in this agreeable company.' Henri, with a twinkle in his eye, forbore from reminding him of his erstwhile opinions. He did however renew his suit with Thyra and this time won the maid.

Meanwhile a messenger had come, bearing word this time from the King to Danbury asking that he, having some knowledge of the northern reaches of the county of Norfolk and indeed owning a small castle there, would undertake a preliminary survey of the area and sound out the humour of the Saxon landowners towards his Kingship and avowed intentions.

'Here's a thing!' cried the castle's lord, hearing the request while he sprawled at ease in his central chair before the board in the Great Hall. All about him seethed the kervers who, as the servitors bore in the various dishes, received their commands to 'breke me that dere', 'dismember me that heron', 'present me that peacock', the whiles the dogs rooted and disputed among the fresh-laid rushes, the huge fire crackled and the jack-boy scorched his face crouching over the handle of the turning spit. Down the table to his left and right all Danbury's family and household sat at meat, the ladies wiping their fingers elegantly upon the insides of their sleeves, the men employing fresh trenchers of bread for the same purpose.

Danbury shouted above the din, 'Men and maids when wed do welcome quietude. Why do we not put your nuptials forward, Henri? Then you could accompany me upon the King's errand and I will duly bestow the ownership of my small Castle Rising upon you.'

'Castle Rising, is that the name of your demesne in Norfolk, my lord?' asked Henri eagerly.

Danbury nodded carelessly. 'So I named it these five years since. I caused it to be built having a liking for the wildness of the terrain and finding good harbourage for my Long Boat along the Blakeney marshes.' His eyes warmed as he referred to his Viking ship. 'Indeed I can offer you some rare sport there too for the wildfowl are prodigious and game abounds inland as well.' He turned in his chair and bent his head to his lady. 'Madam,' said he, 'have you a mind for this? Will you put forward the nuptials? Can you begown the maid and have the feastings in readiness speedily that we may then take the bride and groom to Castle Rising?'

This set up such a chattering among the womenfolk that Henry moved apart. His eyes were sparkling. He murmured, 'Castle Rising, how I like the name!' and he fell to musing upon his fortunes which had so come about that he was enabled to match this lovely sapling to whom he was betrothed; how William had said to him these two months past, 'Henri, beshrew me but you are a landless knight having no parcel of soil which you may call your own! This I will set to rights. Name me your chosen demesne and if it is not already bestowed by me then shall you have it, by my word.'

Henri recalled how he had flushed and stammered in some

confusion, 'I need naught else but to serve you my lord,' at which the King turned grave and nodded his head.

'Thus all men know,' he agreed soberly, 'but we hope for quieter times than you have spent by my side these past few years and you will presently wish to wed. No penniless knight can sue for a great lady, and rumour hath it your eye has already been taken by one who is most finely dowered herself.'

Henri recalled how he had crimsoned, stuttered and at length dissolved into laughter. Finally he had asked ruefully, 'Is there aught, sire, you do not know? Well, for once rumour is not the lying jade she is oft-times said to be,' and then he told the King, who forthwith settled a princely sum upon him; but held his hand at Henri's request that he would not cede to him any existing home, with Henri stammering that he was against any other man's property passing into his hands.

'An I may dare ask your Grace,' he said softly, 'I would find me a place, some piece of land which speaks to me and I to it, for I hold that unless a man has a deep love of the land he owns then both land and man will suffer. If I may be so fortunate as to obtain your sanction I would first find my place and there lay down my foundation stones.'

William smiled. 'So be it, Henri. It pleases me that this should be your wish, though,' and that rare smile lit his dark countenance, 'build no hovel nor no great castle neither, but when your *consel fu pris*[2] then come to me for crowns to make a home.'

Henri attempted to stammer his gratitude, but at the King's behest he finally desisted and as he sat in his favourite pose— lounging against the steps to the throne where his liege sprawled —suddenly he looked up and, greatly daring, clasped his monarch's hand. 'Sire I have it,' he cried eagerly, 'when I build my home I will have carved upon the mantel "*Mis consel fu pris*".'[3] When amid the courtiers later, more than one Saxon lord looked at him curiously, one bolder than the rest was heard to murmur to a group of cronies, 'It seems at least one Norman loves our land.'

Henri swung round on the instant. 'Indeed I do, my lord,' he confirmed, 'or should not seek to wed here and, of mine own choosing, drive my roots down in this your land, in the greatest

2 Mind is made up.
3 My mind is made up.

hope that you gentlemen will one day come to accept me freely among you.'

Was ever man more fortunate! Henri also recalled the murmur of approval invoked by what he had said and in retrospect saw that he had won more that night than at the Battle of Hastings. He ceased remembering, lifted his eyes from the board and encountered Thyra's clear blue gaze. 'What say you, sir?' she murmured shyly. 'Is it your wish that we should do as my father asks of us? For though others all about this board have clamoured their opinions you have said naught as yet.'

For answer Henri rose, grasped the goblet beside him, held it to a page for filling and, in the deep emotion of the moment, his hard-won English deserting him, stammered out in a sorry jumble: 'Miladi, *mis consel fu pris*[4] from the first moment I did see your face and *je veuil*—I would be wed with you *tres orend-toit*,'[5] and the toast was drunk to shouts of sympathetic laughter from the company.

They were wed as Danbury had proposed. Hand-fasted, Norman groom and Danish bride came down the tiny nave of the church, which had been built by the Saxon vanquished. When Henri came to the door he, being of unusual height, by comparison with the men for whom this holy building with its short, square tower had been built, was compelled to bend his head and actually duck to make his exit. Still with hands clasped, like children, they climbed the grassy slope which led to the drawbridge of Danbury's wooden castle, crossed so together and entered. The serfs had spread fresh rushes for their feet, not only within the hall where the great fire blazed centrally, but to the outer limits of the Earl's demesne. So it was that as they walked in enchanted silence, Thyra's robe hem and the edges of Henri's cloak swept across those rushes making a small bridal song to accompany them throughout their passage to the two great, carved chairs which had been set in readiness to receive them.

For the banquet which ensued, the Earl's high table—which by custom stood inside the entrance to his private chamber at the farther end—had been brought forward and to it tables added

4 My mind is made up.
5 I would marry you this instant.

to run down either side of the fire. Thus was the seated company backed by the close-drawn curtains which fronted the alcove bedchambers.

During the feast, Henri and Thyra spoke little to one another and drank sparingly; as was the custom, bride and groom were then bedded, the bedwomen, ripe in ribaldry, shooed all the company before them and, to hasten their departures, finally drew the curtains across again. Then Henri gathered up the strands of Thyra's long fair hair between his hands and wound them round his throat, drawing her close, crying as he did so, 'Now I have you, Madam, in all your beauty and from you will get lusty sons to carry our name forward!'

Later in the night as they lay quietly together Thyra made him her first request, beginning: 'Have you a great love for this my Father's castle, for as you know it is a gift from him?' This won from Henri an answering query, 'Are you in thought with me, my love, that this is not the place where we should put down those roots of which I spoke earlier this night?'

'I am,' she answered. 'I think we should go southward. I feel that we must build our own Norman stronghold for the housing of the many sons which you envisage.' Then she whispered, drawing his head down, 'And when our home is chosen, then let his Grace bestow upon you the Barony he has sworn that you will have.'

Henri smiled, 'Nay my love, methinks that is not quite the way of it. Should we not better say that when you present me with an heir, then shall you "my lord" me for the first time.'

Woman-like, she took the last word from him, saying with a mischievous smile, 'If so be, Henri, you get me with a son.'

They had scant time for solitude together. Within five days a breathless rider was gasping out the dire news that Danbury was dead. It seemed that he, wishing to discuss matters of private import, had ridden off leaving the bridal couple, taking only two gentlemen to attend him. They had been ambushed by an offshoot of the very malcontents he had thought subdued. When the rest of the party came up with them they found Danbury slain and his two companions left unconscious by the louts, who fled on hearing the oncoming thud of many hooves. 'But now,' the panting messenger gasped out, 'my lord's body is being borne back upon an improvised litter with a section of men to protect it. The rest have ridden on to raise further support with which to take their reckoning for this savagery.'

As night fell, so the wind intensified and the womenfolk sat huddled into their furs. The minstrels were silent, the pages drowsing and Henri, chin on one hand, stared into the blue and tawny flames.

'This wind I hate,' said Thyra shivering. 'It was the same two nights ago and sorely out of season.'

'Yet not out of tune with events,' her mother said quietly, 'though I am both surprised and thankful that we have seen naught of Odin's black dog.'

Henri looked up sharply, 'What black dog? I have heard naught of this.' Thyra and her mother exchanged glances, then Thyra spoke, ' 'Tis a most deep-planted belief among our people that the spirit of Odin's great black dog shows himself as herald to impending tragedy. Odin, so the tale runs, brought him here with his Vikings when they settled hereabouts along the Norfolk coast.'

'A great black hound which runs and stops as though in search of someone, bays and runs again, yet do his footfalls make no sound?' asked Henri slowly.

'Yes,' Thyra nodded, eyes widening, 'but what know you of him, Henri?'

'I saw him,' Henri said very quietly, 'the night the wind rose, as it is doing now. The hall was very close and hot and maybe you will recall Courville and I went out to clear our lungs. We took the path that you and I trod earlier today and then I saw and heard your hound; but Courville saw nothing and when I tried to make him see, he called me a touched head and a whimsy and swore I but imagined it. . . .'

'You saw the Hound of Odin?' repeated the lady of Danbury from her place beside the fire. 'He showed himself to you! Why it is past imaginings! And then to cap all, through you not knowing what it presaged, you said naught of it to us?'

Henri's face paled. 'Do you mean, madam, that had I spoke, your Lord could have been stayed from taking his fateful journey?'

'Nay, my son,' she soothed him gently. 'Naught could have stayed my lord, and do you not imagine for one instant that the inevitable could ever have been gainsayed. 'Tis just that I am wondering *why* you saw. Have you seen aught before? Are you given to vision of this mystic nature?'

'Nay, madam,' Henri assured her. 'We are not given to fancies as a family. Nor have we had aught to do with haunting or such mystical experiences.'

No one spake more, but fed upon their thoughts until at length the lady rose and gathered the folds of her robe about her. 'Then I, who have lived with suchlike all my days, will say just this. If the Hound has shewn himself to you he has transferred his unwelcome allegiance to your house. Thyra is now of that house so plays some part in it, yet should I be lacking in my duty if I did not charge you both to heed the Hound wherever possible and forewarn your children likewise. Furthermore, let me have no reproachings for what was both unexpected and uninvited, for my lord was not one to be swerved from any purpose. Deeds, I have had mules who were more capricious by comparison!' And so saying, with a gracious inclination of her head and a faint smile, she turned and quit the Hall followed by her attendant ladies.

Only a short time lapsed before she came in again and resumed her place beside the fire as if it were her widow's vigil station.

Within an hour, tradition had overborne even the recent Christian ceremony in the little Saxon church by which Henri and Thyra had been found together.

In whispers, many of their number carrying congealing gashes on hands and faces and quite a few with kerchiefs tied round their battered heads, the retainers sat about the hall, whispering in little separate groups. One and all were huddled into their cloaks, for it had turned unseasonably chill. Most of what they said was merely a muted murmur but the words 'long boat' and 'Valhalla' sounded clear and were several times repeated.

At length and knowing full well what her late Lord would have elected for himself, his widow rose from her stool beside those blue and smouldering logs and walked across to Henri. 'My lord must have a Viking funeral,' she said looking at him steadily. 'How will you feel, newly joined son to this family?'

Henri rose and took her cold fingers in his own. 'Madam,' he said, 'I am not of your people, though now of your family. I cannot hope to make a balanced judgement in this matter. Therefore thinking at speed, if not thinking well, I would that for many reasons my lord had the blessing of Holy Church upon his passing. Nay,' as she sought to intervene, 'pray hear me out, dear madam. How would it be if I were to intercede with Ufric our priest that he turn his countenance away from the rituals of the actual interment thereafter so that we may give your lord a Viking funeral?'

All eyes were now upon her for her answer. One by one the men rose and moved towards her. Henri heard one mutter, 'Well thought, I say,' and another, 'At such time, a marvellous tactful gesture!' and he also heard the grunts of approval with which the words were supported.

The lady sighed. Then she mustered a faint smile to her white face. 'You may call yourself naught but a soldier, Henri,' she said at length. 'For my part I see in you more than a touch of the courtier, too. It *is* well thought, I do agree, for none should even suggest aught which would add fuel to the fires of strife at such a time as this.'

And so it came about. When all was over, Henri stood hand-fasted with his Thyra on the fringing Blakeney marshes where these ran down so slowly over the mud flats to the sea. The sun was sinking fast to the horizon. The sky was like the coloured plumage of a thousand flamingoes. The sea was cold, grey, very still. Far out now upon the sea the long boat which contained the Lord of Danbury was barely visible as it drifted westward into the setting sun. Against tradition, Thyra had begged to keep her father's sword, which even now was clasped around the hilt by her small fingers.

'Explain me the ritual, love,' asked Henri softly.

She did so, her eyes still fixed upon the vanishing long boat. 'Thus he sails to Valhalla. It is our old belief that when he arrives he will drop anchor there in safety and immortality. It is why his anchor accompanies him.'

'And his horse slain with him in the ambush?'

'That he may be as before in perpetuity.'

Henri sketched a cross upon his breast. 'And that I ask for too,' he murmured. 'For he was a good man and a fair lord. This I think was why priest Ufric stayed me when I embarked upon my request.'

Thyra spoke again. 'Did he know, think you?'

'Of course he knew. He said, "Tell me naught that I should not know, my son, within the rulings of my calling. Let me accept that you and the family, with whom you are now joined, desire a private family interment, with none present save you, Lord Danbury's own blood, and his followers." '

'And thus you told him.' Thyra's voice was a thread on the sudden-rising wind.

'And thus I told him,' Henri confirmed.

An unheralded gust of wind slipped across the strand, tugging at Thyra's hair and whipping up their cloak folds. It stilled as swiftly as it had risen, but came again, this time so grown in strength that the watchers saw it thrust the diminishing outline of the long boat forward. Again the wind died and again it grew, and each time it came the more strongly, until suddenly the long boat seemed to quiver like a freed hound leaping to the course. A bittern boomed, and another took up the sound. A drift of black-headed gulls winged upwards crying peevishly. Then, with a flurry of wings, the many waterbirds took flight, sounded off by a throng of curlews crying their lament. As these all wheeled and eddied they were sundered by a great, rhythmic thrashing. Necks outstretched, a flock of geese drove clean through them to steady above the long boat as if forming an escort to its course.

'The spirits of his ancestors lead him in!' cried Thyra, her own arms outstretched as if she too would join them in their task. 'They will keep surveillance over my father to Valhalla. He has no longer any need of us.'

So saying, she turned on her sandalled heel, glanced up at Henri and 'Come with me, sir?' she enquired.

For answer he clasped her hand again and together they made their way through the singing rushes towards the castle and their own long life together.

Already unknown as yet to them, the seed of her firstborn was planted in her womb.

King William duly elevated his '*tosjors feal*'[6] Henri to a Barony at the christening of his firstborn whom he and Thyra, by mutual consent, named Henri also.

At first the couple had come back to Kent with Thyra's mother and in the selfsame castle where she herself was born, Thyra was safely delivered of a son. By this time Henri, roving the countryside with a small company of men, had probed deep into Essex. There he found, sleeping in a wondrous calm, untouched by the affrays which were common enough elsewhere, the little trio of hamlets called Bestingthorpe and Low and High Aynthorp,

[6] Always faithful. Modern French: *Toujours fidèle.*

where a river ran across the valley and the land sloped back from it to a high rise, in its turn further backed by deep woodlands. He stood beside the fast-flowing water where it made an arm of river and found deer drinking at a pool. He watched the swans glide past, then put his mount to the water, forded the river and climbed the opposing rise that he might view the land from the reverse aspect. Then he came back and went at foot pace through the woods, bidding his men fall back a little as he did so. The peace of it came down upon him like an enfolding mantle. The woodland sounds were passing gentle too, just the scurry of a coney to its burrow, the faint squeal of a wild pig in a thicket, the bird song in the autumn-denuded branches. There was, too, one soundless encounter with a beaver, who sat quite still and gave him eye for eye unwinkingly. At this he threw back his head and loosed a great shout of laughter, which brought his men rushing towards him fearful of what was toward.

'Nay, I but laughed at a beaver who stared at me so insolently,' he assured them, still laughing. 'Time has passed him by in this place and he seems not afraid of man—just watchful. I tell you, *messires*' (he still erred in the matter of language when emotion touched him nearly), 'I shall drive roots down in this peaceful place if so be my lady wills it also. Here is a blanket of peace. Here the tide of affairs sweeps by, scarce ruffling the water ripples on that stream. My sons and my sons' sons will have pause for thought amid these meadows and spinneys. Look,' he turned in the saddle and pointed upwards along the rise, 'we will build there. It is a natural fortress site from which we can command a sufficient eminence to be forewarned of any impending attack. Herewith we shall make a wall, in my French style, to enclose my lady's garden. It shall be planted with apricocks ... as was my lady Mother's ... here shall be stabling for our horses and here will be our bailey. We will enclose all with walls so, in one wide flat sweep, levelling the land to raise it higher still for my *petit château* foundations. Then encircling all, we shall make one deep, deep ditch, cross it with drawbridge and, who knows, perhaps deflect the river later to water it. Certes, we shall cross it with a drawbridge be there water or no. Then, to keep all well protected and under our eye we shall first make the enclosing wall and, within it, hutments for our labourers. The market can be built without the wall, since, by day, all will be sufficiently protected *if* my archers are installed about in watchtowers. Come, let us go and tell my lady . . .' and flushed with excitement, eyes glinting, he wheeled his mount about and galloped off.

'While we shall be hard put to follow him,' one bold member of the company grumbled, bending to tighten a girth before setting off in pursuit. 'I tell you we shall have hard riding for the next three days, mark my words for it.'

He was still wrong, for the journey was encompassed in two. Henri was in a fever of impatience to tell all to his Thyra. This done and her excitement whipped up to match his own, he must set off again immediately. 'I'm for the King now,' he told his family. 'I must sue for his permission and my promised land grants. These obtained, eyes will start from their sockets at the pace that we shall make with our building of the new and permanent Castle Rising.'

He was back within a month to find his wife again well got with child. No sooner had he paid his respects to the womenfolk and elders and he was off again to High Aynthorp where, before the second babe's first lusty cry pronounced his material existence, the foundations were down. The work went on at record pace. By the time Thyra was come upon her time once more, the walls were up and, when the time came to name both sons, Henri's Castle Rising had risen sufficiently for his requirements. Certainly the roof was still gaping to the sky, but the beams which would support it were in place and the inner overhanging wall, which divided his chamber off somewhat from the Main Hall, was almost completed.

'Six weeks, my sweeting,' he told Thyra as she lay beneath her couch furs, 'then we will name our firstborn and I will have his christening at High Aynthorp, and thereafter our coming in will follow speedily. Certes, our chapel is bare and open to the skies! We have no priest! Nor is the chapel consecrated! But this shall all be done and then we shall perform another ceremony of which I have oft-times dreamed.'

He would tell her no more despite her wheedling; but when he returned again he found she had fully recovered from her second delivery. They walked together in my lady's garden in the warm spring weather. It was then he asked a favour of her. 'I would that you consent to bear your father's sword upon this journey,' he told her. 'When you return, as 'tis obvious you must from such a rude habitation as ours will be for a while yet, I shall stay until the roof is finally completed and our entrance secured against marauders. Then I can leave a company of men to guard it while I collect you and take you home at last. Will you agree to this?' And, as always when confronted with his enthusiasm, she did.

Thus it was that they stood within the unfinished hall for the naming of their firstborn Henri, and thereafter for the second babe. When this was done, the priest moved softly from one to another, somewhat awed by the astonishing presence of the black-haired, splendid man who was now his King. William himself was in most easy case, jesting and gracious to the ladies, teasing with the toddling babe whom he proclaimed 'a repetition of his father, upon my oath.' He caught the mite in his great arms and flung him upwards, heart-warmed that the child showed no whit of fear, just gurgled with delighted laughter. 'Wilt thou serve me too, *petit Henri*?' he asked, bending his dark locks over the little fair head. For answer the laughing child put out a tiny hand and caught such hold upon the great chain that hung from the King's throat that William cried, 'He is handfast to me already, Henri, he is my man!'

Henri's eyes kindled. 'All of my house, sire, are your men,' he replied gravely, 'as we ever shall be. I can pledge that with my uttermost confidence.'

William's face softened momentarily, then his hand went to his sword and his expression changed. 'We have trouble in Normandy,' he announced grimly. 'It seems the weight of my hand is needed to put matters back upon their proper footing. Do you then accompany me?'

Henri bent his knee instantly. 'Certes, I do, sire, you have but to tell me the day of our going.'

William gave him a month; they were gone three. But in that month, by the most prodigious effort, the roof went on, the entrance was secured and Thyra's young brother undertook to hold all in safe keeping until his return. Thus it ever was with Henri. His plans came to fruition; but ever and anon throughout his life they waited upon the will of William, erstwhile Duke of Normandy.

The ceremony which followed the christening was a simple one. The assembly formed a half circle before the burning logs. Then, bent almost double in his desire to show due humility, Henri's master carpenter shuffled forward, eyes bulging, hands a trifle unsteady as he gripped the rude ladder which his two sons had set in place above the hearth. Steadying himself he then clambered aloft and duly chipped out the first word of the phrase which in the course of time would become the Lorme motto: *Mis consel fu pris.* With this done Thyra passed her babe into her mother's keeping so that she could grasp her father's massive sword, which even now her page held out to her. She took it, proffered it, hilt forward to her husband, and Henri, grasping it firmly, mounted the ladder himself and with two cords bound the sword to the two strong, wooden pegs which had previously been inserted in readiness for this installation.

The ritual ended and the toastings completed, Henri's own to his King, and the thrown goblet caught and cached safely by his seneschal . . . to his lady and his sons and finally to all the company assembled, his change of mien quickly stilled the rising tide of talk and laughter as he said, 'Sire, mesdames, by your leave and at stress to your patience, there is one more ceremony I would conduct, an you grant me the permission?' He spoke with his eyes on his King who nodded carelessly. Sprawling his splendid person upon a chair, he merely reached out and drew Henri's toddler to his knees.

The seneschal came forward once again. In his hands he carried a casket, that self-same one which Henri's brother had brought from Normandy and passed into his keeping. Henri took it, saying, 'This my brother Edouard brought to me from Normandy. It came from my mother at her dying, for me to have and hold against the time my heir succeeds me. Then, by my mother's wish it will pass to him. She spake certain words which laid a most express and vital charge upon me concerning both the casket and its contents . . . of which I swear that I know nothing. She bade my brother "Charge Henri that he treat the contents of this casket as an heirloom to his descendants and that he pass the word on thus to his own firstborn son." ' For an instant his eyes rested upon the curly, already reddening head which lay against the gold and crimson of the King's robe. Then he resumed, 'And, so she charged, it should go on down the line, for whiles it does, she did prophesy upon her deathbed, "*There will be Lormes who put down good roots, bear fruit and seed themselves beyond the limits of my vision.*" Those were her words.'

The King leaned forward in his chair. ' 'Tis a strange tale,' he commented. 'One is tempted to ask if the Lady Mathilde also imposed the injunction that the contents of your casket should remain secret?'

Henri hesitated, then met the King's eyes. 'Nay, Sire,' he admitted, ' 'tis naught but my own feeling in the matter; certes, should the opening of it be to your desire then shall I do so on the instant?'

Now it was William's turn to hesitate. He frowned, looked away into the fire as if seeking an answer from its leaping blue and tawny flames. Then he shook his head as if disputing silently within himself. 'Nay, Henri,' he said quietly. 'Let matters rest as your instincts prompt you. Such decisions are not within your King's authority.' He shook his great shoulders impatiently as if to shake a burden from them. 'God's oath!' he exclaimed, 'it has suddenly become chill in here! Now either choose to rest in ignorance or break it open now if *you* are unsure. But, an you leave it unopened,' his voice became grave and he spoke much slower as if the words were being drawn from his innermost depths, '*see that you lay the charge upon your heirs to do likewise and keep the contents secret too. The power of such things cannot be denied and once invoked can never be gainsayed without disastrous consequences.*' He spoke with such gravity that others shivered too, and more than one Norman present thought that the King must be remembering Harold's oath taken, unknowingly, over the saint's bones and what that episode had brought in its train thereafter.

Then the King seemed to shake off his mood as swiftly as it had descended upon him. 'Come,' he said in an entirely different tone, 'let us to your ceremony and when we have all witnessed the installing of your Heirloom, without further hindrance lead us to mete I pray, for I am ravenous!'

The spell was broken. The carpenter, who had stood with slack arms and mouth agape, turned his bewildered head from one august countenance to another during this exchange, now rallied into action.

He retested the ladder's strength, went behind the rungs and steadied the sides with horny hands while Henri mounted. The company watched as he worked his fingers along the panelling, swung out a small section of the woodwork and revealed a cache within; they saw him slip the casket in, close up the aperture, dust his long fingers, as it were symbolically, as tribute to a thankful task thankfully completed, then saw him dismount.

He went straightway to the King. 'With your leave, sire, I will unburden you of this mischief,' he said reaching out to the squirming babe. 'Come, lordling, before thy monarch weary of thee.' He swung the child up to sit pick-a-back upon his shoulders and '*petit Henri*' so poised, gurgled with delight, steadying his person by the simple expedient of grasping his father's hair.

The King rose. The small rally of hastily rehearsed heralds blew a not too tuneful fanfare. The King made an amused grimace to them and, taking Thyra's fingers between his own, led the procession to the first fast-break ever to be taken by this young family at Castle Rising.

When '*petit Henri*' was at last laid inside his cradle, the wet-nurse seated upon a stool suckling their second son Gilbert, Henri drew back the curtains of the alcove bedchamber and he and Thyra, arms entwined, went in, leant over the cradle and looked at their elder son whose christening had been graced by a King. They were not, however, thinking of kings. Thyra knelt down and the curtain of her long fair hair fell about her shoulders. Henri leaned across the cradle's covered head and, after they had looked awhile, Thyra looked up at him. 'Well, my Lord,' she asked smilingly, 'art satisfied?'

For answer Henri gripped the hand that held the cradle rim. 'Now, my sweeting,' he said unsteadily, 'we are in truth an English family.'

CHAPTER 3

Of 'Verie Wicked Fellowes'

The characteristics of the Lormes were indeed destined to become as constant as the Hanoverian nose. Hindsight revealed this after only a few generations of the 'English line' had been established on Essex soil. That this constancy also included certain retrograde elements was cause for lament down the centuries, but it had the added Family advantage of closing ranks even more resolutely than for any other cause. Closed ranks were always part of their natural tendency and *bouche ferme*[1] their general policy; this was merely particularised when a younger son evinced such inescapably delinquent tendencies as might imperil the good name of the rest. Then ensued such a hushing, such a clearing of throats, 'ahem-ing' and blank-eyed middle-distance regard of questioners that these were made to feel *farouche*, tactless and somewhat ill-bred, while those who attempted to probe further were left in no doubt that they pursued a totally sleeveless errand.

Meanwhile, under their particular rose the Family met demands, bought secrecy, shipped abroad, subborned priests to hasty marriages and arranged discreet and far distant adoptions with such absolute dedication and meticulous care that scarcely more than a handful of loyal servants ever remained even suspicious of the truth.

The Lormes' French ancestry and connections likewise ensured a strong sexuality in their characters, but they never really possessed the fundamental sentimentality of the English. They strove far more to emulate Chaucer's 'verray parfait gentil knight' who 'loved chivalrye, trouthe and honour', and they evinced little taste for indulging their womenfolk with romantic hyperboles. Indeed, they were very much Chaucer's men for, like his Clerk who was 'Epicurus owne son', they held the pleasures of the table in excessively high esteem.

While Lord John was distinguishing himself at Agincourt

1 Literally, closed mouth, i.e., silence.

under the banner of the fifth King Henry, his youngest brother Alain, another trouble magnet, slew one of Henry's knights in dubious circumstances. Rightly fearing the King's wrath, he took to the forests and there to marauding and killing the King's deer. Even so the famous Lorme Luck, as it came to be known, stood him in eventual good stead. Ever quick to grasp the most slender opportunity, Alain sought and found a chance to perform a service for his monarch and received what his smarting parent deemed 'a mightily ill-advised' pardon. Thus he managed to die in semblance of respectability—in his own bed.

Then again, it became difficult to effect complete concealment of the activities of 'Patch' de Lorme. He it was—on seeing such abundance of gold and jewels laid at the feet of 'Gloriana' by her sailor-adventurers—who deemed it 'a wanton, wicked waste and quite unendurable', as he was wont to state unashamedly when in his dotage. He took to the skull and crossbones, lost an eye in one near-disastrous encounter, yet managed to sail his disgraceful pirate ship and crew into Norman harbourage from whence, top-loaded with Spanish treasure, he dispersed one and all to their Devonian homesteads. His own ill-gotten shares he transferred by 'further wicked deceptions' and many fluent lies to the estates of his French cousins, finally bringing all safely to England. Only when he too had died undeservedly in his bed, surrounded by a quiver of lawful issue—and a far greater attendance of offspring begot in bastardy—did the dreaded truth leak out. But as this was after the richest and best of the looted Spanish gold plate had been made sacrosanct by its use during a visit from the Virgin Queen to Castle Rising; and after the most splendid of the pirated jewels had graced the current châtelaine's throat, wrists, brow and stomach when she sank deep into her receiving curtsy to her monarch—there was naught the Family could do except hush up, as best they might, what would otherwise have brought them all to ruin and certainly some to the block.

The family fortunes soared again and again between these years until the interregnum of the Commonwealth and the loathed Protector. These successes were in the main through their distinguished services in battle to their several monarchs; but trouble was never long removed from them.

Then there was Philip who, to the general Lorme chagrin, became King James I's 'favourite sweeting' and minced the corridors of a Court from which all other members of the Family withdrew to their private lands, lips tightly clamped against the even more distasteful solecism of *lèse majesté*. It was Philip, according to current *on dits*,[2] who first inspired King James to wear a single diamond earring and to protect his white hands within fanciful little muffs! Besides occupying himself with such dubious inventions, Philip won concrete expressions of approval from his homosexual monarch which enabled him to add a further wing to Castle Rising and also what subsequently became the famous picture gallery. This source was of course never mentioned by the Family; but it rankled.

It rankled again when the Dark Boy, Charles Stuart, rode triumphantly into London at last. It was a thorn in the side of every upright member of the Family that they owed the restoration of their home and property in no small part to Julian, 'yet another contamned rogue' as his father groaned. Charles, as was his wont, despite the perpetual monetary strains of those first years in Kingship, ordered the restoration of Castle Rising and instructed Julian to set up a commission for the listing and seeking out of such valuables as had not been melted down or lost during the rule of the 'upstart' Cromwell. In fact it was Julian, pretending that all came from this source, who really provided the gold for Castle Rising's third restoration. Not infrequently he rolled out of the Lady Castlemaine's bed so to do, in no wise abashed that he was thus making his royal patron cuckold. He set up his own private benefit fund inside the pattern agreed upon for the restoration of Royalists' property.

Had Charles caught whisper of it he would certainly have had Julian's head for it; but he knew naught. Julian, having captured the loot, mulcted it happily and, before restoring the rest to its rightful ownership, converted a further percentage into gold for *giving to the King*. These gifts he was wont to make, with bent head and on one knee, murmuring, 'One of your very loyal subjects, Sire, has entrusted this gold to me to offer to your Majesty as a small token for lands ... pictures ... domains ... other valuable possessions .. restored to them by your Grace's generous dictates. Yet have they enjoined me to keep them anonymous, not wishing to impose upon your Majesty the bore of having to remember and further recognise their gratitude.' Scandalous as it may seem the ruse worked every time!

[2] Hearsay.

Julian was of course quick to perceive his King's weaknesses. When closeted with his delinquent cronies he would murmur, 'I earn every groat of what I obtain by that which some would name flagrant and unscrupulous deceits. One instance alone, I spend myself mightily in the quest for ripe plums of womanhood for his Majesty's delectation.' He was referring to his unvarying practice of testing the bedworthiness of each one before handing her over. Besides this arduous chore he worked hard at discovering new games of hazard for Charles' diversion, at burrowing out the latest whiffs of scandal to whisper in the royal ear as the King lounged with his long legs stretched out comfortably chuckling and listening with vast enjoyment. In between times Julian made great endeavour to draw upon his prodigious knowledge of good food and foreign wines. The King, who had starved in Holland, feasted but rarely in France, gnawed crusts in Scotland, named Julian 'my palate' and the wretch flourished despite his sire's expressed opinion within the bosom of the Family that he was 'a thorough out-and-out-paced rogue and shocking scandal having no right to be named any better than a plunderer, deceiver and wanton lecher.' The trouble was that, like his predecessors, Julian saw to it that the Family was handfasted. No breath of his swindlings was heard until *after* treasures were restored and genuine letters of gratitude expressed to the King . . . until *after* restorations had been paid for in swindled gold . . . even as Julian safeguarded his boasting by ensuring that these were never uttered save to cronies whom he made sure were perfectly aware that he knew such of them as would get *their* heads beneath the axe if they said aught of *him*.

The extra devil in all this was that while family consciences were stricken by the goings on of their runts, there were more than a few whose mouths twitched in ill-suppressed amusement at their misdemeanours. Even the famous Lady Margaret, whom Lely painted so superbly; she who had successfully fobbed off the advances of the amorous King Charles, managed so to do without harm to any family chances. Yet she once confided to a trustworthy crony 'the trouble is that with our runtishness goes such a fiendish charm! They are actually *defended* by the very men they make cuckold and the ones they defraud too! 'Tis my opinion people would rather be swindled with panache and cozening manners than treated fair with grave courtesies.'

And so it went on as the centuries slipped by. In due course came the capers of 'Stand and Deliver' Gervaise. He took to the road. He was said to own the finest string in the county. With a band of high-bred cronies he held coaches up to ransom and, so the record ran, had no trouble in winning favours from fair ladies who swooned with alacrity into the strong arms of the man who, mere moments before, had stuffed his capacious pockets with their jewels. Indeed the entire era of Gervaise's domination was made scandalous by the stated claim that no fashionable lady could hold her own unless she could boast of being rutted by the most glamorous highwayman who ever cried 'stand and deliver' behind a pair of mother-of-pearl and silver pistols and a lavishly bejewelled mask.

In due course highway robbery gave place to rum-running under the first King George, with more than a little blackmail included to swell the coffers of the 'bad 'uns'; and runt succeeded runt with just occasional gaps in the sequence when sires and grandsires were lulled into a false and profoundly grateful conviction that the bad thread had snapped and would run no more. Then a further crop would shake the foundations of temporary peace with Richard who sank so far he turned spy during the Napoleonic wars; Hubert who was actually caught and sentenced to deportation for adulterating wine (so heinous an offence that his sire snarled, on hearing the news of it, 'I'd 've hung, drawn and quartered him and that would have been too good!'); the scandalous 'Beau' de Lorme whose sartorial excesses even put Brummel in the shade. It was he who boasted that he had 'never seduced a virgin below m'y own station in life' and who, according to his despairing sire, 'strewed more bastards around the county than there are poppies in one of m'y own cornfields!' Records showed that he spent five thousand upon a single coat for which the silk alone was specially commissioned by a Lyons manufacturer, paid more for his diamonds than was spent on Lady Marguerite's renowned collection, and brought the family perilously near to bankruptcy. Then there was Ralph who became embroiled in the slave trade between Africa and Barbados. Ripples from his infamous conduct with his 'human cattle' ran to the walls of Castle Rising. Though it was gall and wormwood to admit it, Ralph acquired huge properties and filled his coffers with gold with which he returned, possessor of the shameful nickname 'Butcher' de Lorme and proceeded to restore the family fortunes. Then, after slave trading, came the most guarded entries of all when a share-pushing, bawdy-house-keeping descendant of this ancient line ran riot among what were known as the 'cits'; those below-the-salt merchants, whether honest or no, for whom Society was as easy of access as the outer Antipodes.

And then, when the new, twentieth century was but a fledgling and scarcely two years old, that certain Earl was commanded of his Monarch to quit the shores of England forever. In his train went a very young Lorme of whom it was said, albeit in whispers, 'if Wilde had not leaned towards a "golden boy", he would most surely have chosen a copper-headed one instead.' With this Edward Justin Alaric de Lorme[3] away in Egypt, reclining aboard a princely *dahabeeyah*,[4] in all the beauty of his youth and cap of copper curls, the Lord of Castle Rising, knowing himself to be fringing upon his eightieth year, sent formal invitations to all those Family who were close enough to merit such involvement and thus drew them around him for what he chose to call 'an announcement to be made by me on my eightieth birthday.'

[3] John and Primrose de Lorme's only son. Born 1884. Educated Eton and Oxford.
[4] Nile houseboat.

1907, THE SERVANTS

In the Castle

The Housekeeper	Mrs Peace
The Butler	Mr Sawbridge (Sawby)
The Chef	M. André
Milady's Personal Maid	Palliser
His Lordship's Man	Cuff
The Cook	Mrs Parsons
Head Footman	Edward
2nd Footman	George
3rd Footman	Richard
Mr Gyles' Man	Pine
House Parlourmaids	Mason and Pearson
Kitchenmaids	Joan and Eliza
Scullerymaids	Agnes and Mabel
Boots	Sam
Yard Boy	Alfred

In the Laundry

Mrs Sawbridge (gardener's wife)
Sally Sawbridge (their daughter aged fourteen)
Mrs Tompkins (2nd gardener's wife)
Mrs Dick (3rd gardener's wife)

In the Stables

Head Groom	Plumstead
Grooms	Pike and Perry
Stable Boys	Will and Ted

In the Garden

Head Gardener	Sawbridge
Under Gardener	Tompkins
3rd and 4th Gardeners	Dick and Flead
Gardeners' Boys	Billy, Joe and Willy (sons of Sawbridge, Tompkins and Dick)

In the Nursery

Nanny Pringle
Nursemaid Rose
Nurserymaid Violet

In the Schoolroom

Mademoiselle Blanc
Mr Prewitt, Music Master
Mr Sissingham, Lucien's Tutor

On the Estate

Carpenter	Peak
Thatcher	Gillings
Head Gamekeeper	Switch
2nd Gamekeeper	Wittle
3rd Gamekeeper	Postle
Poultryman	Redding
Pigman	Abel
Hedger and Ditcher	Tibbins
Land Agent	

CHAPTER 4

1907, The Servants

Henry de Lorme drew back the bolts of the west garden door with considerable caution as the September sun rose over Castle Rising and sparkled the breeze-ruffled surface of the lake where a sleepy black swan bent her neck to the business of cleaning her feathers. A yard away his elderly cob, already in his forty-eighth year, came slowly to his crabbed, webbed feet. The sun's rays, impacting on the east windows, met the blank refusal of closely drawn curtains, brightened the life of the youngest gardener's boy as he wheeled a barrow towards the long line of stove houses from which plumes of smoke were rising. The sun broke too on the cobblestones of the stable yard and flashed up the gilding on the stable tower's clock, the hands of which showed 5.15 a.m.

Henry, closing the door behind him very slowly, moved out across the west terrace, ran down the steps and took the path beside the topiary which stood sentinel between the long walk and the rose garden.

The air, like a fine, dry white wine, had precisely the tang to tingle up his blood and, as he quickened his pace, he began whistling. It *was* a glorious morning and even the recollection, which intruded dampingly, of the forthcoming, mysterious family dinner party with all its concomitant ceremonies could not dim his pleasure. As he turned into the yard the sun lit up the copper in his hair. ''Morning Master Harry,' called the head groom standing outside the saddle room and inspecting the morning with matching appreciation. This he now directed upon the 'young 'un' as ... ' 'Morning Plum,' Henry shouted back, 'May I have a ride? I want to stretch myself a bit before breakfast.'

'You can 'ave Stardust sir, Mr Henry,' Plum sought to rectify his error and then lapsed again adding, 'but don't you go flingin' yerself into a ditch before 'is lordship's celebrationing. If me memory serve me aright it's '*is* birthday anyway; but rumour 'as it it's more'n that wot's in the wind ... and mark me, sir, now do. If you go on with 'orses like you are you'll get the same label "Hellfer leather 'Arry" as what yer grandfer enjoyed when 'ee was not much more'n your age.'

Henry grinned indulgently and followed the old man to the stalls, as Plumstead shouted to a groom to 'saddle Stardust' and 'get movin' me lad, the gennelman's awaitin'.'

The soft sound of hay being rustled in the troughs and the occasional scutter of restive hooves was orchestrated by the hissing of the head groom as he worked over one of the mares with a curry comb. 'You can stop treating me like a child,' Henry reproved Plumstead. 'Just remember I'm eighteen now.'

Plumstead made no further reply. He followed the boy into the sunlight, watched him put his mount to the paddock fencing, clear it by a foot or more and vanish between the home park trees, some of which had been mere saplings when Charles Stuart sought among them for sanctuary in an elder's branches. Then he turned and went in again, on bowed and gaitered legs, muttering to himself, 'chip off the old block . . . a well-plucked young 'un if ever there was 'un . . . and don't forget old Plum, it was you wot first lifted 'im into the saddle when 'ee was just over two year old.'

In the west wing, which as yet lay in sunless shade, Henry's grandfather, ensconced in his four-poster behind the close drawn curtains, slept the light, intermittent sleep of old age. For him also, as lord of Castle Rising, this was to be a memorable day and not alone because he had first drawn breath eighty years ago. As yet, of all the household, only young Henry was abroad, astride the mount old Henry had supplied; but the hands of the stable clock and of all those other clocks within the Castle walls, which Mr Perkins came every week to tend and regulate, were moving towards 5.45 a.m. when further occupants would be awakening.

As the clocks struck this third quarter Mabel and her fellow scullerymaid, Agnes, shook themselves reluctantly from sleep, stretched, exclaimed, threw back the bedclothes and flexed their toes before standing, barefoot, upon the linoleum covered floor. Then they washed sleep from their eyes, pouring cold water into a flowered basin from flowered jugs—both of which rested on the marble surface of their shared, deal wash-stand. Their scanty ablutions completed, they drew on thick black woollen stockings, dropped striped pink cotton morning dresses over their heads, tied themselves into stiffly-starched, crackling aprons and tucked every scrap of roughly combed hair under frilled cotton caps. Thus accoutred, their feet thrust into black strap and button shoes, they made their way hurriedly down the steepest flight of the servants' stairs like two caparisoned starlings twittering out scraps of trivial chatter, roughened red hands thrust deep into apron pockets.

As the chimes rang out proclaiming the hour, the pair of them removed their aprons, and took down two sacking ones; even upon this memorable day there was the great range to clean, twin residues of cinders to rake out and then twin fires to lay with all the speed they could achieve. The fires were laid with paper, kindling and the little twists of paraffin-moistened coal dust and the small coals piled on top—which Alfred the yard boy prepared every night before his long trudge home and left inside the porch which led to the first of the kitchen outhouses. Then with the fires beginning to crackle Mabel swept up the cinders and ash from the wide hearth and fetched a lump of whitening from a dank cupboard below the vegetable sink. She scraped the whitening down with a knife which Mrs Parsons—Cook—would later that day observe caustically was 'long overdue for the knife grinder, me girl.' This done, Mabel mixed the powder to a paste, took some mildew-smelling cloths and a scrub brush from a further noisome cavity and fell on her knees to scrub in and smooth down the whitening until it glowed with pristine whiteness. She knew better than to start the day by invoking the wrath of Cook of whom all the lower servants stood in awe if not in actual terror.

Meanwhile, Agnes lugged the huge iron kettles to the nearest kitchen tap, filled them and staggered back across the flagged floors with them, setting them over the circular, opened maws of the stove. Between each journey she took the kitchen bellows and blew the nozzle carefully upon the young flames to ensure the fire was 'drawing proper'. Should Mrs Parsons descend to find either fire out instead of glowing redly through the iron bars, Agnes was well aware she would be lucky to escape with a stinging box upon both ears. The two girls scuttled about like demented little squirrels. There were the trays to lay for early morning tea with which they must climb those many flights of stairs to the butler's bedroom, to Mrs Parsons', Mrs Peace the housekeeper and to her ladyship's personal maid, to the vinegary Mademoiselle Palliser who, like her even more temperamental compatriot, chef Monsieur André, and all visitors' maids and valets, rated special service in the below stairs hierarchy. Then there were the thick white cups to set out on the huge servants' hall table and the big brown teapot to warm, the milk to fetch, the sugar bowl to fill and all before those relentless clock hands had reached 6.15!

'Fire's drawing orlright,' Mabel announced, dusting off the front of the sack apron and changing back into her white one once again. 'You get them cups and things, I'll do the trays.'

When Mrs Parsons made her appearance the hands had galloped to 6.30. Both girls scattered like chaff before her as she commanded, 'Scrub them floor stones now . . . get them kettles refilled . . . look sharp there and the copper's not lit nor filled either, so how will George and Richard get their jugs filled when the time comes I would like to know? Fetch Sam this minute.' Meanwhile George and Richard, too sleepy still to even mutter their daily hymns of hate against Mrs Parsons' creaking corseted back, were already hard at it, sleeves rolled back, green baize aprons tied securely, polishing the sixteen brass jugs which the two kitchen maids would carry between them to sixteen bedrooms.

By now these two had made only one brief pause, in which they leaned thankfully against the kitchen table and, with the rest of the under servants, sipped their strong hot tea, sweetened with two surreptitious extra lumps while Mrs Parsons' back was turned.

By now the kitchens and sculleries were seething with activity. The kitchenmaids were scudding about setting out the trays, lining up the various 'early tea services', which the house parlourmaids —Mason and Pearson ('like them 'airbrushes', as they were wont to joke in lighter moments) laid on the traycloths, set out the china and silver and then busied themselves cutting the paper-thin, alternately laid slices of brown and white bread and butter which also went up on every tray.

Then Mr Sawby entered, shrugging himself into his below-stairs alpaca jacket. 'Agnes, my girl,' he said severely from the doorway, 'look sharp there *please*, my sitting room fire is not yet lit nor the breakfast laid and where is Mabel may I enquire?'

'Coming Mr Sawby,' cried Agnes, bringing in the last tea set, and 'Coming Mr Sawby,' cried her opposite number Mabel dashing in from the corridor which led to the cleaning cupboards.

'Hurry along then, girl, you too, Agnes, and see to it you wash your faces again before you sit down to breakfast. A nice thing for our staff reputation if you were to be seen by our guests with smuts on your nose.' His sharp eyes glimpsed Mabel's back vanishing around the corner and he raised his voice, 'Mabel, straighten your stockings, girl, they're all awry and twisted.' Then in the same breath but with a total change of voice, 'Good morning, Mrs Parsons, and how do you do on this eventful morning?'

'So so,' said Mrs Parsons, not well pleased by Mr Sawby's topping of her authority with the kitchen girls, 'A twinge of rheumatism I fancy. I'll need to go steady to get through a day like this,' thus avenging herself with the reminder that if *that* was his attitude he could expect no extra help from *her* today. So saying, she refilled her cup and carried it into their sitting room where the fire was beginning to crackle. Thus she was able to supervise the laying of the breakfast table, at which Mr Sawby, she and the rest of the upper servants, would eat in splendid isolation, and at the same time she was able, through the open door, to 'keep a sharp look out' at the table preparations in the servants' hall.

Beyond these two rooms, in the main kitchen, staff breakfasts were in train while George and Richard laid the table in the servants' hall and Mrs Parsons kept up a running commentary upon the importance, even at a family house-party, of the precedence which each member's personal servant should enjoy in the servants' hall, be he valet or personal maid. The nursery staff under the iron rule of Nanny would breakfast in the day nursery and all their trays would be carried up by the two under footmen. The head footman Edward was already in the breakfast room setting out a fourth table and checking the spirit stoves under hot plates which, even in this French-influenced household, supported the standard of early nourishment with such an array of dishes as totally covered the sideboard and two butler's trays as well.

'Omigawd,' ejaculated George suddenly, stopping in his tracks with a handful of silver, 'the newspapers!'

He dived for a flat iron, set it on the hob, and shot out of the kitchen door. Mrs Parsons rose. 'He's late,' she announced magisterially, 'and no one told me,' and so sailed like a small galleon in the wake of her errant footman. She was referring to an overdue daily ceremony.

Outside, a gig was drawn up as it had been each morning from the inception of the daily newspaper delivery round. At the reins, only now dismounting, was the 'newsboy' Samuel Groby, who looked like a rosy, withered pippin and who had already seen some sixty summers go by. Mrs Parsons helped herself to two sugar lumps from the bowl on the 'hall' table and tacked on to greet Mr Groby with a very sharp, 'Groby, you're late and morning tea ready to take upstairs.'

'I'm sure I'm very sorry ma'am,' apologised the pippin dismounting on legs so bandy that they seemed to be two drawn bows coming together at a pair of remarkably small, neat feet. 'Tom shed a shoe a hundred yards short of the smithy. I had to wake smith up and wait while he heated anvil up afore we could reshoe him.'

'Well, you're here now,' said Mrs Parsons, apparently appeased, 'and here's Tom's sugar.' She toddled to the horse's head to hold out her hand. 'Take your sugar, Tom, and remember it's not at all the thing to cast a shoe afore the Castle papers is delivered.'

Samuel reached into the cart and handed the newspapers over to George who snatched them up and ran back to his flat iron to go to work upon them before Mr Sawby could fold and set them on the trays. Then, mindful of his other overdue responsibility, he rushed back with the 'something warming for Samuel' which Mrs Parsons supplied each morning from September 1st to June 1st, changing therefrom to 'something to quench the thirst' in the warmer months between.

Slowly, but in an aura of hustle and bustle, the servants executed their preliminary duties, putting on pace towards the end as those relentless clocks moved on to 7.00 a.m. Promptly, as the hour chimed, the visiting maids and valets descended and with Monsieur André looking, to them, morning-peculiar in an alpaca jacket similar to Mr Sawby's and with his scant wisps of thinning hair exposed by the absence of his High Bonnet which, as he was always telling these English was properly called his *Coq de Cuisine*.[1] Whenever he so did Mrs Parsons would say, deep in her throat, 'Doesn't sound quite naice to me!' and then Monsieur André would lift his shoulders high in a Gallic expression of defeat and exclaim, '*Mon Dieu, les Anglais*' before

[1] Virtually untranslatable—and suitably so! F.C.

marching into the kitchen to supervise the baking of the croissants he had prepared the night before for his own and Mademoiselle Palliser's delectation.

Back at the table, the lower staff were now all seated at breakfast with the head parlourmaid at one end and the head footman at the other. Chef, in the Housekeeper's Room, would dunk his croissant in his coffee, ingest and gulp with considerable noise—this never failed to make Mr Sawby and Mrs Parsons flinch—but, save for these 'vulgar sounds', quiet would reign for the precise twenty-five minutes allotted for this meal by Mr Sawby.

At this same time, with one and a half hours' work behind them, the gardening staff and the stable staff, from youngest stable boy to head groom and gardener, could be seen—if anyone were interested—trudging back the minimum half mile to the nearest of the staff cottages; the while Mr Sawby snapped open his gunmetal half-hunter and glanced at his sitting room clock to confirm the synchronisation of both. Then he opened the door. 'Time to get moving,' he announced. 'Housemaids look to their boxes; kitchenmaids clear the tables; scullerymaids to their dishwashing and footmen with me to the breakfast room.'

Mademoiselle gathered up her voluminous skirts, Mrs Parsons rose and she and Chef moved towards the kitchen. Mr Sawby merely processed—such stately movements could scarcely be called walking—in the van of his footmen up the staff stairway, as he called it, or 'them dratted steep stairs', as the lower servants called them, en route for Family Breakfast.

Then things began to hum. Mrs Parsons stationed herself at the outer kitchen's door in readiness to receive her sworn enemy, Mr Sawbridge the head gardener. She hitched her shawl closer around her shoulders for, as she had earlier observed when feeding Tom, it was 'a trifle parky for the second day of September'; then Sawbridge appeared, accompanied by the boy Ted, both pushing the 'house trolley' upon which the first consignment of kitchen garden requirements for that eventful day were stowed in their special containers.

Mrs Parsons acknowledged Sawbridge with a grudging nod. 'Stack them down 'ere please Mr Sawbridge,' she pointed majestically with one hand, 'my maids will collect and distribute.'

In silence Sawbridge withdrew the trays of trimmed leeks, young carrots, prime shallots and the first picking of the last crop of *petits pois*—concerning which Mrs Parsons was wont to state to her cronies, with knowledge brushed off on to her by Monsieur André, 'none of your bursting, pellet-sized, bright green ones for this Frenchified household!' The pile grew apace: slender three-inch-long courgettes, French beans as narrow as match-sticks, small, beautifully rounded baby turnips, and a surmounting trug with all the herbs, *fines herbes* and garlic heads that M. André would require for his stocks and sauces. All these were taken out and set down, washed and trimmed, under Mrs Parsons' critical inspection. Then, 'Where's me greens?' she demanded sourly.

'Coming, Mrs P,' replied Sawbridge equably, 'on the next load with the tomatoes, 'ot 'ouse veg and after them the fruits what Tompkins and Dick is picking now. Then I'll take care of the peaches, neck-tarines and me pines wot 'ave come on splendid for the occasion.'

Mrs Parsons grunted. 'Well, I want them greens for staff to 'ave for their dinner. Sharp at twelve it will be today.' Turning about at the opened doorway, 'Joan,' she shrieked, 'Mabel, Agnes, Eliza, come 'ere this instant,' and a covey of kitchen and scullery maids appeared as if conjured up from space.

When the trolley was emptied, Sawbridge touched his cap, about-turned and went off with Joe, the second gardener's son. He was not going to be antagonised by 'that ole dragon, whomsoever 'as their bowels fermented by her wiciousness' as he was wont to confide to his helpmeet when, at the end of a long day he sat, in carpet slippers which she had made, toasting his gnarled, splay-feet at the crackling fire in their rag-rug-floored kitchen; an exercise which he was wont to acknowledge ruefully 'is comfortin' but in winter sets up me chilblains something crool.'

Mrs Parsons, scarlet with chagrin at having failed to draw blood during this encounter, returned to the kitchen and promptly took it out on the girls.

Having set matters in train in the breakfast room to his own, if not to the footmen's satisfaction, Sawby gave a last glance around before returning to the servants' hall. His eye roved critically across the three sideboards where not even he could find fault with the polished surfaces of the oak, nor the sheen upon the silver which had been made during the reign of the first King George. He turned his attention to the second sideboard where he noted the positioning of the stands, the 'cold collations' from ham to raised pies, then he inspected the third which even won a slight nod of approval for the arrangement of fruits on pewter platters, and he finally permitted himself a slight scowl at the sight of Miss Patience's dish of stewed prunes. Then his eyes warmed again as he glanced around the linenfold panelling, the 'small portraits', the high-backed Stuart chairs and the long narrow refectory table, centred by a low bowl of *Maréchale Neil* roses whose name he did not actually know.

Arrived 'below', Sawby 'went through' the post and then extracted a piece of paper from his alpaca pocket and summoned the two housemaids. The early morning tea trays were now lined up on the erstwhile breakfast table from which the kitchenmaids had already cleared away, having also done the washing up. A pile of freshly ironed newspapers were set beside the letters. Sawby always enjoyed sorting these since he was thus enabled to obtain his first-of-the-day gleanings on family activities.

The scullerymaids were out in the vegetable room tackling the mountain of pot vegetables issued to them by M. André ... leeks to wash, top and tail, onions and shallots to peel, very ripe tomatoes to plunge in boiling water and then skin under cold water, young heads of celery, not the best since as yet there had been no frost but good enough for André's basic liquors. Like two dejected Niobes they wept into their work—the cause not sorrow but onions!

In his kitchen M. André was trotting to and from his *garde manger*[2] carrying copper terrines and casseroles of pre-prepared basic items which had already been cooked for his *diner d'anniversaire*.[3] On his baize board, which hung below the barred windows, the day's luncheon and dinner menus, in his spidery handwriting, were pinned neatly into position. Luncheon, by decree, was to be a truncated meal of a mere six courses; the dinner eleven elegant ones with the usual range of alternatives.

Over his head, the *Jambons de Bayonne*,[4] blackened and very hard, dangled from the beams with the special herbs, bunches of which were replaced each week. At the opposite end, on a much smaller board and written laboriously by Mrs Parsons,

[2] Cold larder.
[3] Anniversary dinner.
[4] Bayonne ham used in classic cookery in place of salt for imparting a special flavour to certain sauces etc.

were her round pot-hook type meal lists. These ranged from Nursery breakfast, through luncheon to supper and included the breads, scones and suchlike for the day, together with tea in the library, all staff meals and the sandwiches and beverage lists for the bedrooms which had to be installed 'last thing', after dinner had been served. Thus it was ensured that no fears of night starvation could arise. Mrs Parsons always referred to these as the 'bedside nourishments'. She had, in fact, remarked about this last chore while in a mood of rare expansion, 'Well, at least we don't 'ave to serve 'em lobster salads for tea what His Majesty 'as to 'ave, God Bless 'im. On the same subject young Stephen was to be harshly reproved by his papa later in the day for remarking at the table—albeit after the ladies had withdrawn— 'If you ask me, I'd say the old king is digging his own grave with his teeth and his phallus.'

At this precise moment Mrs Parsons was too absorbed for any extraneous conversation. She was too busy 'setting' the first crumpets of the autumn season, baking the already proven Chelsea Buns, spooning her mixture into sponge finger tins (for the nursery) and supervising the weighing out of ingredients for sand cake, seed cake and what she called 'me pin der peace' which M. André corrected at the shriek into *Pain d'Epices.*[5]

The hands of the kitchen clock registered six minutes to 8.00 a.m. The housemaids warmed and filled the teapots, fitted on the small teacosies with their linen slip covers all bearing the white, embroidered de Lorme crest.[6] The three footmen clattered down the stairs. Mr Sawby cleared his throat and began reading from his piece of paper and after each order he paused to hand over a pile of letters.

'His-Lordship-*The-Times*-and-the-*Telegraph*-and-here-are-his-Lordship's-letters' (pause) 'Her Ladyship . . .' and so on through the list ending, 'Mr Henry—the *Sporting Pink* and what looks remarkably like a string of bills and invitations in about equal numbers.' The staff sniggered. He quelled them with a single glance over the top of his steel-rimmed spectacles, then removed them from his nose, inserted them in his jacket pocket, gave The Nod and the cortège moved upwards with their bur-

---

[5] French gingerbread.
[6] An astrolabe won by the first Henri's father. It was an instrument formerly used to take altitudes and to solve other problems in astronomy, besides being used in the draining of the Norfolk fens.

dens. They were met on the first landing by Mrs Peace the housekeeper, a well-upholstered figure of fashionable hour-glass shape, encased in black from throat to toes, her hair swept up and coiled in marvellous imitation of a popular current sweetmeat called by Nanny—the whipped cream walnut. Mrs Peace settled her pince-nez on the bridge of her pinch-pointed nose and, at the sight of the first tray bearer, turned round with a tremendous swish of petticoats, rapped very discreetly upon the first door, listened, then turned the handle and held it open for the maid to enter. Then she listened again until she heard the sounds of shutters being folded back and curtains being drawn. This was her cue to open the door once more, push in a kitchenmaid with her 'box' containing sound-insulating gloves as well as hearth-clearing and cleaning implements, duster and scuttle of coals. Her duty was to lay and light each fire so that the welcoming crackle and the pretty leap of flames should further encourage the occupant towards the effort of getting out of bed and being dressed.

Once this routine had been repeated sixteen times, and the kitchenmaids had vanished from the upper floors, Mrs Peace hurried off to make sure all personal maids and valets were ready to assist their employers in the arduous matter of getting themselves ready for the 'nine o'clock gong'.

Those returning to the lower regions were now titillated by the fragrance of frying bacon, sizzling kidneys, baking *croissants* and above all M. André's coffee. 'One of these days,' confided George to Richard, 'I'll 'ave me breakfast at nine or 'arf past, lolling back with a plateful of cold game pie instead of porridge.' Mrs Parsons overheard and snapped, 'Well, it won't be terday, so stop yer nonsense and look slippy me lad.'

Boots was being titillated too. He stood within three feet of M. André at the enormous kitchen range. This Sam, as he was properly called, was a poor, withered leaf of a man, dwindled, as one could fairly say, by having been a chimney sweep in his very early days. The long hours up chimneys, half-stifled with soot, had wreaked havoc with him, even destroyed his genitals; but he was rescued by the family and given a cupboard under the back stairs in which to sleep and the boots and shoes for the entire household to clean for five shillings per week and his food. This he regarded as a sinecure, although in reality he was employed ceaselessly from 5.00 a.m. until close on eight o'clock at night.

He had already snatched what he called 'a breather', gulped a cup of scalding hot tea with plenty of sugar in it, downed a large plate of the porridge despised by Richard and just struggled in to M. André with two hods of coke which he poured into the avid maws of No. 2 fire on chef's range. Now he stood back, enjoying a second 'breather' and watching with fanatical admiration chef's deft, unhurried movements as he prepared his *Oeufs Brouillés à la Forestière*,[7] skinned and split his kidneys for *Rognons en Brochette*[8] and broke eggs with one hand on to the base of cream and diced ham in the bottom of a dozen miniature cocottes. Sam watched, as always totally riveted in attention upon this culinary alchemist. He saw chef wind a fresh frill around the bone of a *Jambon de York*, insert sprigs of Sawbridge's freshly picked parsley in the central cavity of a *Pâté en Croûte*[9] and slip cutlet frills over the vee-shaped bone ends of tiny pink cutlets which were also to appear on the breakfast table as *Les Côtelettes à la 'Reform'*.[10] Suddenly, chef glanced up at Sam and the creature smiled sheepishly. 'Wunnerful to watch,' he said hoarsely. 'Right down marvel you are, sir, and that's the truth.'

For the first time that morning chef smiled, gave a tiny shrug, tugged at his Imperial and vouchsafed graciously, *'Cela se voit mon vieux*,'[11] then he glanced around. ' 'Ere, take thees...' he said, surreptitiously slipping a surplus cutlet into the little creature's hands. *'Allez y*,'[12] he commanded. 'Pees off,' and, so saying, he picked up half a pound of farm butter and began running it through his fingers into a copper pan for the cooking of his French scrambled eggs.

The pace was mounting. Mrs Parsons, at her end (and never did the twain merge), was handing over grain-separate rice for straining in order to assemble her kedgeree while, in the same cause, Joan chopped separated hard-boiled eggs into little mounds of white and yellow. Eliza sliced mushrooms for Chef, 'and hurry up with that nonsense, girl,' snapped Mrs Parsons, 'I've got me finna 'addies to watch and someone'll 'ave to grill them

---

7 Scrambled eggs with mushrooms.
8 Skewered kidneys.
9 Pâté enclosed in a crisp pastry crust.
10 Served in manner of Reform Club when Alexis Soyer was head of the kitchen.
11 Literally 'it sees itself'—that's obvious,
12 'Off you go,'

kippers. It's more'n'me life's worth to boil 'em the easy way in *this* Frenchified 'ousehold.'

The pace increased still more. Richard scuttled up the stairs with napkin-covered wicker baskets of freshly baked, piping hot scones and croissants. George pelted after him carrying a long silver tray laden with jams and jellies and a single pot of Cooper's Oxford Marmalade which only Miss Prudence liked. Miss Prudence was the lapsed member of the family who had acquired 'strange English habits'. These the majority of the family had calmly withstood for eight hundred and forty-one years. They merely endeavoured, when in some English households, to avoid, without offending the normal tenets of good behaviour, such horrors as the service of cheese after pudding—this they overcame merely by always refusing the latter. In the main, however, they were the first to admit that standards were now higher than they had ever been before.

At this precise moment in time French chefs and French waiters were glad of the privilege of working in London which was acknowledged by them as being '*une centre gastronomique et culinaire*',[13] though few, including Chef André, could resist the appended rider '*à cause de nous*'.[14] This situation was of course accelerated in an hitherto unprecedented manner by the arrival in England of a man destined to immortality. His name was Georges Auguste Escoffier. He was so small that he had to wear high heels in his kitchens in order to raise his face above the blazing heat of the old coal oven. The impact of the book which he actually wrote in London, *Le Guide Culinaire*[15] (1902) was enormous and it was available in very good, original translation, it exerted a powerful influence throughout the catering trade and was Monsieur André's bible; even as Mrs Marshall's Cookery Books were nonpareil to Mrs Parsons, who never lost an opportunity of recalling how she had actually attended classes at Mrs Marshall's School of Cookery in Great Mortimer Street.

Up went the cutlets, the kidneys, the bacon and at long last up

---

[13] A centre of gastronomy and the culinary art.
[14] Due entirely to us.
[15] Escoffier's greatest works are *Les Eloges de la Cuisine Française*. These are virtually unobtainable in England, but the author has been able to study them because she is an honorary member of the Escoffier Society for which a special building has been erected in the great man's birthplace, Villeneuve-Loubet. Sold in fine English translation as (pre-1908) *A Guide to Modern Cookery*. The author has given up trying to find her way about in later editions.

went Sawby, now changed into his morning apparel. As he walked across the hall he drew on his white cotton gloves. The clocks began to chime and ring and tinkle their chimes and delicate carillons. Edward slipped into position beside the enormous brass gong, picked up the drum stick and watched Sawby, who now stood beside the opened breakfast room door, gunmetal half-hunter open in one gloved hand, the other upraised in readiness. As the last stroke of nine was sounded Sawby dropped his hand and snapped down the lid of his watch.

Edward struck. With the ease of long practice he sent the rolling sonorous din echoing and eddying upstairs, downstairs and along the corridors of Castle Rising, as down the great staircase came Gyles de Lorme, his Lordship's forty-five-year-old son and heir.

THE FAMILY AT BREAKFAST

Monday, September 2nd, 1907

Bishop Alaric de Lorme
Mrs (Dorothy) de Lorme
Countess Marguerite de Tessedre
Miss Prudence de Lorme
Mr John de Lorme
Mr Eustace St John
Mrs (Henrietta) Delahaye
Mr Sinclair Delahaye
Mr Christian de Lorme
Mrs (Claire) de Lorme
Mr Henry de Lorme
Mr Gyles de Lorme

CHAPTER 5

The Family At Breakfast

Henry de Lorme heard the gong as he hurried back from the stables. His mud-spattered breeches and jacket, tousled hair and filthy hands were the result of having stopped by the river bank to give Stardust a breather. On dismounting he had noticed a very slight movement in some bushes from which he had flushed out his old playmate, the local poacher Tim. After some initial protests from this disreputable friend, the two settled contentedly to tickling some of Lord Aynthorp's trout until, looking up from the bestowal of a trout in the cache of grasses Tim had made, Henry saw that he had forgotten his watch and that the sun had risen ominously high. With a hurried, 'I must go, Tim, I'll get hell if I'm late for breakfast,' he gathered up the reins, raced back, and returned the mare to 'Plum' who gave him a drubbing for riding her into a lather. Then Henry hurried off to change.

As the gong sounded he broke into a trot, taking the terrace steps three at a time, flinging himself around the garden door and skidding along the corridor where he narrowly avoided cannoning into George, the second footman, who flattened himself against the wall and apologised for what was not his fault. 'Begging your pardon, Mr Henry, I'm shaw.'

'Not your fault, George,' panted Henry. 'I'm late for breakfast . . . I'll get hell. . . .'

He knew that he must clean himself, effect a suitable change and present himself in the breakfast room not more than fifteen minutes after the hour or else he would suffer for his unpunctuality from his father. He had a very clear picture of Gyles de Lorme as he wrenched off his boots and breeches. There he would sit, groomed, brushed, polished, monocled, smelling faintly of Johann Maria Farina Eau de Cologne and impeccably dressed in what his French great-aunt always called 'les sales tweeds', with a fastidious wrinkling of her high-bridged Norman nose. As Henry wrenched open drawers and cupboards he mentally saw his father dip into his pocket, snap open his gold repeater, glance at it and enquire quellingly as he made his tardy entrance, 'I trust you are not ill, Henry?'

After three successive collar studs had rolled 'under things', Pine, his father's valet, had failed to answer his frantic tuggings at the bell pull, and one of his braces had come clean away in his hand, he must prick his thumb on his chosen tie-pin, ooze blood upon his clean shirt and have to begin all over again.

When, eventually, he slammed the door behind him, leaving a shambles which would not have discredited Caius Marius at Carthage, the clocks were striking the half hour. Down the great staircase the boy thudded, muttered, as he put one hand to the breakfast room door, 'OmiGod' then went in wearing a brave face which he felt was no more than a triumph of hope over experience.

His father was not in his usual seat. Instead he occupied Lord Aynthorp's, the old peer having been persuaded, with enormous difficulty, to eat breakfast in his dressing room in preparation for the rigours of this very special day.

As greater men than he had done before him, Henry decided that the best line of defence was attack. So, 'Good morning', he began generally, then looking directly at Gyles, 'Good morning sir, I really do apologise.' Thus launched, he gained confidence and ran on, 'There is nothing the matter with me ... never felt better in m'life. I woke early, took Stardust for a stretcher—with Plum's permission of course—then I ran her a bit hard so gave her a breather at Rupert's Pool and started watchin' the trout. There's a woppin' wily old 'un there as I expect you know, sir, and I expect you also know the bank's a trifle steep in places. Anyway I slipped, lost m'y balance and fell in. I was in such a state by the time I got out I had to clean up before presentin' m'self. Then I lost three collar studs, broke m'braces, and, as if that wasn't enough, pricked me thumb on m'tie pin and mucked up m'shirt so I had to start all over again ...' he ended lamely, 'that's why I'm so late, sir.'

Having looked down at his plate during this saga, primarily to conceal the glint in his eyes, Gyles looked up and observed surprisingly, 'Done it all m'y self. The more one hurries the worse matters become, eh?'

'Exactly so,' Henry agreed weakly.

Gyles then enquired, 'Might one ask do you not carry a watch?'

'Forgot it sir, know that is not an excuse.'

'Precisely.' Gyles pushed back his chair and rose, plate in hand. 'Well,' said he, 'as long as you were not sleepin'. Too much sleep's demoralisin'. Now get yer breakfast and say good mornin' to the ladies, I want some more of that excellent ham.' So saying he moved towards it and began carving, observing to the hovering footman, 'This ham is exceptional. York, of course?'

'Indeed yes, sir.'

Henry did the rounds, greeting first his great-aunts, since neither his mother nor grandmother were present, moving on to his aunts, planting chaste kisses on the ladies' cheeks, working through his great-uncles from Bishop Alaric, Lord Aynthorp's eldest brother, to John the youngest and then his uncles Eustace, Sinclair and Christian until, duty completed, he was free to lift lids from chafing dishes, inspect and select from their contents.

Conversation became general. Sawby slipped into the room, bent over the Countess Marguerite, who presided over the coffee pots, to enquire whether these needed replenishment. Obtaining an affirmative, he despatched Richard for fresh supplies; after which he consigned George to the nether regions in search of hot water for the teapot over which Marguerite's severe elder sister, Miss Prudence de Lorme, held sway in her mannish dress.

Henrietta Delahaye was recounting the latest scandal. 'Did you hear, Marguerite, that Sally Winterton has been struck from the Court List?'

'No, my dear,' replied Marguerite, equably relinquishing to Bishop Alaric the peach she was peeling. 'What persuaded the King to do such a thing?'

'Because she attended the last ball in a dress which nipped her cruelly and wore besides a train so heavily embroidered that she could not manage it.'

'Surely Sally did not confide such matter to His Majesty?' Marguerite raised an astonished eyebrow.

'No, not at all, she merely fell flat on her face in front of him and the Queen. Incidentally, I must say Her Majesty is quite amazing. They rumour she is over sixty-five!'

'She is,' Gyles observed.

'Well she looks like thirty-five and quite lovely.'

'Chocolate-box looks,' snorted Prudence. 'Ah, thank you, Sawby,' as the boiling water appeared at her elbow.

'Royalty,' murmured Gyles, 'do not realise the existence of accidents in their presence. They merely make irrevocable decisions. Freddy Ponsonby was tellin' me the other day at the club what happened when one of the grays in the royal escort foamed at the mouth and a spot floated off and landed on the old Queen's veil.'

Henry looked up. 'What did happen, sir?'

'A notice appeared outside Buck House the followin' mornin',' Gyles recounted drily. 'It ran, "In future, horses in the Royal Escort will not foam at the mouth." It was signed Victoria Regina.'

Amid the general laughter, Henry received a cup of coffee from his Great-Aunt Marguerite, whom he adored, plus a little loving pat from her and he sat down, noticing for the first time that his cousin Stephen Delahaye's chair was empty and that his uncle, Sinclair Delahaye, had heard nothing of the tale, and instead was endeavouring to catch Sawby's eye. He then did so. 'Sawby,' he said.

'Sir?'

'Have you seen anythin' of Mr Stephen this mornin'?'

'No, sir,' said Sawby, 'I'm afraid not, sir. Shall I make enquiries, sir?'

'If you please, and pray inform him that his presence has been anticipated at the breakfast table since the gong sounded at 9.00 a.m. It is now nine forty-five precisely.'

Sawby withdrew, motioning the other two servants to precede him. As he closed the door, 'What are the final arrangements for the car, Gyles?' enquired Prudence. 'Do we know when it arrives and what other plans your father has made for today? We are entirely in the dark and I for one would be obliged by a little information. I might also add that, while I do know that Gabrielle and Primrose are taking breakfast in bed—a habit which I deplore —I know nothin' of Robert, Damien, Rosemary or Priscilla.'

The Bishop's wife Dorothy came to her aid. 'I heard Alicia sayin' late last night, dear, that they were comin' down by motor in time for luncheon.'

'Indeed!' Prudence registered strong disapproval. 'I'm sure I admire your courage in trustin' your gels to one of those nasty horseless carriages but....'

'It is quite all right, Prue,' soothed the Bishop. 'Damien is drivin' and he is, I do assure you, the most cautious of men.'

'You can say that again!' muttered Henry under his breath. Fortunately this was not heard.

'And if the motor breaks down?' Dorothy faltered.

Alaric resumed smoothly, 'Then we have a further modern innovation to advise us of the fact, the electric speaking tube.'

'But supposin' it happened where there was no such form of what I call "frightenin' communication" available?' Dorothy countered.

Alaric placed white fingertips to white fingertips and answered his wife by the oblique method of addressing the table in general, which was well used to such exchanges. 'My dear wife,' he said, with a smile which owed nothing to amusement, 'my dear wife would, I am assured, if offered the choice of two evils, always take them both. There is no reason, my dear, to suppose any ill-event and I dare prophesy that all four will be with us for luncheon as arranged.'

Henry, busily polishing off croissants and cherry jam at an astonishing rate, amused himself with his own thoughts while this exchange ensued. *That old 'Miss'* (meaning Damien) *will take care nothing happens. Silly old fusspot! All the same I shall be surprised if they get here before the afternoon. He drives at about two miles per hour.* Wisely he kept his reflections to himself and re-concentrated on the conversation in time to hear Great-Uncle Alaric brush off his wife's alarums with, 'And now if you please, Dorothy, let Gyles tell us what the arrangements are which he has made for Justin's gift. I am sure we are all agog to know.'

'Gyles?' queried Dorothy, clearly indicating that in her opinion Alaric should have been the one to make such arrangements as were necessary.

'Yes, Gyles,' repeated Alaric, a trifle nettled. 'We settled it together last night. Gyles is, after all, Justin's heir. Now pray let us listen quietly.'

Gyles had been polishing his monocle on a corner of his table napkin during this exchange. Now he looked up at his uncle who nodded encouragingly. 'As you know,' he began, 'Father has agreed to take things very quietly until luncheon and so has Mother; but we all know what *that* means! Our present, the motor, is due to be delivered about eleven o'clock this mornin'.

Allowin' for the ever-present possibilities of some unexpected hitch, it should at worse be here well before luncheon.'

'Oh, sir,' exclaimed Henry, 'there are no hitches with Rolls Royce motor cars. A chap in my College was tellin' me they claim nothin' ever goes wrong.'

'Yes, yes, we know,' said Alaric testily, 'but if I were a writin' man I would write a book on "breakdowns I have experienced since the innovation of the horseless carriage" . . . however. . . .'

They were not to know what his next observation was for Sawby reappeared and stood waiting deferentially.

'Well, Sawby, is my son coming?' asked Sinclair impatiently.

'I fear I cannot say, sir,' said Sawby, 'I went to Mr Stephen's room only to find that his bed has not been slept in. The smoking jacket he wore last night is hanging in his wardrobe but,' Sawby coughed deprecatingly, 'I ascertained from Mr Gyles' man, who unpacked Mr Stephen on his arrival yesterday, that his hacking jacket, breeches, boots and other riding appurtenances are not to be found.'

'Thank you, Sawby,' said Sinclair dismissively.

'Thank *you*, sir.'

'Now what in the world,' fussed his mother as the door closed once again, 'is that boy doing. Has some accident befallen him I wonder?'

'Henrietta my dear,' said Sinclair soothingly, 'we do not have the remotest grounds for such a conjecture so pray let us set about finding out where he is first, instead of worrying ourselves unnecessarily.' He turned to Henry. 'Do you know anything of this?' he enquired.

'Not a thing, sir, I do assure you.' Henry's face had registered first surprise, then slight anxiety. 'After dinner we played a couple of frames of snooker and went to bed. We were both deuced tired after the ball the night before.'

'Deuced tired,' murmured Gyles with a twinkle, 'yet recovered in your case by 5.00 a.m.'

'Oh dear,' exclaimed Marguerite, 'I trust we are not beginning another *Something*.' Which obscure remark drew a most unladylike snort from Prudence and quelling glances from her brothers.

Alaric again intervened. 'Can we not return to the matter of the motor car? I am sure nothing is amiss with Stephen; after all, Henry was very late for breakfast and there is nothing wrong with him.'

Sinclair grunted, 'Oh, very well,' and Gyles resumed. 'I have arranged to send for Plum as soon as the motor arrives and have him conduct the car and chauffeur to the stables. Then the chauffeur can be given some luncheon and after we have had our own he can bring the motor back to the main entrance. I thought three o'clock would be a suitable time and I have arranged for a photographer to be here so that we can combine the giving of our gift with a photograph or two with which to commemorate the occasion.'

There was a general murmur of approval. 'Now is that not a capital arrangement, my dear?' enquired Alaric, beaming at his spouse. 'Which brings me to another matter. I really must crave attention for some moments for this is of paramount importance.' He patted his wife's rather mottled hand with his own white one. 'Not,' he ran on hastily, 'that it is any concern of yours. Indeed, it does not concern any of you girls.' He smiled a trifle archly and Dorothy obediently took the implicit direction.

'Just so,' she observed, putting down her napkin, 'I have letters to write and Mrs Peace wishes to see me on some matter. Then I have promised Alicia that I will look in on her before she dresses.' So saying, she rose and turned towards the door which Henry hurried to open for her.

Prudence rose too. 'And Alicia has also sent for me,' she announced, marching towards the door. She was followed by Marguerite who smiled at her favourite great-nephew, nodded and said, 'And me too, dear, so it cannot be anything very important,' and vanished with a delicious whispering sound of petticoats.

'Really,' thought Henry, returning to his seat after closing the door upon the last of his female relatives. 'She is quite the prettiest great-aunt anyone could wish to own.'

Christian de Lorme, who had been markedly silent throughout the meal, now said gloomily, 'There's somethin' in the wind, I can feel it in m'y bones. Claire has been summonsed too and I dare suppose all the other female members of this family turn in turn.'

'You would not be wrong,' Gyles said curtly. He and Alaric again exchanged glances, then, 'You tell them, Gyles, dear feller,' said Alaric, looking portentous, an appearance he was well qualified to present.

'No,' said Gyles. 'You do it since it must be done.'

The Bishop was adamant, insisting, 'It is only right and proper that as the Heir it is you who should speak.'

Sinclair's patience was wearing thin. 'Well, whatever it is,' he said testily, 'I for one am not goin' to spend the rest of the mornin' at this dishevelled breakfast table while you two back and fill like a couple of unsatisfactory fillies. I want to find my son.'

Gyles turned to him. 'My dear chap, we are most inconsiderate, I really do apologise; but this is a matter of some gravity and, for me, of some delicacy too.'

Henry's eyes were fixed upon his father. He experienced a faint prickling at the back of his neck.

'Well?' said Sinclair, unrelenting.

Gyles cleared his throat. 'Father,' he said quietly, 'is handin' over.' Ejaculations of astonishment and disbelief ran round the table.

'Handin' over.'

'Good God!'

'Whatever started that strange hare?'

Henry tackled his father bravely since he seemed unwilling to embellish the bald statement. 'But can you not tell us why, sir? I mean, the old man was out ridin' yesterday, spry as a linnet, in the pink, first rate fettle I should say. ... Is there somethin' wrong with him that we do not know?'

All eyes were on Gyles now. 'To the best of my knowledge and belief,' Gyles answered, 'there is nothin' wrong with him at all. I will tell you all I know, but as you may imagine this has thrown me too. I had thought Father good for many years yet— if I thought at all—which I am now beginnin' to wonder.'

'After all,' Alaric mused, 'dear old Justin is eighty.'

'What's eighty to us?' flashed Gyles. 'We are long-lived stock. Right back and back to Norman times, why when everyone was dyin' off in their forties, Henri de Lorme, who had our Barony from King William, lived to be over sixty and then only died of sheer loneliness, bored with livin' alone.'

'Perhaps,' speculated Eustace, 'he wants to give you the reins now so that he can school you a bit?'

'That is a capital thought,' exclaimed Alaric, ever one to grasp a consoling straw. 'I'm sure that is a splendid suggestion. Rest assured that is what your dear Pater had in mind.'

'I rather think not,' said Gyles frigidly. 'Father has never lacked the initiative to school us at any time, had he a mind for it. Most certainly he need not *hand over* to do so now!'

'I agree,' said Christian sombrely. 'There's more to it than that.'

John got up to pour himself yet another cup of coffee. There was a short silence, into which he said 'stone cold' as he tasted the cupful and put it down.

Alaric tried again. 'Could your dear old Pater be feelin' the weight of years, even though he presents such a splendid face to the world?' he speculated.

'I wish,' said Gyles, frayed beyond his usual rigid self-control, 'you would not keep callin' m'y father "the dear old Pater" as if he were some dodderin' old country parson, when all of us know he has the fiend of a temper, all too easily aroused, rules us with a stockwhip if necessary to keep us in line and has a crimson flow of oaths when driven to 'em. After dinin' he can sink a bottle of port with the best of us and has never had a day's illness in his life.'

Alaric made no reply to this, just allowed his fingers to stray towards the heavy gold cross which dangled across his more than slightly convex paunch.

Gyles resumed more mildly. 'He only told me last night. He said that he had decided some weeks ago and, incidentally, I entirely agree that somethin' must have happened. He said that he had chosen his eightieth birthday as a suitable time for tellin' us, hence the summons to all the immediate, adult members of the family. He has it all worked out as usual. We are merely to follow the lines he will lay down. Tonight, after dinner, Mother will take all the ladies into the white drawing room and explain in full to them. When they have withdrawn, Father will invoke his ancient right to hand over while he still lives.'

'Did he say that as if he thought he was not to be with us much longer?' John queried. 'Did he give you any indication as to his thoughts?'

Gyles looked at his youngest uncle and lifted his eyebrows faintly, 'Did he ever?'

John nodded. 'Point taken, we are still in the nursery and if we are good little fellers we shall be told as much as is good for us tonight.'

'That's about the size of it,' said Eustace with a sigh. 'Sinclair, what do you make of all this?'

'A deuced odd affair altogether,' he confessed. 'But then remember I am only married into the family and not of it.'

'Poor Sinclair,' Gyles sympathised. 'First Stephen's prank and now this. I cannot help thinkin' you will come to regard this in retrospect as a very disagreeable day.'

'Oh, not at all, not at all,' said Sinclair hastily. 'Pray do not imagine such a thing for a moment. I am just out of m'y depth and gropin'. It's a deuced great honour to be asked...most signally aware that this is so I do assure you.'

'What does Aunt Alicia think?' Christian wondered.

'Whatever she thinks she's ridin' it easy' said Gyles, grinning at his recollections. 'I looked in on her on the way down. Palliser had already dressed her hair and taken away her breakfast tray. There she sat, bolt upright, wearin' a peignoir which mightily became her. She looked ridiculously young and was busy makin' the table plan and sketchin' out the design to be used for the flowers on the dinner table and in the *épergnes*.'[1]

John chuckled appreciatively, Sinclair exclaimed 'Fanastic' and Christian answered him. 'Not for her,' he said, 'just normal. She is a very remarkable old personage, which I know is shockin' disrespectful, but her command and energy enslave me and I only hope that my Claire will be one half of what she is by the time she's nearin' eighty.'

'No one,' boomed Alaric, 'will ever be the half of what our generation are. They do not have the stamina today. Dear me, but this is a distressin' business! Not,' he added hurriedly, 'that in the...er...eventual course of events I...er...will not be proud to serve the family under your stewardship, Gyles, do not misunderstand me.'

Gyles flung him an absent-minded grin and continued examining a Rockingham coffee cup before him as though he had never seen it previously and now found it a remarkable object. 'He did say one other thing,' he vouchsafed finally.

'Who? The guvnor?'

'Yes, he said he thought I might enjoy havin' time to accustom m'yself to the idea and then he added this—I hope I remember it aright—"tonight after dinner I will exert my ancient rights in handin' on both the Heirloom and the administration to you. I shall then remain the titular head of this family until my time

---

[1] Elaborate tiered baskets in silver gilt, gold or silver, containing vases for large spreading flower arrangements which rose to prodigious heights.

comes to go." Havin' so said, he reached for another cigar and began talkin' about the badgers who, in his opinion, are becomin' slightly too prolific.' He shrugged, 'Anyway, that still leaves me wantin' to know *why*.'

'Then, tell me if I have it right, sir,' stammered Henry. 'From tomorrow you will run the place? Handle all the affairs? Do the estate rounds? Deal with the Agent?'

'Exactly so,' said Gyles evenly.

'And does it mean you will be havin' the Heirloom too?'

'Yes,' said Gyles, 'I suppose ... it does ... I had not ... considered that ... as ... yet.'

Sound subsided as they all reflected. Then into the pool of silence young Henry flung his stone.

'Do you suppose,' he asked, scarcely above a whisper, 'that Grandfather has seen Odin's Hound?'

Before anyone could reply the door opened and Sawby entered. 'Excuse me, gentlemen,' said he, 'but there is a chauffeur at the main entrance with a motor. He says he has been instructed to deliver a yellow Rolls Royce and is asking for you, Mr Gyles.'

CHAPTER 6

The Yellow Rolls Royce

Throughout the day Henry's question haunted the men of the Family who had heard it posed at the breakfast table. It was still there when they gathered in the great hall before luncheon and watched as Lord Aynthorp handed his wife down the staircase up which Patch de Lorme had once set his favourite hunter when bayed to desperation by the Bow Street Runners. It set their necks prickling as they raised their glasses in a birthday toast and drank the peer's health and, as the murmur rose, 'Happy birthday grandfather ... father ... Uncle ... Justin ...' it was oppressively so.

As Lord and Lady Aynthorp reached the bottom tread the family surged forward and engulfed them. Because this was still very much a French family, scarcely more than tempered by England and her tradition, in moments of otherwise carefully suppressed emotion they automatically kissed or shook hands. The old peer stood smiling, acknowledging each one, clearly enjoying the fuss; an erect figure, so lean and similar to his son Gyles, his old eyes sparkling under their craggy brows, upright as an old tree whose roots still gripped very firmly.

'What're you all drinkin'?' he enquired.

Sawby stood at his elbow with a decanter on a silver salver. 'Your favourite *Verdelho*,[1] my lord,' he murmured, permitting himself a slight twinkle—with due deference.

'Splendid, pour me a glass if you please.' Lord Aynthorp turned to his wife, calling her by the name only he used, 'Meg, will you take a glass with me—it's the *Verdelho*?'

'Indeed I will,' she replied briskly, twinkling at him, 'if only for my health's sake, dear Justin.'

Henry, watching intently, gulped and emptied his glass too fast.

[1] One of the two dry Madeiras in the four grouping *Sercial, Verdelho,* and sweet *Bual* and Malmsey.

'Precisely,' agreed the old peer, handing her a glass, 'and now I will make my little speech.' He raised his glass and a hush descended upon them all. 'Brothers and sisters,' he said clearly, 'children, grandchildren, nieces and nephews . . . all my Family, thank you for your good wishes and may you have a very pleasant day.'

'The old boy looks as chipper as ever,' whispered Henry to his very young Aunt Rosemary who had arrived safely a few moments before, wearing a large hat tied under her chin with an even larger veil and covered by a long beige 'dust coat' which fell to her ankles.

'Why should he not?' Rosemary whispered back, puzzled.

Henry stared a moment, then realised and said, 'Of course, you do not know. Come in a corner with me away from them all, you too, Priscilla' (to his other young aunt who was only six years older than himself), 'and I will explain.'

The trio turned towards the mullioned windows seats and here settled themselves, heads together.

The girls' escorts, Damien and his brother Robert, were handing over their gifts to their uncle who, having exclaimed in pleasure, passed them on to Richard. 'I have decided to enjoy the openin' of all my presents after luncheon in the library,' he explained, 'and now, Sawby, you may replenish my glass with some more of that splendid Madeira.'

Damien lingered. 'You have a great fancy for Madeiras, Uncle Justin?'

'Indeed I have. I acknowledge that this is an English custom, and one for which I have a great predilection, as had m'y father, grandfather and great-grandfather before me. How much do you know about 'em—the Madeiras, I mean.'

'Lamentably little, sir,' Damien acknowledged, 'but I have always been greatly taken by the ones you have given me to drink here.'

The old man looked at him sharply from under those shaggy white eyebrows. He did not particularly care for 'the boy' who, as he had confided to his Meg, was 'too missish for my likin', too finnikin' altogether'; but these comments sent Damien's stock up as it was intended to do by the 'boy' who was rising forty.

'Fascinatin' study,' the old peer added. 'We have as fine a collection in m'y cellars as you can hope to find anywhere today except in the Blandy, Cossart, Leacock or Zino cellars.'

'And who are they, Uncle Justin?'

'The four great English families who rule Madeira,' he replied, 'but that's another story. Now, what was I sayin'? Oh yes, m'cellar, of course there have been no vintages since the two scourges.'

'Scourges?' Damien raised delicate eyebrows. 'You must think me a fearful ignoramus, sir.'

'Not at all, not at all, but it's a fascinatin' study which I commend to you, m'boy. There were two diseases which demolished the vines in Madeira. First the *Oedum* in, let me see, I think I am right in sayin' it was 1852. Come along, let us check that with your cousin Gyles. Marvellous knowledgeable feller about wines is Gyles, includin' the fortified ones. Most creditable!'

He threaded the way through the family like some great old warship with Damien following in his wake. *Bobbin' about*, Henry observed to himself, *like some fussy tug behind the old man. Bet he's plannin' somethin'*. The two dropped anchor alongside Gyles and his Christine.

'Beautiful as ever,' Lord Aynthorp nodded approvingly at his daughter-in-law. 'Excellent turn-out too, permit me to say, suits you admirably, m'dear. Mind if I ask your husband a question?' Thus he inserted himself and, unobtrusively, Henry left his aunts and attached himself to the men.

His grandfather was saying to Gyles, 'We were discussin' the dates of the *Oedum*, pray correct me if I am wrong, Gyles, but was it not 1852?'

Gyles grinned affectionately. 'Of course it was sir, you are never wrong on dates,' and won a pleased, darting glance from under the brows.

'Well then,' Lord Aynthorp resumed to Damien, '*that* took a dreadful toll—a special fungus which attacked the vines so that they had to be destroyed. Then in—now do not prompt me, Gyles—I think it was 1872, the remainder were wiped out by the dread phylloxera, eh?'

Gyles just nodded, eyes warm but somehow shadowed too, as Lord Aynthorp noted and regretted, knowing the cause.

'What happened then?' Henry asked. 'Please go on, grandfather.'

'Never quite the same again,' Lord Aynthorp grunted. 'Had to graft with American stock, happened all over Europe too. Don't like Americans . . . no staying power . . . healthy enough, but not stayers . . . so the vines lost their capacity for producing grapes which made wines of the old, remarkable longevity. They just lost their full capacity for age in bottle, just like Americans, who tend to mature paunchy.'

Edward beat the gong, more gently than for breakfast since the family was already assembled, with one exception. He, the missing Stephen, now came pelting down the staircase in the nick of time.

Justin Aynthorp took Christine in, the rest of the family paired off and followed, with Stephen darting in beside Priscilla, first easing his way alongside his father to murmur, 'Not now, father. I will explain later, it's all right really,' and then falling back again to take his rightful place.

Seated at the table, Gyles mused softly to Marguerite de Tessedre, 'Now where the devil has that boy been?' as he and every other man turned to the left while she and every female present turned dutifully to the right as the first course was presented.

Marguerite managed to whisper back, behind her raised napkin, 'I do not wish to know, but I fear that we shall hear soon enough. So be a good boy, do, and avoid ruffling the surface of this particular pool with any more alarums and excursions. We have enough problems already.' After which she lowered her napkin, picked up her forks and began dissecting a *Truite en Gelée*, while enquiring of her nephew Sinclair, 'Have you seen my new rose? It is called Violette.' She was responsible for the ordering and planning of the famous roses and this was her especial passion and pleasure. 'Indeed, roses,' she continued a trifle wistfully, 'are so much more rewardin' altogether than humans. You only have to site them properly, feed them properly, give them a bit of prunin'. . . .'

Sinclair managed a rueful smile. 'It looks pernicious probable I shall need to do a bit of prunin' on Stephen after luncheon,' he commented.

'Now, Sinclair,' Countess Marguerite warned. Her plate was then withdrawn, so on cue, with a quick, sweet smile to Sinclair and a tiny nod, she turned automatically to her left-hand neighbour.

Lord Aynthorp and Stephen Delahaye were the only two members of the family who seemed entirely free from the shadow which lay so heavily upon the rest. Lady Aynthorp had clearly said something to the 'gels' when they called upon her in turn in her boudoir during the morning. Thus they were all a trifle *distraite* over this luncheon—which was today taken in the Little Dining Room, used at balls as an extra card room—despite the fact that conversation was as bright and determined as it was necessary for it to be *'devant les domestiques'*.[2]

In the Great Dining Room druggets had been laid down over the Chinese rugs and parquet so that Sawbridge's house trolley could be wheeled in, this time laden with stephanotis, tuberoses, trails of pale yellow flowered Cape Ivy, strands of smilax, yellow lilies and the starry whiteness of what Sawbridge always referred to as 'me gypso-felium'. All these now awaited Countess Marguerite's attentions. The table had been spread with its green baize, then covered with the pale yellow damask woven with the Aynthorp coat of arms by the Beauvais nuns. The matching table napkins, folded into the starched complexities of the *eventail à quatre pointes*[3] awaited placement on a temporarily erected butler's table as did the 'infamous' gold plate which Patch de Lorme had pirated. The silver gilt salts were there too, one-time property of King Henry V and presented by his descendant James I to his 'favourite' de Lorme.

At the head of the table lay Lady Aynthorp's placement plan, the place cards, the menu holders—tiny gold hands framed in mother-of-pearl—and the rough sketch which was to act as *aide memoire* to Countess Marguerite. Concerning her talents, Mrs Parsons had vouchsafed the unwelcome opinion to Sawby: 'No one has quite the Countess's touch and heaven alone knows who will fill 'er place when she is gorn.' To which Sawby had answered tartly, 'Time alone will show, Mrs Parsons, so let us meet that bridge when we come to it.'

He was quite confident that when the time came he would be more than capable of taking over since he had spent over twenty years watching and learning from the supposedly irreplaceable flower arranger.

'It is my opinion,' he then observed, in the privacy of the Steward's Room where he took his luncheon with the senior staff, 'that there is something up.'

'*Bien sûr.*' André spoke, as usual, with his mouth full and his elbows out.

[2] In front of the servants.
[3] A four-fold fan. A classic Edwardian folding of a starched table napkin.

'And what is more,' Sawby continued, 'tonight will reveal all, I dare say.'

'Well,' said Mrs Parsons heavily, 'wot with the yellow out and the gold plate what 'is lordship 'as never used for 'is birthday dinners in my recollection' (in the heat of emotion her aspirates went wild), 'there *is* more than something in the wind and it's something 'ighly portentous.'

The reference to 'the yellow out' was of course because yellow with white hoops were the family colours, carried by the men of the family when they went 'chasin' ' and by their jockeys during the 'flat' season. It was also the family custom—save when at Lords for the Eton and Harrow match, when cornflowers were *de rigueur* for Harrovians and carnations, tinted pale blue, for Etonians—for them to attend Ascot, Goodwood, Ranelagh and Hurlingham with the men sporting yellow carnations and the women carrying bunches of carefully retarded yellow primroses, then freesias and finally in late summer, rosebuds, tied to the handles of their parasols. It was also for this reason that the older members of the family had elected to subscribe towards a yellow Rolls Royce for Lord Aynthorp's birthday present.

Stephen, insensitive to the underflow of distress, was eating cheerfully and copiously and was even now enquiring in a very clear voice, 'Has the car come?' He was shushed so loudly by his great-aunt Prudence that even the cause of this now slightly macabre celebration broke off his protracted Madeira perorations to direct a surprised glance towards his sister, simultaneously registering another inward twinge of distaste at her mannish attire.

'Later, Justin, later,' said Prudence sharply.

'So, as I was sayin',' Lord Aynthorp obligingly resumed, astonishingly complaisant, so clearly guessing something was in the wind for him. He did not complete whatever he had intended for he then broke off to say, 'No thank you, Sawby, no more. I shall exert a modicum of consideration for my taste-buds' (but none for his age Henry noted) 'and let them rest now until dinner.' So saying, he waved away Sawby's proffered decanter. 'We must not disappoint chef tonight, whatever else we do.'

'Quite so, my lord.' Sawby withdrew the decanter and waved Robert away as he approached with a dish of *Tartelettes aux Fraises du Bois*.[4]

[4] Wood-strawberry tartlets.

'Oh Gad, and now where was I?' his lordship exclaimed, a trifle put out at last.

'The Terrantez, sir,' Damien prompted, fully determined to extract every iota of information from his Uncle Justin, who was happily unaware that all was being gleaned merely to put sparkle and authority into Damien's own dinner table dissertations thereafter.

'Ah yes, well you will find there is a splendid 1790. It is superb now and will I dare say be equally superb in another sixty or seventy years. Then there are a few dozen of the '95 too. Look, why not come down to the cellars tomorrow mornin' and form your own opinion? Damme it's far too long since I examined those bins! Sawby.'

'Yes, my lord.'

'You can conduct us both tomorrow mornin' and perhaps we might broach a bottle or two.'

Sawby coughed gently. 'Would it not be advisable, my lord, to postpone your lordship's visit until say, Wednesday, as Mr Damien will very fortunately be remaining here for a week?'

Lord Aynthorp looked puzzled for a moment, then laughed. 'Oh, Sawby! *Et tu Brute*, do ye imagine m'y palate will be too exhausted after a mere dinner party?'

'Oh no, your lordship,' Sawby sounded horrified.

'Even if we drink a trifle deep I fancy I shall be in fair shape by, shall we say eleven o'clock, for discriminatin' between a parcel of Madeiry wines.'

'Exactly so, my lord, it shall be arranged.'

'Father,' Gyles at last managed to draw his parent's eye, 'are you plannin' to take a rest after luncheon?'

'Rest! Good Gad, Gyles, now you are tryin' to coddle me, bin restin' all mornin'. Too much rest can be the death of a man. I feel in prime fettle, thought I might have a canter before tea.'

Like Sawby, Gyles could only reply, 'Quite so, sir.' Then, 'Could you, I wonder, spare us a few moments before you ride. You may have noticed that some of us have not yet given you a birthday present.'

Lord Aynthorp nodded. 'Thought somethin' was in the wind. Of course. I am yours to command.'

At this, even Alaric passed a hand across his mouth to conceal something suspiciously like a grin. Henry choked on his wine and won a sharp glance from under shaggy eyebrows. John explained,

'You see, sir, some of us older ones have clubbed together to give you somethin' a bit special.'

'Well, is it ready?'

'Yes, sir,'—this became a chorus.

'Then what the devil are we waitin' for?' Lord Aynthorp banged down his table napkin, drained his glass and stood up. 'Always did like presents,' he confided in Henry who rushed to the door to hold it open for him. 'Come on, m'y boy, let's see what the old 'uns have got for me, somethin' special eh?' and so saying he led them all through into the Great Hall. Here he rapped out to George who was hovering nearby, 'My compliments to the ladies, George, and pray tell them their presence is requested . . . Gyles, where do we go?'

'Outside sir.'

'Say outside and say wraps, George, and hurry, man, hurry, don't keep me waitin'.'

Wait however he did until his Meg appeared, a sable cape draped across her shoulders. He took her hand, tucked it under his arm and saying, 'Come on, Meg, they have got a surprise for me,' turned across the hall. Then, on a rising note he ordered, 'Come along, Sawby, come along everybody, open the doors, Sawby, look sharp there,' all, as it were, in one breath.

Sawby, unruffled, and well used to such performances was enjoying this one. He merely nodded to George who flung open the huge double doors and the whole party came streaming into the hall to follow their leader who continued muttering the impatient repetition, 'Open the door, damne, open the door . . . wonder what it is, eh, Meg m'dear . . . wonder what in the world it can be . . . a horse?'

After the presentation came the photographs. The somewhat awed photographer, having made some initial plunges under his black drapes, emerged flushed from his last plunge to put forward the stammering comment that the group 'while most tasteful reely' would be even more improved if 'the recipient of this magnificent gift, and the donors too, were to be disposed casually upon chairs, while the rest of the distinguished houseparty remained in standing positions behind.' This invoked an instant click of the fingers from Sawby, a Gadarene rush by the three footmen and their breathless emergence thereafter with some very fine Spanish chairs from the Great Hall which they carried and proffered rather as if they were the keys of some nebulous city being presented to some fabulous nabob. The effect was so hilarious that Henry became unaccountably overcome with hiccoughs which displeased Lord Aynthorp who turned and addressed the company in general and Henry in particular upon the subject of young men who could not hold their liquor.

The remainder of the photographic session was punctuated by hics: ... 'Now pray smile a little' ... 'hic' ... and an interpolation from Lord Aynthorp to 'stand that flamin' boy upside down!' ... then the photographer again 'Pray might I trouble you, my lady, to let us see your head tilted slightly? ... that is precisely right ... thank you, my lady' ... 'hic' ... until Sawby came out with a glass of water on a salver and thus arrested the proceedings completely while he extended the glass and Stephen assisted Henry into an inverted position from which he tried to sip the water ... 'hic'. At which Lord Aynthorp exploded 'Damme, Gyles, I am bein' kep' waitin'. Send those boys to the devil,' and Henry overbalanced and collapsed in a wave of choking laughter which did at least dispel the hiccoughs.

The little photographer, reckless with success, intervened, 'Could we perhaps persuade her ladyship, your lordship, to enter your magnificent motor?'

'Persuade!' shouted the excited peer, which sent the photographer backing up alarmed. 'Come on, Meg, I am sick to the withers with this confounded uproar, let us go for a motor ride. Where is the whatyoucall 'em, chauffeur, Sawby...?'

The brand new chauffeur, resplendent in his brand new livery —bottle green with the Aynthorp brass buttons gleaming— sprang from behind the motor and rushed to hold open the door. Then, as Gyles had already given his father a brief résumé of the Rolls Royce and its capabilities, his father moved towards it and handed his wife in, shouting, 'Capable of sixty miles an hour Meg, splendid affair, look at that hooter, they call it a boa constrictor. Well, get in, man, and drive her, get in,' to the deferential chauffeur as he closed the door. This sent the agitated man scurrying round to the nearside, into which he inserted himself and worked his way across to the driving seat, tucking in his coat skirts. He settled himself behind the wheel and blew an exploratory toot on the 'boa constrictor'. Lord Aynthorp shouted, 'Louder, man, louder! Pray do not tickle that splendid brass affair, and now move off. I say, Meg, isn't this splendid...?'

He sat back, hands upon his knees, eyes fixed upon the chauffeur's back. 'Goodbye everybody,' he roared as the engine started, cranked by a deliriously contented Plum who had been standing by in hopeful anticipation of this privilege, and the car moved off. Still Lord Aynthorp shouted, 'It's called a Silver Ghost, Meg . . . no, dear, not Silver Toast . . . Ghost, Meg . . . Ghost . . . appeared for the first time at somethin' called the Motor Show, only last year. . . .' And, as the car rolled on, totally carried away, Lord Aynthorp rose, as it were in the stirrups, and roared at the top of his still considerable lungs, 'Yoiks, Tally Ho. . . . Come on, me beauties. . . .'

On a fading note they rounded the drive's first bend and entered the avenue of elms. The Family saw their 'grand old man' seize his wife's parasol and use it like a lance to jab the chauffeur in the small of the back.

Very faintly, as they disappeared from sight, Lord Aynthorp's voice floated back, 'Her ladyship says stick to the middle of the road, my good man . . . stick to the middle of the road.'

'Well,' said Gyles, a trifle unsteadily, 'that I think we can assume is an unqualified success and, I may say, most gratifyin'.' He slipped one arm around his wife's slim waist, took a pocket handkerchief from his sleeve and blew his nose rather more loudly than was his wont. Christine patted his hand. 'An unqualified success, dear,' she repeated, lifting a pair of brimming violet eyes. 'He really is a darling, Gyles.'

'Herumph,' Gyles replied, replacing the handkerchief. 'Possibly, possibly, but I don't recommend yer tellin' him so, m'dear. Now how about a stroll? I have one or two matters I would like to discuss with you . . . alone.' And so saying, he led her towards the topiary.

With the yellow Rolls Royce safely embarked upon its first journey and even Lord Aynthorp's voice silenced by sheer distance, the family split up. Countess Marguerite processed gracefully towards the dining room. Prudence marched upstairs to a rendezvous with Mrs Peace. The men, excepting only Gyles, drifted towards the library to which, in due course, Lord Aynthorp would return to open the enormous pile of presents which had been assembled on the big circular library table. The younger ones went off to play croquet and Stephen vanished in the wake of his incensed father to a grilling interview in the breakfast room.

Sinclair positioned himself before the morning room chimney piece, nodded as Stephen asked cheerfully, 'May I sit down sir?' and watched, grim-faced as his son settled himself in a deep chair and crossed his long legs. 'Now may I explain, sir?' Stephen enquired equably.

'If you please.' Sinclair's voice was heavy with the weight of past history which pressed upon him. 'I will be obliged if you will furnish me with details of your extraordinary departure,' he said frigidly.

'Well, I went to bed rather early, just played a couple of frames with Henry and then turned in.'

'And then?'

'Just as I was gettin' into bed I missed somethin'. I searched for it quite unsuccessfully so I pulled the bell. George answered and I learned from him that Pine had unpacked me. I then sent for him and asked if he had unpacked a parcel from my cases. He swore there had been no parcel, was most insistent about it, so there I was . . . up a creek without a paddle as you might say. I mean, what else could I do?'

His father stared at him blankly. 'About what?'

'My parcel—grandfather's birthday present, rather a fine set of carved ivory chessmen, although I say it m'self.'

'Are you stallin', sir? snapped Sinclair. 'If not, then pray elucidate and give me some good reason for all this fandango about parcels. I fail to see what any of this has to do with absentin' yourself all night, our findin' your bed not slept in when I enquired after you half an hour after breakfast had been served, and your finally consentin' to reappear at the precise moment that luncheon was announced.'

Stephen stared incredulously. 'I'm tryin' to tell you, sir. You mean you do not understand?'

'Not a single syllable.'

'But when I found the parcel was not here I had to get back to town and collect the chessmen from m'y rooms.'

'In the middle of the night?'

'Yes, sir. I changed, borrowed old Plum's bicycle—had to knock him up to get it—than I bicycled over to The Priory, threw some pebbles at Charles Danement's window, he woke up and came down. When I told him what a fix I was in he agreed to borrow his pater's Renault and drive me back to London. We found the chessmen all right—must have left the parcel on m'y bed. By this time it was mornin' and we were devilish hungry so we popped into the Cri' for a bite of breakfast and finally, fiendish bad luck, we ran out of petrol in Leytonstone village and had to get a canful to get movin' again. Then the confounded car wouldn't start and when it did we had to go back to the man's garage to get her filled up properly. But even so I made luncheon, sir, and gave grandfather his present after all.'

Sinclair drew a long breath and expelled it through his nostrils which quivered with ill-suppressed anger. Then, 'Stephen, are you tellin' me the truth?'

'Absolutely, sir . . . ask Charles . . . ask Plum . . .' Stephen met his father's blazing blue eyes with his own clear and seemingly untroubled ones. 'I mean . . . you see . . . there was absolutely nothin' in it really . . . what else could I do . . . honestly sir . . . I couldn't appear without a present for m'grandfather on his eightieth birthday . . . not at all the thing.'

The boy held his father's scrutiny unflinchingly and, as Sinclair told Henrietta later, 'There he sat, cool as a cucumber, perfectly at ease, yet, Hetty, all the while I had the feelin' there was not a vestige of truth in any of it.' He added glumly, 'But provin' it is a horse of an entirely different colour.'

'Well, what *did* you do?' asked his wife distractedly.

'Dismissed him,' said Sinclair curtly, 'went down to the stables and chatted with old Plum for a while about this and that. Managed to refer to the bicycle episode without seemin' to question him. That part of it *is* true. He did borrow Plum's bicycle. There's no room for any doubt there. I then spoke on the electric speakin' tube to old Danement, mentioned Charles with reference to the first meet of the season and he volunteered that Charles was workin' with their chauffeur on the Renault, so he would ask him when he returned to the house and get him to write me a note. He told me the boy had borrowed the car last night and brought it back with somethin' wrong with a piston or somethin'. You know how interested Charles is in machinery.'

'So it all fits,' mused Henrietta. 'Are we perhaps so over-shadowed by the past that we are imaginin' things I wonder?'

Sinclair sighed. 'We were not imaginin' over that episode at his first preparatory school, nor at Eton over that affair with the tea-shop girl in Windsor . . .'

'Neither of them terribly serious,' defended Stephen's mother. 'But straws which show the way the wind is blowin'. . . . Things do add up, m'dear,' reminded her husband, grimly aware of the recurring tendencies among some of his wife's ancestors.

Gyles and his wife were discussing the self-same matter from a somewhat different angle as they wandered out of the topiary garden and strolled towards the lake, down the long sweep of grass which Lord Aynthorp had planted with rare, flowering saplings when a young man. Now these were tall trees shaking their autumn leaves into little heaps of saffron and gold, crimson and russet, crisped by the dry weather and making soft crunching sounds as their feet touched them. Gyles was saying, 'A very disturbin' thing happened a few days ago when I went down to the Aynthorp Arms to see Stubbins. He had complained to Tony that his roof was leakin'. Tony told me so in his office when I went to see him on some triflin' agent's business Father had asked me to handle. Tony asked me if I would look into Stubbins' complaint for him. Seems he does not care much for him and wanted a second opinion. So I rode over to see for m'self. Stubbins was well within his rights in complainin'. The roof was leakin'. One or two of the rafters were dickey too and there were a number of slipped and broken tiles; not a big job but a necessary one. I told the man it would have immediate attention and was just remountin' when a toddler ran out of a side door and a girl came out in pursuit—that young niece of Stubbins who has come to live with him and help out in the bar. She called after the child, "Come here to mum and don't bother the gentleman, you naughty boy." She had to chase him and by the time she had caught him up I had seen quite enough. He was a sturdy little chap, with hair the family colour and he was the spittin' image of Stephen . . .'

Once escaped from his dissatisfied parent, Stephen hurried across the home park on foot, not wishing to draw any more attention upon himself. He was bound for a tryst with Charles Danement whom he knew intended spending the afternoon with a rod, working from the river bank where this flowed through his father's land. Once clear of the Aynthorp estate Stephen began working down stream, stopping occasionally to whistle a phrase of *Little Dolly Daydream*—a pre-arranged signal by which he hoped to put up his quarry. He was rewarded eventually. Indeed he almost fell over the recumbent form stretched out on the grass beside his rod and creel, sound asleep. Stephen prodded him. 'Wake up, Charles, I must talk to you and I cannot stay long.'

Charles opened his eyes, groaned and then sat up yawning. 'Omigod,' he complained, 'and now I'm stiff as well! I had a devil of a job with that motor too—worn out I am, done brown!'

'Listen for heaven's sake,' said Stephen urgently. 'M'y pater's far from satisfied with m'y story. He smells a rat but can't quite place it yet and if the truth gets out he'll never let me go up to the 'varsity and *I must get away*, that damned girl's pesterin' me.'

Charles blinked and ran his hand through his hair. 'What am I supposed to do now?' he asked wearily. 'I'm achin' in every limb, shouldn't wonder if I hadn't caught a streamin' cold and all for your poodlefakin' antics. What about the gel, think she'll go to your old man?'

'If she were goin' to do that she'd 've done it already. The brat's goin' on for three.'

Charles chuckled. 'Which makes you fifteen when you ... er, I say, Stephen, that's not bad goin'.'

'No,' Stephen grinned back, 'well, perhaps; but never mind that now. I want you to go over our story again to make sure you've got it right. You know what a blamed addlepate you are.'

'Oh lor,' said Charles vaguely, 'well then ... how's this? ... you chucked some bricks at m'y window after I'd gone to sleep ... woke me up ... I came creepin' down ... you told me about yer grandpater's birthday present, so after a bit I agreed to borrow my guvnor's car. I drove you to London, we had a bit of grub at the Cri' and then the car broke down.'

'No, no,' shouted Stephen, 'we ran out of petrol in Leytonstone village ...'

'And then we ran out of petrol in Leytonstone village,' Charles amended. 'Is that it? Yes, well, and it's why we didn't get back until just before luncheon.'

'That's right,' said Stephen, 'By the way, where were you while ...?'

'Sittin' in that draughty car. That's where I was,' Charles answered sourly. 'Freezin', cramped ... What happened anyway? It was dawn when you came out.'

Stephen grimaced, 'Well, first she ranted a bit, then she threatened a bit, then I gave her some money I'd managed to wangle. That softened her up a bit and then ...' He tailed off lamely so Charles finished for him, 'And then I suppose you both drank from the same trough, so to speak, and you dozed off a bit afterwards.'

'That's about the size of it.' Stephen was tearing at the grass with nervous fingers.

'Supposin' you get her the same way again?'

'Never mind that now—what matters is that no one saw us creep back to bed. You did bribe your man properly?'

'You know I did. What a deuced demandin', fussin' chap you are! Unfortunately the fool let us sleep on far too long and I had to lead you out over the roofs to those burned-out stables. Got m'self in a deuced awful mess.'

'I tore m'breeches,' said Stephen gloomily. 'Anyway I got home undetected and if you stick to your story we'll be all right. But please,' (up came another torn handful of grass)' 'don't go embroiderin' it or you'll get in a tangle and then we will both come unstitched.' He glanced at his watch. 'I'll have to tear off now, can't afford another flamin' row. See you tomorrow and . . . I say . . . thanks a lot, old man.' Somehow Stephen managed to raise his smile—that devastating Lorme smile which he had inherited from his mother. This worked, as it always did. Charles smiled back and said hastily, 'Think nothin' of it, push off and good luck . . .'

As the two young men struck off in opposite directions there was a slight movement in some bushes immediately behind where Charles had slept. A pair of rheumy eyes peered out, inset in a creased, dirt-engrained countenance and Tim the poacher looked to left and right very carefully before easing his disreputable person into the open. Once satisfied that the coast was clear he made off, darting like a stoat from cover to cover, somewhat uncomfortably encumbered by capacious pockets jam-packed with cold, dead fish, the property of Sir Andrew Danement. His little ferrety mind was probing and rootling through the conversation on which he had eavesdropped so fortuitously. As he made his sporadic flashes out of cover into the open and back again to such cover as the bushes afforded, he examined and assessed the various benefits to himself which just might accrue from what he had overheard, a ploy which greatly minimised the discomfort in which he travelled the lengthy way between the Danement lands and his noisome shack in a spinney on the farther side of the village which he called home.

CHAPTER 7

Pandora's Box

Below stairs, the mounting pace and concomitant tension evinced itself as much in the curious silence in which the work was being done as in the speed with which it was being executed.

Above stairs, the table waited in the subdued glitter from the cherry logs burning under the huge marble mantelshelf. Behind the double doors which Le Brun had painted, and under his ceilings, a separate table was set for the service of dessert . . . the silver gilt compotes and tazzas were pyramided with Sawbridge's nectarines and pineapples, studded with little green figs and late ripening Reine-Claudes, cascaded with grape tresses from the great vine. The Crown Derby and gold dessert knives and forks flanked the Stuart finger bowls on each gold plate, each bowl a miniature lake of rain water scented with orange and rose waters supporting a tiny flotilla of yellow rose petals.

Even in the fading light the log flames caught the shimmer of silver gilt upon the great marble-topped table. The warmth of the room drew out the scent of the tuberoses; the firelight even shone a little in the dark green hedera and smilax. It flamed up on the polished crystal and made the formally folded napkins into motionless white birds, poised for flight.

Back in the kitchen the heat was now intense and chef had already exchanged one sodden-banded high-bonnet for another and replaced his sweat-soaked neck linen.

In the servants' hall the staff dining table was covered from end to end with *bains marie* in which were packed crushed ice blocks. Already some supported gilt dishes laden with the garnished *Plats froid*.[1] Chef André was spinning *sucre filé*[2] for the *Croquembouche*[3] with two table forks tied back to back.

[1] Cold dishes.
[2] Spun sugar.
[3] More usually chosen in France as a wedding cake, an elaborate confection of choux paste, chantilly cream, liqueurs and sugar roses.

On the first floor, the ladies maids and valets were dressing their charges. White ties, black waistcoats, clocked black silk socks, patent leather pumps, stiffly starch-fronted dress shirts, tail coats and black dress trousers with two rows of braids down the sides, all for the valets to hand to each man; and for the maids, all the complexities of the ladies' *toilettes*, from evening stays, corset covers of fine lawn, chemises run through with narrow *bébé* ribbons, under and evening petticoats, silk stockings also elaborately clocked, or trimmed with drawn thread work or with lace insets in colours which matched the satin 'Louis-heeled' slippers, and finally the gowns: low in décolletage, drop-shouldered, nipped in like skins over the corset lines and flowing out in folds of chiffon, velvet, lace, satin, *toile de jouey*[4] and *mousseline de soie*.[4]

Also upstairs, Henry let himself into his Great-Aunt Marguerite's boudoir in answer to her 'Come in—is that you, Henry?'

'There is no doubt about it,' he decided, watching his great-aunt resettle herself in a chaise-longue, cross her still very slender ankles and arrange the billowing skirts of her tea-gown to her satisfaction. 'This room is at any rate different from any other in the castle!'

'I'm just taking a little rest, dear, after arranging the table-flowers,' said the owner of the room. 'I am delighted to have the pleasure of your company, would you care for a cup of *tisane*?'[5] Henry shuddered inwardly but accepted. 'Because if you would, dear, be kind enough to hand me another tea-cup and saucer from that *petite commode*[6] and I will pour it for you.'

The *petite commode*, as Henry observed with amusement, was Louis VI and by one of the most famous *ébenistes*[7] of the eighteenth century. It now supported a glass-domed arrangement of wax fruit and flowers, a small Russian glass and ormolu candelabra, a piece of rock crystal and two shocking boxes stuck all over with shells. Concealed behind its satinwood door lay his objective, a Chinese cup and saucer. 'So fragile,' crooned Countess Marguerite, taking the object, 'sweetly pretty. I am very Chinese at the moment.'

4 Fashionable evening dress fabrics of the period.
5 Herbal tea.
6 Small chest.
7 Cabinet-maker.

'So I have observed,' Henry permitted himself, glancing round at the miscellany of fans, screens, bamboo furniture, ivory fishes, priceless Chinese Immortals, pictures of the Furies painted on rice paper and scrolls, all mixed together with Ch'ien Lung Kettles on spirit lamps, ivory tea caddies (used for dried camomile), bobbled, velvet-covered "occasional tables" and peacocks' feathers.

'Ulysses been moultin'? Henry enquired mildly.

'Yes dear, was it not fortuitous? I spent hours pursuin' the wretched bird to be sure his beautiful feathers were not ruined in the damp grass. Most exhaustin'.'

Henry chuckled, then responded dutifully to his aunt's reproach. 'You have not yet said a word about my screen.'

He had hoped to avoid this, but now, cornered, he said resignedly, 'Forgive me but ... er ... what *is* it exactly?'

'Valentines, love, all the valentines my beaux sent me when I was your age. Ah, men were so romantic then.' Countess Marguerite put down the cup she was about to fill, and rising, crossed to the screen. 'Come,' she invited, 'let me show you the ones my husband sent to me. He had them sent specially from England you know.'

Henry followed his aunt obediently and together they pored over the screen.

'Here,' said she, 'is the first one I ever received from your Uncle. This—with the dove, all feathered, bearing the message in his mouth. See how the arrow is feathered too and look at this delicate silver lace frilling which surrounds the pierced heart ... Here is another in a copy of the old Knot work.'

'Knot work?' Henry queried. 'What on earth is that?'

'It was greatly done by gentlewomen in the seventeenth century, whole conversation pieces! We have some in the Blue Room. The delicate materials are pushed and caught with fine stitches, to make figures, clothes, background, even faces. See how cleverly it is done."

'Oh, I have noticed it,' Henry agreed, 'but I never knew it was called Knot work. . . .'

'Then see this one, Henry,' the Countess exclaimed. 'Look how the satin heart is minutely quilted and the tiny real Valenciennes lace frilling surrounding it. Jules, your uncle, told me later that he had enlisted the assistance of his sister, Celestine, who died in '89, to find the lace for him and he in turn sent it to

England to have it used in that, the most beautiful of them all I think. . . .' Her eyes suddenly filled with tears and she turned away. 'Come, let us sit down again. Our *tisane* is chilling and I am nothing but a silly sentimental old woman.'

Henry put one arm about the frail shoulders and led her back comfortingly. 'You are nothing of the sort,' he assured her. 'You are my favourite, beautiful, romantic Aunt. Come, sit down and let me give you your cup.' He poured for her, passed her the cup, and she obediently sipped. Then, as she calmed down, 'I suppose you have never been told about your Uncle Jules?' she queried.

'No, no one has ever mentioned him to my recollection.'

She reflected a little, then said, 'The story is brief enough and you are the heir so all things about the Family should be known to you. I will tell you.'

'Not if it will distress you further,' Henry said quickly.

'Nonsense,' she said, with a return to her usual manner. 'It is all so long ago and I am being silly.'

She tucked her handkerchief into a hidden pocket of her tea gown and Henry said softly, 'He died?'

'Oh no,' she surprised him, 'he is still alive.'

Henry frowned, 'Away from you?'

'Yes, my dear. We had a most wonderful and romantic relationship which lasted twenty years.' She tilted her head like a small bird with her usual coquettishness. 'We were the darlings of French and English society from 1865, when we were married. . . .'

'Here?'

'No, my dear. I went to Paris to stay with distant cousins for a great ball. We met there and I stayed to marry him. Most unorthodox in those days; but I was a wilful girl and Jules wholly swept me off my feet. He was, of course, a completely eligible partie—we just fell in love. Oh Henry, how we fell in love! We had everything. He had great estates, wealth, position and we were young. He was so handsome. . . .'

As the old will, she lost herself for a while in her narrative, then with a little shrug of those expression shoulders, came back to the present and the boy's young face bent close to her own.

'Then,' she said sadly, touching his cheek, 'when Jules was fifty—in 1883—he came into my boudoir, much as you have done this afternoon. He fidgeted about the room picking up little things and putting them down again. And then he told me. He wished to go into a monastery. He wished to have done with the world, with me even. He had already seen the Abbé of the Order. He just came to ask me if I would agree to an annulment, as the Abbé insisted this must be done before Uncle Jules could become installed in the Order.'

'Good God,' Henry exclaimed, 'just like that?'

'Just like that,' she echoed, staring over his copper head. 'My pride sustained me, of course, and my blood. I remember as if it were yesterday saying, "If that is your wish, my love, it must be done. If you feel now that the religious life pulls you so strongly and you would have done with the world, it would be wrong for me to stand in your way, very wrong." Then he took my hands and kissed them. He said, "Thank you, my love. I knew you would understand," and that was the last time he ever touched me. I . . . just . . . came . . . back . . . to . . . Castle Rising.'

There was a long silence, broken only by Henry's last question.

'And are you, then, not even married to him anymore?'

'For him, I am not. His instrument of annulment was automatic and, as I have said, essential. In due course he took his vows. Your Grandfather, Uncle Alaric, all of them, tried to persuade me to do my counterpart in this country where the French annulment is insufficient for me to marry again. But I knew then, as I know now, that after Jules there could and would be no one and somehow I have always felt a little closer to your Uncle by doing. . .' she spread out her be-ringed little hands in a gesture of infinite pathos '. . . *absolument rien de ma part.*' Then she added irrelevantly, 'We always spoke in French together. That is why you all say my French is so unexceptionable.'

'You *look* entirely French too.' Henry reminded her, accepting a cup of *tisane* with an outward show of pleasure.

'I regard it as the greatest possible compliment,' she nodded. Then she gave him a further coquettish glance out of her still very fine eyes and patted her elaborate coiffeur with a small hand which, even at this hour, sparkled with diamonds. He thought how beautiful she must have been when she was young; how, even now, unmistakable traces lingered. Of course, as with all the Lormes, high-bridged nose and pointed chin were showing signs of coming closer together, but the delicate bone structure was eloquent.

Henry said abruptly, 'You have inherited the family beauty.

What a pity it failed in Great-Aunt Prue,' which proved an excellent red-herring.

Countess Marguerite made a little moue, then said hastily, 'Oh, but it was not always so. Believe me when I say she was a very strikin' gel, very strikin'—*une espèce de jolie-laide*.[8] But then, you see, she took to those dreadfully mannish clothes, deplorable hats and quite despoiled her appearance.'

'What got into her?'

His great-aunt dropped her voice. 'That frightful Mrs Pankhurst,' she said sepulchrally. 'She became *suffragiste*.' Somehow she managed to give the word a certain grace which made Henry grin. 'No, I assure you it is no laughing matter, quite deplorable . . . her room full of leaflets, and pamphlets, and things called posters. She has even banished the beautiful furniture for a typewriting machine which *clicks* and *clicks* on a terrible rolled-top desk of enormous proportions . . . wears paper cuffs too . . . I only hope and pray she does not become the thing she and her dreadful cronies are beginning to threaten . . .' She hesitated, groping for the word.

'Militant?' Henry made it a question.

'Yes, that is the word and I tremble to think what it implies, but I am perfectly sure it will be even more horrid than just suffragism. Let us say no more about it for it is singularly unromantic and quite horrid altogether.'

Henry grasped this proffered straw. 'Talkin' of romance,' he said, seeing an opportunity to divert the conversation, 'What has happened to Patch de Lorme's snuff box?'

'I have it, look, over there on that *bouille* table—they are all there, the Lady Marguerite's, wicked Julian's, the gold filigree one which belonged to Patch and the blue enamel one King James gave to Philip.'

Henry picked up the little gold box and closed one hand around it as if he were wanting something from his pirate ancestor to flow through to him. The little Countess stopped chattering and watched him curiously. At length, 'What is the matter with my favourite great-nephew?' she asked very softly.

He started, replaced the box with great care, returned to his chair and drew it closer to her. 'Tonight,' he said, taking one old hand in his, '*tonight*. Can . . . can I ask you an awful question—please? It is a terribly important one— I think.'

[8] Quite untranslatable! Literally—pretty/ugly!

She nodded, clearly enchanted. 'Of course, of course, what is it that you want to know?'

'The Heirloom,' he said flatly.

'What about the Heirloom?'

So he told her, and further disturbed himself by noting that he too had dropped his voice and was now speaking in whispers. 'Darling Aunt Maggie, *what is it*?'

She patted the hand which enclosed her own. 'Now you know perfectly well we do not know. We have never known. That is the tradition. Why worry yourself with the impossible?'

'But why should it be impossible? What makes it so?'

'I do not know,' she leaned back, closed her eyes and admitted, 'I have sometimes wondered, as indeed I am sure all of us have done at one time or another. It might be some personal trinket or a cross maybe or perhaps a lock of hair.'

Henry looked at her incredulously. 'In that great leathern box?'

She sat bolt upright and stared. 'How do you know it is a great leathern box?'

'Because Grandfather told me when I was a little boy. He was explainin' Family to me and tellin' some shockin' marvellous tales about some of 'em. He said it was a great leathern box, black as pitch and hasped with rusted iron. On the lid he said there was a device which—I can remember it as clearly as if it were yesterday—it was *argent*, a *fesse gules* between, two *chevronels* of the second,[9] and something else I clean forgot.

'Part of the arms of our Norman originals,' she murmured automatically.

'Ah, I see,' said Henry. 'Well, Grandfather held out his hands to show how great the box was and I clearly remember his sayin' to me, "One day, Henry, it will be in your trust and keepin'." When I asked him how that would come about he stroked my head and said, "When your father takes the Swan's path and I am long gone to my ancestors." I also remember that I interrupted him to ask what was the Swan's path so he went off at a tangent to explain. He talked a lot about our ancient Viking link and how the first English Henri wed the daughter of a Dane called . . .' he struck his forehead and her soft voice supplied, 'Danbury, descendant of the mighty Cnut.'

'That's it! Clever you. And how because of this she insisted upon a Viking funeral for her father after she and Henri were

9 Part of the arms of the author's family in 1070.

wed and he told me just how this was done and how that Dane took his "Swan Path".' His voice tailed away and after a while he added ruefully, 'I played Viking funerals all that hols with Charles Danement and Stephen and quite forgot about the box. *Why* do we not know what it contains? Did the Lady Mathilde decree that this was to be so? And if not *why* has no one looked inside in all these centuries? It makes it seem like some evil Pandora's box and not a cherished Heirloom at all!'

Marguerite de Lorme sighed. 'I can see,' she said with manifest reluctance, 'that I shall have to tell you how it came into being and the mystery of it havin' been given to Henri who was the fourth son and not to the heir.'

She paused, lay back again and so reclining, told of the dying of the Lady Mathilde and how the gift of prophesy seemed to come upon her in her hour of passing as she lay shriven in her great bed. She told of Guilbert's reluctant journey, of his meeting up with Henri and the King and then she rose and went across to a little rosewood escritoire. Here she took a key from a drawer and with it unlocked another, concealed by some panelling.

'The eighth Lord Aynthorp kept this book throughout his lifetime,' she told Henry as she turned the pages. 'Now listen carefully. "Herein enscribed are suche pointes of grete matter to the family as are fitting for me to name," ' she read aloud. Then, turning many more pages—she was clearly familiar with the faded penmanship, 'Now listen very carefully here Henry. "Here are the wordes spake by Edouard de Lorme when he brought this caskette"—dear me the spelling—"to this lande after the dying of his mother the Lady Mathilde. This Edouard he gave it to Henri his younger brother and in so doing recounted the manner of his mother's passing." '

She read him the deathbed story, closed the book, returned it to its cache, closed this too, locked it and put the key away. There was silence for a while in the over-crowded, scented room. Suddenly, startling them both, her parrot squawked, flapped his wings and went wobbling from end to end of the perch to which he was tethered. 'Pandora's box', he shrieked, 'Pandora's box . . . Pandora's box.'

Marguerite de Tessedre turned her head to him and her face whitened. 'But why?' she whispered. 'Poor old Jamie, he has never said that before. Oh, what in the world made him say that at this time?'

Henry rose. 'Dear Aunt Maggie, I must go; and we shall never know why that bird took it into his head to say Pandora's box. But there is one thing I do know and you may as well know it too. If and when I become the trustee of that box *I shall open it.* That I can undertake, and what is more, even if I am the youngest adult member of the family bidden to this dinner tonight, I intend askin' why the Box should not be opened now.'

'Oh, Henry, should you?'

'Why not? Accordin' to you, who are steeped in Family history, there is no . . . oh what is it the prayer book says?'

She quoted, 'No just cause or impediment—is that what you want?'

'Yes, that's the bit, so anyway there can be no harm in askin', for *if* there is a reason I will respect it as all we Lormes have done; *but I must know.* Perhaps m'y father is also curious about the contents and what I intend to do may release a few family inhibitions about it. . . .' He turned towards the door, 'But why, oh why above all, did the Lady Mathilde die . . . laughin' . . . is what I should most like to know.'

LADY AYNTHORP'S TABLE PLAN

Lady Aynthorp

Bishop Alaric de Lorme	Mr John de Lorme
Mrs John de Lorme	Mrs Christian de Lorme
Mr Eustace St John	Mr Henry de Lorme
Miss Priscilla de Lorme	Mrs Sinclair Delahaye
Mr Damien de Lorme	Mr Robert de Lorme
Miss Rosemary de Lorme	Mrs Eustace St John
Mr Christian de Lorme	Mr Stephen Delahaye
Miss Prudence de Lorme	Countess Marguerite de Tessedre
Mr Gyles de Lorme	Mr Sinclair Delahaye
Mrs Alaric de Lorme	Mrs Gyles de Lorme

Lord Aynthorp

CHAPTER 8

The Birthday Dinner Party

The sun went down in flamingo splendour over Castle Rising. The peacocks flew into the trees to roost, the gardeners plodded home. In the stables the boys, under Plum's direction, were filling loose boxes with armfuls of soft hay, sweeping and hosing down the cobblestones and closing up stable doors.

The yellow Rolls Royce, in a temporary stable-home, was being polished by the chauffeur, divested now of his livery and working with his sleeves rolled up. The rooks in the elms cawed goodnight to one another and the elms turned black as the sun slipped over the horizon. Even the shadows were gone and an aura of tranquillity spread over the gardens and the home park. Somewhere in a distant spinney a cock pheasant loosed his plaintive call. The secure, domestic sound of a dog barking drifted to the walls. In the windless stillness, swords of grey smoke from chimney after chimney pierced the fading light with two great Excaliburs dominating all the rest as a tired Boots emptied hodful after hodful of coke into M. André's twin kitchen ranges.

On the upper floor, hands came out to draw leaded window panes together before closing curtains and shutters. All was calm, immensely tranquil; all spelled order, security; and an age-old peace which had withstood the onslaught of many centuries. It now exuded a most powerful confidence in itself and its immortality, as if the pores of the old stones breathed it out, declaring that as it had been, so it should continue to be for many centuries to come. The evening star came out and hung like one of Lady Marguerite's splendid diamonds in a sky which turned dark blue as though a bolt of Lyons velvet had been flung across it. The air was heavy with the scents of hay, roses and bonfires. Then a light breeze stirred around the topiary, strengthened and soared, taking the rose scents and wafting them inwards to a bemused kitchen maid who leaned from an upper window. She inhaled this intoxicant gratefully, then with some reluctance closed the latch down and returned to her labours.

There was nothing special about this twilight scene. It was no more than a token of things past and things to come, unhurried, recurring, making an unbroken rhythm down the weeks and years, pregnant with confidence in its own inviolability. Only the most fevered imaginations could persuade themselves that they heard this perfect English late summer evening sigh with immeasurable sadness and persuade their imaginations that they could feel the chill of impending change.

Gyles and Christine came on to the south terrace together and stood there looking out over the lake.

'Gyles.'

'Yes, my love.'

'You know this, too, is my love,' she said quietly, 'this home, this land, it is all so quiet and so beautiful. I do not think I could ever bear to live anywhere else.' She turned her face to his, 'I felt like this when you brought me back after our honeymoon. Castle Rising has bewitched me. Every day serves to tighten the thraldom in which it holds me.'

'Passin' poetical,' he teased her gently.

'Yes I know. I cannot recall that I have ever spoken like this before; but the power of beauty is a very potent one. I am suddenly aware, I do not know why, of the centuries of wealth as well as taste which have made it all possible. I read somewhere the other day the only definition I have ever liked about wealth. It seemed to me to sum up exactly what your family has created with it.'

'Tell me.'

She hesitated, watching the ripples a late-homing water bird made upon the surface of the lake. Then she quoted, 'Wealth is a high wall round a quiet garden shutting out the cries of noisy people.'

Gyles was silent for a while before reminding her, 'Our ways have fallen in very pleasant places. We are greatly fortunate. Even so, you know only too well that this does not mean we are free from sufferin', pain, grief, all the stresses and anxieties.'

She moved her shoulders a trifle impatiently. 'I never meant it to do anything else. I took that for granted. I simply meant that even when one *is* bayed by problems, Castle Rising's strength and security lessens them with the power of...I think "continuity" is the word I want.'

'And that,' Gyles agreed, 'I can fully comprehend. I came past the laundry after ridin' the other mornin'. The women were ironin'. I looked in through the open doorway and saw the creases in the linen disappearing as the iron passed over them. That's what this house,' he corrected himself, 'after tonight our house, has always done for me—ironed out the creases. Now I'm the one who's gettin' poetical! When I was in Africa sleepin' out under those extraordinary stars on the veldt I used to shut my eyes, remember the single evenin' star hangin' over that lake, hear the rooks and imagine I was home. It was a most sustainin' feelin'. There was death and fire and cruelty and pain all around me; with men and horses dyin', women sufferin', but somehow Castle Risin' in m'y mind was a reassurance.'

'No,' she interrupted him eagerly, 'a confirmation of stability and safety. Gyles, we must go in or we shall be later for dinner.'

He bent and kissed her hair lightly. 'At the risk of bein' sentimental, Christine', he murmured shyly, 'you were as much a part of all this as the place itself. What is that song they sing in music halls? Oh, forgive me, you would not know of course; but I think it is called *The Miner's Dream of Home*. Well the only difference is that this place represented my "dream of home"...and it always will....'

She pressed his hand, the moment slipping away already. 'Yes, my dear,' she echoed, 'pray God it always will.'

The stars were coming out fast now, bejewelling the night now turned to black velvet. Somewhere behind them an owl hooted, then another took up the lost, disembodied sound, making Christine shiver. 'Owls are like lost souls I always feel, they make my skin prickle. Oh, Gyles, I do hope this night will not be as sad a one as we anticipate.'

'Amen to that,' said Gyles fervently. 'Come on, my love, we must dress for this rather dreadful celebration.'

Lights were springing up inside the castle as they turned off the terrace and went back slowly to the drive. Hands were still closing window coverings across lighted windows, but for every one they shrouded, two more sprang up to make the window panes sparkle in challenge to the stars. As they stepped inside, a young crescent moon rose. As if it had called to her, Christine turned for a last lingering look. ' "And the young moon," ' she quoted, 'look, Gyles, "like to a silver bow new-bent in heaven, shall behold the night of our solemnitudes." '

He opened the doors for her and they went inside to prepare for the solemnitude of the de Lorme family dinner party.

The magic of those moments on the terrace lingered as Christine surrendered herself to the attentions of Pearson the parlourmaid who came in to do her hair and dress her. As the girl brushed out the long, fair strands with a monogrammed ivory hair brush in each hand, mistress and maid chatted together in a companionship made harmonious by years of association. Pearson chattered about the servants' excitements, the wonders of Monsieur André's confections, the beauty of the table appointments: 'Cook, I beg pardon, madam, Mrs Parsons was saying as she has never seen the table so splendid since His Majesty was staying here. Of course I wasn't allowed above stairs so I never saw that,' she added regretfully, 'but Mr Sawby took us upper servants into the dining room just now and he lit the new 'lectricity and we saw it all. Oh, but it looks wonderful. We're ever so excited we are, below stairs, madam.'

Christine smiled, put up her hands and adjusted the aigrette which Pearson had affixed behind her wide, rolling pompadour, 'A little to the left I think, Pearson, would be better,' she suggested.

Pearson stood back and examined the airgrette's position in the toilette table's looking-glass. 'Lovely, madam, it wasn't quite right before.'

'But you've done my hair beautifully,' said Christine with a smile. 'Thank you, Pearson.'

'Oh, it's a great honour, madam, I'm sure. Miss Palliser was saying as how she thought I was getting above my place doing your hair and she could well do yours after attending to her ladyship.'

'Oh no!' exclaimed Christine involuntarily. She much disliked her mother-in-law's vinegary attendant. 'You and I manage famously together, I do not need anyone else.'

She rose and Pearson helped her out of her wrapper so that she could step into the cloudy circle of frilled evening petticoat which Pearson had made into a circle upon the carpet. As she tied the strings Christine said abruptly, 'Pearson, would you like to become my personal maid?'

Pearson gasped, 'Oh madam...' she stammered, 'you mean you would have me to look after you all the time and accompany you when you travel, like Miss Palliser does with her ladyship?'

'Yes I do.' Christine stepped into the dress and submitted to the intricate back fastening of a myriad hooks and eyes, by which her slim figure became encased as if in an exotic satin and lace skin. 'We could make the arrangements very quietly. Of course I would not like you to discuss the matter in the servants' hall until it was all settled.'

'Oh no, madam', Pearson sounded shocked, 'I would not breathe a word.'

Christine turned, kicked out her skirts with a satin-slippered foot and sat down again at her toilet table. Pearson went for her jewel case, set it in front of her, all a-twitter with excitement. She pulled back the tiered trays so that the winking jewels were displayed, gave an almost hysterical little gulp and exclaimed, 'Oh my goodness, what a chance for me, madam! Of course it might show! On the other hand, perhaps cook and Mr Sawby would put it down to the excitement of the occasion.'

'I'm sure they will,' Christine replied tranquilly, 'but first let us consider the question of your replacement in the servants' hall. Then we shall have to establish with Mrs Peace what we are planning. She would obviously have to re-engage you, as I am sure you will appreciate.' Christine was turning over her jewel trays as she spoke.

'Oh, of course, madam, I really do quite understand what is expected of me and what I must do.' Pearson was by now so excited she was chirruping like a starling, 'Though I am sure there is no one below stairs at this time whom Mrs Peace would consider as a replacement for me as a senior house parlourmaid.'

Christine held up a parure of fire opals, laid them against her dress, nodded, then held them around her throat so that the maid could secure the clasp. 'Well, we shall have to look further then for your replacement,' she said equably. 'Do you perhaps know of anyone who might be suitable?'

'Indeed I do, madam', Pearson said. 'I have a cousin who has been in service with old Lady Parkinson at the Hall. She, my cousin I mean, is expecting her notice daily since her ladyship's death. Of course all the servants have been kept on as yet. The family solicitor called them to the library and assured them that their positions were secure for the present, but he gave, as it were, a *warning*. I saw my cousin on my monthly "day off", and she confided in me that she was expecting her notice all the same, for it seems as if only a skelington staff will be retained by the heirs who, as you know, madam, are distant relatives who spend most of their time abroad. My cousin is a very experienced parlourmaid.'

'What is her name?' Christine was experimenting with a pair of fire opal drop earrings.

'Appleby, madam, Pansy Appleby. She is so hoping she can find a new place before she is dismissed, hers being a very sad story and places hard to find for senior servants. Places are so often *inherited*, they pass to sons and daughters who begin as scullery- or laundry-maids and work up through the years getting their training ready to step in when their relatives retire. Times are very hard for senior servants who are, as it were, suddenly cut off by a death like is the case with Pansy.'

Christine slipped on her rings and rose. 'What is this Appleby's background, Pearson?' she enquired, moving towards a pier glass to inspect her reflection.

'She is a widow, madam. Her husband was Lady Parkinson's butler. Then he fell down the cellar steps what someone had inadvertently took away and he broke his neck leaving her a widow. Now he, Appleby, had been a widower, so Pansy had three step-children, two little boys and one girl which Appleby's mother cared for in readiness for them going into service with her ladyship in the natural course of events. Pansy still gives her mother-in-law money for their keep and she will be hard put indeed if she has no place and no money coming in.'

'Supposing,' said Christine, examining her reflection, 'I asked Mrs Peace to see her, and also requested that she keep the matter private at this juncture. Do you think you could arrange for her to come and see Mrs Peace when she has her next monthly "day"?'

'Oh, dear me yes, madam.' Pearson clasped her hands to stop their excited waving about. 'Of course she would, and grateful all her days for the opportunity.'

'Then,' said Christine, 'I shall see Mrs Peace in the morning. Now I must go downstairs and indeed so must you.' She was beginning to find herself a trifle dazed by the Appleby saga and also somewhat moved too by the woman's sad situation. She put out her hands and Pearson collected herself sufficiently to loop the small fan over her wrist, hand her a gossamer-fine, monogrammed handkerchief. 'Now, do you think you can manage to put all this out of your mind until I have spoken to Mrs Peace?'

'I will try, madam,' faltered Pearson, 'and thank you, madam, thank you from the bottom of my heart. I can undertake, madam, to serve you to the last vestige of my strength.'

Christine nodded smilingly, 'You do already, Pearson, you do, and I am grateful. After all is it not why I made the suggestion?'

Pearson made no reply but just stared at the vision she had helped to create. Then Gyles walked in through his dressing room door, saying cheerfully, as he slipped a cigar case into the pocket of his tail coat and tucked his pocket handkerchief up his sleeve, 'Well, are we ready? I think we should go down. You look ravishing, my love, congratulations, Pearson.'

Pearson bobbed her curtsey, rushed to the door, held it open and watched them as they went through. Then she did a little dance all to herself in the disordered room and fell to whisking things away and bestowing them in drawers and cupboards humming a little tune as she did so.

'And where 'ave you bin?' enquired Mrs Parsons sourly as she came down the basement stairs. 'There's an 'undred and one things lef' for you to do and me rheumatism is terrible tonight.'

'Dressing Mrs Gyles,' said Pearson. 'Just you sit down and take a little rest. Now tell me what you want doing and I will do it for you. My pore father suffered something cruel with the rheumaticks and I can sympathise.' This somewhat mollified 'old sour-puss' as Sawbridge called her—out of earshot. 'Well that's a good girl,' Mrs Parsons thawed, 'but first you must change that apron girl, it's creased in one corner.'

The white drawing room was filled up now. Prudence was there, standing sipping lemon water wearing an unbecoming maroon dress with a high, stiffly-boned neckline, and no jewellery save for a heavy, early Victorian hair brooch, which was a gift from one of her suffragette cronies and, therefore, far more important than what she called 'family gee-gaws'.

The two girls, Rosemary and Priscilla, wore lemon and white *toile de jouey* caught up in flounces below the knee. Rosemary's was fastened at the point of each flounce with yellow rosebuds, and she wore a spray of rosebuds in her hair. Priscilla, as befitted her youth, wore white with pearls and little lovers' knots of white falling ribbons on the puffed, off-shoulder sleeves. Christine, too, wore white, lace over satin—for she took her own line at all times; having found that white still enhanced her beauty, she wore it in defiance of accepted form. Marguerite sailed in wearing a tight collar of diamonds at her throat; a paradise plume swept across her white hair. She carried a tiny, hand-painted, chicken's skin fan. She wore a lavender satin gown and, by what miracle only she and her maid could tell, her waist appeared almost as small as those of her nieces. The fact that she was excruciatingly uncomfortable was of no import since her reflection met with her approval. She was followed by Gabrielle, dressed by Poiret in an apricot faille with *pointe d'Alençon appliqués* and a fichu of the same lace falling from her shoulders; then by Dorothy, in mustard yellow, which ill became her sallow looks and self-effacing manner; and then by Primrose in palest blue velvet, her dark hair supporting a spray of sapphires, which quivered as she moved. Last but one came pretty Claire in a peacock blue frock by Worth all sewn with minute bugles, and then came Lady Aynthorp, tiny but regal in grey velvet, wearing the famous emeralds.

Henry, buttonholed by his Great-Uncle John—fervent devotee to cricket, was listening dutifully to a summary of the great Doctor Grace's innings taken and runs made. While managing suitable replies and inserting a 'how remarkable' to his Uncle John's 'in '95 he scored a thousand runs between the 9th and the 30th May', Henry kept a weather eye upon his parents, saw that his mother's face was tranquil, his father's a mask, giving nothing away as he bent his head to his mother, who sat, very erect, in a chair covered with Gobelins tapestry.

Lord Aynthorp was discussing bloodstock with his son-in-law Sinclair, looking, Henry decided irreverently as spry as an Empire stroller, and as the footmen and Sawby moved among them the Family in general presented a totally unruffled appearance, although, as Henry knew full well, 'the flamin' lot were teemin' underneath.' 'What is more,' he thought gloomily, 'the worst has yet to come for we have not yet embarked upon the crux of the matter and heaven help us when we do.' And while Henry was thus reflecting, Sawby announced from just inside the doors —which Le Soeur had travelled to England to paint in 1652— 'Dinner is served, my lady.'[1]

Then came the bombshell. They proceeded towards the dining

[1] For dinner menu, see Appendix.

room. They took their appointed places, studied the menus with totally unaffected interest and shook out their '*eventails a quatre pointes*'.

The footmen handed the oysters, the parlourmaids proffered paper-thin bread and butter and little water lilies cut from lemons, which were the only support the family permitted for oysters. Sawby poured the champagne, Lord Aynthorp waved the lemons away, grunting, 'Even a drop of lemon juice is the thin edge of the wedge of heresy in my opinion,'[2] and then he lifted his glass, smiled brilliantly and said, 'Meg, my dear, your very good health.' He turned to his daughter-in-law and commented regretfully, 'Shockin' pity it is no longer *comme il faut* to smash one's glass after toastin' one's lady,' saying which he drained the glass and Sawby replenished it immediately.

The old peer lifted an oyster shell to his mouth and swallowed from it, wholly abhorring what he regarded as the malpractice of using a fork. Then he spoke again and this time, seemingly deliberately, raised his voice and spoke with unseemly loudness. 'And now I hope you all have a splendid dinner party as I intend to do, if only to mark the beginning of a new era for me in total freedom from responsibility.'

This time the replenished glass was lifted in Gyles's direction. The words electrified them all. There was a sudden, shattered hush. Then, as the head of the house had very clearly intended, the import of his words became like a charge of this new fangled electricity to them. *He had no intention of dying yet* . . . he could have had no import of such an ending and with the dawning of comprehension for all of them anticipation took precedence over dread. Sadness stood down for infinite relief, while one oyster after another went down that lusty old throat and the perpetrator of all these alarums and excursions settled back with manifest pleasure to the enjoyment of a gargantuan meal.

A positive chatter of conversation broke out and only Christine, on whom the shaggy brows were bent, discerned the appreciative glint in those bright old eyes.

'Wicked,' she murmured softly, 'wicked, naughty, bad old man, but bless you and may you live to persecute us for many years to come.'

---

[2] Acknowledged plagiarism, as said by the late, much-loved M. André L. Simon, who was my husband's and my own gastronomic Papa. F.C.

'Hey,' he rallied, 'persecute did you say? Me? What shame on you, madam.'

She gave him an untroubled nod, 'You rule the roost, you call the tune, and every single one of us dances to it. I only hope my Gyles will be as splendid when he reaches your age.' One hand lay in her lap and to her astonishment, Lord Aynthorp slipped his right hand under the cloth and gripped hers for an instant.

'To beauty,' he countered, raising his glass again and beaming on her with what approximated, for him, to benevolence.

'If the old boy tipples through the meal at that rate,' Henry murmured to Claire, 'he'll be in his grave faster than any of us had anticipated.'

Claire made a tiny move. 'Never tell him I said so,' she confided, 'but I think he's a gorgeous old boy, he frightens the life out of me at times but I think he's deevey.'

'Deevey,' Henry took up the word, 'Oh yes, the court slang, so now you have got it! And now I suppose everything will be "Deevey" ...'

'Oh no,' she refuted, 'but do you know them all I wonder?'

'Try me,' said Henry.

'What is a tea gown?'

'Haven't the faintest,' he confessed.

'There you are, you ignoramus. Well, it's a teagie, and who is a man-man?'

'A Royal Personage?' he hazarded.

'Good. And a perfect fit?'

Henry tired of the game. 'You tell me,' he suggested.

'Fittums, of course, and while I am on that subject, Christine's gown is positively fittums fittums, don't you think?'

Prudence de Lorme was boring Sinclair to extinction with a long peroration about the Suffragette Movement. 'As you will see, my dear Sinclair, they have only begun their campaign for women's rights. By next year, unless they are satisfied, we shall see militancy and then we will show them.'

'We?' said Sinclair, moving uneasily in his high-backed chair.

'Yes, we,' said Prudence emphatically. 'Old I may be, but healthy I *am* and I intend to support the Movement to the uttermost. As Mrs Parkhurst was saying. . . .'

She was interrupted by the removal of the caviare and oyster plates, compelled to make her choice between Almond Cream

Soup and Consommé and thereafter to turn to her left hand neighbour. 'We will continue this later,' she promised darkly. 'Consommé, please, Richard, these cream soups are deleterious to the digestion.'

'*Crème Normande*', said Sinclair clearly, bent upon sustaining at least one male prerogative.

With a nod to Henry, Claire too turned to her left while at the head of the table Lord Aynthorp, sustained by his oysters, prepared himself to converse with his sister-in-law Dorothy, whose redeeming feature, her passion for horses, matched his own. Dinner was progressing famously.

When at length, with the hands of the Sèvres lyre clock showing close upon 11.00 p.m., Chef André reached the dining room doors, and Richard opened them. Then chef came in proudly bearing the *Croquembouche* which he carried round the table. The sugar veiling was like spun gold in the brilliant lighting.

' 'Pon my soul, André, you have excelled yourself,' exclaimed Lord Aynthorp, and the entire family clapped their hands in spontaneous tribute to the pretty thing which they knew well enough had taken their chef hours to prepare.

It rose before Lord Aynthorp, a phallic column of tiny choux buns, joined together with golden, caramelised sugar, diminishing in circumference as it soared to its narrowed summit, which André had filled with shaded spun sugar roses in varying tones of yellow. Between the interstices, André had driven lemon roses so that the whole confection was studded with them. The interior was filled with liqueur flavoured *crème chantilly* and over all was flung the delicate veiling of *sucre filé*. Lord Aynthorp beamed with pleasure and let it be said, anticipation, which if no more was undoubtedly a tribute to his digestion.

André produced the knife, and offered it like a sword saying, '*Et maintenant*, Milord, if your lordship will make the first incision, for good luck, I will then give myself the honour to cut your lordship's birthday cake.'

Lord Aynthorp grasped the knife murmuring, 'Monsieur André, it pains me to destroy your beautiful work but if it has to be done, then let it be so,' and he drove the knife down with a flourish. André removed the *Croquembouche* and the ritual of service went on behind him with footmen hovering and Sawby setting aside the first slice for André to put before 'his lordship'.

The *Croquembouche* went round. Sawby poured the champagne and with a faint interrogatory lift of his eyebrows placed an extra glass before his employer. Lord Aynthorp waved it away. 'No, Sawby, I know that Chef would prefer to wait until we broach the *Terrantez* and then you shall pour a glass for him and another for yourself.' Sawby bowed. Alaric demanded a second serving and demolished this too at speed. The covers were drawn and the decanter of old Madeira put before Lord Aynthorp. 'Remember,' he said with gravity, 'all of you, this wine was in bottle three years before Marie Antoinette was beheaded,' he caught Damien's eye, 'and you, Damien, will doubtless appreciate it since you have such an affection for my old Madeiries.' The dessert was put upon the table. The servants withdrew. André, who had waited in the background, carried his glass as if it were the holy grail. The family was left alone.

Henry rose, lifted the glass of glowing amber liquid and said, 'By your leave, sir, and as the youngest present, I now have the honour to propose your health and happiness for many years to come on this your eightieth birthday.' The family drank the toast, Henry sat down, sweating slightly, and under the general hum of conversation, Lord Aynthorp murmured to Gyles, 'Very neatly done, the boy shapes uncommon fine. My congratulations, Gyles, the line extends itself with security guided by your hands and when your time comes I believe we may repose a like confidence in Henry.'

All Gyles could manage was a soft, 'Thank you, sir,' and then, after a slight pause, he added 'and God bless you, sir.' His spirit, vastly lightened and heartened by what had transpired at the onset of dinner, waxed bolder and then spurred him to un-precedented *lèse majesté*, 'And may you live, sir, to curse us crimson for many, many years to come.' They touched glasses for an instant, drank and fell silent.

Presently, Lady Aynthorp collected eyes, a sinecure this night as all the females had been well prepared by her for a speedy withdrawal. She said, 'And now, dear Justin, we will leave you to —ah me!—the terrible inroads upon your livers, concomitant with the enjoyment of the *Terrantez*,' she glanced briefly at the dinner menu, 'and then your port and finally your brandy. After which we shall anticipate with some pleasure your joining us in the drawing room.' So saying, she left the men of her family alone.

When Henry had closed the doors behind his young aunts,

the last to make their departure, he returned to the table to hear his grandfather saying briskly, 'And now let us close the ranks, Henry my boy, come here and sit beside me—so—Gyles, stay where you are,' and the rest of the men obediently moved, filled empty places and drew close.

Lord Aynthorp settled himself and with some leisure selected a cigar, then setting it close to his hand, he launched the port upon its first tour. In silence the men poured the wine and passed the decanter on until Gyles served himself and returned it to his father. Then with a sign of extreme satisfaction the old *fine bouche* carefully removed the band from his cigar, picked up with some deliberation the cutter Sawby had set beside the cigar box, and cut the tip, before setting the decanter to his left to launch it upon its second tour. He then sent the cigar box down and dipped one veined white hand into the pocket of his black waistcoat and withdrew the little gold box in which were his swan vestas.

As if he had been awaiting this cue, Sawby entered, turned off all the lights, glanced at the candles to confirm that all were burning steadily and stood a pace back from Lord Aynthorp's chair. 'Will that be all, your lordship?' he asked.

'Yes thank you, Sawby, oh no, just a moment, go to the cellar, get two bottles of champagne, give my compliments to Mrs Peace and ask that she and all the staff take a glass for their own pleasure and to drink my health, if so be they've a mind.'

When Sawby had made his final departure and the flame from the swan vestas had touched off an even glowing end to his cigar, he resumed speech, in short, somewhat jerky sentences, as though to overcome his distaste at even broaching what was manifestly an emotional subject. Thus, 'I will not detain you all for long,' he puffed appreciatively, 'just a few points to tie up ... nothin' to disturb us after those fine wines ... and that most admirable dinner. ...' The cigar was drawing evenly and he was clearly satisfied, so much so that his lean frame relaxed slightly, which was more than could be said for the rest. As was to be expected, they appeared relaxed, a group of men, sipping their port and enjoying their cigars. In fact they charged the atmosphere and by their fixed attention upon the speaker, their implied alertness and their aura of tension, registered all the anticipation of greyhounds straining at the leash.

Lord Aynthorp continued, 'Point I want to make concerns the runnin' of the estate, which you know well enough is a small one by the standards of our great landowners—a mere thousand acres, a parcel of home farms, a handful of cottages, a string of gees, and a few servants—nevertheless it is a demandin' responsibility and likely to become more so as time goes on.' He shot a keen glance over the cigar smoke at Gyles. 'So I decided to kill two birds with one shot and give Gyles here a chance to get his eye in while I'm still above ground and can be reasonably active in the background. Henry, the port's with you, m'boy, kindly circulate. . . .' Henry started and hastily passed the decanter. All round the table the white shirts in the candlelight resembled gulls upon a rock watchful, waiting, still. As the head of their family had leaned back in his chair, so did they, thus placing their faces in shadow. These same shadows blurred out the outlines of their black tail coats. The port went round. Christian passed, the Bishop filled his emptied glass, while, to occupy his hands, Henry picked up the nutcrackers and cracked walnuts, peeling each one with the dedicated concentration of a surgeon performing some crucial operation.

'So far as my health is concerned,' Lord Aynthorp went on, 'it seems that I have a reasonable expectation of goin' on for years, not surprisin' really. We're long-lived stock and old Sir Matthew gave me a thorough goin' over, checked me withers, examined me hocks and sounded me wind, last time I was in Town. He assured me I was in the pink of condition, "astonishin' " was the word he used, cannot imagine why.' A slight strangled sound came from the throats of the younger men and even John permitted himself a tiny chuckle. 'Come to think of it, he's rather an old fool when it comes to advice, must be gettin' past it, advised me not to inhale cigars, I know it's unorthodox, . . . imagine! and me smokin' the best in the world, good enough for m'y monarch anyway.' His eyes sparkled indignantly at the recollection, 'Which is neither here nor there. What matters is I have time enough to see everythin' ship-shape before I go to m'y forefathers.' Again he paused, examined the glowing end of his cigar and took up once more, 'I've bin goin' over old ground and seein' a bit forward if you like, same as old Mathilde did but nothin' so mysterious and dramatic as that old gel! Now don't mistake me over this, there's time ahead yet, but somehow I have a feelin' we should begin to rein in a bit, conserve our wind and ware wire. What with income tax at a shillin' in the pound, *doubled* mark you since the 1880s, and on top of that the iniquitous imposition upon other people's property this scandalous death duty at two per cent we could find ourselves in the hands of the Jews or totterin' on the verge of bankruptcy in a few decades; less than should see you out, Gyles, in my considered opinion. All in all, runnin' this place, keepin' an eye on the damned politicians, sniffin' the wind and takin' up the slack with due consideration and forethought is no damned sinecure, look at it whichever way you like, and that in a nutshell is why I have elected, as my prerogative, to hand on durin' m'y lifetime and not wait until I'm carried out in m'y box. Now rein in for a bit longer, I've nearly done. I have always depended upon m'y agents, never have had much of a head for figures, but Gyles here—and meanin' nothin' derogatory to you dear boy but times change—Gyles here is like a flamin' bank clerk when it comes to figures. . . .'

'Curiously enough, father, so is Henry,' Gyles murmured, his eyes now bright with enjoyment and all fear gone.

'Is he indeed? Well that's even more encouragin'. Now as I was sayin', I'll be able to slough off responsibility, have more time to escort Meg in that splendid motor machine . . . get a bit more huntin'. . . .'

'Ware wire y'self, grandfather,' said Henry softly.

'What? eh? oh faddle boy! I'll see you off, young feller me lad, for many seasons yet. . . . Now where was I? Oh yes, restock m'y cellar, which is parlous neglected and needs replenishin' . . . and what's more Henry,' the warning rankled and he reverted abruptly, 'I fancy I can still lead the field without takin' any harm. I'm talkin' too much and really will have done in a moment but I have one more vital point to settle. Alaric, the port. . . .'

The old peer leaned forward and looked around at the shadowed faces, 'It is a matter of due ceremony. Now ceremony is no bad thing, used properly. Not this twaddle that France is usin' for the replacement of the rituals of rank and chivalry, gettin' themselves a lot of crimson and purple robes, dollin' them up with miniver and puttin' orders around their necks,' he snorted at this point, 'nothin' but pifflin' replacements for the real thing, all for a parcel of writers, or wine growers or suchlike, which I don't hold with nor ever will, for it's nothin' more than a twaddle-replacement for their forbears' just and proper state. Poor France, she deplores her loss of kingship and all that goes with it so she plays childrens' games with substitutes. What I am talkin' about is the ceremony with which our ancestors went to the guillotine in their finest clothes, patched, painted, powdered and with total indifference, in those disastrous carts, to the howling of the rabble. It gave them stamina with which to die. In the services it has another name—discipline—the discipline which held those thin red lines and suchlike,' he coughed, slightly embarrassed at his own show of feeling, 'so let's come to the crux of this matter . . . and it concerns you, Alaric.' His brother was happily refilling his port glass from the last of the wine in the decanter.

Justin Aynthorp grunted, 'Get another decanter—it's over there—Damien, you fetch it, boy, you know how to handle wine. . . .' Damien hurried to do his bidding, placed the full decanter beside his uncle and resumed his seat.

'What do you want from me, dear boy?' Arlic enquired mellifluously. 'You know that whatever it is I shall surely acquiesce.'

'Well, that's as maybe,' said his brother a trifle tartly. 'Just let me explain. The crux of this matter concerning ourselves and the present situation I have imposed upon you is what I like to think of under the simpler headin' of good behaviour.' His old eyes automatically flickered briefly in Stephen's direction and he slowed his words down to give them proper emphasis, 'It is good behaviour and its observance that has held this family together for over eight hundred years. Good behaviour has bin the Lorme bastion against adversity; and the only Lormes who have battered against these bastions—praise the Lord unsuccessfully—have bin the ones who lacked a proper consciousness of what good behaviour constituted and thus depraved themselves.' He here resumed his ordinary pace of speech, 'Therefore, Alaric, I submit —only submit, mark you—it comes under the headin' of good behaviour for me to ask you to officiate and for all of us to repair in the mornin' to the chapel and give us your official blessin' on the handover, and the constant survival of the casket which now passes into Gyles safekeepin'. Would you consider this a presumin' upon your office?'

'My dear Justin,' the Bishop boomed, office transcending port, 'nothin' could do you greater credit, dear boy, and I for one shall be honoured to . . . er . . . officiate. I take it though we shall not enlist the assistance of our worthy Vicar?'

'Heaven forfend!' his brother confirmed, 'a private *family* matter and a brief one, just for a simple dedication of the family to the family and all it represents. . . .'

The Bishop nodded, 'Agreed. Dear me, what a mercy I have

that christening on Thursday, and my dear Dorothy packed for me everythin' I shall need.'

'Then I take it you agree?'

'Of course, and respect you for the suggestion.'

'And the rest of you?' he looked around the table. With their assent confirmed, Lord Aynthorp ended, 'Then let us say at 8.30 tomorrow morning,' he paused, took out his watch glanced at it, corrected himself, 'this mornin' . . . mercy me, we must join the ladies, 8.30 it shall be, then we can have our breakfast afterwards.'

He made as if to rise, but Henry who had been 'ripening' steadily under the influence of his grandfather's wines now came upon as much courage as was needed. 'Grandfather,' he said clearly, 'sir, may I have lllleave to ssspeak a moment. . . .' His courage flickered and he manifestly stuttered.

Lord Aynthorp examined him dubiously. 'Don't say anythin' you will be regrettin' afterwards,' he said startlingly.

'Nno, sir, of cccourse not, sir, but I mmmust say it.'

Lord Aynthorp sat back again, 'Then pray do so, but for pity's sake be brief, I have talked an unconscionable time already.'

Henry drew a deep breath. 'Well, sssir, . . . it's jjust this . . . why do we not know the contents of the bbbox? Why have we gone eight hundred odd years in ignorance of what the Lady Mathilde bequeathed to the first of our line in England?'

'Aaaah,' Lord Aynthorp echoed, 'why indeed m'y boy. I have wondered the same m'self and lacked the courage, damme, to take the decision. There seems something irrevocable after all these centuries . . . at all events I will not be the one to open the box. . . .'

'Bbbecause yyyou ssee in it ssomething of Pandora's box?'

The old man looked at him keenly. 'Could be, m'y boy. Yes, could be,' he mused.

Gyles spoke. "Since Henry has raised this, sir, may I add that I too have wondered. In all my researchin' I have failed to find a *reason*. Have you one, sir? Will you now tell us?'

'I have no reason,' he spoke sombrely, 'except a curious reluctance to prank with what has lasted for so long . . . there *is* nothin' in the shape of an embargo . . . there is in fact nothin' to stop the Head of the family,' he laid emphasis upon the word, 'examinin' the Box, nothin' indeed to stop all the men of the family . . . but somehow . . .' Again he tailed off and again Henry came in.

'Father, would *you* open the Box?'

Gyles moved restlessly, 'Frankly,' he said, 'I do not know. Wonderin' why my father has not, is a different matter from speculatin' on whether I would when my time comes. . . . I shall have to have notice of that question.'

'Good,' this time Lord Aynthorp rose with some resolution, 'then shall we join the ladies?'

CHAPTER 9

The Children

Christine de Lorme awoke on the morning after the dinner party with a slight tingling of pleasurable anticipation. The children were coming home. The nursery wing and the schoolroom, under the autonomous rule of Mademoiselle and Nanny, would be filled again and, with the new term looming for the older ones, there would be school uniforms to replenish, tuck boxes to plan and 'treats' to be arranged. In the meantime, for over two weeks, the full complement of children would be there to delight and occupy her. They were returning in time for tea.

Gyles would, of course, be closeted with his father and the family solicitors, firstly for luncheon, after the scheduled 11.00 a.m. descent with Damien to the wine cellars, and thereafter in the library where they would occupy themselves with the solely male affair of estate transference from father to son without let or hindrance from any females.

Christine's mind ranged over the day's carefully scheduled arrangements. As soon as breakfast was over, Bishop Alaric and his Dorothy would go by carriage to her sister's house at Over Bunting where they were promised for luncheon. After this, Alaric would officiate at the christening of a new nephew, at which a minor royalty was to be chief godparent.

The three Delahayes were leaving to join a shooting party in Sandringham. Prudence would in all probability have made her departure already, to spend a few days in London with what Christine, within the privacy of her own thoughts, assessed as 'those extraordinary women, in some dusty Suffragette head-quarters, eating nut cutlets and getting covered in ink'; while John and Primrose were catching an early train to attend a horse sale at Newmarket. It added to her pleasant expectations that only her three favourite 'Family'—her mother-in-law, her Aunt Marguerite and Henry—would be sharing the day with her until the children arrived.

They had, as usual, left for Bognor at the beginning of August, to spend a bracing five weeks by the sea in the house which was rented for them annually. This establishment was run by a retired butler and his wife who, on becoming possessed of an unexpected windfall from a miserly great-aunt, had merged this with their own meagre savings as butler and housekeeper to a family in the County and retired to Bognor. Here they had set up a pattern, similar, in a modest seaside way, to the boarding house enterprise which was proving so rewarding to another retired couple—Mr and Mrs Claridge. Mrs Dewberry cooked for her 'families' as she had been a cook, a position from which she had finally graduated to housekeeper with her late employers. Dewberry 'did' the rest of the house which, between them, they ran with all the efficiency resulting from a lifetime of training among what Nanny described approvingly as 'the very best families'. Thus Mrs Dewberry won Nanny's essential and highly fortuitous approval.

Nanny took with her both Rose the nursemaid and Violet the nurserymaid to assist her in the arduous and rigid routine which she imposed upon 'her nursery'. These two hand-maidens were also responsible for a large part of the work concomitant with the well-being of the schoolroom brood which made up the majority. They comprised Gyles de Lorme's younger children, thirteen-year-old Ninian, Andrew aged ten and Anne who was nearly nine; one of the three St John boys, James, who was the same age as Ninian, and his sister Lucy who had just passed her eleventh birthday. With the two Delahaye girls, Stephanie aged fourteen and Rosalind eleven, this made a total of seven, leaving five in the nursery proper: five-year-old Lucien St John, the Delahaye's youngest, Gilbert, aged three, and Gyles and Christine's baby, the wilful but enchanting two-year-old Richard, together with the two babies of Christian and Claire de Lorme, four-year-old Peter and baby Priscilla, just two and already a raging beauty. Ralph St John, who was fifteen, was spending the holidays with a school friend in Suffolk and was thus the cause of both envy and acrimony on the party of Ninian and James. They bitterly resented being, as they described it between themselves, 'lumped together with a lot of kids and most of them silly girls.' However, with their pockets suitably lined with gifts of money, they had departed with the rest in reasonably good humour. The same could not be said for Nanny who was distinctly tetchy at having to cope with the schoolroom contingent for the first week while the French governess spent her holiday with an aunt in Brittany.

It had taken three carriages to bear this brood and their custodians to Lower Aynthorp station, with the shooting wagon following the cortège piled with a huge assembly of trunks and valises, cots and hampers, buckets, spades, cricket bats, diabolos —the latest craze—and the appurtenances of battledore and shuttlecock for which the nets would duly be erected in the Dewberry's small, high-walled garden. By the time the last item had been loaded on to the waggon—with a mad dash at the moment of departure by George for Nanny's vast red sun-umbrella, which had almost been forgotten—the uproar from the carriages had resembled the parrots' cage at the London Zoological Gardens and even Christine, turning away after a last wave, drew a slight sigh of relief at the concomitant diminishing of noise.

Now, below stairs, on this the morning of their return Mrs Parsons was handing out the 'rough edge of her tongue' to all and sundry under her command as she worked away at the components of special nursery tea—another ritual which was repeated annually, as was Mrs Peace's meticulous supervision of the final cleaning of the nursery wing. Woe betide anyone who left so much as a single speck of dust or a single unpolished surface for Nanny's sharp eyes to light upon, as Mrs Peace reminded the two slightly perspiring housemaids.

At a quarter to twelve the library bell rang in the servants' hall. George, the under footman, was assisting Sawby in the delicate matter of decanting port. Sawby poured, while George stood, candle held in the claws of its long wooden holder, so that the flame was behind the neck of the bottle and thus clearly illumined its contents as they flowed into the decanter. Sawby, steel spectacles perched on nose, was therefore in no possible doubt as to when to stop pouring, as he could see very clearly the sediment rising gradually from the base of the bottle.

'That will be Mr Gyles.' Sawby spoke as the bell rang, but his eyes never wavered from his task. 'There is a package from London which he wishes you to collect from Lower Aynthorp station.' He raised his voice very slightly, 'Richard, come and replace George, he is wanted in the library,' and continued pouring with infinite care and slowness.

Richard obediently replaced his colleague while George hurried himself into his striped waistcoat and began running up the steep stairs, fastening the Castle buttons as he went. Then, presenting himself inside the library doors, 'You rang, sir?' he enquired of Gyles who was seated in one of the embrasures. The morning sun, slanting through the leaden panes, highlighted his hair and fell in a bright pool on the old Persian rugs.

'Ah yes, George,' he said looking up from the document he was reading. 'I have already spoken to Sawby. He says he can spare you, so will you please go down to the stables as soon as possible? Mr Plumstead has the pony and trap ready waiting. Take it to Lower Aynthorp station and ask the station master for a package for me which came on the 11.25 train.'

Thus it was that George, a few minutes later, went spanking down the drive in the trap, holding the ribbons and whistling between his teeth. 'Nice to get away,' he thought, 'nice to be out in the sunshine. Think if the parcel don't take too long to find, I might manage a quick 'un at the Aynthorp Arms on the way home.' Thus thinking, he touched up Dorrie with his whip and bowled out into the country lane.

When George returned, metaphorically at least, licking his chops, it was not solely in retrospective appreciation of the pint of porter which he had downed. The package being ready and waiting in the hands of the station master, he went to the 'Arms' and there heard a ripe and fruity piece of gossip which he gleaned in the 'tap' from that 'leery old bastard' Tim the poacher who was likewise indulging alongside him. Tim had opened the ball with his customary furtive cheerfulness. 'Seen the little 'un, gaffer?' he nudged George who edged away a little and looked down his snub nose.

'What little 'un?' he enquired, registering absolutely no interest whatever.

'Nelly's, that's wot,' said the old rogue, whispering hoarsely and thrusting his face close to George's thereby releasing a noxious waft of stale breath over the young footman.

'Nelly ain't married,' countered George, taking another pull at his porter, 'don't talk so silly, ole Tim, get back to yer poachin'.'

'Poachin' is it?' bridled Tim, stung by his indifference. 'Yer goin' ter sing a different toon up at the Castle when yer claps yer beadies on that chile. That I can tell yer.' His voice dropped to a whine. 'Wot about 'arf a pint for the pore old man?' he wheedled.

'Carn't afford it,' said George shortly, 'what's all this ragga-marole about what child?'

'Nelly's, you great silly, who she 'ad off *someone* at the Castle. None of 'em seen it yet, but it's Lorme orlright and she weren't got into it hereabouts but up in that sinful Lunnon.'

George paused, lifted tankard suspended in mid air, 'You don't mean it? Yes 'avin' me on! and ooo, pray, up at the Castle? Mr Sawby I suppose?' and he let out a great roar of laughter.

Totally goaded by this time, Tim told him, with the result that it was a very reflective footman who unhitched the pony's reins, turned the trap and went bowling back, brooding with shocked incredulity upon what he had just learned.

In the meantime when one of the Aynthorp carriages, driven by Plum himself, had passed the Aynthorp Arms bearing the 'legal gennulmun from Lunnon', Plum had observed George's trap with some wrath. So he, too, drove home in no very good frame of mind, determined to waylay George 'afore this day is out', and have from him an explanation as to what 'My pony and trap was doin'' outside the boozer.' The Lorme pot was once again coming to the simmer.

Justin Aynthorp, having dusted his knees and elbows fastidiously, after emerging from the cellars with his nephew Damien, strolled across the Great Hall, encountered Sawby in the act of closing the library doors and demanded, 'Hey, Sawby, have you decanted our port yet?'

'Indeed yes, my lord, it is resting on the sideboard in antici-pation of it quite settling down by the time your Lordship will require it.'

'Good, good, what about the Madeiry?'

'Awaiting you in the library, my lord. Is it your pleasure that I should pour it now?'

'Certainly, certainly.' The old man passed him at speed, 'Come on in, man, we shall all be the better for a glass,' and so saying changed mien with amazing celerity, entered the library and made his guests welcome with grave courtesy.

Gyles was standing with them by the round central library table, a map spread out upon it. He broke off to welcome his father, 'Mornin', sir, nice to see you in such good fettle.' Thus he won himself a warm and surprisingly gentle smile, so he smiled back, then went on to explain, 'I am just goin' over the boundaries sir. . . .'

'Ah yes, our boundaries, what is it exactly, just a thousand acres?'

'Exactly so,' Gyles confirmed. The white head, whose owner was freshly nicknamed by the irreverent Henry 'our remarkable octo-geranium', joined the red one and the bald pates of the lawyers as they all bent over the map again. Sawby dispensed the Madeira. He then bestowed a benevolent parting glance upon the group and withdrew closing the doors softly behind him.

Lady Aynthorp, the Countess Marguerite and Christine took luncheon at a round table set by Sawby in the windows of the small breakfast room. They were attended by Edward, the head footman, assisted by Pearson who whisked in and out with plates and dishes; a Pearson who was still so excited by what she called her 'prospeks' that from time to time as she went about her duties she gave little skips and sang 'tra-la-la' when absolutely certain neither Mrs Peace nor Mrs Parsons could see or hear her.

She knew Christine and Mrs Peace had been closeted together for some time in the 'office' which led into the linen rooms. She had passed the door just as Mrs Peace was evacuating two laundrymaids with a 'shoo' and the stately instruction to 'return when Madam has gone'. Now, Pearson had to contain herself, in so far as she was able, until Mrs Peace should enquire of her the date of Pansy Appleby's monthly day. She had already resolved to write Pansy a long letter, a task she earmarked for after staff supper and when Upstairs dinner was over. Then she would be safe from the prying eyes of 'ole rule-the-roost' Mrs Parsons who would, by then, have shut herself into the stewards' room with the rest of the upper servants and she would be free from all save the heavy badinage of the footmen and the curious glances of the maids.

'Let 'em stew,' she thought vulgarly as she whisked into the breakfast room with one of Chef André's soaring brown-topped soufflés.

When Lady Aynthorp and Countess Marguerite had drunk their *tisanes* and Christine her coffee, the latter escorted her mother-in-law to her boudoir and left her in Palliser's safe keeping, to undress, wrap in a peignoir and put to bed with a hot water bottle and a book; meanwhile the sprightly Countess assumed a large chip hat, collected trug and pruners and trotted off to her beloved roses.

Christine then returned to Mrs Peace. In the morning she had delicately and tactfully raised the subject of Pansy Appleby and Pearson. By dint of careful flattery and a pretty display of deference, she succeeded in winning Peace over to the scheme. 'Indeed, madam,' Peace went so far as to say, 'I am extremely grateful to you for your kindness to Pearson, who has always been a good girl and willing. If this person, her friend Appleby, proves satisfactory it will give me great pleasure to engage her and thus release Pearson for better things. I shall ascertain Appleby's "monthly day" immediately and invite her to interview with me.'

Christine, of course, saw clean through all this persiflage. She knew well enough how much Palliser was disliked and realised that the prime motive behind the acquiescence stemmed from the opportunity it provided for an implicit snub to Palliser and the elevation of a malleable young woman who would never, Mrs Peace was reasonably sure, 'give herself la-di-dah airs graces like that old cat Palliser'. The diplomatic rod so indisputably available was, of course, that 'poor Palliser was doing too much.'

Now, as Christine returned to the housekeeper, she began to realise that she was doing so as the newly created mistress of Castle Rising. She was already fully conscious that the tranquil running of the Castle's domestic areas would depend upon her having Mrs Peace as an ally.

She found the housekeeper already reseated at her desk, a small card table drawn up alongside on which were ranged a number of lists, catalogues, invoices and household books.

'You will have to instruct me, Mrs Peace,' Christine resumed diplomatically, 'I have much to learn. Her Ladyship tells me you are such an expert.'

Mrs Peace's severe face softened a little. She even unbent sufficiently to reminisce. 'I was taught, madam,' she said with sudden gentleness, 'by my dear father. He was a strict man, but just. He used to say "order is heaven's first law" and from very small children we were taught "a place for everything and every-thing in its place".'

'You learned well,' Christine commented, glancing round at the orderly, pigeonholed papers, the stacks of cardboard boxes all neatly labelled—footmen's buttons, maids' caps, maids' cap ribbons, coachmen's epaulettes, white cotton gloves, kitchen maids' sacking aprons, dusters, polishing cloths, carriage lamp wicks, oven cloths—all rising in tiers from the packed shelves around the room. She noted too the smaller boxes with single buttons sewn to the outsides, ranging from black shoe and boot buttons to mother of pearl and linen-covered ones, these last for replacement on the women servants' underwear, each with the remaining number inside the boxes marked clearly on the outside.

Mrs Peace drew a clip of lists towards her. 'I have presumed, madam,' she began, 'by making out some notes on our autumn replacement requirements. If you would be so good as to glance through them. . . .'

Christine smiled. 'Why not just read them to me and explain as you go along, then I will begin to understand your pattern?' Mrs Peace made a slight courteous neck inclination, glanced down at the first page and began. . . .

'Well, first of all, Madam, perhaps I had better explain that we have been in the habit of sending our replacement orders six months ahead to the Beauvais nuns for the hand-embroidered Family table linen.'

'Then let us accept that this practice will continue,' said Christine.

'Thank you, Madam.' Peace made a little pencilled tick on the page. 'Then, we have for many years bought our everyday table napkins from the Stores—the Army and Navy Stores I mean. We generally buy the Louis XVth design in finest Irish table damask. Twenty-seven inches wide, costing fifty-nine and sixpence per dozen and we really do need a further ten dozen if we are to maintain our stocks at the usual standard.'

'Then please order them. But do go on, for I am learning all the time.'

'We buy the same Irish damask for the larger breakfast room tablecloths. They measure two and a half yards by seven yards and the current catalogue shows them at seven pounds, ten shillings and sixpence each.' She glanced up, Christine merely nodded, so she resumed, 'Cloths for the senior staff tables and for the servants' hall we just buy by the yard, four and eleven, seventy-two inches wide. They are then hemmed here by the laundrymaids. Then I was wondering, the tablecloth used in the servants' hall for their leisure periods is getting sadly worn. We really should buy another, if only because it would cast discredit upon the Family with visiting servants if we were seen to be using a shabby one.'

'Unthinkable!' Christine agreed.

'There are servants' liveries to replace too. Mr Sawby requires a new dress coat, waistcoat and trousers which will cost four pounds, seventeen shillings and sixpence. We also require a replacement of coachmen's breeches in pigskin, these would be one pound eighteen shillings each, a new coachman's greatcoat in box cloth, which would be a further three pounds seven shillings and sixpence, and a five-lap cape which would cost three guineas.'

'How long do these garments last normally?' Christine asked interestedly, but before Mrs Peace could reply there was a scratch upon the door and Pearson entered.

'Yes, Pearson?'

'I am sorry to disturb you, Madam, Mrs Peace,' she said, 'but I thought that Madam should know, the carriages are coming up the drive.'

Christine rose, 'How quickly the time has gone,' she exclaimed. 'You must forgive me, Mrs Peace, but I must go, perhaps we could resume work at say eleven o'clock tomorrow morning if that will be convenient?'

'Of course, Madam.' Mrs Peace rose, went with Christine to the door, held it open for her and watched the slim, straight back disappearing down the long corridor. Then she closed the door, went to the small, rather pitted looking-glass which hung on the wall, examined her reflection in it and vouchsafed the information to herself, 'She'll do. A proper lady. You're lucky in her ladyship's successor.'

Christine hurried down the main staircase to the Great Hall into which the children were pouring, heedless of Nanny's and Mademoiselle's exhortations. In a moment she was engulfed.

'How you have all grown!' she exclaimed plucking her baby Richard from the press and holding him close, 'My darling, what a big boy you are now.' She stroked his curls and he nuzzled into her neck. 'Missed you,' he mumbled. 'Where's Papa?'

To ecstatic cries of 'Mother...Auntie Christine', and the more sober greetings of Nanny, 'Good afternoon Madam, we think we are all well, if a little turbulent after the journey,'... Rose and Violet's excited and slightly awed curtseys as, with eyes decorously lowered, they murmured shyly, 'Good afternoon, Ma'am,' and bobbed about like small corks. Phrases like, 'Mother, I swam a hundred yards, honestly I did,' . . . 'Aunt Christine, can we come in to dinner tonight, we are almost grown up now?'— this latter in plaintive chorus from the two thirteen-year-olds— drifted out of this general uproar while Nanny bustled about ordering the disposal of the luggage as it came off the brake, flinging curt instructions at her handmaidens, 'You, Rose, take Master Peter upstairs to the nursery this minute and wash his sticky face. Violet, pick Miss Priscilla up, she is crawling under that console table . . . George, that wicker hamper goes to my room and not to the night nursery, IF you please.'

In the middle of the uproar Gyles strolled out from the library, caught up his baby son from his wife and rumpled his curls to delighted shouts of 'Papa, dear Papa, *my* Papa,' at which his daughter Anne flung herself at him screaming 'Me too, me too, kiss me,' and baby Gilbert, toddling in her wake, fell on the marble floor and set up unearthly yells. At this precise moment Lord Aynthorp made his appearance. By merely standing in the library doorway and ejaculating, 'Hey, what's this Bedlam? Good afternoon, Nanny,' he obtained total silence.

Then the children crowded round him and the shouts began again: 'Grandpa, how are you?' . . . 'Can we come down to dinner, we *are* thirteen?' . . . and from Richard, set down by his Father in order to console his daughter Anne, 'Up, Ganpa . . . up . . . piggy back.'

Lord Aynthorp laughed. 'Too old to pick up great boys in my arms,' he said smilingly. 'Now listen, all of you. I have had a birthday since you went away and I have been given a yellow Rolls Royce motor car. If you all go upstairs and have your tea quietly I will take you out tomorrow mornin' in turns. But if Nanny tells me you have been sinners I shall refuse to have you in my splendid motor.'

Richard, always one to know on which side his bread was buttered, now gave the lead. Murmuring, 'Tea, now, I'll be good,' he set himself against the first tread of the great staircase and began clambering laboriously upwards, his bottom sticking out, his little chubby hands gripping the treads, shouting, 'Me good boy.' Lord Aynthorp burst out laughing. 'That's a chip off the old block, Gyles,' he said approvingly, then to the children, 'Begone with you all and remember what I said, or I will be after you with a riding crop.' The older children stampeded upwards. Gyles picked up his Richard and swung him on to his shoulders. Christine followed with her daughters clustered around her and the hall emptied gradually.

There were other undercurrents below stairs on this day. George had returned in very abstracted mood. The truth, as he acknowledged to himself, was that he did not rightly know whether to dismiss old Tim's leery confidences as a 'load of codswallop', a term which he had once used in Sawby's presence and had been roundly rebuked for his ' 'orrible vulgarity, not to say downright coarseness!' 'However, be that as it may,' he thought, 'I'm still in a fix.' In the end he drew Richard into the butler's pantry and confided in him. Richard, of course, immediately passed on the information to Edward, for although Edward was so superior to him in the below-stairs hierachy, they were great cronies. As was more or less inevitable, Sawby overheard them whispering, caught the name 'Mr Stephen' and ordered the three of them into the Housekeeper's room where he demanded an explanation.

When he had at length wrenched it out of them he read them a severe lecture on the virtues of loyalty, the limited prerogatives of servants and ended his homily with the words 'See nothing, 'ear nothing, speak nothing, and now you can go; but let me catch you passing a word of this to anyone else and it will be as much as your places are worth and that I can promise you.'

He sat bolt upright in his chair after they had gone, staring ahead of him and thinking hard. He had never been known to do other than set an example of correctness to the lower servants. His axioms were well-known both below stairs and throughout the outside staff.

'We have our place and they have theirs,' he was wont to lecture them periodically. 'If we are lucky enough to find a good place, such as this is—and never could anyone hope for better employers—then we should be doubly circumspeck. The ways of the Almighty must never be questioned. We have been called to lowly positions but we only set ourselves lower still if we betray them. We are NOT among the lilies of the field who toil not, neither do they spin. We are the drones in the hive; but if we look around us at the sufferings of some, like little children working in mines, chimneysweeps like Boots was—now there's an object lesson for us—we should give daily thanks for our lot and for the pleasant places in which it has fallen. There is one law for the quality and another for servants. That is as it should be. No one should ever entertain ideas above their station.'

He was prone to the delivery of this familiar peroration just before evening prayers, so that as he ended, he could reach out for the family Bible, lay it on the table, change his coat, adjust his spectacles and then carry the book to the head of the long table in the servants' hall where a small lectern was set ready for him every night. All the servants would be lined up at the farther end awaiting him on such occasions. When he had delivered himself of his credo, he would look around at the assembly and fire his last Parthian shot: 'We have our prayers in the servants' hall. The family go to the chapel. We are Low Church, the family are High. So it was ordained.' Then he would open the Bible at an appointed place, leave it ready and dropping to his knees begin, 'Our Father which art in heaven.'

At this moment in time he was recalling his credo for his own benefit. It did not help him greatly in his present dilemma. *What should he do?* He was, as he confessed to himself, 'bamboozled'. Then there came a tap at the door. He called out, 'Come in.' A scared kitchenmaid, Rose, bobbed in the doorway and said, 'It's Mr Plumstead, Mr Sawby, he is at the back door. He asks if you could spare him a moment, he says as 'ow it is somethink important.'

Sawby glanced up at the clock on the stone mantelshelf. It proclaimed 7.30 p.m. He rose. 'In fifteen minutes, Rose, I am due in the dining room. Tell Mr Plumstead I will come immediately, but can only spare him five minutes. Then I shall have to prepare myself for dinner.' Rose bobbed again, fled to the back door with the message and Sawby followed more slowly.

Plum, in off duty jacket, was standing twisting a cloth cap around in his gnarled fingers. 'I'm sorry to trouble you, Mr Sawby' he began, 'but as this is a private matter and you 'ave work to do I wondered if so be I could ask a favour of you?'

Sawby liked Plum. They were old cronies, and therefore detecting something grave in the man's demeanour Sawby replied, 'How would it be if I came to your cottage after dinner, Mr Plumstead? Would your good lady permit that I joined you for a short while?'

Old Plum coloured up with pleasure. 'If so be you would consent to take a glass of 'er cowslip wine wot she is mortal proud of I can think of nothink we would both like better, so to speak,' he added as an afterthought.

'Then shall we say 9.45 sharp so as not to keep you out of bed to all hours? Will half an hour be enough for what you wish to say?'

Plum nodded, still torturing his cap. 'Three minnits is enough to say it, Mr Sawby; but it's not the saying but the resolving what troubles me.'

Sawby's face sharpened. He peered at the man in the growing dusk, 'I might,' he said regretfully, 'I say I just might, have a wind of what you are about to say. But now it must wait. Shall we say after dinner then?' His majestic demeanour softened, due partly to his own shocked suspicions and partly to his affection for the sincere old man, so he added, 'Don't worry too much, Plum, two heads is better than one and we'll put ours together.' Then he turned back to his duties and old Plum plodded off on his bandy old legs into the descending darkness.

Working his way homeward, Plum reviewed yet again the enormity of the situation in which he had unwittingly involved himself. In his slow assimilation he eventually arrived at a conclusion which oppressed him with a strong sense of guilt. *He had supplied Stephen with his bicycle.* His proportionate anger at Stephen's lies and deceit coupled with his own conviction that the bicycle episode was indeed a part of the 'goin's on at the Arms', were so infuriating that, like Tim, he fell to muttering unlovely comments as he made his way between the trees in the home park, striking a crow's flight line between the Castle and his cottage in the growing darkness, with all the assurance of a homing bird, albeit a distressed one.

CHAPTER 10

Stephen

The tenor during dinner was positively bland. Lord Aynthorp, exhilarated by the relinquishing of responsibility, familiar through long years of association with the lawyers who were conveyancing his wishes, was positively benign; so much so that Gyles, after a thoughtful look at his uninhibited parent, murmured to his wife, as they sipped their sherries in the small drawing room, 'One must suppose that after so much amiability there will be an almighty explosion before many days have passed.'

Christine twinkled at him and demurred, 'Not necessarily, my love. I have a suspicion that he is not too well pleased with himself at keeping us all in such dreadful suspense. If such a thing were possible for your father, I would say he is faintly uncomfortable at discovering how deeply we care about him, naughty old man that he is!' Gyles acknowledged the possible truth of this, then, mindful of his duties, he turned to engage the lawyers in conversation.

They were father and son, Trusloves, both partners in the old firm of Truslove, Pennyworth and Copthorne, whose offices had for several generations been situated in Lincoln's Inn Fields. They were, Christine reflected, as she watched them amusedly, extraordinarily like two pelicans, with their long, beaky noses, their very bony legs and their shared habit of darting their faces forward when talking. 'The White Tufted Pelican', she invented to herself, and 'the Brown Tufted Fledgling Bird', who would clearly be the replica of his desiccated parent in another thirty years.

Then her attention was drawn towards her Uncle and Aunt, John and Primrose. They were talking animatedly with Henry about the success of their purchases at Newmarket. Henrietta and Eustace likewise seemed in splendid humour for they had returned from a luncheon party well in time to catch the entire nursery and schoolroom brood still at the tea table and were charmed with the appearance of both their little snubnosed darling Lucy and her brother Lucien. This difficult child put them in the best of humours by telling of his battledore and shuttlecock achievements. It was the first time the boy had ever shown the faintest interest in any game. It acted like a tonic on both parents and, even if only temporarily, quelled their growing suspicions already voiced anxiously on more than one occasion: 'Alas! Lucien should have been a girl!'

Henry was in high spirits, too, for he was to go up to Oxford for the Michaelmas term in October. Moreover, he would go to Balliol where his father had been before him.

The general mood was further emphasised by the Bishop. He was well-pleased with the way the christening had gone off and full of what the Royal Personage had said to him and what he had said to the Royal Personage. Under cover of his sonorous voice, naughty old Countess Marguerite whispered to her favourite nephew, 'Henry, I have at last found the correct description of your Uncle Alaric's voice when he is pleased with himself. He booms—like a bittern on the Norfolk Broads.'

Thus the meal progressed in a general atmosphere of felicity.

Sawby was the only one who did not enjoy 'his' Family in their content. His unease, his knowledge, his rendezvous with the old head gardener all weighed upon him more heavily than any of the trays he carried, or the great dishes he held out. It was therefore with a sigh of relief and a few sharp words to each footman—who in their own opinion had never acquitted themselves better and were at a loss to understand what could have earned them rebukes—that he eventually descended to the housekeeper's room, ate a sparing and speedy meal, changed into an ulster, observed that the evening had 'turned unexpectedly sharp', and set out across the Home Park in a mood of the utmost despondency.

When he returned, the rest of the servants were abed. He then did an unprecedented thing. He went up to the dining room, opened a cupboard, took out a bottle of *Roget et Delamain* cognac —the 1830 which had been served at the birthday dinner— poured a generous quantity into a balloon and returned with it to the housekeeper's room. Behind the closed door he shrugged off his coat, settled himself in a chair and tried to calm his agitated thoughts.

He climbed back upstairs to his bedroom as the assorted clocks began striking 2.00 a.m. with the result that the following morning he was still very tired, still undecided, short of sleep and even shorter in temper when he appeared at 7.00 a.m. This his luckless juniors soon discovered for themselves.

It was only when Gyles was carving himself some of his favourite York ham at the cold table that Sawby drew a deep breath and took the irrevocable step. 'Might I ask, Mr Gyles, the favour of a very private word with you, sir, after breakfast? The matter, I believe you will agree, sir, is vital.'

Gyles turned, surprised. One brief glance at the butler's drawn and worried countenance was sufficient to draw the response, 'Of course, Sawby. Shall we say immediately I have eaten my ham? Go to his Lordship's no, of course, I forgot, *my* office and I will join you within a few moments.'

The result of this exchange was that the ham tasted like sawdust. Gravely uneasy by this time, Gyles made his excuses as soon as possible, went into the office which he had so recently taken over where Sawby turned sharply from the window as he entered, then stepped forward to close the door. Five minutes later Gyles pulled the bell.

To the footman who presented himself he said, 'Ah, George, my compliments to his lordship and the legal gentlemen. Tell them I have been unavoidably detained but will join them as speedily as possible.'

Then, as George closed the door, Gyles said to Sawby, 'And now, Sawby, be good enough to begin at the beginnin' and tell me everythin'. I am deeply in your debt for your loyalty. I fully appreciate what it must have cost you to tell me what you have done so far; but now we shall have to confer together, which can only be done if you put me fully in the picture. Just one thing before you begin, I may as well tell you that I have seen the child at the Aynthorp Arms.'

When Sawby ended his painful tale, told with many anxious glances at his new master, in between riveted attention upon his own tightly gripped hands, he was bereft of the last vestige of his professional pomposity and sadly depleted composure too.

He had declined Gyles' request that he sit down in his presence with a stiff, 'I would prefer to stand if you please, sir, as is my wont,' so remained, well forward on the balls of his feet, as all

men learn to do who spend the majority of their working hours
upon them. That part of his narrative which concerned the
gossiping footmen seemed to cause him the greatest distress and
also the cowslip wine exchange of confidences with his friend
Plumstead in the front room of his cottage.

It was at this point that Gyles interrupted him for the first
time. Until then he had listened in silence, his lean legs crossed,
one hand gripping the stem of a pipe which went out, unnoticed.

'Can we repose any confidence in the footmen?' he enquired.
'I am reluctant to dismiss good servants due to no real fault of
their own.'

Sawby recovered sufficiently to say with severity, 'Gossip is
always a fault by my standards, sir.'

'Yes, quite! But can we keep them or are they to become a
major consideration? You take my meanin' of course.'

Sawby gave his faint inclination of the head which was so
familiar to the Lormes. 'Yes and no, sir,' he admitted, thinking
out each word before he delivered it. 'If I may be permitted an
opinion, sir, they are becoming well trained footmen *in my terms*.
They are indisputably loyal to the family and appreciate the
great privilege of being attached to this household.' He paused,
but as Gyles made no comment, he resumed. 'If I may go further,
I would say that, being young, they could not contain themselves
over such confidences as old Tim breathed over them. They are
also fairly simple minded, having had little or no education. If I
were in the slightest doubt I would recommend their instant
dismissal. As matters stand and, on reflection, I respectfully
suggest it would be wiser to let them stay. All they need is a
thorough dressing down from me. If I may presume to ask a
question, would you not consider it would exaggerate the whole
affair out of all proportion to their lowly positions if the family
were to involve themselves in any way? It will strengthen my
hand if I can pour scorn on that drunken old poacher who his
Lordship, as Chief Magistrate, has sent to prison on many
occasions; but I can imagine how they would view the family's
involvement.' Sawby began to ruminate aloud: ' "Phew," they
would say, "it must be serious for his Lordship or Mr Gyles, to
be sufficiently anxious to discuss the matter with mere footmen!"'
If you will trust me to make their ears burn, I think I can undertake to make them objects of derision and mockery, silly boys,
witless and so forth, and not to speak of their being guilty of

presumptuous and impertinent domestic vulgarity. I have always found, sir, that if you can make the young look sufficiently silly *that* will close their mouths faster than any other way, for they cannot endure ridicule. To give them money or send them away or both would be fatal.'

Gyles tapped out his dead pipebowl and stood up. He took out his monocle, polished it, replaced it, then said, 'I accept your reasonin' and on behalf of the family will abide by your decisions. There is one more point I must ask however, what of poor old Plumstead?'

'Bowed down with shame, sir. Feeling that he is responsible in letting the family down. He kept muttering last night sir, "My bicycle, for such an 'orrible errand".'

Gyles nodded. 'Well then, would you advise me to call on him or would that upset him more? I think I can tell that good old man swiftly enough not to give him a heart attack how much we value him and respect his integrity.'

Sawby's voice was the merest trifle unsteady as he replied 'He would cherish it to the very end of his days, sir. He really is in the deepest distress and last night, until I made reason prevail, was all for wringing old Tim's neck.'

Gyles nodded. 'Well then, would you advise me to call on I will visit him and, Sawby, you can leave Tim to us too if you please.'

Gyles de Lorme, thinking that it did begin to appear as though this particular scandal could be fairly easily contained, unwittingly spoke aloud saying, 'Which leaves only that rogue landlord, Tim and the girl.'

Sawby coughed and Gyles looked up sharply. 'If I could presume, sir, there is one more.' He spoke with extreme diffidence, implying that while he could hope and be grateful for graciousness in respect of the Lower Orders, when it came to the Gentry it was an entirely different matter.

'Who on earth . . . ?' Gyles stared.

'Mr Charles Danement sir.'

'Oh, Charles,' Gyles laughed a trifle grimly. 'If you can account for our footmen I think you can leave me to undertake Mr Danement without undue stress and strain upon myself.'

He turned towards the door with a heavy sigh. The weight of weary repetition, both of memory and family history, rested heavily upon him. Even so, what he said to the butler, very quietly, before closing the door behind himself, left that worthy so profoundly moved that for the first time in his life he failed to hold open a door for a member of the family, so Gyles both opened and closed it behind himself. Then he walked slowly down the long corridors towards the library.

He was in no state of shock. He had guessed, the instant that little copper-headed boy toddled out of the Inn door, what was in the wind and now experienced far more of a sensation of relief that the business had been brought out into the open than any other emotion. He was steeped in his family's history. His father had shared with him what the old peer summed up as 'the disgustin' affair of gettin' John and Primrose de Lorme's Justin out of England with his scurrilous and eminent friend and no damned repercussions'—by which he meant, as Gyles understood: before the tide of scandal washed over the Name and all associated with it. Therefore he now experienced only a deep despondency that no amount of education, dissemination of the blood through marriage, example or upbringing had succeeded in eradicating such flaws.

He reviewed the relations who were involved this time and those who would have to be brought to the conference table over this, the latest debacle: Sinclair, of course, Stephen's father, Stephen himself and, as was the custom on these damnably recurring occasions, the other older members of the family, in this event signified by his uncles Alaric and John, Eustace and Gyles' cousins, Christian, Damien and Robert, because they too were Lormes. Bilking at the last fence, Gyles walked even more slowly, giving himself time to decide whether—since he was now the working head of them all and his were the shoulders on whom family responsibilities now rested—he was right to involve his father, even now barely released from eighty years of such burdens and clearly anticipating a final run of what he would consider to be peace and quiet.

Gyles weighed the odds. Finally he came round to the fact that these were too great, even if he did elect to 'go it alone', due to the awful proximity of that little copper head. This taken in conjunction with Lord Aynthorp's habit of riding around the estate visiting all and sundry made it well nigh impossible to ensure that he did not see the boy even as Gyles had done himself.

He paused outside the library doors. His shoulders drooped again as if some unseen hands had gripped them. Then he dismissed such fancies, experienced a swift surge of anger at his own fear, closed his long, thin fingers resolutely over the massive, carven handle and went in, taking with him, as he crossed the great Bokhara rug his grandfather had brought back as a gift from his famous plant-hunting expedition in Turkey, the acceptance that now it would all begin again ... the bargains to be struck ... the arrangements to be made ... the manipulating to be done ... the money to be wasted ... for it was not just the matter of a local bastard, as he could see only too clearly. But he could not bring himself to admit, even within his own thoughts, the word which represented the crux of the matter.

The men gathered round the library table looked up as he entered. The dessicated lawyers registered polite pleasure at his appearance. Bishop Alaric greeted him with habitual unctuousness. John de Lorme murmured, 'Ah, Gyles,' registering—as is so frequently the case with dedicated 'horsey' men—his own peculiar brand of deceptive vacancy; but the old peer, darting a quick glance from beneath those shaggy brows, even as he said, 'Come along, Gyles, we are in need of you,' registered like the barometer that he was, 'Somethin's up damme. What's toward now, I wonder? I dare swear it's wet and windy ahead!'

Gyles laid his hands on the back of his father's chair, in readiness for drawing it away from under him. He cleared his throat, 'I am sorry to have delayed you all. If it had not been a matter of considerable import, I would not have been so discourteous.'

Lord Aynthorp held himself rigidly erect in his chair. He made no comment but just drummed his fingers on the tooled leather table top. 'Somethin' has come up and I fear I must beg leave to hold up proceedin's for a few moments longer. I think it would be advisable for my father to join me for a few moments—just a turn or two on the terrace—a matter has arisen which is I believe ... er ... relevant.'

Lord Aynthorp stood up. Gyles drew back the great chair. 'Then,' said the old man, looking suddenly very much older as he addressed his eldest brother, 'Alaric, pray pull the bell, order whatever refreshment everyone requires and let us take a fifteen minutes' recess.' He turned to his old lawyer. 'Mr Truslove, I apologise; but I could never describe Mr Gyles as an alarmist, so at this juncture, if you will forgive me, I feel compelled to accede to his request. We will be back with you just as soon as is possible.' Saying which, he strode through to the terrace with Gyles at his heels.

Behind them, Alaric rose, pulled the bell and gave the requisite orders to George, who looked so profoundly shaken that his face alone could have confirmed to Gyles that Sawby had already been about the business of making *his* ears burn. Then Alaric crossed the room to the opened windows through which father and son had passed and for a while stood there, his fingers passing and repassing over his big gold cross, a proclamation to all who knew him intimately that he was profoundly 'put out'. His family instinct was by now well aroused. As John put it typically some hours later, 'Dammit by now the scent was breast high'.

Father and son descended the terrace steps and entered the knot garden. When they were completely out of earshot Lord Ayn-thorp broke the silence. 'Which one?' he asked curtly.

'Stephen, sir.'

'Ahhh. So it comes again, Gyles?'

'Yes, sir, I have every reason to believe it does.'

'Any evidence?'

'All too much, sir. Not that what has occurred so far is in the higher echelons of past family scandal as our forbears experienced it.'

'Then before you explain I think we will sit. I am not as young as I was.

They chose an old stone seat which had once been occupied by that little, allegedly six-fingered witch with the slender neck called Nan Bullen, during the period when she was exercising her talent for victory through retreat from her Royal suitor[1] whom she thus deliberately enflamed more than ever and further stiffened in his resolve to possess her.

'May I first say, sir,' said Gyles, 'that at the onset I was all for handlin' this myself. Then I recalled that you had called me in when you were facin' the affair of John and Primrose's unfortunate Edward Justin...' he paused and contributed a curious addition, ' "Awful Eddie" they used to call *him* at Harrow, I learned the other day... met a chap who confided his study was more like an actress's dressin' room.'

[1] King Henry VIII.

'Faugh,' exclaimed his father distastefully, 'but this, you assure me, is not the same?'

'Oh no sir, merely a matter of bastardy. Taken alone it is not, as I said, among the more heinous of Lorme descents from grace. We must however add to it our coloured hair which proclaims this *bar sinister* expedition to all and sundry upon the estate.'

'Upon the estate!' Lord Aynthorp swung round to face him, 'Foulin' his own nest! Good gad, what shockin' bad breedin', a bastard here among us!'

'In the village, sir... er... can I ... er... begin at the beginnin'!'

The old man nodded and so Gyles went through the details from what Tim had claimed to have overheard and told the footmen, through Sawby's part in the affair and Plumstead's confidences, always being careful to stress what honourable ways these two had taken in the matter throughout.

'Highly commendable. We are well served and they shall be suitably rewarded; but have you seen the implicit danger in this affair?'

Gyles hedged. 'I have seen several, sir, but which one have you in mind at this moment?'

'Blackmail, sir, that's what, damned confounded blackmail! Here's a boy not yet sixteen lays a village female—what is her age now?'

Gyles hesitated. 'Difficult to be certain. If she has roughed it then twenty-five or -six; if not, then thirty, which is what she looks.'

'And the lad?'

'Somewhere between three or four.'

The old man rose slowly, straightened his back and to Gyles' astonishment the vestige of a twinkle crept into his eyes. 'Well at least we may acknowledge that the strain remains lusty even on the distaff side,' he observed with slightly salacious irony. 'Further, one is tempted to conjecture, was this woman the first to receive the benefit of Stephen's sexual appetites?'

Gyles nodded. 'One can speculate,' he agreed, 'but surely even for Lormes, it's startin' early enough?'

'Not a bit of it, m'boy,' Lord Aynthorp took his son's arm as he turned to retrace their steps. 'Why I can recall your Great-Uncle Philip who laid our housekeeper when he was thirteen and she passed thirty-five. Only housekeeper we ever had who was installed one month, sacked the second and gone the third! Another shockin' business, but he was even lustier than Stephen.' He quickened his pace.

'What are you going to do, sir?' Gyles then asked, startled at the swift return to vitality.

'Cope, m'boy, that is what I am goin' to do. Put the whole thing to the Trusloves. This is a matter for the lawyers, not just the Family alone! God knows it is not the first time they have been drawn in, as you well know.'

Unwisely, Gyles protested, 'But, sir, should we not reflect a little? This is no time to be precipitous.'

'Precipitous, is it?' Lord Aynthorp was working towards the fringes of one of those whirlpools he could create so easily. 'That boy seduces a trollop under one of MY roofs (Gyles prudently forbore to remind him that the roofs were all his now), lays her, pays her, discusses the details under a hedge like a country bumpkin and could be said to have taken the gel's virginity.'

'Oh no, sir!'

Aynthorp rounded on him. 'Don't you "oh no, sir" me. I'm enterin' into the line the pack of 'em take, not what *we surmise* to be the truth. . . . Now come on in and we'll tell Truslove. No other course open to us! That blisterin' fool Stephen has been proclaimin' parenthood and acknowledgin' guilt with every penny piece he's handed over to the trollop. God, what a mess! And not the only one that boy has caused! Either way he's headin' for disaster. Possibly I may not live to see it but disaster will be the outcome. I only wish I could get a line on the turn that it will take.'

Predictably, the 'Pelicans' asked for time too. The situation was increasingly complicated they opined, due to the absence of Sinclair and Stephen. Gyles, John, Alaric and Eustace were unanimous in support of Lord Aynthorp's angry barking, 'This is a family affair and as family we need you all.' He added, as the rest remained silent, 'Dissemination is unthinkable, so what have they or we to fear? As for Mr Truslove and Mr Timothy Truslove, *they* are our family advisors as were their fathers and grandfathers before them, so nothin' need be added on that head.' He resumed his finger drumming on the table-top. After a long pause he added, 'We owe it to Robert and Damien that they should be brought into this as has been our custom for centuries.

If the young are old enough to command, co-habit and administrate, they are old enough to take the strain with us, so, Gyles, pray summons Henry.'

'Heir apparent experiences first testing,' Gyles murmured ironically, adding, 'Well, no time like the present I suppose.' He continued, 'As Mr Truslove and Mr Timothy have asked us to give them time to discuss the matter together, would it not be wiser if we returned to other business and resumed this discussion, with Henry and the rest, after luncheon?' He glanced at the old Pelican who was seemingly asleep.

'That will suffice, Mr Gyles,' Mr Truslove barely opened his eyes to answer. He then addressed his son, 'Timothy, I wish you to communicate with our office. Address yourself if you please to Mr Pennyworth, of course. Obtain for me the answers to the following questions.' He passed across a small piece of paper with some minute hieroglyphics inscribed upon it. "Once we have the answers to these I believe we may resolve this matter with both speed and the necessary discretion.'

'What the devil!' even Lord Aynthorp was factionally shaken. 'But how on earth . . .?'

The old Pelican's parchment face creased into what, with his curious physiognomy, passed for a smile. 'We had information already my lord which I had not of course suspected would be relevant to this matter, but now it may well transpire to be so. Once my son has employed the electric speaking tube we shall know. . . .' Timothy Truslove rose, as John de Lorme offered to conduct him to the relevant machine. The rest sat rigid in their chairs digesting in their several ways what the old lawyer had said.

It was an uncomfortable luncheon. Sawby and the three footmen went through their duties with almost theatrical perfection, despite the red-rimmed eyes of George, the youngest. Conversation flowed with customary smoothness too as course followed course. The only material evidence of anything amiss was the consistent and lamentable paucity of appetites. André, in the kitchen, worked himself into a state of near hysteria as his confections came down again, one after the other, almost untouched, the plates containing traces of miniscule portions taken, pushed around and left.

Mrs Parsons, sipping tea in the steward's room, pronounced

with predictable non-clairvoyance, 'If you arsk me,'—whom no one had of course consulted—'I'd say as 'ow somethink is UP and That Somethink is Family matters, which no matter how 'ard we probe won't never be allowed to reach OUR ears! So, it's no use your getting yourself into a State, Mr André, at what 'as nothing to do with your cookery whatsoever, which for all your fine sauces probably tastes like sawdust in their mouths.' This exposition of diplomacy sent André straight over the edge of reason and screaming, 'Saw-dust, *mes sauces—nom d'un nom!*' He then poured out such a stream of abusive French as happily none of the other servants understood. Thus attentions were diverted. So very much was this the case that it needed all Sawby's remaining skill—the man was exhausted already—to stop the temperamental Frenchman from packing his bags and returning to France forthwith. When at length he had succeeded in pacifying him, Sawby went to his room and closed the door.

There was trouble in the schoolroom too. A number of the inhabitants had graduated to luncheon with the family. Frilly pinnies had been ironed, goffered and laid out ready for the girls to wear and clean trousers set ready for the boys, so Ninian and James, Stephanie, Rosalind and Lucy were reduced to a state of sulks by the information that their presence would not be required.

'It's a rotten shame,' claimed the two boys, who were, as ever, inseparable.

'Foul old rice pudding in the schoolroom instead of lovely things to eat in the dining room,' added Stephanie, while Rosalind just burst into tears and refused to be comforted even by Lucy, that prime mistress of the combined arts of soothing and pouring oil upon troubled waters. Ultimately, both the dining room's and the school room's completely unwanted and unwelcome luncheons went downstairs again and the men of the Family returned to the library.

Lady Aynthorp, preparing for her rest ritual, confided to Christine, who accompanied her to the door of her boudoir as usual, 'What a very good thing, dear, that Prue is safely out of the way today,' and with a naughty little chuckle surrendered herself to Palliser. This worthy took down her hair, brushed it, her lips tightly closed all the while, which was intended to indicate to her ladyship that she was very much out of sorts. Regrettably, her ladyship's own thoughts were far away and the deliberate display of displeasure went unnoticed which only served to make Palliser crosser still.

The men of the Family drifted one by one into their appointed places at the table. Lord Aynthorp was the first to his chair. He sat there in rigid silence until all the rest were present. Old Truslove had requested him privately that the ones who had not been present in the morning were made *courant* by him with the details as they were then known, after which the lawyers undertook to come in and present the results of their protracted telephone calls and whispered conversations.

So once more the tale was told. Then in stalked the 'Pelicans', looking, Henry opined, rather complacent. When they had settled themselves side by side and disposed their stalk-like legs beneath the table, the father cleared his throat.

'I will,' he began, 'be as brief as possible. I have obtained the information I required and I will say straight away that it concerns the Aynthorp Arms.' He addressed himself throughout to Lord Aynthorp, but as Gyles sat beside his father he managed to convey that he was deferring to both the old peer, who had relinquished the reins and the new head of the family into whose hands they had been thrust and thus—no mean feat with this family—managed to keep the peace with both.

'The Aynthorp Arms,' old Truslove intoned, as if they did not know of its existence, 'is an ale house on the Tollgate Road situate on the edge of Lower Aynthorp village. Anent it I have here four separate notices of complaint—endorsed in each case. These notices are couched,' he coughed deprecatingly, 'in what are tantamount to slanderous terms employed by somewhat illiterate persons, stating that on four separate occasions these persons have been unable to obtain their ale at the aforesaid inn, due to this being bolted and barred during licensing hours. I need scarcely stress that in the terms of reference by which any Inn landlords are employed, the one most heinous offence against the law governing the running of such establishments is that which states that at all times and in all circumstances, the hours of opening must be adhered to *or the tenant landlord exposes himself to instant dismissal.*

'It had been part of our ordinary agenda with your lordship and you Mr Gyles, to bring up this matter for review in the course of our current business today. When this other matter was

mooted I glimpsed a possible solution from the same source. It
seems that Albert Stiggins, the present licensee, has also proved
unsatisfactory on other counts over the period of his tenancy.'
Mr Truslove riffled through some papers, selected one and read
from it. 'On April 14th, 1904 the local constabulary, comprising
Police Constable Perkins and Police Constable Stott, were summonsed from their beds by one Mrs Dewberry of Rose Cottage—
which is adjacent to the Inn—on a complaint of noise and abuse
emerging from the Aynthorp Arms at 1.00 a.m. On assuming
their uniforms these two constables found a brawl in progress
in which someone called "Old Tim"—he seems to have no other
name, gentlemen—was a prime offender. The matter was dealt
with—as I understand is quite often the case in rural village life—
without recourse to legal action. What concerns us vitally at this
juncture is that there are altogether,' he riffled through a bundle
of assorted letters and papers tied up with bright pink tape, 'seven
such genuine and authenticated instances of disturbing the peace
etcetera, etcetera.

'Therefore it is our considered opinion,' he pecked forward at
his son who pecked back in silent confirmation, 'Yes, quite so';
Mr Truslove lifted a veined, attenuated hand pontifically, 'that
if so instructed, we can on your behalfs, my lord and gentlemen,
take the matter to counsel just to be sure before making any
move, and thereafter act. We are already reasonably assured that
we have more than adequate grounds for *terminating Stiggins'
tenancy forthwith, although the statutory notice, on either side,
is one calendar year.* We therefore advise,' a further exchange of
pecks and nods between father and son at this juncture, 'that you
take one of two courses. Either dismiss the man forthwith and let
him do what he may; or give him one month's notice of your
intention to replace him at the end of this time and also make it,
er, worth his while to go without trouble, either now or at any
time in the future. This we believe we may arrange for you
without undue difficulty.

'Thus, gentlemen, should you take the latter course, the
woman engaged as his barmaid, who is his niece Dora, will,
together with her child, be rendered homeless and without any
means of support. You on the other hand would be left without
a tenant to keep the village "Arms" open according to law. BUT
should you follow the perfectly legal course open to you in such
circumstances and instal a temporary manager—one who has

already had experience as a publican and possesses a blameless record—he can take over instantly and you can then either apply at the next Licensing Session for his name to be accepted as the permanent landlord under your aegis, or submit another name and dispose of the temporary employee. In a short while I expect to hear from my office that the latter kind of person has been found for you.' He paused at last to draw breath. 'As I have one or two notes to make on what I have already explained, I would like my son Timothy to continue while I draw myself level again.'

Timothy opened his beak-like mouth in readiness for his papa's last spoken word and took over without pause. 'Your lordship, gentlemen,' he began again, 'you may recall that some years ago you employed us to act on your behalf in the matter of one Joseph Stapley, your old head gamekeeper. If I may remind you, this man broke his leg in a poacher's trap, there were subsequent complications and unhappily the man had to have his leg amputated which rendered him useless for the only work he knew. You then behaved with the utmost generosity and put him as assistant to a publican so that he could learn the trade. Thereafter, he having the necessary capital through your generous provision, he would be able to take up an inn himself as tenant licensee. You will be pleased to know that his further record is equally blameless. He passed in due course from being a trainee to the post of temporary manager and from thence to becoming licensee of an inn which, alas for him, or so he thinks at this moment, is being demolished to make way for a railway. My father and I were reluctant to speak to him of this matter until we obtained your consent to our suggestions, but we have absolutely no doubt that both he and his wife would be elated at the prospect of being in the employment of the Family once again and would serve you in the new capacity of licensee and wife at the Aynthorp Arms as faithfully as they did heretofore as gamekeeper and laundrymaid.

'I must emphasise that no man can be a temporary manager unless he has a clean record plus experience of the trade. Then, whomsoever he is, and however suited to becoming a permanent tenant landlord, he cannot so be until his name has been put before the Licensing Sessions and by those present given proper sanction. But he could be the temporary manager immediately and later could assume a permanent position if all went as we believe it will. Then, with Stiggins gone, Stapley installed, *we*—

but, we beg of you, not any member of the family—can arrange matters for the girl and her child so that they are suitably provided for, on condition that they are prepared to be removed to a place so far distant that never again can they cause any of you the slightest trouble.

'As for the wholly distasteful word which none of us cares to mention, Mr Stephen's behaviour has, if you will permit the observation, been—in our joint opinion—in excess of stupid. However, in the shock of the news you perhaps overlooked the fact that he was a minor when he seduced this very adult female, a minor when he gave her monies and therefore not responsible in law. All that can be dealt with by us, but it is our bounden duty to warn you that it will cost a great deal of money.'

Mr Truslove looked up from his notes. 'And I, Timothy, would add a rider to that statement. Such matters always cost money. The ... er ... last one was excessively, yes excessively, costly and a most unjust drain upon the estate. This will be a lesser matter but should not Mr Stephen's parents be made responsible?'

During all this recounting Gyles and his father had both eased themselves from their chairs and gone over to the windows where they both stood, hands clasped behind their backs, listening. Now both swung round, Gyles' eyes flashing, Lord Aynthorp's face dangerously red and his eyes blazing. 'Let me make somethin' quite clear to you, Truslove,' he said furiously, 'since you seem to have forgotten what we said last time. It matters less than anythin' concernin' this family,' his voice rose perilously, '*what it costs to protect the name*! It will always be protected and to hell and damnation with the costs of whatever is involved. The Lormes have protected their good name, despite the unfortunate flaw which runs through their litters with devilish consistence for goin' on nine hundred years and they will continue to do so until all men wed sterile women and the line ceases to exist. Now, Truslove, tell us again the value of our estates and properties.'

Truslove did not swerve his hooded gaze from the incensed old man. 'Three millions, five hundred thousand and forty-three pounds precisely, your Lordship,' he reported, 'excluding the pictures which are pending valuation. That is entailed property and does not include the private means of the individual Lormes.'

'Then,' snapped Lord Aynthorp, 'I will remind you that Mr Sinclair Delahaye has little private means. He and my niece occupy a suite of rooms in this castle, and as you are likewise perfectly aware, will continue to do so for so long as it stands. Moreover, such additional funds as they may require will always be drawn from the Family purse.' The colour began to mount upon the old peer's cheeks. His eyes became intensely bright. He continued on a rising note, 'As you may not perhaps fully comprehend, even after all the years in which we have reposed our confidence in you, we are essentially a French family in our outlook. Castle Rising is basically a French Château, in that, when a property of this size is owned by the head of the family, it is regarded as natural and proper that the immediate descendants and closest relations take up their habitation within its protection. If you ponder for a moment or two you will realise that this establishment is staffed, maintained and ordered in such a fashion that the autonomous occupation by my brothers and sisters is expected. Thus, while Bishop Alaric maintains his own establishment under the direction of his ecclesiastical superiors as is right and proper, nevertheless he and his wife's suite of rooms is kept in constant readiness where they may enjoy privacy and comfort and at the same time take part in the communal family life as and when they so desire to do. When my sister, the Countess Marguerite, suffered *her* tragedy—for so I see it—*she* came home. Mr Gyles, who is head of this family by agreed transfer, save only for the peerage which he cannot inherit until my death, Mr Gyles knew, as we all know, that this was as much part of his administrative responsibility as anything else. It is also that of his wife, my dear daughter-in-law, Mrs Christine. My son would not have it otherwise. Good Gad, Lady Aynthorp and I would rattle about like two dessicated peas in an enormous pod if we inhabited this vast place in solitude . . . it would become a mausoleum not a home! If you look deeper you will see that the nursery and schoolroom are run on the same pattern. Family children drawn into a family relationship, become a Family responsibility.' He paused, and met his grandson's steady gaze. 'I am happy,' he then snapped, 'that you, Henry, find your grandmother and me humorous when described as dessicated peas.' He turned to his eldest son, 'Gyles, I have usurped your new position for long enough. You will pay the piper; Mr Truslove and Mr Timothy Truslove will merely call the tune and,' he rose abruptly, 'you, Gyles, will now carry on. I shall withdraw. I am incensed.' On which superb understatement he left the room.

Gyles opened his mouth to speak, but before he could Mr Truslove held up one of those bony claws. 'Please, Mr Gyles, I have served your father for many, many years. I know him and I should have known better than to invite that storm upon my head. Habit dies hard,' he shook his head regretfully, 'and it just goes against the grain for me to see money wasted on wastrels.'

Gyles smiled, the rest relaxed and Alaric spoke, 'What you have said, Mr Truslove, is masterly, what you have left unsaid leaves me very anxious and I am sure the rest of us are feeling the same.'

Mr Truslove nodded. 'You mean the disposition of the young woman and the little boy, your Grace?'

'Precisely.'

'Immediately after Stiggins has been dismissed, a little man in a large new motor car will call for some ale and will engage the niece in conversation. He will flatter her. He will enquire as to what such a good-looking woman is doing wasting her looks and talents at a village inn. She will have been rendered vulnerable by the knowledge that she is suddenly about to be homeless. He will then disclose that he is a theatrical impresario. He will offer to provide the money and arrange for the woman to go to London and be "seen" with a view to her joining a tour to Australia which he is promoting under the control of a highly ... er ... "genteel" is the word he will employ—"lady" of the stage who chaperones all his young actresses.

'The tour will last for two years at least. If the girl shows little talent then she will remain in subsidiary roles; but she will be paid handsomely by the impresario, *though* the additional sums over normal salaries will be drawn from your monies. Eventually she will disclose the existence of the boy, or the impresario will contrive to see him and he will put to her that this is *an advantage to her chances,* since this particular company is to put on several plays in which small boys are necessary. He will confess to her that these are difficult to find, thus putting the wherewithal into her hands for bargaining with him for more money than he could possibly offer otherwise without arousing suspicions. Eventually she will be gone and none of you will ever hear of her again.

'I know this man. As the profession goes he is respectable. You know what I mean, sir, there is no fear of her being used as bordello material or the boy for any immoral purposes, either. Furthermore he, the theatrical impresario, will have a link with her and with me and I will see that a regular check is made on what is happening to both mother and child.'

'Are you absolutely sure of all this?' Alaric asked with great eanestness, turning what Henry basely suspected was a Nelsonian eye to the matter. 'One could not have it upon one's conscience as a Christian . . .' Alaric rumbled.

'Absolutely certain, your Grace, otherwise Truslove, Penny-worth and Copthorne could not bring themselves to be a party to the matter.'

'Quite so, quite so,' Alaric accepted eagerly.

'Then,' said Henry, intervening, 'there seems to be only one more hurdle to cross.'

His elders eyed him severely, except for his father, who managed a slight twinkle. 'Tim, eh Henry?'

'Yes, father—that old gossip, windbag, poacher, ne'er-do-well and thief. If Mr Truslove and Mr Timothy have not reached a solution on the problems he creates, I do have a suggestion to make.'

'Do you now, Mr Henry?' said Mr Truslove interestedly. 'Well, will you please give it to us?'

Henry picked up a pencil and began doodling with it. 'I was talkin' with the Colonel of the Duke of Cambridge's Own[2] the other day. He's a nice old boy and forthcomin' when not in his own ante-room! We got on to the subject of delinquents and he told me about a ranker who was such a perennial dam' nuisance that in desperation he, the Colonel, recommended as a sort of last resort that the wretch was promoted and given responsibility —from which you can judge the old man was a very fine soldier— in fact, he told me the chap never looked back after that. What really interested me though, was that he said he knew a Padre chap who worked in the East End of London with boys who were thieves and thugs. Padre claimed his best success was with a downright tough, crooked boy of sixteen. He put him in charge of funds at the welfare hall he had set up for a group of 'em. That boy dam' near killed one of his mates when the chap stole a penny. Fella was ill for weeks, and the delinquent turned out the best treasurer the Padre had ever had.'

Gyles, whose nerves were by this time frayed to the point where he could cheerfully have committed murder at his son and heir's preamble, broke the pencil he was turning end over end in

[2] Originally the 17th Lancers. Later merged into the 17th/21st Lancers.

one hand as if it were a drum major's baton. The snapping sound was loud as a pistol shot in the quiet room where the shadows were already beginning to lengthen beyond the wide windows.

Below stairs, Sawby was fretting like a broody hen ejected from her nest of warm eggs. He was pacing up and down, half-hunter in hand, muttering, 'Half an hour past the time for tea! ... orders from her leddyship not to disturb the gentlemen on any account. So what do I do?' and by his looks indicating that anyone who attempted to tell him was bound for the gallows on the instant.

Upstairs in the library, Henry paused at last, said, 'Sorry, sir,' came back from his immersion in what he had been saying and added, 'I *am* comin' to a point.'

'Not, I trust,' Gyles found an outlet for his tension in irony, 'in proposin' reform for old Tim, dear boy?'

Henry grinned. 'Yes, sir, but not perhaps in the way you think.'

The elder Pelican leaned across the table with an enormous peck, managing to indicate that while aware of the boy's age and presumption he was still addressing the heir apparent. He said, 'Then perhaps, Mr Henry, havin' given us the ... er ... valuable background to what I assume is to be a proposal, you would be so good as to cast a leetle light on this envisaged pattern, for we are all sadly at a loss to follow your thinkin' at this juncture.'

Henry apologised. 'Deuced confusin', sir, I agree. I beg your pardon.' He looked steadily at Mr Truslove. 'What I have in mind is in fact Clangowrie.' He continued to speak directly to the old lawyer whose eyelids flickered at the name. His nose, if such a thing were possible, seemed to become even sharper.

'Ahhh, I begin to get your meaning. Pray continue.'

Henry, whose hands were damp and continuously twisting together under the table, now drew a pocket handkerchief from his sleeve, wiped them, replaced the handkerchief and shot a grateful glance at the perceptive old man.

'Right, sir, here we go.' He gripped his hands together and gave his outline. As the sense of it became apparent, his father, broken pieces of pencil discarded, watched him with such changed expression in his eyes as would have caused him endless embarrassment had anyone else observed it.

'Clangowrie,' Henry resumed, 'is a huge parcel of fine timber, a small shootin' lodge in no great state of repair and a stretch of heather across which we enjoy some of the finest, if not the

most luxurious, grouse shootin' in the Highlands. It is, I believe
some five hundred miles away from here. There is nothin' about
it but crofters' dwellings and tumblin' streams all bristlin' with
trout and there's that superb bit of salmon water which you all
know better than I. There is besides some good sport, deer
stalkin' in the high land—a poacher's paradise in fact. Why do
we not transfer Tim there? There is a shack, I recall, where I
have more than once taken shelter from the storm. It is far and
away better than that noisome badger's lair which Tim inhabits in
our woods here.

'*If* we offer him the alternative of either facin' a whole string
of charges concernin' the Inn, those brawls and his incessant
poachin'—to which half a hundred hereabouts can and will bear
witness—and as a result a severe stretch in prison, *or all charges
dropped, on condition he agree to go and is seen to do so with an
escort*, then I think I know which he would choose. He could
never get back. He would be livin' the life he likes and if we
put him under the protection of one of our old ghillies and
actually gave him a small but regular weekly wage, it is on the
cards he might discover in time that it was pointless to poach
when, as an employee of ours, he could come by more than his
needs without riskin' imprisonment and would most certainly be
facin' a brick wall if he tried to sell what up there is tantamount
to sellin' coals to Newcastle. As I see it, we should chuck in some
warm clothin' and a pair of stout boots and I respectfully submit
we get Uncle Alaric to do the whole thing for us on the savin' of
a Christian soul level.'

At this last, Gyles choked. Some strangled sounds, hurriedly
suppressed, ran round the table. Henry went on, seemingly un-
moved. 'We could then get rid of him for good, *with* a clean
conscience and to a land where he would be so little understood
and where the Scots tongue would be so incomprehensible to him
that he could never put over a story such as this with any hope of
anyone understandin' or believin' him. Furthermore, when Uncle
Alaric has done his part, I would undertake to escort the old
villain. There should be time enough before the Michaelmas term.
Then I could see to it that the shack was made habitable and,
much more important, I could allay any doubts Tim might have
by sharin' a day's sport with him and that, I submit, gentlemen,
would then be that.'

He hesitated, but only fractionally, then stood up. 'And now I will go. I believe you may discuss what I have said with greater ease if I am not here. I fully realise my juvenile impertinence, but this is a family matter and in family matters anythin' is better than the exposure of conduct which casts a shadow upon our name.' And so saying he turned, made a funny little bow and marched towards the door.

The ensuing silence was profound. It was eventually broken by the old Pelican who blew his nose, cleared his throat, fiddled with his papers and then said rather more loudly than was his wont, ' I can see ... er ... no possible cause for failin' to accept Mr Henry's ... er ... ingenious proposal. I would venture to remark that Mr Henry has found a most admirable and ironically humane answer to this particular problem.'

Still no one spoke. So after a further pause the Pelican enquired mildly, 'Would it be proper to suggest we took a family consensus of opinion?'

Emotions were running high. Any display of them would have been abhorrent and unthinkable. Gyles' eyes were sparkling but in the end it was Alaric, for once in his life without a vestige of pomposity, who said quite quietly. 'You can count upon me to play the part my nephew has outlined for me.'

Typically, John then asked, looking more vacant than ever, 'When does the Michaelmas term begin?' and within a few moments the details of the matter were being examined.

It was only when all had been put, as Mr Truslove described it, 'in some sequence of order', that Eustace enquired, 'Just one more small point which I feel it incumbent upon me to draw to your notice. How and when do we tell Sinclair and should he be summonsed from his shootin' party?'

CHAPTER 11

Nanny

There were three women among the household staff who possessed pronounced matriarchal qualities, Mrs Peace, Mrs Parsons and Nanny. Of these, Mrs Peace concealed her iron hands, which were no whit weaker than the rest, under her flowing black skirts. From there, whenever she was about to apply her particular brand of pressure the fingers of her right hand would start playing with the bunch of keys which depended from the châtelaine at her waistband.

Mrs Parsons was almost entirely incapable of restraint. She knew she had a 'nasty temper'. She depended upon it. She made no concessions whatsoever to the appeasement of anyone. On appointment she had forced her way roughshod to the van and there had remained, despite Mr Sawby, despite Chef André's gallic eruptions, despite even the waspish oppositions of Miss Palliser.

Nanny belonged to neither of these bully categories. She was on her own as an autocrat, from the false piece which she pinned under her bonnet to the last button on her black boots. She took herself at her own valuation. This was not only immensely high but was based upon the undeniable premise that she had already brought up one generation of Lormes, had been entrusted thereafter, with the second generation which, indeed, occupied her currently and was in no doubt whatever that in due course she would be entrusted with a third. She regarded parents as a necessity since they were the providers of her life's requirements —babies. Having so acquitted themselves, 'her' parents were expected to abide by 'her' rules with the same unquestioning compliance as her babies. Nanny would take care of everything. Nanny would discipline these babies from the first moment they were placed in her care—at one month—into obedient and well-behaved toddlers. She would further ensure that these evolved in due course into obedient children. She would dominate their lives, their bowels and their diets. Even when they achieved schoolroom status she would, could and did over-rule any governesses if she considered this to be necessary. She merely declined responsibility for any damaging influences experienced by the male Lormes at preparatory and public schools which she insisted were solely responsible for the back-slidings evinced by certain of the male line.

'If only they had been left to me!' was her perennial cry always followed by the supplementary, 'Proper whippings and my home influence was what was needed; but then no one ever listens to me'—a self-delusory aside which should have evoked the feet of Ananias.

The truth was that Nanny enjoyed privileges which, in any other member of the domestic staff would have been categorised as unpardonable impertinence. However, privilege was considered by Nanny to be her natural prerogative, even among what she dismissed, when even fractionally crossed for an instant, as 'this Frenchified lot'. In point of fact the Lormes were, in this respect, totally anglicised. They were indoctrinated and had been for centuries and they upheld Nanny Rule with murmured 'Do as Nanny says, dear', and 'Nanny knows best', as was only right and proper if children were to be brought up 'correctly'.

Thus, when Christine was still in bed, recovering from the rather difficult delivery of her youngest son Richard, she said something in Nanny's presence which caused her to erupt. 'That you will *not* do, Madam,' she snapped wrathfully. 'Over my dead body will you go to that Gala at Covent Garden in two weeks' time! The very thought of any mother of any of my babies showing herself in public before she has been churched! I am surprised at you, Madam! It is very naughty of you even to suggest such a thing. You are old enough to know better! So let me hear no more about it.' Then, merely pausing to draw breath, while Christine regarded her with twinkling eyes, 'And now it's past time for your afternoon nap so I will leave you.' So saying she marched from the room in a huff muttering as she went away with creaking stays, 'Gala . . . Grand Opera indeed! I don't know what the world is coming to!'

Christine chuckled, snuggled down among her goffered pillow slips and slid into a delicious drowse; but she did not attend the Gala and, according to the tenets of her period and position, left the Castle for the first time in order to be churched.

Nanny was so completely certain of herself and her powers that she even confided in her nursemaid Rose. Rose was her toss-pot over whom she emptied her opinions, confident even when these were positively slanderous that the girl would repeat nothing.

She regarded this 'vessel'—('Now remember, my girl, your mouth is sealed or you will find yourself out in the world without place or reference and will starve to death or come to a worser fate.')—as her safety valve, so when pressures inside herself were building up dangerously she used Rose to reduce the pressure and also enabled herself to clarify her future actions in respect of all who came under her jurisdiction.

Nanny was also a great one for the trite comment. Each was uttered with the greatest solemnity and used with unfailing success on all occasions. The older children, when they graduated from nursery to schoolroom, were apt to chant derisively—when safely out of earshot—the more common of Nanny's sayings: 'Laugh before breakfast, cry before supper', . . . 'I'll thank you not to take that tone with me, miss!' . . . 'Little children should be seen and not heard!' . . . 'Bread and butter before cake, *if you please*', . . . 'Everyone must eat a peck of dirt before they die', . . . and the one they all adored, 'Always pick blackberries above dog-leg-lifting-height'.

Nanny's confidences, like everything else in her life, were reserved for special occasions: 'There's a time and a place for everything'. The *mise-en-scène* was always the day nursery. The time would come after the nursery staff had been served with their supper and when she and Rose were left to themselves in front of the nursery fire. Then Nanny would lower herself into her rocking chair and extend her feet to Rose. Rose would unbutton her boots for her and put on the slippers with the heart-seases embroidered on the toes, during which operations Nanny would murmur with unfailing regularity, 'Remember there are three kinds of sins, big sins, little sins and taking off your shoes without unbuttoning or unlacing them'. She would then lift her feet on to the rim of the black iron fender inside which rose the high fireguard topped by assorted small garments in process of airing. She would settle herself comfortably within 'turning-reach' of these items and then would empty her repressions over Rose, duly settled close beside her in an old nursing chair and sewing industriously.

Generally the tenor was harmless enough and took the form of astringent comments upon the day's events, but the comings and goings of the past forty-eight hours had undoubtedly spread their outer ripples to her aura. She was uneasy; she was also completely uninformed. Even so her beady little eyes had not failed to observe George's red-rimmed ones, nor Sawby's drawn face, nor the lawyers' protracted stay. She had also happened to be peering through the bars of the nursery window at twilight the day before and had seen Plum crossing the park *in the wrong direction* for 7.30. in the evening! She put two and two together when, after darkness had become complete, she looked out again and saw a hunched figure in an ulster taking the same path, carrying a swinging lantern. 'And what is Sawby doing crossing the Park at this unlikely hour?' she ejaculated, turning away from the window and reassuming her in-bedded position among the patchwork cushions of her rocking chair.

Her instincts were well alerted by this time. These developed into some painful reflections, crystallised eventually into speech as, turning a pair of drawers with bands of frilling on the legs, she launched herself into an analysis of the brood under her command.

'I shouldn't wonder,' she began abruptly, 'if Master Richard was to go the same road as that young varmint Stephen, what a regular good hiding would most likely have put to rights if he had had it often enough when he was younger. Now he's set upon his road and only heaven knows where it will all end.' This alone clearly indicated her remarkable combination of perspicacity and guesswork in respect of the current goings-on. She added, after a short pause, 'He's had the devil a-whispering in his ear all this day and only a good slap on his bottom has cured his ills for the time being.' Rose looked up aghast. 'What, Mr Stephen?' she mumbled, alarmed and with her mouth full of pins.

'No, you silly girl, Master Richard. As far as Mr Stephen is concerned it'll be the least said the soonest mended from now on, but if I have *my* way there'll be no repetition. Master Richard may be only two, but he's a young limb of Satan already. Handsome he may be, but handsome is as handsome does and charm he may have too; charm the birds off the trees that one, I do admit he would already, given more than half a chance! *But I know, my girl, and never forget my words.*' She twitched her shawl a little closer around her shoulders, 'Nippy it is for the time of year I must say. Put a bit more coal on the fire, there's a good girl.' Rose obeyed; Nanny glanced at the nursery clock, 'Very nearly time our cocoa came up,' she observed, 'and a nice finger of Mrs Parsons' plum cake wouldn't come amiss with it neither. ... Now where was I, Rose?'

'You was telling me, Nanny, to mark your words.'

'Just so,' Nanny wagged her head portentously, 'and mind you do, my girl. Then there's that Mrs Gyles' Andrew. Only ten, but born to be a sojer. Takes to discipline like a duck to a pond. Tidiest play box in all the nursery cupboardful was his, even when he was only tiny. A good, dear, little boy he is, what never gave his Nanny a moment's trouble not even when he was teething. He's like that little sister of his.'

Rose looked up. 'Miss Anne?'

'A course, but never you run away with the idea that that little miss won't get into a pickle or two before she goes to her grave, because she will.' Nanny lifted a work-worn finger in emphasis and stabbed the air with it. 'She's a born flirt she is and likely to be a beauty like Lady Arabella what I helped Nanny with when I was a nursemaid like you.'

Rose was so overcome by this disclosure that she dropped her work and was taken with a fit of the giggles through which such words as 'never ... nursemaid ... you ... well I never!' emerged indistinctly. Nanny automatically reproved her; but her mind was not wholly upon this task. She resumed, 'That was the Lady Arabella—never you mind the rest of her name—what grew up and earned herself the awful nickname of the Bolter below stairs and above too, but there,' she pulled herself up hastily, 'such is not for the ears of a young girl like you! I'm just placing it on record that our Miss Anne will be bound to set off a squib or two later on. She'll set a few too many hearts on fire, like Master Ninian, or I'm a Dutchman.' This evoked another stifled giggle from Rose.

'Now 'im, Ninian, and young James are a most extra-ordinary pair. Thick as thieves, never apart if they had their way. Anyone'd think they was twins instead of first cousins. Nothing of the lone wolf in them, unlike the young Delahayes. For instance, that Stephanie, she worries me. Makes my corns ache sometimes. A girl of fourteen with a pray dooer[1] in her bedroom and forever kneeling at it, praying. I think she might come down with religion later on. So serious, she could become a nun. Now you know,

[1] *Prie-dieu.*

Rose, in four years' time, eighteen she'll be and bound for her coming out. I tell you frank and fair, I don't predict no success for her at it and that's the plain unvarnished truth. I reckon she's too shy and too religious. Proper modesty is nice and fitting in a well-brought up young girl but she carries it all too far already. She goes into her shell for all the world like she was a little snail should any man who isn't family so much as speaks to her, if it's only to ask her how she does or will she have another piece of bread and butter.

'Not like her sister Rosalind. Only eleven but all squirmy and will-o-the-wispy if there's so much as a man in sight. There's something about *her* what draws men's eyes already. Only eleven, of course, but *Nanny sees*. Very strange she is too in another sort of way; but then them Delahayes have got some odd blood in them from Mr Sinclair, what with Mr Stephen, who will bring his father's grey hairs down in sorrow to the grave. I don't say there's anything actually wrong with Rosalind except a slight tendency to anaemia, but always with brimming eyes, those 'uge blue eyes everlastingly dripping tears if anyone so much as says "Boo" to her.

'It'd be no more than the truth if I wos to tell you, which I am not, of course, that even their little Gilbert shows signs of developing into a proper little Mr Money Bags. A hoarder at three! Just imagine! As well you know, if he gets so much as a sixpenny tip we have to wait until he's asleep before we can prise it out of his chubby little fist without him getting purple in the face and stamping his little foot and screaming, "It's mine, no, Nanny, it's mine." ' Nanny's voice had dropped to a monotonous murmur. 'Remember Mrs Gabrielle carn't have no more, not after what happened the last time.'

'All the others is all right though isn't they, Nanny?' Rose asked very softly, head still bent over her sewing, as if she was fearful of stopping this enraptured spate of predicting and premonition which Nanny was emptying over her.

'Some is and some isn't,' Nanny replied, still in the monotone, 'and the members of this copper-pated family isn't all done with spawning yet, not by a long chalk. Mrs Gabrielle may have done with it and her eldest will be steady enough I shouldn't wonder, but he'll breed like a white mouse once he gets down to it. *He's* got the hair, we must remember! Then there's nice Mr James, a steady lad and all round a good boy. You know, try as I will I can't see much for him either way.

'It's when we come to the two next youngest St Johns that I can feel some unusually inclement weather ahead. Sort of not natural somehow. There again, I can't put my finger on what it will be when it comes, but come it will. There's that little snub-nosed darling Lucy, what spreads little rays of sunshine wherever she goes and then there's that Lucien. He's a lovely little boy and I'd be the last to deny it. Gentle and docile, more like a girl than a boy! Lucy is like a shadow to him. Find one and you'll sure enough see the other lurking, never wanting to be in the way but *near*. There was something funny and por-tentous about the first naming of them too. Lucy and Lucien! More than just foreign fancy!

'But it's not their being always so near to one another, and speaking one *for* the other. After all that's the case with Ninian and James, but them two boys is what you'd best describe as a couple of horsey youngsters who naturally stick together having identical tastes as it were. Never out of the saddle if they have their way. Taking their fences together. When they're not riding then they're swimming together or climbing trees, or playing badminton or tennis or boating—always doing things for two. They don't neither of them like rugger nor cricket neither because it can't be done together and I hear now they are even sharing a study at Harrow; but it's all outdoors and fresh and natural. Do you know Rose, a most peculiar thing happened the day after we came home from our holidays. You remember you set our Miss Lucy's new party dress for her to wear downstairs to make her goodnight curtsey?'

'Yes, of course, Nanny.'

'Well, you'd never credit it if I wasn't to tell you, but I went into Lucy's room to see all was prepared and proper, like I always do.' Rose shot her a knowing glance under her eyelids but abstained from any comment. 'Who should I find in there but little Lucien and you'll never guess in a million years what he was doing so I'll tell you. *He was kissing that dress,* stroking it and standing all alone saying, "Pitty, pitty, Lucien kiss-kiss"— a big boy like him too! Well, I mean, it isn't natural! He's a most peculiar little boy, never gets hisself dirty, never climbs trees, never even when he was crawling did I have to fish him out of the coal bucket. Always spotless, always complaining if his hands get so much as sticky with a bun. He and Lucy—for I can't see them two separate, not no-how—bewilder me and I don't feel comfortable about either of them, in relation to each other that is; time alone will show.'

Time, at this moment, showed Richard standing in the doorway with the cocoa tray and Nanny's desired fat fingers of Mrs Parsons' rich black plum cake.

While Nanny indulged herself with these analyses and thereby expurgated some of her instinctive unease by her own peculiar form of verbal crystal-gazing, it fell upon Gyles to write to Sinclair. He enclosed a personal letter to his sister but, after a preliminary paragraph, in which he expressed the sincere hope that Sinclair would not think the men of the family had been presumptuous in handling the Stephen affair as best they might in his absence, Gyles confined himself to a brief statement of the facts and an extremely careful report on what had been set in motion. These letters he despatched by the noon post on the morning following the library conference, having spent half the night writing and rewriting his rough drafts.

Sinclair's response came swiftly, in the form of a telegram which the village postmaster brought on his bicycle. The message read, 'Profoundly grateful for swift and generous actions. for obvious reasons will complete stay here. letter follows. (signed) Appreciatively, Sinclair and Henrietta,' which caused the little postmaster to scratch his head as to the possible meaning, which was, of course, what had been intended.

In the interim, various sealed envelopes were brought down by messenger from the Pelicans' place of business and this messenger waited each time for the sealed replies which he carried away with what Christine described mirthfully, 'all the reverence of an Archbishop handling the Regalia at a Coronation'.

By the time the three Delahayes returned to the Castle the first of the boys had been despatched to school with bulging tuckboxes crammed with pound cakes, potted meats, fruits, jams and pickles put up for them by Mrs Parsons who steadfastly refused any assistance from M. André.

Henry, who had been in London equipping himself for his first term in Oxford, made what he described to Marguerite in the privacy of her boudoir as 'a most embarrassin' bloomer'. He described how, with the assistance of the guard who had flung his baggage into the nearest first-class non-smoking carriage, he, Henry had hurled himself in after it as the train gathered speed. He then found to his horror that he had picked the carriage which had been reserved for the three Delahayes. 'I suppose the guard thought this was the right thing to do, he must have recognised them,' he exonerated the man glumly. 'It was,' he recounted, 'a deuced uncomfortable journey. Stephen obviously knew he had been found out though the Lord alone knows what had transpired. Henrietta looked thoroughly ill. Even through her rather thicker-than-usual veil I could see her eyes were quite swollen with weepin'. Sinclair was, I think, thankful to see me. He talked away valiantly throughout the journey which seemed as if it would never end. Stephen looked glum, and after saying "hello", he flipped over the pages of a book, keepin' his head well down behind it, but I don't think he read a single word. Two or three times I caught him lookin' round the side at me, but he looked away at once when he realised I was lookin' back. When we got out, Stephen climbed on the box with Plum who sent his tiger back on the station wagon with the baggage.'

'And where are they all now?' enquired Countess Marguerite. 'I cravenly took to my couch after luncheon with a headache and have remained here, equally cravenly I must admit, ever since.'

Henry managed a slight smile. 'For someone with a headache I must own you look in remarkably fine fettle. Anyway,' he added loyally, 'I don't think you were craven just tactful. In case you don't know, Mother found urgent affairs with the vicar and I haven't even seen her yet. Aunt Prue sat straight-backed behind the teapot and of course Gran was present. She kissed Aunt Henrietta very lovingly when she came in and patted her hand, then she said very calmly, 'I expect you are fatigued after your journey, my dear. Come and sit quietly beside me and drink a nice refreshin' cup of tea.' After that she went on chattin' away about Castle news in an absolutely magnificent manner.'

'Where are they now?' the little Countess enquired, looking even more guilty.

'Oh, back in the library with the octogeranium and papa.' Henry paused and stared at his hands. 'I went in to tea first while the others went to their rooms and Grandmother made some remark which sparked Grandfather off. He exploded in wrath—you know how he does quite suddenly. He said, "It's the sheer idiocy of this affair which maddens me. When a feller has means and opportunity there is no excuse for messin' about with estate amateurs. If he wanted assistance over ... er ... women— damme (yer not children now so stop looking shocked, Prue), we would have provided him with a suitable *demi mondaine* as my father did in *my* young days." Then there was a sound outside and Aunt Henrietta came in. The rest you know.'

Countess Marguerite chuckled. 'Did your Grandmother say anything to this outburst?'

Henry grinned. 'She twinkled at him, said "Such revelations!" and Aunt Prudence made little clucking sounds of disapproval.' Henry paused and then spoke depressedly. 'Where will it all end, Aunt?' he queried.

'It will not, my dear,' said Marguerite sadly. 'These things do not. I have been examinin' some of the ... er ... cypher notes your dear Grandfather gave to me. He always said I had a good head on my shoulders despite the fact that he considered it to be a very pretty one; but of course that was many years ago when I was very young. Now what was I saying?'

'That it never did end.'

'No it cannot. Records of over nine hundred years are unlikely to cease being repetitive. Stephen will do something else, probably more dreadful. At least we have been alerted.' She sighed. 'We shall have to keep our eyes open from now onwards. I wonder,' she widened her eyes at Henry, 'do you imagine Sinclair will send him to Australia?'

Henry rose to his feet and looked down on the elegantly coiffed white head. 'Judgin' from his aspect during the journey I would say he doesn't know himself but I am pretty convinced that he was in a towerin' rage. He just had himself well in hand.' He picked up one small be-ringed hand, kissed it, excused himself and went away to dress for dinner. Countess Marguerite remained on the chaise-longue staring unseeingly through the leaded window panes until Palliser scratched upon the lock and enquired in French, 'What dress may I lay out for dinner, if you please, Milady?'

By the time the men had dispersed to their various rooms to prepare themselves for dinner, Sinclair's already seething rage had reached white heat. His hands were even a trifle unsteady as he tied his own bow tie, having dismissed, rather curtly, George's offers of assistance. Henrietta begged to be excused and took to her bed where Pearson came on tip-toe to undress her, draw the blinds, close the curtains and finally leave her with a handkerchief soaked in eau de Cologne. 'I'll bring you a nice cup of chef's chicken consommé and a few fingers of dry toast later, Madam,' she promised. 'Just you rest and let your head and stomach settle. There's some as can train travel and some as can't support it. My aunt was always the same, but she being of the lower orders, her's was not such a delicate constitution.'

Henrietta thanked the girl in a slightly choked voice. Then Pearson tip-toed away without an inkling of what had laid her charge so low.

Sinclair, on the other hand, told one or two distinctly risqué *on-dits* at dinner, culled from the recent house-party, recounted one or two entertaining scraps of gossip, drank deeply and ate nothing. By the time the women had left the dining room Lord Aynthorp shot an uneasy glance at his son-in-law from under those craggy brows. Stephen sat twisting the stem of his port glass, still with eyes lowered, saying nothing and having also only picked at his food. When the old peer rose at last, he cut short their customary length of stay in the dining room. Sinclair, white-faced and grim, looked up and said, 'I wonder, sir, and Gyles, if I might have your further attention for a few moments in the Library?'

'Of course, of course,' agreed Lord Aynthorp, 'as long as you like, dear boy.'

'And Gyles?'

'Of course.'

'Thank you both. Then perhaps you will permit me to ask Stephen to withdraw now and await us there?' Both men nodded.

Stephen rose, thrust his hands in his pockets and slouched out without a word. Everyone else then rose and when the doors had closed none too softly behind the miscreant, Sinclair moved quickly to open them again for his father-in-law. He then excused himself too. The rest went to the billiards room.

Feeling unable to cope with female society, Gyles and his father moved with infinite slowness towards the library doors and thus saw Sinclair coming down the main staircase again with a riding whip in his hands.

'Ahhhh,' like a whisper the sound came from Lord Aynthorp's throat. Gyles' face muscles contracted slightly but he remained silent. When Sinclair reached the last tread, the three went in together and Henry, who was last, closed the great library doors.

CHAPTER 12

Interregnum

Henry came down from Oxford for twenty-four hours in November to attend the coming-out ball given by Sir Charles Danement for his youngest daughter Petula to celebrate her eighteenth birthday.

Despite young Charles Danement's minor involvement in the 'Stephen affair', as it was now known among the family, the Danements and the Lormes had been close friends for centuries. Their estates were adjacent to one another. Charles and his late wife Melissa had grown up with Gyles, Gabrielle, Henrietta and Robert, though neither Henry's parents nor indeed his uncles and aunts had more than vague hopes of a romantic attachment between the two 'children.' Even so, it was taken for granted that Henry would attend the ball, so Gyles wrote to his college for the necessary permission. Henry arrived after luncheon on the great day. Plum met him at the station, where he promptly ousted the footman and settled himself beside Plum on the box. After a couple of miles he persuaded his old crony to hand over the reins so that the carriage came up the drive at a spanking pace driven by the future owner.

Plum paid Henry the compliment of saying rather grudgingly as he dismounted on his little bandy legs that he had 'fair hands, considering', and was duly thanked. Sawby, with Edward at his side, witnessed the arrival from the top of the steps, then watched Henry pick up a parcel containing his gift to Petula and dismount. After greeting Sawby, he asked, 'Where are m'parents, Sawby?'

He was told, 'Mrs Gyles is with Mrs Peace, sir, doing the Christmas Orders and Mr Gyles is out with his Lordship making arrangements for the next shoot with Switch and Wittle.'

'That's all right then, Sawby. I won't disturb mother if she's busy. Is the Countess in her rooms?'

'Yes, Mr Henry, taking her afternoon's rest.'

'Good,' Henry smiled. 'I'll go up. How have things been by the way?'

Sawby inclined his head. 'Quiet, sir, nothing untoward to report, I am happy to say.'

Henry grinned. 'That's a nice change. Give my compliments to Mrs Parsons, will you, and tell her that some hot, buttered muffins would not come amiss at tea. My luncheon basket on the train was shockin'.'

Sawby started to open his mouth to say that Mrs Parsons had already anticipated this requirement, knowing Mr Henry's predeliction for muffins, but the young man had already gone, taking the stairs two at a time and vanishing around the leftward branch at full tilt. Sawby thought, turning towards the corridor which led down to the servants' quarters, 'He can't wait to pump Milady for what has happened about those Delahayes, I'll be bound,' as he went off to chivy the parlourmaids.

Henry scratched on his great-aunt's boudoir door. Pearson opened it beaming and resplendent in her new personal maid's black with neat white collar and cuffs, for she had newly assumed her position with Henry's mother and was also taking over the care of Countess Marguerite thus replacing the enraged Palliser. Pearson's eyes sparkled with pleasure at the sight of her favourite.

'Welcome back, Mr Henerey,' she bobbed at him respectfully. 'Please to step in, sir. I have just settled Madame for her afternoon nap.' Then, over her shoulder, 'It's Mr Henry, Milady . . . yes, Milady . . .' and to Henry, 'Please to come in, sir. Milady will receive you.'

Henry was left in no doubt of this as Marguerite's voice floated out all too clearly. 'Pray, Pearson, tell me with whom you parley in that opened doorway? I am in a draught and as you know very well I detest draughts. If it is Mr Henry, just show him in, girl.'

Henry grinned. Gaining access, he strode across to where his quarry was reclining upon her chaise-longue, dressed as usual most becomingly, in a lacy peignoir.

'Sorry, my pretty one,' he said, taking one be-ringed hand between his own. 'I was just congratulating Pearson on her promotion. Who has taken her place in the household?'

'A nice woman who is called by the unsuitable name of Pansy Appleby. Pearson spoke for her to your mother, Mrs Peace engaged her and I am told she does very well. Rather a sad story, but it will keep. Have you seen your Mother?'

'Well, no,' Henry confessed. 'Sawby said she was closeted with Mrs P. over the Christmas Orders and I know what *that* means so I thought I would leave her undisturbed until tea and come straight to you.'

'So that you,' the Countess supplemented, 'can bring yourself up to date with all the gossip as quickly as possible. Pearson, you may leave us now. Just put that tantalus at Mr Henry's elbow. He will doubtless take a glass of brandy with me while I sip my camomile.' Then as the door closed behind the maid, 'How much do you know?' she enquired. Both were aware of precisely what she meant.

'Very little since *they* left,' Henry confessed, removing the cut-glass stopper from its container of rich amber fluid.

'Well,' Marguerite put down her cup and saucer, 'just let me look at you.' The wide shrewd eyes appraised him. 'You are growing up,' she pronounced a trifle tartly. 'Less uncertainty, more assurance. After a mere month at Oxford I see you are already a fair way towards developin' like your Grandfather. I should not wonder if in a few years time you will be ridin' roughshod over the lot of us, just like Justin!'

'I shall have to wait a long time then before I do it,' Henry commented, swirling the small balloon cupped in his hand. 'Don't forget I have m'pater to reckon with. He may be a quieter man than the old octogeranium but he won't stand any nonsense. I don't fancy m'chances if I tried ridin' roughshod over him.'

Marguerite nodded. 'Your father has bred true,' she agreed. 'He takes a quieter line of course, as you say. There will be none of the soul-shatterin' outbursts on which Justin thrives, but, nevertheless, you are right to assess his mettle before tryin' conclusions with him.'

'I have no intention of tryin',' said Henry. 'I don't want my ears scorched. Now don't hedge, darling; tell me the score.'

'Pray do not be vulgar, Henry.'

Henry sipped and waited. At length, 'Well as you know,' she began, '*they* stayed here only a very short time; indeed I assume only just long enough for Stephen to . . . er . . . recover.'

'That's the only bit I do know.' Henry confirmed.

'Then they went to London. They took a suite of rooms at Brown's and set about equipping themselves. It is really rather curious, but Sinclair seemed to change after . . .' she faltered, 'well, that . . . er . . . scene in the library.'

'In what way?'

'A few days later he announced that he was not sendin' Stephen anywhere. He was takin' him. He did it in such a way that even your Grandfather could not see how he could possibly raise any objections. Sinclair made his case very firmly. He maintained that what Stephen needed was *supervision by someone who knew all the facts*.' She broke off. 'You do know about the earlier episodes?'

'At Eton and at his prepper?'

'Yes, I see you do. Well, Sinclair explained that he had no inclination for any tutor, whatever credentials he might possess. So, having consulted with Henrietta, they decided that the only wise course was to take the boy in hand themselves. They have gone on a world tour which will keep them away for two years. By that time Stephen will be of age, indeed well over, and Sinclair said, "By then I shall hope to have drummed *some* sense into him." They have naturally taken a very great many letters of introduction with them and they have friends all over the world. What *I* think Sinclair intends is to engender a suitable marriage for Stephen. I am sure he thinks that the only way to curb him is to get him tied to an acceptable, strong-minded wife who will bear him plenty of children. Then Sinclair will do what he can, with our help, to settle him in a position where he has sufficient responsibilities—plus his two years of parental indoctrination—to help him quieten down.'

Henry was silent for a while, staring into his glass. 'It won't work, you know,' he said at length.

'Of course I know,' said Marguerite vigorously. 'We all know it. It is curiously interestin' really if one can make oneself sufficiently objective to take the dispassionate and unbiased view.'

'What? Stephen's behaviour? But it runs in the blood!'

'Not from the distaff side,' said Marguerite firmly. 'I have been looking through old records. On the sire's side, as we all know, the vein runs clean through from the original Lormes in Normandy, but this is only the second instance in over eight hundred years of it comin' out on the dam's side.'

Henry looked at her quizzically. 'Is there anythin' in Sinclair's lot to account for it?' She shook her head.

'Absolutely nothin'. They are all quiet men. None of them have ever set the Thames on fire, but there is absolutely nothin' shady, messy, nor as far as I can discover, has there ever been. They have a solid, but relatively undistinguished past record, every one of them. Dull men of unassailable probity, would be my description ... er ... in confidence, of course.'

Henry put down his glass and walked towards the windows. He stood there looking out over the angle of the south and east terraces where the rise and fall of the land still showed the line of the moat Henri de Lorme's son had incorporated into the plans of the first stone Castle Rising which replaced the original one for which his father had decimated the surrounding forests. As he looked over the sweep of lawns and terraces to the maze in the distance through which Henry VIII had chased Nan Bullen, he tried to imagine what the view might have looked like to the founder of the English line.

'It has not, let me assure you, changed the Castle's character by one iota,' said Marguerite from her sofa.

Henry turned. 'Great-aunt, you are a witch!' he exclaimed. 'How could you know that I was thinkin' of this place and tryin' to imagine what it must have looked like when Henri first came ridin' through the forest and decided to build his home here?'

'It was a natural sequence of thought,' she said calmly, 'at least for one such as you, Henry. You must realise,' she sat up and spoke with unaccustomed force, 'that all we Lormes are indissolubly bound to our history. Our consciousnesses are permeated with it. We are as much the children of Castle Rising as we are of the union between our parents. Old buildings have immense power. Never forget that, for it is a fact. Have you ever been to Loches?'

'In the Touraine? No.'

'You should go. It would make my point for me. There were terrible things done inside those ancient and beautiful walls, which housed such unspeakable dungeons where men suffered so much that their sufferings came to be imprinted on the character of the building. Their miseries seep through the stones. I sometimes fancy that it was something of this that William Shakespeare had in mind when he wrote that line, "Sermons in stones". ...'

'And "good in everything",' Henry reminded her drily.

'It is the greatest foolishness,' she retorted, 'to claim that good cannot come out of evil. The point I am tryin' to make is that the walls breathe out their own history.'

Henry reflected. 'I know,' he admitted, 'that trees have a life of their own. If you lay your arm against an ancient one and rest your forehead up on it you can hear the tree throbbin'. When I was a child I used to wonder if trees came to life and moved about,' he shifted himself, restlessly. 'Anyway, it is not relevant. Can you describe to me how things are here now that this particular storm is over?'

'Not over,' Marguerite corrected him, 'just abated. Yes I can. Sinclair and Henrietta are in Egypt. They wrote to both your father and grandfather. They intend spending Christmas there on some *dahabeeyah* on the Nile. In due course they will let us know what they plan to do next. It appears that they have met a privileged archaeologist who has obtained permission for a 'dig' and Stephen is helping him. So his days are at present spent without benefit of female society and at night he returns to the hotel in which they have made their headquarters.'

'Shephards, of course,' said Henry absently.

'Yes, of course. Mrs Peace has taken over their rooms here and she alone has the keys. She airs regularly, sees that the rooms are always in readiness for their return, but no one else has been near them to my knowledge. It is as if they had never lived here. No, not quite that, it is like a whirlpool at sea, yes, that is it exactly! The sea becomes torn and ravaged, the water swirls higher and higher taking with it every single thing which comes across its path. *But it moves on.* When it has gone it is as if it had never been. The sea is too strong for it. The waters subside, the waves run over where it had been, as they did before it came and there is nothin' to show that it was ever there. So it is with all of us here.

'And so it was when they had been gone a few days. There was another shootin' party, then the first meet of the season. Hounds met here. Your grandfather turned out. Sawby and the footmen carried around the trays with goblets of our stirrup cup. Everyone drank to a good season, clear runs and clean kills, then they moved off to draw the first covert. The Pendleburys gave a ball and your mother had thirty guests stayin' in the house. She gave a dinner party of course. Everythin' went on as usual.

'Now we are beginnin' our Christmas preparations. Your mother with her lists, then on Wednesday next the travellin' man comes here with the Christmas samples. I have already been to London, which is still comparatively quiet although it is the silly season. I have done a great deal of my Christmas-present shoppin' already. Aunt Gabrielle has ordered a black velvet dress from

Paquin for our Christmas dinner party and one from Worth for our New Year's Eve Ball. All the women of this family are concerned with their winter frocks and furs and furbelows. The men talk of nothin' but huntin' and shootin'. Oh yes, we have settled down again.'

Henry drained his *ballon*, glanced at the tantalus, hesitated and then poured another half-inch of liquid into the glass. 'The mixture as before,' he murmured glancing down at the 'legs' in the glass as he swirled the old brandy. 'Then,' he looked up for a moment under his lids at his great-aunt and looked down again quickly. 'Well, I don't think the next bombshell will cause them quite as much distress, even though they are simply certain to be a bit put out!'

Marguerite eyed him in sudden consternation. 'Next . . . bombshell . . .' she faltered, then as she saw the twinkle in his eyes, 'you *are* a bad wicked boy to frighten me so! What in the world do you mean?'

'It won't be until January anyway,' Henry hedged. 'It's quite simple really, but I must wait at least until I'm nineteen before I tell them.'

'Tell them what? I shall have an attack of the vapours if you do not stop hinting like this; *tell me what you mean, this instant.*'

'I mean,' said Henry with maddening slowness, 'that I intend to find out tonight if Pet feels the same about me as I do about her. If so, well of course we shall have to wait—I thought probably the best thing was to suggest until I was twenty-one—but, darling Aunt Marguerite, I want to marry Petula Danement more than anything else in the world and I thought you would like to be the first person to know.'

Henry said nothing to either of his parents and they said nothing to him, but the number of times he stood up with the girl did not go unnoticed. When Pearson had undressed her, Christine lay back among the elaborately goffered pillow slips, looking not only extremely wide-awake but also extremely thoughtful.

Gyles came in from his dressing room and finding her so obviously alert, sat down on the edge of the bed. 'That was a most agreeable ball, my love, do you not agree?'

'Oh, most agreeable,' Christine responded.

'Then,' Gyles enquired mildly, 'what is causing you to look so profoundly thoughtful at this hour?'

'Gyles,' said Christine abruptly, 'what would you say to having Petula Danement as a daughter-in-law?'

'I haven't even given it a thought,' he answered, beginning to unfasten the frogs on his dressing gown. 'Henry is a long way off marriage yet. He's not nineteen until January and Petula has grown up far too close to him for that sort of thing I should say. They have always been like brother and sister, in and out of our respective houses like a couple of puppies.'

'Even so,' Christine persisted, 'you have not answered my question.' Gyles stood up, kicked off his slippers and removed his dressing gown. 'All right, I will. Frankly I do not think, if it ever came to it, that I should have the slightest objection. Oh I know there was that business of young Charles' involvement with Stephen, but I saw him afterwards you know and he behaved admirably. Looked me straight in the eye and asked, "If you were needed to cover up for a pal, sir, what would you have done?" When I didn't answer he went on, "I know it was wrong, but there is such a thing as loyalty. I was run ragged, not knowing what the devil to do for the best, but in the end I decided to back Stephen up." Then he made me laugh. He added, "After all, sir, I never expected to be found out! Now it's all come out I'm pretty ashamed of myself, but I'm bound to say I am also certain I should do the same thing all over again. I'm just damned sorry." There's nothing wrong with that. The line's clean. They're capital fellers the Danements, always have been, and the girl's as pretty as a picture. What's more she's intelligent with it. I know it's far from fashionable for young gels to think, but I'd say she had a good head on her shoulders. She moves like a thoroughbred too. All in all I think Henry could do a great deal worse. I'm assumin' of course, this is a purely academic question?'

'Oh yes,' Christine yawned at last, 'purely academic, but remember I asked you, because it just might happen one day and it helps me a lot to know what you think and how you would react if ever it did.' Gyles looked at her in the soft light. 'Well then, let's be really serious for a moment,' he said gently. 'If you are right, women's intuition and all that, I should not want to oppose their marriage on any score. In fact when she is a little older I think we would both welcome Petula Danement as a daughter-in-law; but, my love,' he bent over his wife and kissed her, then turned off the light and concluded in the darkness, 'I am bound to admit I speculate on just how many prospective daughters-in-law we shall have to consider before Henry speaks his marriage vows. Even then there will be the same performance all over again with Ninian and Richard, too, whose romantic attachments, I strongly suspect, even though he is only a baby, will claim a good deal of our attention in due course.' A slight chuckle escaped Christine in the darkness and they were both silent for a while. Finally in a sleepy voice, Gyles murmured, 'I wonder . . . whom we shall have . . . as daughters-in-law . . . in . . . the. . . end. . . .'

CHAPTER 13

Christmas

Christmas at Castle Rising was considered by Lord Aynthorp to be a matter which had been arranged by Almighty God and himself for *his* personal entertainment. As to the precedence, the opinion of the younger members of his family was that Lord Aynthorp only put God first as a matter of good manners. In fact this child of eighty clearly held the opinion that he had a personal monopoly of Christmas and that it really only pertained to himself, his wife, his castle, all who bore his name and his dependants. In consequence it was a very grave matter to him that his daughter Henrietta, his son-in-law Sinclair Delahaye and his grandson Stephen should elect to absent themselves from *his* celebrations. In the welter of arrangements for what Henry called 'the octogeranium's Borgia Orgy', the cause of this absenteeism was of absolutely no importance! Only the effect mattered—that a to-him-monstrous-and-totally-unreasonable breach had been created in the family's solidarity!

In one sense his passionate enthusiasm for Christmas was not in character. It was not French. His Norman ancestors had paid little or no attention to it by comparison with the English. On the other hand, early English Lormes had subscribed whole-heartedly and as, above everything else, Lord Aynthorp dearly loved a party, it was accepted as a most agreeable excuse for lavish spending, intensive organisation and above all, a welcome opportunity to chivvy and order, command and supervise. This kept him happy and amused for many weeks beforehand. He extended to himself the utmost leniency, spent with reckless abandon, gave with characteristic, if grandly seignorial generosity and thereafter devoted most of the month of January to vociferous complaint at the avalanche of bills which descended upon Castle Rising.

By the end of November his plans were very well advanced. The vicar had come in for his annual roasting. He had been thoroughly instructed in the order of service for Matins on Christmas morning, told what hymns would be sung, and been made to realise that anything but the briefest of sermons would be considered both unsuitable and distasteful to his patron. Further fiats went forth. At 8.00 a.m. precisely the vicar would attend a short family service in the castle chapel. This service, at which all dependants were expected to be present, would be conducted by Bishop Alaric. Communion would be celebrated while the early service at Aynthorp church would be taken by the curate. The vicar would then take breakfast with the family and thereafter be graciously permitted a carriage to take him back to the Vicarage in order that he might be ready for 'elevenses'. By Aynthorp edict there would be no marriages, no christenings, no 'irrelevant fripperies' on Christ's birthday. It was a Lorme Day and nothing must interfere.

Understandably, the details of the Family service were left entirely to the Bishop. Lord Aynthorp bored easily. He had a low threshold to this discomfort and Alaric came perennially near to crossing it. Rather than run the risk of being bored to extinction with hair-splitting perorations from his brother, Lord Aynthorp left the matter severely alone. A wave of the hand, a bland, 'Leave it all to you, my deah fella', and all risks were neatly avoided.

The Order for The Day was done in conjunction with Lady Aynthorp who alone knew exactly how to handle her intransigent spouse. As she commented drily to Christine, 'The line, my dear, is quite astonishin' in its consistency. I never allow myself to forget that our Lady Mathilde's lord and master not only died of an arrow in the spleen but had his obituary spoken by his relict when she commented to her ladies, "My lord's was always a somewhat overworked spleen". So it is with Justin. This is just an annual bridge which I have trained myself to cross without the slightest mishap. To be perfectly truthful,' the famous twinkle sparkled momentarily, 'I rather enjoy it all myself.'

So, closeted together in her boudoir, she and her Justin did The Plan which was no great matter anyway as it was the same every year. Luncheon would be a buffet at which chef André would be given full opportunity to exercise his undeniable culinary genius, while responsibility for the traditional items was given to Mrs Parsons, who ran the gamut of her few emotions in both the receipt of her instructions and the execution of them. Firstly, she would be traditionally and marvellously deferential while the audience briefing was in progress. Then she would descend to the Steward's Room and there, among her domestic equals, would let herself loose with pointless and self-pitying invocations as to 'where in the world I am expected to find the time for all this! ... atop the Christmas puddens which I have to make for her ladyship to present to all and sundry'—by which she meant to those who inhabited cottages upon the estate—'how I shall ever mannidge all them pies! ... what I am expected to do at this time of the year when my rheumatism is something crool already! ... and so on ad infinitum, honing herself, as it were, into a state of sharp perfection for the greatest lower-servant-nagging-orgy of the entire year.

She had a further cause for complaint in the weeks prior to Christmas in that M. André was 'forever doing silly drorings in the Steward's Room, working up fantastical notions out of that foreign head of 'is and then 'aving to rush round screaming like a cageful of parrots trying to catch up when it comes to 'is meal-times which he did never ought to do with so much on all our 'ands.'

This being interpreted meant that, as usual Mrs Parsons was jealous of André's ability to make exact and detailed drawings of *pièce montées* which he would produce for the highlights of his culinary year, the Christmas Buffet and the dinner, than which nothing gave him more pleasure, with the sole exception of his *Soupers des Bals*. Nor did he content himself with culinary designs. Armed with handfuls of papers he would quit the kitchens for long sessions in the housekeeper's room where he would submit his table drapes and dressings to Mrs Peace. She would then pass on these designs and make it her pleasurable business to supervise the special sewing women who were brought in annually to execute the swags and flounces, pleats and pelmets, over- and under-drapes with which M. Andre's cold collations were to be framed.

Nor did the footmen escape these advance preparations. They stood ready, in order of seniority, until Mr Sawby in the van opened up the cavernous safe in which the 'plate' was cached. This they bore away for cleaning and rewrapping in tape-tied green baize bags so that all should be in readiness for a final rub up with jewellers rouge and their thumbs, on Christmas Eve and after the family had dined.

At Lord Aynthorp's meeting with his spouse, the matter of their Christmas cards had been mooted. Lord Aynthorp examined the Meet picture, pronounced his approval and then observed mildly, 'Curious, ain't it, Emmy, to think that when I was born, there were no such things as Christmas cards!'

Lady Aynthorp smiled reminiscently. 'They are such a well-established part of Christmas that one forgets,' she acknowledged. Lord Aynthorp stroked his waistcoat complacently. 'Well, I was lookin' it up the other day so I'm fairly bristlin' with the facts,' he twinkled. 'The English never change and I dare suppose they never will!'

If Lady Aynthorp was surprised at this manifest *non-sequitur*, she gave no sign of it and waited for him to explain. 'A chap called Dobson invented 'em in '44,' she was told, 'then in '46 two fellers called Cole and Horsley brought out the first commercial ones. This caused the devil of an uproar! Seems that the first one depicted a family drinkin' wine and if anyone can tell me a more suitable occupation for Christ's birthday, I shall find it highly interestin'. Damn fools of English prissies complained it encouraged drunkenness! It was a cryin' shame. Yet who turned water into wine, I would like to know?' He glowered quite unnecessarily at his wife.

'Well, we all know, dear Justin, do we not?' she countered carefully, seeing the warning signs developing which presaged one of her husband's explosions into wrath. 'Indeed we can go on for a long time quoting Holy Writ on the subject.'

'Precisely . . . that's me point: "Wine that maketh glad the heart of man." A very right and proper sentiment. All these pussyfoots revolt me!' Then suddenly he forgot his rage and chuckled instead. 'Ours will be all right anyway, it's got the stirrup cup well into the fore and that, as we know, is strongly laced with alcohol.'

Suddenly he became bored, so began to talk about the tree which had already been chosen. He merely informed his wife as to the details and she made notes on the pad at her elbow in her neat little Greek handwriting. He had attended the selection and had supervised the measuring of the tree he finally approved, *in situ* and on a distant corner of the estate where a plantation of young trees had been installed for the use of future generations; all of them in this particular area being *Saxe-Gothaea conspicua* which, as Lord Aynthorp pointed out to his forester, was Prince

Albert's yew and therefore the only permissible tree to be employed for Christmas celebrations by anyone, since it was this and no other which Queen Victoria's consort had introduced into England from his native Germany.

Lady Aynthorp checked the height against further notes concerning the height of the ceiling in the Great Hall, agreed that the measurements were eminently satisfactory and then was put further in the picture by an explanation of the custom, to which she attended patiently, although it was in fact she who had inaugurated it when as a young bride, she first came to Castle Rising.

In due course the tree would be hauled to the steps of the Castle and then installed in the enormous tub which had been built for it many years ago. On the day, the youngest footman, Richard—as was also traditional—would station himself beside the decorated tree, with a wet sponge tied to the top of a long cane, held like a lance. This precaution was taken to ensure that he could douse any erring candle the instant it lurched at an angle and thus imperilled the adjacent branches. Before this the tinsel and the glittering icicles, the snowballs and the ribbon-caged snowstorms, the pomanders, masks, diabolos, stars, spangles and transfer-decorated shiny brown and white parcels would be affixed by the school-room brood—another ancient tradition, always executed under the supervision of two footmen, one to hold the steps securely, another to hand up the required items.

All this would be done on Christmas Eve afternoon when tea had been served and before the ladies went to dress. Then, after all the children had retired, Lord and Lady Aynthorp would return to the Great Hall where, by this time, Sawby and Mrs Peace had brought down all the Christmas-decorated larger parcels. These would then be stacked around the tree to the rim of the tub, spreading out for many feet around it. This was always the occasion for Lord Aynthorp to eye the completed encircling mountain with growls of misgiving. He would then mutter, 'Are you *sure* we have got enough, Emmy?' and his Emmy would annually assure him that no one had been forgotten and there was a plentiful supply of gifts for everyone.

Quite separate of course from all these were the children's stockings, stuffed in their scarlet felt toes with oranges, rosy apples and gilded nuts and thereafter with little cone-filled twists of shiny paper containing brandy balls and humbugs, while pink and white sugar mice would be affixed up the outsides of the felt stockings with little gold safety pins. Then there were the pillow slips, stuffed with smaller toys and games for hanging up against the feet of cots and beds to confirm that Father Christmas (or Père Noël as distant French cousins called him) had indeed paid them his annual visit during the night.

Lady Aynthorp also dealt with a barrage of questions fired at her by her Justin as these squirrelled around in his mind. 'How has Giles got along with the staff gifts?' he demanded. 'What's happenin' about the cheeses? Has he said anythin' to you about the sirloins? Is he usin' the ballroom for staff gift presentations?' Lady Aynthorp just patted his hands and soothed, 'I know, dear, that it is extremely difficult for you to hand over such matters after so many years of complete responsibility,' (she hoped as she said this that it was only in imagination that she heard the feet of Ananias), 'but I can assure you that Gyles and Christine are doing splendidly. The cheddar cheeses have all been ordered for the cottagers. Christine gave her cheese orders to Paxton and Whitfield as usual, though what on earth André does with all that Gruyère and Parmesan is really a trifle difficult to comprehend. However, our Stiltons are ordered too, including the ones we are sending as small gifts. Your Roquefort is of course arranged for, and the sirloins too. There is really absolutely nothing for you to worry about on any of these scores. Paxton and Whitfield will also send all the hams, and Christine has consulted André as to the exact date for their delivery. The ballroom *will* be used, as is our custom. In fact, Gyles has done everything possible to leave things unchanged now that he has taken over.'

The old peer grunted. 'Well I don't mind for meself, it's only all of you that concerns me, as you should know. Heaven alone knows there is enough for me to see to, anyway. We ain't going to part with the Yule log ceremony if I have anythin' to do with it. Then I have to see about the lake and arrange for the usual tests before we can give permission for the children or anyone else to set foot upon it. I'm goin' to London on Wednesday. Sotheby's are sellin' some rather good snuff boxes accordin' to the catalogue they sent me and I want one or two as gifts. Then I am engaged to have luncheon with young Berry. Going to him in the mornin', he's putting on a tastin' for me and then we'll have luncheon. I'll probably stay the night at m'y club, thought I might go in the Royce motor if it would not inconvenience you to be without it, m'dear?'

Lady Aynthorp assured him it would be perfectly all right. He nodded, well-pleased. 'Then I can bring back some of m'shoppin'. Never like leavin' parcels at this time of year. Much better to bring 'em home and besides I've another appointment with Spink.[1] There are some pieces of Fabergé and one or two old Chinese pots I want to run m'eye over, and I have to go to Cartier's.' He rose rather hurriedly as he said this. 'See you at tea m'dear. I realise you can manage splendidly without me so I shall take myself off and see what can be done about gettin' a new hunter for Gyles,' he paused and looked back anxiously from the doorway, 'thought it might make an acceptable present, do you think he will be pleased . . . ?'

Lady Aynthorp sat quietly for a little while after her husband's departure. She realised that her Justin was well and truly launched on his annual spending spree. She was feminine enough to wonder if the Cartier's appointment concerned herself and decided that her wisest course would be to choose a gown which would make a suitable background for whatever jewel she might receive on Christmas morning. She thought amusedly, Justin will insist upon paying for my frock too and Gabrielle tells me he has already issued the command to her, and I suppose to all the rest of the gels, that the bills for their Christmas gowns are to be sent direct to him.' Eventually she rose, smiling gently. 'What a mercy it is,' she thought tranquilly, 'that we can afford Justin's excesses! It would be dreadful to have to worry about them because the purse pinched.' Then she rang the bell for Palliser and engaged her in a discussion about clothes.

The interregnum between dramatic incidents last longer than usual. Letters came intermittently from the Delahayes who, so they informed the family, were intending to go on to India where the list of Maharajahs who had invited them to stay in their palaces was an explicit confirmation that the Indian visit would be a protracted one.

---

[1] Spink & Son Ltd, Mayfair, established in 1666. Fine art, Medal and Coin (numismatics) dealers.

A sharp frost heralded December. By the second week in the month it became so severe and the going both so hard and so perilous that it put an end to hunting. By the fifteenth of December the lake appeared to be solidly frozen, so a plough was drawn up to it and after this had been pulled across by two of the famous Aynthorp Shire horses, Plum reported to Sawby, and Sawby to Gyles that 'the ice was holding fast and skating could commence'. He likewise passed on the message that he would set about polishing and refurbishing her ladyship's sledge forthwith. This was a most elegant and elaborate affair: a source of pride and joy to Plum. He had barely completed this happy duty to his satisfaction when orders were brought down and pinned to the stable walls setting out the days and times for carriages to be at Aynthorp station to collect the returning family.

The highly seasonable weather, as it was regarded by those who did not hunt, made it quite impossible to hold the usual Meet on Boxing Day. Lord Aynthorp was greatly put out by this. One of his famous explosions into wrath against the whimsies of God, in not taking into proper consideration the requirements of 'huntin' men', was only narrowly avoided by a fortuitous suggestion from Lady Aynthorp that they should hold instead a skating party: 'A modest version of what went on when the Thames froze so hard in the winter of 1683. We could have chestnuts roasted in braziers,' she proposed. 'Perhaps we could even roast an ox? Then we could have of course a buffet beside the lake and any number of amusin' entertainments, dear Justin. Wouldn't that be a capital thought?' And thus she cajoled him.

After a few preliminary growls he came round to the idea, accepted it as his own, and immediately embarked upon a further spate of orders involving the staff in a vast additional amount of work but keeping himself amused while so doing. Little notes were despatched to all and sundry of their acquaintance in the county. The carriages were in excessive demand. Sawby was also put out by having his third footman commandeered to deliver a number of these notes by gig.

The arrangements for the annual Costume Ball on New Year's Eve had long been made, Chef André's *Souper de Bal* menu drafted and approved, the orchestra engaged and all instructions despatched to them for the playing of the traditional Sir Roger de Coverly and for the final Gallop with which these balls were always concluded. Down to the last item for the post-ball 'breakfast' all this was well advanced. Even the dance programmes had arrived and were sitting in their cardboard boxes upon Mrs Peace's desk awaiting her attention, for she it was who attached the delicate silk cords from which the little white pencils depended.

The woodcutter had been taken from his normal employment to cut down and bring in holly, mistletoe, bay, and to deliver separately to the stables, box branches for the kissing boughs. These, somewhat strangely, were made by Boots. Little Sam had evinced a strange talent for this ploy many years ago. Thereafter, each year, he took up his position in a corner of the harness room and worked away in great content almost submerged by wire hoops, box sprigs and reels of scarlet ribbon.

Eventually Christmas came and for the first time Gyles and Christine mounted the dais in the ballrom for the present-giving ritual. The castle dependants, the men in their Sunday suits and hats, red-faced under the restrictions of unaccustomed high collars and the women a little sharp drawn about their mouths due to the nipping of their corsets amid-ships and their many-buttoned Sunday boots below, filed past to receive their gifts. To each married man Gyles presented a token for a barrel of beer, then he handed each one a gold sovereign; whilst Christine bestowed upon all the wives, one prime sirloin, one cheddar cheese and one hamper, containing assorted groceries together with one of Mrs Peace's plum puddings, a pot of her mincemeat, a rich black plum cake and a tin of Huntley and Palmer's assorted biscuits. Each woman, married or single, further received a shawl, a warm pair of stockings and a pair of woollen gloves. Then it was the children's turn. They formed a long line, in which they chattered and fidgeted and were repetitively shushed until it came to their turn when they reached out eager hands for their large parcels of toys and sweetmeats. They all had a word or two from one or other of the new heads of Castle Rising, every child being correctly addressed by its Christian name.

When the ceremony was over Sawby stepped forward, called for three cheers for Lord and Lady Aynthorp coupled with Mr and Mrs Gyles de Lorme and the hip, hip, hurrahs well-nigh raised the roof.

Then they all repaired to the old barn for tea. When this gargantuan repast had been ingested and the majority of adults were burping surreptitiously behind their hands, the turn came for the schoolroom-brood to officiate. They appeared in their simplest frocks and both organised and took part in games for the children.

When darkness had fallen and the sky was glittering with stars, the Castle put on her own jewels and was transformed into a fretwork of sparkling lights. Then great white flakes of snow came tumbling down. By the time the exhausted parents had tied their progeny into a multiplicity of scarves and shawls, grabbed little sticky fingers and rammed them into woollen gloves, the grounds were white with the newly fallen snow, and the light shining out upon this glistening whiteness.

Thoroughly invigorated by the contents of huge steaming punchbowls of mulled ale, the country voices sounded louder than was their wont as mothers, fathers and children streamed out of the west door and hurried around to the main entrance. There they formed a dense semi-circle on the edge of the drive. This was the moment when the lantern-swinging carol singers came out on to the steps, wiping their mouths after the refreshments with which they had been supplied. They then arranged themselves in tiers on the steps. The curate promptly re-marshalled them, and then raised his baton in mittened fingers. Simultaneously heads popped out of the upper windows to look down upon the scene as with 'Hark, the herald angels sing...' the carol singers rejoiced with extreme vigour, their voices floating out over the Home Park and up to those opened windows.

Gyles in an Inverness, and Christine swathed in furs, leaned from their bedroom window side by side. ' "As it was, is now," ' Christine murmured softly, her head against her husband's tweed-covered shoulder. 'And,' supplemented Gyles, 'if I have may way, as it "ever shall be". Look, my darling, Plum has kindled the bonfire.'

In the distance a light was quivering. As they looked it broadened, split into flame points and, despite the fat snowflakes which were tumbling down, developed a glowing core while the smoke spiralled upwards and the flames danced higher and higher.

This was traditional too. It was begun during the Napoleonic Wars when the then Lord Aynthorp had ordered a great bonfire to be laid on the brow of Puck's Hill, an eminence which was suspiciously like an ancient barrow and from which the bonfire could be seen for miles. When the rider galloped in with the news that the Wars were ended, the fire was kindled. Then the villagers streamed through the Castle gates to dance a wild fandango about it and from that time, whenever a state of peace existed in England, bonfires had been lit every Christmas Eve. In times of war the fires were duly laid but they were never kindled. When the news was bad and England learned that the tide was running strongly for the enemy, the villagers would each pay pilgrimage to the unlit fire, carrying branches to lay upon the stack, in token of their unassailable confidence that on one not too far distant day peace would reign once more and the fire would crackle merrily.

Even now, some old instinct at work and tired as they all were, the Castle folk turned away as the carols ended and hurried to where the flames now tossed their sparks high into the air, illuminating the watchful men who stood about it and throwing into dark relief the water cart, drawn up nearby as an extra precaution against any erratic sparks. In the darkness, with the veil of snow, the effect was wholly primitive. 'Small wonder,' murmured Gyles wryly, 'they call that mound Puck's Hill. They look like wild folk from some savage clan, not peaceful country men and women!'

Christine frowned. 'I have never been quite sure how the legend runs,' she confessed. 'It is one thing about our Castle which I have omitted to find out.'

Gyles shrugged. 'It's an old tale, lost in the mist of time, but there are still folk hereabouts who cling to it. They say Puck lives under that hill in caverns down in the womb of Mother Earth. They say he comes out on All Hallows Eve and plays tricks upon them still.'

Christine watched the gyrating figures, the whole crazy scene. 'It is fascinatin'' she said, stretching out her arms in an unaccustomed gesture of exhilaration. 'Oh, how I love my home and all about it!'

'You are carried away, my love,' Gyles said amusedly, putting one arm about her slim shoulders. 'You look as if Puck had possessed you himself. Come away in and dress for dinner or we shall face worse than the fire from m'father, should we be late on this night of all nights in the year.'

Custom also had it that the household dined late on Christmas Eve in order to give the staff a brief respite after the tenants' celebration. Then, when dinner was over, the family would process on foot or by carriages to the church to join in the singing at the Midnight Service and to put their envelopes into the offertory bags.

Nothing changed, and nothing was changed from the old pattern either that year or for the next two successive ones. The children grew older and changed schools as 1907 gave way to 1908 and then to 1909. Henry's Petula had chosen to be elusive and would not consent to an engagement. She admitted to caring for him but displayed a streak of caution which enabled her to withstand his most ardent pleadings. 'I want to be sure,' this brown-eyed girl had insisted at her eighteenth birthday ball. 'I want to have a season anyway, meet everyone, curtsey to the King and Queen, go to all the balls, to Epsom and Ascot, Hurlingham, Ranelagh, Goodwood and Cowes. Ask me next November, Henry, then I will tell you truly whether or not I have fallen in love with anyone else.' But she did not tell him anything of the sort. When Christmas came round again, with a brilliantly successful season behind her and a number of very eligible suitors having offered for her hand, she both refused them all and persisted in telling Henry that she was not yet ready to decide.

CHAPTER 14

Uncalculated Risks

Two years later, when everyone had grown used to the idea that Henrietta and Sinclair would be absent for many years, they were advised of their return to the Castle by only the briefest of warnings—a telegram stating, 'In London, returning by train arriving 5.10 p.m. Stephen not with us. Love Henrietta and Sinclair.'

This set up such a spate of conjecture and speculation, such a crop of absurd and impossible explanations as engrossed not only the family but the servants' hall as well, to the point where Mrs Parsons actually burned her sponge cakes whilst standing holding the oven door in a patchwork-gloved hand, debating the situation with Miss Palliser. This worthy, animosity set aside the better to savour such a prime news bonus, was hissing and murmuring like a kettle which had almost burned dry. All this continued, orchestrated by thoughtful grunts from Parsons until she suddenly came back to reality with a start, wrenched at the oven door, hauled out a tray of blackened objects and 'There now!' she exclaimed in vexation, 'look which I done and no one but myself to blame! RUINED that's wot they are and all to be done again!' She raised her voice still higher. 'IVY,' she bellowed, 'come right here to me, girl, and get me sponge cake mixture ready all over again while Miss Palliser and I restore ourselves with a nice 'ot cup of tea in the steward's room.' Suiting action to words, she bore Palliser off as if she were a 'spoil' from the wars, only to be pulled up short as she opened the door by the sight of Mr Sawby (without even his alpaca jacket) and M. André (in his shirt sleeves) both seated and clasping glasses which had quite obviously contained generous measures of their employer's brandy.

'Wot a sight indeed!' she exclaimed, astonished. With arms akimbo she surveyed the guilty pair. André leapt to his feet, made an exaggerated bow and drew up two chairs for the ladies. Mr Sawby coughed, then murmured, 'we were discussing the news,

ladies. Pray come in and join us.' This was delivered at his most
pompous, clearly inferring that *he* was the lawful occupant of the
steward's room and *she* was the intruder.

Mrs Parsons hesitated, then ravaged by curiosity and spurred
by the thought that Sawby probably knew something which she
did not, she capitulated, took the proffered chair, indicated to
Palliser that she do likewise and merely murmuring, 'Such goings
on!' composed her voluminous skirts and looked expectantly at
Sawby. That worthy gentleman coughed again. 'It is my belief,'
he told the new arrivals, 'that there is more trouble brewing over
that young limb Mr Stephen.'

'*Bien sur . . . bien sur . . .*' murmured André, '*scèlerat;*'[1] but as
none of them knew what he meant by this judgment upon the
absent Stephen, none could take exception to it and the word
passed into limbo.

Meanwhile, the family, having elected to take their coffee in
the dining room, were also at it, if not exactly 'hammer and
tongs' then with considerable vitality. As Sawby recounted to his
attentive audience, 'That young cousin tried to get the ball rolling
while we were waiting at table but her leddyship said something in
French, par de-vong something. . . .' André, with eyes twinkling,
supplemented, '*Pas devant les domestiques*—was that eet?'

'That's it, Frenchy,' Sawby nodded. 'What does it mean?'

'Not in front of the servants, mister Sawby, that ees what it
means.'

'Ahem,' Sawby merely coughed. 'Well,' he concluded,
'nothing more *was* said while we were in the room.'

What had happened then was that as the doors closed behind
them, Gyles said, '*Now* we can speculate till hounds turn purple,
but I may say I doubt that anythin' will accrue from it, since
none of us has the remotest idea why Stephen is not comin'
home with them.'

Lord Aynthorp herrumphed. 'You may be bound m'y boy that
whatever it is it will be some tarsome pother or other. On that I
am prepared to gamble!' Henry snorted into his raised wineglass,
apologised immediately at the expressions of amazement which
greeted this unseemly noise and murmured *sotto voce* to his
visiting young cousin, 'Since the old octogeranium has been known
to bet on two flies crawlin' up a wall, that's no great shakes to m'y
mind.' Prunella merely giggled, looked at him in round-eyed

[1] Villainous.

amazement and queried in equally muted voice, '*Is* Great-Uncle really such a terrific gambler? Oh how deevy, do tell more. . . .'

Bishop Alaric cleared his throat portentously, placed finger-tips to finger-tips in his old familiar pose and then pronounced. 'I am reluctant to prejudge the case,' he boomed. 'In so young a man it is surely within the bounds of possibility that Stephen may have turned over an entirely new leaf?'

Lord Aynthorp snorted but of course no one reproved *him*.

'If you ask me,' John said abruptly, surprising himself with his own loquacity, 'I must confess to a certain uneasy belief that all Stephen's "leaves" are irretrievably soiled even before he turns them over! However,' he made a funny little bow towards his uncle, 'doubtless sir, yours is the more charitable view and one which wholly becomes your calling. For my part I shall rein in, ware wire, and tuck in m'y horse's heels.'

'While I,' said Lady Aynthorp, 'shall order the carriage to meet the ten minutes past five train. Christine my love, perhaps you will be good enough to implement these instructions for me?'

'Of course, Mama,' Christine acquiesced.

'Well then *that* at least is settled. Christine and I have already seen Mrs Peace about their rooms, Marguerite will do the flowers for them presently and I have composed an extended dinner menu with which to welcome them home. André will discuss it with me while I am having my afternoon nap.'

'What time did the telegram say?' Gyles wished to know.

'Their train,' replied his mother, 'is due in at ten minutes past five as I have just said. Plum will drive the carriage I think, and Christine dear, would you be good enough to order one of the luggage brakes as well? They may have a prodigious amount of luggage after travellin' for two years.' She sat back in her high, carved chair, smiling a little, 'And now I recommend all of you to contain yourselves in such patience as you can muster until about 5.30 p.m. this afternoon. Justin, may I trouble you . . . your arm if you please.' She rose to her feet, took her husband's arm and together with Henry doing what he called 'door duty', they left the dining room.

In the event it was a great deal later in the evening before their shared curiosities were satisfied. The carriage bowled up the drive, setting down a very elegantly dressed Henrietta at the foot of the steps. The two older footmen went out to hold doors and assist descent. The family flowed out behind them and in moments

Sinclair and Henrietta were engulfed in greetings, kisses, hand-shakes and cries of welcome.

Henrietta then expressed an urgent need for a bath and change of clothing. Sinclair passed a hand ruefully across his chin and observed, 'I shall need a shave before I change for dinner. Really sir,' looking at his grandfather-in-law, 'it is splendid to be home, we have missed you all and are very grateful for all your help.'

Thus it was that with Christine escorting and Gyles following with Sinclair, the pair were shown directly to their rooms—where Christine told them that dinner would be at eight o'clock, so if it would be convenient they would all meet for a glass of Father's old Madeira at 7.45 p.m. On which impersonal note she with-drew. She went straight way to her own rooms where Gyles was awaiting her. 'Well?' he asked, eyes twinkling, as she came into the private sitting room, 'did you get any clues?'

'Nothing,' said Christine shortly, 'and I predict we shall not hear a word on the subject of Stephen until after we have dined. Henrietta is in looks I thought and Sinclair very bronzed, but . . . there is something . . . a definite constraint. . . . I have to admit, my love, my impression is that they have bad news to impart. We shall just have to wait and see.'

Dinner on the night of Sinclair's and Henrietta's return bore more than a touch of ceremony: ten courses, ten complementary wines, Sawby and the two footmen in the dining room, two parlour maids bringing dishes to the dining room doors—since, like King Edward, the Lorme family refused to allow women servants to appear at table.

Henrietta wore a new Paris gown, the conversation ran through their travels and experiences and through family and estate news. It was only when the menservants had withdrawn—the Meissen dessert service set out in all its splendour—that Lady Aynthorp said cheerfully, 'And now my dears, as we can talk freely at last, what news of Stephen and when is he coming home?'

Sinclair's curt reply, 'He is *not*', threw a girdle of silence round the assembly. His face became taut and pale. Before he said more Lady Aynthorp caught the young, visiting cousin's eye. She set down her table napkin instantly. 'I wonder, Great-Aunt,' asked the cousin with a small, charming smile, 'if I might take a brief turn on the terrace, I am feeling the heat a trifle . . . if you would permit me...?' Thus she disposed of herself with that all-important semblance of being unaware of any undercurrents and, according to Hoyle and the tenets of 1909, merely following the inviolable rule of civilised behaviour.

When Henry had closed the doors once more and returned to the table, dabbed at his mouth with the fine lawn napkin and settled to the matter of peeling himself a peach, Lady Aynthorp resumed as if nothing toward was afoot. 'Not coming back, dear?' she queried gently. The ready tears were already welling to Henrietta's eyes. She seemed suddenly to have shed her 'in looks' appearance and aged tremendously.

'No,' answered Sinclair heavily. 'If you can bear with me I will recount everything as is befitting to my kind, loyal, absolutely splendid parents-in-law.'

Lady Aynthorp, who had placed him on her left, patted the hand that lay with clenched fingers against the Meissen plate. Her spouse interjected, 'Carry on m'y boy. Damned graceful tribute, I assume there is more trouble?'

Sinclair nodded. 'I have been an utter fool. I might add I have also been the victim of the sharpest confidence trick in my experience. I never imagined... could not conceive....' He began to stammer, collected himself and continued, looking now at his father-in-law. 'It was not possible to credit that one's own son would pose, connive, dissemble for over two years without ever givin' the slightest impression other than he was comin' to heel splendidly, had found a ploy which interested him enormously and was wholly absorbed in it.' Sinclair paused for a moment and then launched himself into his sorry narrative. 'As I believe either I or Hetty told you in one of our letters, we spent our first Christmas at Monte Carlo and moved on to Cairo for the New Year.' Lord Aynthorp nodded, helped himself to a cigar, pierced it—another fad of his—and began to light it.

'Well,' continued Sinclair, 'so did the explorer Harry de Witt —a splendid chap, he's a baronet y'know, has a string of letters to his name, and is a capital feller.' Lord Aynthorp's cigar was now drawing satisfactorily. He shot Sinclair a Look under those beetling brows but wisely abstained from any comment.

'Well,' Sinclair resumed, 'we all celebrated New Year's Eve in the Residents' Club in Cairo. Stephen seemed to have great shine to Sir Harry in Monte and Hetty and I thought he was deuced good for our son. At any rate Stephen spent the whole evenin' questionin' him about his exploits until I remonstrated gently. Sir Harry insisted m'boy charmed him, said he was very happy to talk. Stephen never even so much glanced at a petticoat. He never danced, just lay out on a rattan chair on one of the verandahs listening to Sir Harry whom I heard say at one point, "Now I'm givin' up big game huntin'. Sick of slaughter I think, and mebbe feelin' my age a bit." I then had to go and do a "duty" dance and when I came back they were deep in exchanges on "digs". Stephen was most deferential to the old boy, admitted he had been invited to take part in a small local "dig", asked for advice, listened carefully and generally seemed to be totally engrossed in the whole affair.

'There matters stayed for some time. We all went our separate ways. Sir Harry to Burma while Hetty, Stephen and I went on to China. Some months later we ran into the old boy at a great Chinese banquet. Phew! Justin, one of those would tax even your lusty appetite. Sir Harry was the principal guest, much fêted and *salaamed* to and it came out that he was in the first stages of planning a dig in Africa where he had picked up some stuff about the Lost Continent of Atlantis, and our host was in the thick of it. Neither Hetty nor I had the faintest inkling that matters had gone any further until we went to India not above four months ago and there were the guests of old Bingo,' he corrected himself, 'The Maharajah of Sawarka—you remember we shared a study when we were both at School?[2] Well, the upshot of it was that old Bingo was lendin' Harry five thousand pounds for his forthcoming expedition. This was half the amount he needed to raise. We learned too that he would be up country for a minimum of two years. He then put the suggestion to Stephen that he would be glad to have him with him as part of the official party. When Stephen heard this, his face lit up with pleasure and eagerness.

'Oh I cannot put it into words! But all this developed *over nearly two years*. I had never seen him with a petticoat in all that time, except when he steered very suitable gels into the dance. He always brought 'em back to our table afterwards. I rode with him each morning to his little dig. I collected him in a carriage every evening after which he seemed quite content to dine, discuss the day's "finds" and "turn in early". He would

[2] Harrow.

say, "We've got to make an early start, dear Pater, in the morning." '

Sinclair passed a weary hand over his smooth head, which, they now observed with a slight shock, was faintly greying at the temples. He resumed. 'Hetty here seemed delighted, I *felt* delighted and everyone who met the boy was full of praise for his diligence, his enthusiasm *and his charm.*'

'The Lormes' deadly inheritance,' Lady Aynthorp murmured. Then, 'I beg your pardon Sinclair, pray continue.'

The whole table was still, eyes fixed upon the speaker. Sawby at one point just put his head round the door, but Lady Aynthorp made a faint movement with one hand so he closed it again. Two minutes later the steward's room was seething once more with speculation and conjecture. By the time the dining room bell sounded, there was not a single member of the household who did not know that there were ructions in the dining room and none had any doubt that the cause of it *must* be 'Mr Stephen'.

Meanwhile, above stairs, Sinclair ploughed on drearily until he arrived at the crux of the matter. It seemed that Sir Harry de Witt had traced the Delahayes. He had sent them a lengthy cable. In it he reiterated that the exploration was on just as soon as he, de Witt, could raise the other five thousand. This it seemed was proving somewhat difficult. Sinclair and Henrietta discussed the matter for over five days. Then Sinclair questioned Stephen, 'as closely as I possibly could', and Stephen succeeded in convincing them both that he was as keen as mustard and did not see anything at which to cavil in saying goodbye to civilisation for a minimum of two years. He talked his parents dizzy with stories, records and theories concerning the Lost Continent, emphasised the potential fame and fortune which would result if they found the slightest traces of the allegedly Atlantean city, 'Let alone', as he put it, 'if we found treasure. Then I could possibly repay you both and Great Grandfather for all the shockin' mischief I have got myself into in the past.'

The couple were hooked. Within three days Sinclair had despatched two lengthy cables of his own, one backed by another from Henrietta. In short Sinclair and she cabled home instructions for the selling of her remaining investments, while a second cable sped to Johannesburg informing Sir Harry that *they* would advance the requisite five thousand, equip their son and give him the *lettre de cachet* to the Johannesburg bank nominated by her own, and then more cables sped back and forth. Finally, a month ago, they put an excited Stephen on a ship, waved him goodbye and planned to spend another six months together travelling before coming home to roost.

Inside the first six weeks a further, and this time highly agitated, cable arrived from Sir Harry revealing to them the awfulness of their folly. Stephen, it appeared, had quitted the boat without being seen and thereafter had vanished into thin air with all his equipment, his mother's five thousand pounds plus the thousand Sinclair had added for Stephen's own personal expenses. Sinclair cabled again, and again received a prompt reply from Sir Harry. 'J'burg bank confirms Stephen obtained all moneys lodged by you. He has not been heard of since. Regrets. Sincerely, De Witt.' The letter which followed told the rest. Stephen had bribed a purser to get him off the ship earlier than her docking time. He had bribed the man heavily, there was no possible doubt about that. The wretch broke down under interrogation and confessed to his 'infamy', as the letter stated all too convincingly.

Sinclair wound up in a dry, hard voice. 'It then became manifest to both of us that Stephen had waited and planned for over two years so as to be quite certain he had dispelled every parental doubt, and had regained our confidence simply in order that he could "escape" when the opportunity arose.'

As matters transpired they were not to have sight or sound of him until the August of 1914 after a number of mostly painful occurrences had cast long shadows over Castle Rising and its inhabitants.

CHAPTER 15

Stephanie

It so happened that none of the Delahaye children saw their parents on the night of their return to the Castle. Before the telegram arrived, both Stephanie and Rosalind had been taken by Claire de Lorme to spend the night with their maternal grandmother at Stanhope Gate in order to pay their routine six-monthly visit to the dentist on the following morning. The remaining male, five-year-old Gilbert, was recovering from a feverish cold. He had been 'quite poorly Mummy' and was now sleeping, Nanny assured Henrietta when she presented herself at the nursery door. That worthy added that 'Nanny for one would be most obliged, Mummy, if we could let him sleep the slight fever out and waken to the glad news tomorrow morning.' To this, Henrietta naturally acquiesced so Nanny, who could now afford to be generous, invited the Mother to come and see her own child and together they went into the night nursery.

The red merino curtains were closely drawn. A coal fire glowed and crackled behind the fire-guard. A nightlight swam in a saucer on the cot-side table, watched over by the small china rabbit who presided on the rim. A hump in the middle of the quilt was all that bore testimony to Gilbert's presence. Nanny bent over the lowered bars, eased back the bedclothes and very gently turned the little boy on to his side. She managed this manoeuvre without causing him even to remove the thumb which he had wedged into his little crimson face. Henrietta stood watching. 'He's more beautiful than ever, Nanny,' she breathed. Nanny nodded. 'That he is, and a proper varmint with it.' She finished tucking Gilbert into a cocoon of bedding, and firmly led Henrietta away. When the night nursery door was closed, 'He'll not wake until morning,' she said reassuringly, 'but he is a handful, Mummy, into everything, up to all sorts of scrapes.'

'Scrapes! Oh Nanny, not another one!' The careless words

slipped out but Nanny gave no sign of reading anything untoward in them.

'Scrapes,' she repeated, 'scrambling on to window ledges, playing with a sack of soot, handing himself down all them stairs to find Mrs Parsons and wheedle her for some of her sponge fingers—and in the middle of the morning too, when he should have been at his pothooks!'

All Henrietta said was, 'Oh, those sort of scrapes,' in a voice of infinite relief. 'And how are the girls? I was so worried by Gilbert's chill I have quite neglected to enquire after my daughters.'

'Miss Rosalind,' Nanny told her guardedly, 'is a very good girl, most obedient. When I was a girl, ma'am, we called her sort biddable. Never given me a moment of trouble nor her governess either, she hasn't, but sometimes Miss Stephanie worries me. The governess tries to reassure me—but I *am* uneasy. . . .'

'And who is the governess now?' Henrietta enquired, confident that with the Castle brood it would undoubtedly be someone different after a lapse of two years.

'A Mademoiselle Lisse,' said Nanny. 'She has a great influence upon Miss Stephanie, both of them being so devout.'

Henrietta twinkled. 'Is Miss Stephanie devout?' she asked amusedly. Nanny thought about this for a while with her head on one side like a robin. Eventually, 'Would you like to see her room, ma'am? You know she has her own room now.'

Henrietta was not deceived. Nanny did NOT approve of the 'devout' aspect in her daughter's character; it was as plain to see as was the equally obvious reluctance on her part to being drawn into making any unnecessary statements. Therefore Henrietta deduced, 'seeing' Stephanie's bedroom would be the most speedy and satisfactory way of summing up the offending 'devoutness'. However, all she said was a meek, 'Yes please, Nanny,' after which she followed the old woman down the long corridor. In doing so she seemed to see her own younger self, pacing that self-same corridor, strapped to a backboard lest during her studies she became round-shouldered.

Nanny opened the door, stood aside for Henrietta to enter and then, drawing the handle inwards, closed the door again.

'It . . . is . . . like . . . a . . . cell . . .' said Henrietta slowly. 'Oh dear, Nanny, whatever shall we do?'

She sank down on the narrow white cot with its plain white

cotton bedspread and looked towards the bedhead where hung a very passable copy of Melone's *Madonna and Child.* Then, turning slowly, she looked round the room, taking in every detail. Between the two wide windows, against the stark white wall stood a *prie dieu.* Above it a small ivory crucifix dangled with, a little to the left of it, a rosary. On the inner wall there were book-shelves. At this point she rose from the bed and crossed the room. All the while Nanny stood, erect, unmoving, her little beady eyes shining with curiosity, but she said nothing. Henrietta examined the titles: *The Rosary . . . Lives of Great Saints . . . Re-Discovering the Tomb . . . The Vision of St Bernadette . . . St Francis of Assisi, his life and work . . . The History of the Vatican. . . .*

'When did this begin Nanny?'

'When I fust taught her to say Gentle Jesus . . . even then she prayed on silently after we was all done.'

'And this room?' Henrietta made an all-embracing gesture of distaste and shivered a little.

'Not so long after you was gone. She went to Miss Christina, I should say Mrs Gyles, and she said what she wanted. Mrs Gyles very properly took my advice afterwards. 'What should I do, Nanny?' she asked me in that soft voice of hers. 'It's not,' she said, 'the question of her having a room of her own. She is entitled to one when she is fourteen.' Nanny broke off to add an explanatory rider: 'You will remember, ma'am, she was turned fourteen when you left and is now coming up to her sixteenth birthday.'

'Yes, I know, Nanny.'

'Now where was I up to? Oh yes, well she said, "It's not the room but the *reason*." I can tell you what that is, I told her,' said Nanny. 'I said, so as she can have privacy to pray, to spend hours kneeling on all that *petty poing* a-praying to the Virgin Mary.

' "Yes," sighed Mrs Gyles, "that's just what it is." Then she asked me, point blank, "Shall I give it to her, Nanny?"

' "Well," I says, "it's no mortal use giving her the excuse to develop a persecution compleck, she'd only go around looking like one of them old Christian martyrs because she was being ill done by all of us. So," I says, "give it to her madam and leave the whole thing until Mrs Henrietta comes home. You carn't do nothing on your own even though she does turn to you first when her Mama is away." '

'Does she?' Henrietta sounded wistful.

'Thinks the world of her', Nanny nodding like a mandarin. 'She'll do things for Miss Christine what she would not do for no one else.'

'Like what?' asked Henrietta.

Nancy looked so surprised that Henrietta said quickly, 'Oh Nanny, I'm just trying to find out something about my own daughter which might help me to reach her. She's turned to all this because we, her parents, have neglected her.'

'Not a bit of it', said Nanny briskly. 'Now there's no need to make a bigger drama of it than what it is. She was like this as a toddler. Anyway, it's silly to take about negleck. Ladies of your station is for visiting and respecting their children. It's us Nannies as has the raising of them, as is only right and proper.'

Henrietta sighed mightily. 'Oh, I suppose so. It's what we have always been brought up to believe.' Horror again darkened her face. 'Nanny,' she came swiftly across the room and grasped one of her old nurse's knotted, veined hands, 'Nanny, you don't think she intends to take vows . . . become a nun . . .?'

'There there, my pretty.' Nanny drew her across to the bed once more and made her sit down again. Then she pulled her to her and began stroking her hair.

'Now you listen to Nanny and you'll be all right. She's close on sixteen so next year she could do the running up bit to being presented: pretty frocks, parties, young people. Thank your lucky stars it came about when it did. Every girl has her head turned by her first season; perhaps her Ladyship could be persuaded to give a little sub-debutante dance for her in the summer. Then she could go to some parties in the silly season and before you can find time to even mention nuns and convents to her she'll be in the thick of it with no time no more in front of any *pree-jer.*'

'Oh, do you really think that would work?' The ever ready tears were swimming in Henrietta's eyes.

'Well, if that won't we are in a pickle and no mistake', said Nanny briskly, 'so let us find out and put it to the test. Now what is that Mr Gyles says about hope and travelling? Can you remember for me?'

Henrietta smiled at the old woman and wiped her eyes. 'It is better to travel hopefully than to arrive. Is that it, Nanny?'

'Yes it is,' Nanny agreed tartly. 'So take it to heart, Miss, I mean Madam, and let us have no more tears. Now run along and talk it all over with Mr Sinclair otherwise your face will not be fit to be seen when the dinner gong starts its thunder.'

Henrietta went away Nanny returned to the nursery wing. It was late that night when she stopped her rocking. She even dismissed Rose who was normally her confidante on these occasions. To and fro she rocked alone. Had she done right to say no more, or had she been wicked? The refusal to wear silk or anything soft, the insistence upon plainness, Stephanie's condemnation of all jewels, that bit of coarse rope she wound round her waist, her disapproval of all 'those sinful orgies' as she called her grandparents' dinner parties, her own abstinence, her determination to take only bread and water on Fridays and her tramping with Mademoiselle across the park to take Communion at 8.00 a.m. at the village church and not at the family service in the chapel. Her further traipsing back and forth for matins, to assist at the afternoon Bible Readings for the children of the villagers and finally her return for Evensong. 'Should I have told?' was the problem which fretted Nanny now, but when at length she put herself down and hobbled out of the room, she had been unable to 'see a way through it all either one way or the other.'

It was not until after Henrietta had seen her daughter Stephanie, that she plucked up courage to say something to Sinclair. Born and brought up, as she had been, surrounded by women of considerable beauty—save only for "poor Prue", it was clear enough to her mother that Stephanie held out little promise of sustaining this natural Lorme inheritance. When she presented herself in her mother's boudoir on the afternoon of her return, Henrietta first observed that she had grown enormously. She judged that in her walking boots she must be at least five feet seven. 'Very difficult for dancing partners,' flashed the thought. 'She will always have to wear slippers with ball gowns!' Then, dismayed, as her daughter walked composedly towards her, 'Big feet, too! Oh dear!'

The girl bent forward to kiss her Mama, gracefully disposed on a dove grey chaise-longue.

'Well, Mama, are you rested after the fatigue of the journey?' she enquired much as if she had been asking her Mama to pass the breakfast toast.

Henrietta put up a ringed hand to her hair. 'Still very fatigued my love, but pay no attention to me, I will soon rally. Let me look at you. Dear me, how you have grown, you are actually taller than Mama now!'

'It is not important one way or the other,' Stephanie replied with a definite note of rebuke in her rather colourless voice. 'Tall, short, fat, thin, we are what we are and that is how the Lord Jesus decreed it.'

'With the best will in the world, my love, I scarcely think the Lord Jesus has the time to ordain the length of your hair, or finger nails, or your height either,' Henrietta protested. 'I have always been given to understand He was more interested in things spiritual than things material.'

'Possibly so,' Stephanie conceded. 'I merely wish to make the point that I am indifferent to my exterior and it is my inward soul and spirit with which I am concerned.'

'Really,' Henrietta, quite out of depth and floundering, made a valiant effort to rally, saying rather weakly, 'I do not consider that such vehemence is *quite* within the tenets of behaviour for young gentlewomen who are not yet "out".'

'Out!' exclaimed Stephanie scornfully. 'If you mean that monkey parade you all go in for, sticking feathers in your hair and crowding up the Mall to curtsey to that poor, deaf Queen and her libertine husband . . .'

The *lèse majesté* was well timed. In an instant Henrietta was on her feet, eyes flashing and not a sign of tears. Then, very quietly and slowly, she said, 'Never again let me hear a daughter of mine stoop so low as to criticise the Monarchy. Never, do you understand, Stephanie, never! And now go to your room and remain there until you hear from me that you may come out. And,' she added unwisely, 'use that *prie dieu* of yours to ask God to forgive you for such unfilial behaviour, such disloyalty to the Crown and such gross bad manners in yourself.'

Stephanie turned and ran from the room, crying as she went, 'You never give yourselves time to think . . . you are all too busy dressing up for each other . . . no . . . time . . . to . . . think . . .'

This alarming little scene so disturbed poor Henrietta, who was already in some degree suffering from shock at Stephen's latest defection, that she promptly and with no more hovering, set out through the Castle in search of Sinclair. She traced him eventually to the gun room where she surprised him discussing the details of some new gun which Claire's Christian was expounding for Sinclair's benefit. Both men looked up in surprise as Henrietta stepped into the doorway.

'Good evening, Christian,' said she, coming forward with some semblance of composure. 'You look very well. I may hope you do as well as your looks. Does not Christian look well, Sinclair, my love?'

Sinclair put down the gun. 'Yes, very well,' he said somewhat drily, 'but you know you do surprise us by your visit. With your declared abhorrence of firearms in general and this gun room in particular, it must be a matter of considerable urgency for you to beard me here.'

Henrietta nodded. 'It is,' she said, simply.

'Well, we cannot talk here,' Sinclair slipped one arm through hers. 'Christian, you must excuse me, my dear chap. I am truly sorry to treat you in such a cavalier fashion. Perhaps we can resume my instruction at some other time?'

'By all means,' Christian concurred, 'pray do not give it a thought.' He hesitated, 'but why do you two not stay here and I'll take myself off . . .? It is absolutely no trouble.' He looked at them expectantly.

Henrietta shuddered. 'No, not in here thank you, Christian. We'll go into the Blue room; no one ever goes in there at this hour'. And so saying, she moved away eagerly, with so much urgency in her movements that Sinclair found the amused thought flicker through his mind: 'I am being led away. Wonder what the devil's up now.'

Henrietta left him in no doubt. She took him through the initial conversation which she had had with Nanny, and the subsequent visit to Stephanie's cell-like bedroom. She repeated more or less verbatim both what she had said and what Stephanie had said in her boudoir. Sinclair listened attentively, staring at his hands. He heard her out. Then he brushed one hand across his head and said one word, 'Children!'

Henrietta nodded. 'You mean why do we have them? If we had any idea when we first married that they would prove such heartbreak we would not, surely could not have brought them into the world!'

'And thus', Sinclair added sadly, 'entirely fail to fulfil the one purpose for which marriage came into being.' They were silent for a while and then Sinclair said, 'You know, I think that I am in no way equipped to deal with this matter.'

Henrietta stared at him aghast. 'You mean you wash your hands of Stephanie . . . ?'

Sinclair took her hands gently. 'Of course not, but what I do mean is that I think this is a petticoat affair. No man can tackle the problem satisfactorily; you should take your troubles to the women of this family. This IS a feminine issue you know, my darling, so how can you expect a mere man to deal with such a situation. In any event,' he added, 'surely at a time like this, IF she really IS contemplating getting herself to a nunnery, the mere sight of any man, even her own father, could be anathema to her. No, take this to your mother, take it to Prue, to Marguerite, to all of 'em. Their composite knowledge and, above all, their special intuitive instincts will help you as I never could. I would be perfectly content to rest upon their judgment and to concur in whatever is finally decided to be the way in which the situation should be handled, but advise you myself I cannot.'

Henrietta's face suddenly cleared. 'I could not see that at first', she confessed, 'but now I do. Of course you are right, dear, clever Sinclair. We will have ample opportunity after dinner whilst you are at your port. Mother can send Sawby away quite quickly and then I can tell them. Naturally one sees that nothing can be resolved in one evening but once they know and are sharing the problem with me I shall feel quite different. I know I will.'

Sinclair stood up and then bent to kiss his wife's hair. 'Though it is curious', he observed in a hard voice, 'that we should encounter such a moral and spiritual issue immediately after . . . er . . . Stephen.'

Stephanie was released from her room in time for the ritual descent from schoolroom to drawing room after tea and before the 'grown-ups' dressed for dinner. Nanny, who released her, showed no surprise at finding the girl on her knees again. She merely said briskly, 'Come along now, we must wash our face, brush our hair and change our frock. It's very nearly drawing room time. You and Rosalind are to go down with Lucy.'

'No one else?' asked Stephanie in an indifferent voice. 'Oh, it's all so silly.'

'Grown ups aren't silly, Miss,' snapped Nanny tartly. 'Just you remember you are still only a child and mind your manners. I can see I shall have to have a word with Mademoiselle.'

'Mademoiselle is *my* friend,' said Stephanie. 'She is the only person who understands me.'

'I reckon I understand you all right.' Nanny shepherded the girl out of the door and virtually shooed her along the corridor. 'There's little wrong with you that a dose of cold baths in the morning and plenty of healthy exercise wouldn't cure. It's all these niminy piminy ways with young girls all of a sudden that I don't hold with. Now, into the bathroom with you and remember, I shall expect to see you in the day nursery in not more than fifteen minutes' time.' Saying which she toddled away in high dudgeon muttering, 'Silly indeed! What is the world coming to I would like to know!' Then, native shrewdness overcoming wrath, she told herself—between the bathroom and the day nursery—that *she* was not the right person to 'have a word' with Mademoiselle so resolved to 'put a word' in the ear of the one whom she had cast for the duty: Mrs Christine.

Mrs Christine was in fact a fair way towards being consulted, appealed to and quoted in times of stress as if she were some lesser Delphic oracle. Stepping, as she had done into her mother-in-law's tiny shoes as Henry had described it 'while Granmama's feet were still inside 'em', she was well aware of the hazards which lay ahead. Serenely, at least outwardly so, if fraught within by manifold uncertainties, she gradually approached the various vital members of the household. By dint of superb domestic diplomacy, a suitable amount of subtle flattery and further aided by a most beguiling face and manner she suddenly discovered herself not only to have won potentially prickly customers over to her, but to have gained such an unenviable reputation for wisdom and infallibility that 'Ask Mrs Gyles' . . . 'Christine will know' . . . 'What does Madam say about it?' . . . were part of the common daily round in one way or another and everyone turned to her. So it was now.

Nanny, greatly daring, trotted resolutely onwards, past the nurseries, down the short staircase, through the green baize doors and so out into the Long Gallery. At the farther end she turned right, then left, sorted herself through a maze of short steps and unexpected turns and brought herself up short outside Christine's private sitting room door. This she opened gently. 'Begging your pardon Mrs Gyles,' said she, putting her capped head around the door. Christine was lying down reading a magazine. She looked up, saw Nanny, set the magazine aside and with a quick 'Oh come in, Nanny, please', she patted the bed and invited Nanny to be seated.

'No thank *you*,' said Nanny, grabbing an upright chair and hauling it into position. 'I never did hold with sitting on beds, Mrs Gyles, as well you know. Now, I'm in a bit of trouble. Time is short, so you might say I have played truant from the nursery wing and must get back before I am found out.' Her old face creased into the semblance of a grin and Christine laughed. 'Say on, Nanny, and I will listen, I promise.'

The descent to the drawing room before dinner gave Henrietta and Sinclair an opportunity to study their daughters. The first thing which struck them both when the girls entered the room was the extraordinary lack of resemblance between them: Stephanie was distinctly big-boned, while tiny Rosalind had clearly inherited the 'family' small bones, from her narrow little feet to her elegant hands. Nanny had dressed her in Grecian style and put a fillet into her long fair hair. These things became her very well and made cruel contrast to Stephanie's yellow serge banded with navy-blue braid. This merely stressed her sallow colouring, in the reverse of little Lucy whose pale blue shaded chiffon dress, caught on the shoulders with satin bows, enhanced her delicate prettiness. The girls bobbed their way around the room ... to grandmama, aunts and mama ... then took up their positions, Rosalind on a footstool at her Papa's feet, making a very pretty picture with Lucy close beside her but Stephanie, feet firmly planted together, her back ramrod straight, sat rigidly in an upright gilt chair, hands folded in her serge lap. Her expression was similar to that of an early Christian martyr about to be boiled in oil.

Lady Aynthorp eyed the girl thoughtfully as she too sat completely erect, working at her embroidery frame. 'This is a beautiful room, is it not, Stephanie?' she observed questioningly.

Stephanie looked surprised. 'Is it?' she said indifferently. 'I know it took a long time to decorate, it employed great talent, it is old and it was also very expensive.' The tone of voice was perfectly unexceptionable but the implicit criticism was annoying.

Lady Aynthorp resumed. 'Do you know by whom it was done?' she enquired.

'No, Grandmama.'

'Then let me tell you, for we should all know and understand the beautiful things with which we are surrounded and thus come to respect them with a connoisseur's eyes and not just for the cost.'

'Thank you, Grandmama,' Stephanie murmured dutifully and without a flicker of either pleasure or enthusiasm. She merely folded her hands in her lap and looked down at the carpet.

'Well then', Lady Aynthorp began, setting aside her *petit point*, 'the style of this room is called Rococo and it is French. The then Lord Aynthorp was staying with friends near Paris in 1723. He had occasion to compliment his hosts on the superb workmanship done to the designs of a very gifted Italian from Piedmont called Meissonnier...' She recounted the old story, of how Meissonier had come to Castle Rising with three of his own men, and how with two workmen from Upper Aynthorp they had all spent eighteen months on the decorations. She ended her tale: 'Why child, even the Aubusson carpet was Messonnier-inspired... this very one at which you are staring so intently now.'

Stephanie lifted her head and looked levelly at her grandmama. There was a flush on her cheeks suddenly, as if she were in the throes of some violent emotion which she strove to conquer. 'And how much did it all cost, Grandmama?' she asked quietly.

'Oh dear me, child, I do not know, a very great deal of money I daresay, but then at that time we...er...had a very great deal of money and were content to spend it in embellishments to Castle Rising.'

'I see,' said Stephanie, wondering *when* this terrible drawing room ordeal would end. Then Mademoiselle appeared in the doorway and....

'Ah, there is Mademoiselle,' exclaimed Henrietta gratefully. 'Come children, say your goodnights and go with Mademoiselle.' She began chatting to the woman in her native French whilst the three girls once more went the rounds, bobbing and murmuring courteous goodnights, which ritual had been ground into them by Nanny. She had for many years assumed the mien of whomever was germain to her lesson, then she invited her charges to state how they would greet, depart, thank and bow or curtsey to that person.

Once outside the door, 'Phew,' exclaimed Stephanie, 'I'm so thankful that is over. All those silly, overdressed women sitting there like lap dogs, waited upon, fussed and mollycoddled while some overworked village women is very like scrubbing out a midden.'

Mademoiselle sighed. '*Chèrie*,' she expostulated, 'you must not these things say. I understand, but for the rest it is not clever to talk so loud and angrily. It is not *comme il faut* for a demoiselle in your position.'

'Everything I believe in is not *comme il faut*, I wish I had absolutely no position,' Stephanie murmured rebelliously. Mademoiselle looked at her pityingly, 'Only because,' she said in her strongly accented English, 'only because you do not know what it is to be without any position or any money either.'

CHAPTER 16

The Mixture As Before

While the Family were once more repairing the gaps in their defences as they had done with monotonous regularity down the centuries; while Lord Aynthorp replaced the six thousand pounds and Christine enlisted willing allies among the indoor staff to invent small duties which only Henrietta could execute to perfection, life went on. Meanwhile Stephanie sank deeper into a morass of religious fervour and simultaneously a small *château* situated just outside the Touraine village of Azay-le-Rideau was being prepared for an engagement party.

News of this reached Castle Rising in the form of two letters addressed respectively to the Honble Mrs John de Lorme and the Honble John. The former was from Primrose's daughter Rosemary announcing her engagement to Charles, Vicomte de la Coutray. The latter was an elegantly couched request for the recipient's permission to take his daughter's hand in marriage. Telegrams were promptly dispatched congratulating the couple. John's carried the further appendage 'Welcome to the family, letter follows'. Lord Aynthorp saw fit to be equally benevolent to a young man whose forbears had fought with Henri and his Duke in Normandy. There was general rejoicing. Regrettably, as Rosemary informed her mother, the wedding would take place in France. Charles' very eminent Tante Clarissa-Marie had consented to act as *chaperon* and Rosemary would stay with her after the engagement and until her wedding, save only when making trips to Paris for clothes. This she would do under the aegis of her future mother-in-law.

Rosemary wrote: 'Charles is fascinated by women's dress and very knowledgeable. He knows exactly how he wishes me to look. He and his mother are already full of plans for me with their hairdresser, bootmaker and so on. And what do you think, Mummy? The Marquise congratulated *me* on my *accent* and she speaks the most beautiful French I have ever heard except

Grandmama's! Now isn't that splendid? We are, according to my future *belle mère* strictly en famille here, but I suspect from what I have heard that they keep great state on all formal occasions and certainly their family way of life is elegant enough. The footmen wear soft slippers—for the parquet is famous as you know. Their feet make no sound; this was a bit creepy at first. The slippers are velvet and look elegant, as do the footmen who still wear their powder at night, and, what do you imagine? *They will not have electric lighting.* All the reception rooms are candlelit and when the great chandeliers are alight, as they will be for my engagement party, Charles says it looks *"magnifique"*. Now you will come over just as soon as you can and stay for as long as you can, won't you, Mummy, because it just wouldn't be a wedding if you and Papa were not there, much as I love Charles . . .?'

All this was very much to Lorme taste. By common consent Lord and Lady Aynthorp would not attempt the journey, though there was an ominous glint in the old man's eyes and Giles, having encountered it, experienced some misgivings. However, it was agreed finally that Gyles and Christine would go with John and his Primrose. Bishop Alaric expressed the wish to accompany them with or without his Dorothy and a subsequent letter from Henry summed the affair up as 'what a lark! Rest assured I shall be there somehow, though I imagine it will take a bit of wangling'. The engagement was celebrated that night in a general atmosphere of felicity and with the last of the Lafitte '75.

It all worked out perfectly. Gyles, diary in hand, gathered the family around him at the breakfast table. Old Lord Aynthorp, still suffering from frustration at not being allowed to go but secretly acknowledging the sweet reason in such a decision, was all the crosser because of it and in a tiresome state of mind. 'Why on earth a weddin' should take two days I do not comprehend,' he grumbled, 'A lot of civic mumbo jumbo is what I call it!'

Gyles dropped his monocle, replaced it, and said patiently, 'But, sir, you know the reason perfectly well and how it began.'

'With a lot of flamin', seditious regicides who could barely write their names,' Lord Aynthorp exploded. There followed ten minutes of blistering invective on the French Revolution and all its consequences. 'Demmed civil wedding ceremonies required by a miscellany of counter-jumpers,' he snorted.

'Now father, do be reasonable,' Gyles appealed, his patience still holding despite the recent assault upon it. 'It has all come about in a most fortuitous manner. The weddin' is in mid-June, so it misses the Eton and Harrow match at Lord's. It also misses the Court, to which you have been bidden, and likewise Ascot. We will all be back in ample time to cope with everythin' for the Annual Fête. I can still handle the ribbons for you if you wish to do Goodwood in your usual style. Henley is clear too and we are both looking forward to that, so even if you do change your mind and decide after all you would like to be in Scotland for the 12th, it just about sorts out your arrangements.'

'Hrrumph!' snorted his lordship, further frustrated by the inability to find a simple flaw in his son's reasoning. 'Don't mind me, just make what arrangements you see fit. What I would like to know is what any of you think would make a suitable weddin' present for the gel?'

Thankfully grasping at this straw in the hope of reintroducing some amiability into his father's mien, Gyles entered into the debate whole-heartedly, knowing full well that there was nothing his temperamental parent liked more than an orgy of spending and mentally thanking his creator that 'funds were up to a rousin' depletion for this forthcoming weddin'.'

John de Lorme, on being drawn in by the barked-out question 'Hey, John, what's the gel's birthstone?', vouchsafed 'Er... sapphires I think, sir.' He turned to Primrose: 'Isn't it sapphires, m'y dear?' Primrose nodded. 'Pity Rosalind is such a poor horsewoman,' she commented. 'I saw just the mount for her at Tats the other day.' Which set them all off at a tangent discussing Rosemary's seat. This, if the truth were told, left much to be desired.

Eventually, after drumming impatiently upon the table top while Sawby hovered in the background watching him anxiously, Lord Aynthorp banged on the table and said in a roar, 'I shall give her sapphires and diamonds! Sawby order the carriage for nine in the mornin'. I'm going' to London, Cartier's I think, and then perhaps a bit of chinchilla. Nothin' becomes a pretty woman more than a bit of chinchilla,' and so declaring he stomped from the room.

'Phew' said Gyles, 'that was a near thing. He nearly overboiled. Sawby, please may I have some fresh coffee, I am quite exhausted.' Sawby's face creased into something remarkably like a grin. However he only murmured, 'Immediately sir...

Thomas . . .' and the coffee pot was launched upon its journey of replenishment.

'Now for the rest,' said Gyles more temperately, '*if* we can find out what the old man has bought—and *that* should not be too difficult—would it not be a pretty touch for some of us at any rate to contribute? He'll spring a magnificent parure, no doubt whatever about that, but it does leave brooches, earrings, bracelets . . . they don't wear stomachers any more do they, Christine?'

'No . . . they . . . don't,' Christine choked. 'Really Gyles! They went out with Queen Elizabeth! After Gloriana they became the prerogative of wealthy Cits' wives and completely *pas de rigeur*, but, darling, the idea IS a good one, though whoever plumps for the earrings must remember that they should be long ones as Rosemary has a long, graceful neck.'

John intervened. 'I rather thought, Christine,' he said gently, 'that Primrose and I would do a bracelet and a matchin' brooch if that would not be considered gross poachin' upon Gyles' splendid idea. Then we could slip in a cheque of course.'

Lady Marguerite then spoke. 'No one has thought of MY thing,' she exclaimed contentedly, 'so it belongs to me. I shall give the child sapphire pins and diamond pins for her coiffeur and a set of combs too. That pale coffee- and cream-coloured tortoiseshell with a narrow band of diamonds on the one and sapphires on the other, charmin' dontcher think?'

Sawby brought the coffee. They were all enjoying themselves immensely. After all, the majority of them were descended from Julian Lorme which was synonymous for saying they adored spending, even by proxy, almost as much as Lord Aynthorp. Eventually they went their separate ways, so with the breakfast room finally emptied, Sawby and his footmen were at liberty to draw covers and each other for any gleanings on what had actually happened to 'Mr Stephen'.

Sawby told them heavily. 'They're playing this one very close,' he said dolefully, 'very close indeed. Miss Prunella, she did make one attempt last night and was promptly snubbed in no uncertain manner by her ladyship. Since then, not one single word has been uttered on the subject in my presence. It must be a bad one or they would not be so careful!' Then he recalled himself, rapped out an order and followed it with 'Look sharp there and no dawdling, we're behind with our work as it is, with breakfast running close to elevenses and . . . oh drat, that's the White

Drawing Room bell.' His hearing had always been acute, yet although the bell system was below stairs and only lights operated in back corridors on the floors above, Mason appeared in morning pink at the breakfast room door to say, 'The White Drawing Room bell is ringing, Mr Sawby.'

Sawby sent her packing too. The footmen exchanged grimaces and the butler paced off towards the room in question, wondering who on earth was in there at this time of day. From the united chatter he heard, 'Well, I do think Mama we could spare the Sèvres'... an interpolation of 'Coals to Newcastle Aunt'... and the statement... '*I* shall go to Worth this time...' He deduced what he could of these scraps while making his presence known in his own inimitable manner.

'Oh Sawby,' Lady Aynthorp was the first to observe him, 'can you please obtain information for us as to what time boat trains leave Victoria Station for Dover and at what time these trains arrive in Calais? Also I would like to know what allowance for transit is made between train and boat and what delay there is at Calais before the boat train leaves for Paris.'

'Will your ladyship require reserved carriages and if so how many am I to bespeak, milady?' Sawby then wished to know.

'A good question; one carriage should be sufficient, maids and valets to travel separately as usual.'

'Very good, milady. Might I also enquire does your ladyship wish to make a very early start by staying the previous night in London?'

'I am not going, Sawby,' Lady Aynthorp said a trifle tartly. 'Christine, what do you think, my love?'

'Oh, for my part,' said Christine, 'I would stay the night in town as Sawby suggests and then make an early start the next morning. Otherwise it will mean breaking the journey again to spend a night in Paris. That would be delightful for the return journey but I would prefer NOT to arrive for one night in Paris in a state of dishevelment and exhaustion. Will that arrangement satisfy everyone else do you imagine?'

'I do,' said her mother-in-law firmly. 'Then so be it. An early train from Victoria, Sawby!'

Sawby, thus dismissed, made his way slowly down the back stairs. 'The plot thickens,' he muttered. 'New dresses, nights in Paris, private carriage, so that means six of 'em and her leddyship said "valets and maids" so the gentlemen is going too.' Nevertheless he could make little of it and no one above stairs thought fit to enlighten him—as yet.

In fact he did not find out until Christine told Pearson while she was dressing her hair and Pearson—having enquired earnestly if she was permitted to tell the rest of the household staff—came scuttling down the back staircase positively pregnant with the news. She enjoyed a reception somewhat more awesome than she had expected. Palliser flew into a rage at not having been told by her ladyship and Sawby gave Pearson a 'damper' with his well-controlled, 'Oh yes indeed, how very interesting Pearson, now I wonder might I trouble you to take your work into the sewing room?' So saying he hauled up a frilly petticoat from the back of the chair he was occupying. 'I almost banged my hand upon this needle,' he said severely, and held up the offending garment as if it were a dead mouse.

'He's a Vicomte, that's what he is,' said Mrs Parsons shrilly. 'He come here for the Ball last New Year's Eve.' André took hold of the conversation. '*Monsieur le Vicomte de la Coutray,*' he said, 'that is his name. He has a charming *château* in the Loire, now let me recall its name ... a moment please ... ah yes, of course, I have it, it is just outside *Azay-le-Rideau.*'

'A *château,*' repeated Mrs Parsons. 'Isn't that a sort of castle?'

'*Mais oui,* of course it is, and a very famous one too. Not large like this but *tres elègante* and famous.'

'Well, she certainly waited long enough,' observed Miss Palliser acidly. 'Rising twenty-nine, I do declare.'

'Oh no she's not,' snapped Parsons. 'She's past thirty and everyone had thought her quite on the shelf. She's a lucky girl that's what she is. Will you make the cake, Monsieur André?'

André only shrugged. 'Ow do I know? No one has said anything to me.' He feigned indifference. 'I have much to do anyway. After all, they are being married in France where superb *pâtissiers*[1] are available on every hand.'

In fact, Lady Aynthrop was at this precise moment reading a letter from Rosalind in which the girl said: 'We would both like it so very much if André could make our wedding cake. *Belle-mère*[2]—she used it like a pet name—'suggested we should have

[1] Pastrycooks.
[2] Mother-in-law.

two because you know how very different a French wedding-cake is from our own! Do you think it would be possible, dear Grandmama?'

And thus it came about that eventually André took his own cake to *Azay-le-Rideau* where he assembled it before the admiring eyes of the *château's* staff and was permitted to stay and witness the church ceremony. This was impeccably rehearsed. It was likewise beautifully presented, with a full complement of brides-maids and pages in white satin knee breeches being approved and patted by dowagers in huge hats. The happy couple were photographed upon the lawns, photographed at the top of the famous staircase and photographed on the drawing room parquet after which everyone was sent out into the garden to be photographed in one enormous group.

The ripples of the wedding widened and spread leaving behind them the most pleasant memories, innumerable photographs and eventually a commission from Lord Aynthorp to Sir John Lavery.

The wedding photographs, with divers cuttings taken from both French and English magazines, had been for the nth time riffled through by all and sundry that they positively littered the White Drawing Room and drove the servants demented. From them Lord Aynthorp had selected an informal photograph of the happy couple. In it, Rosalind was still wearing her wedding gown. She had laid aside her bouquet. This having been made in what was technically known as a 'shower' spilled down elegantly over an elaborate fountain in the *château's* water garden.

'Y'know, that really is a capital picture,' the old peer exclaimed yet again. 'Alicia just you look at this. I'm more than half a mind to commission some fellah to paint 'em both exactly like this,' and he waved the picture at his wife. 'We could put it in the Long Gallery if it was anything like good. . . . I think I know whom I should get to paint it too. . . . What was the name of that chap who was the rage of the Academy last year? Oh come Alicia, you know perfectly well whom I mean.'

'Yes dear,' she agreed, 'I know I do. But do you not think, my dear Justin, that it would be better for you if you were to recall his name for yourself?'

'Oh very well,' he said crossly. 'Lavenham . . . Lister . . . Lawson . . . Livery . . . damne I've got it!' he shouted tri-umphantly. The noise awoke Marguerite who had been drowsing. 'Gracious me,' she sat up with a start. 'What in the world . . . ?

Oh it's you, Justin. Why do you always have to make such a noise, dear boy?'

'Fine thing,' snapped back the 'dear boy,' 'if I can't make a bit of a racket in my own house. Wake up Meg, I've got something to tell you.' He rubbed his long, heavily veined hands together and looked immensely pleased with himself.

Marguerite took her time. She first put up her hands to her hair. When she had satisfied herself that she was in no state of disorder, she smoothed the silk of her gown and announced, 'If you're as pleased with yourself as you look then we may be sure it has something to do with spendin' . . .'

That dashed him, but only momentarily. 'I'm goin' to have Rosalind and Charles painted by Lavatory, I mean Lavery. Chap got a knighthood and I recall, Sir . . . wait a bit, it's on the tip of my tongue . . . Sir John Lavery, that's the feller's name. He paints women to look like women, feminine, charmin' and graceful and that is more than I can say for some of the work these eccentric lunatics are gettin' on the line. Absolutely scandalous that's what they are!' He paused to draw breath, took a handkerchief from his sleeve and mopped his brow. 'Gad it's hot in here . . . come on Alicia, let us take a turn on the terrace. . . .'

The morning was still fresh and sweet, with the promise of full summer's heat to come. Henry, just down from Oxford for the long Vac, had come down ahead of everyone else, in riding breeches, bolted his breakfast—which annoyed Sawby—and was up and away on his new grey 'Morning Star' while the dew was still bejewelling the paddock grass and sparkling like crystal in the hedgerows. More often than not Lord Aynthorp rode with him, the pair of them mounted and gazed after adoringly by Plum. Then they would canter off side by side, the rapidly soaring sun glinting on the copper head and the white one as they disappeared between the trees.

But this morning Henry rode alone, savouring the incredible freshness of the morning. He cantered delightedly through the surrounding lanes where a film of dust, thrown up by a multiplicity of horses hooves lay like a faint reproach upon the dog roses and the banks pierced by the plumes of foxgloves. Low down among them that probing sun caught crimson as it found tiny wood strawberries playing the modest game of violets in springtime. Once out of the lanes Henry gave the mare her head. . . .

Returning an hour later, walking Morning Star now as they dropped down King Charles' Hill and into the valley, Henry was in a mood of profound content. He tuned in deliberately to the song of summer being chanted by a myriad insects and small birds. He blinked at a dragonfly explosion of colour as it arrowed down upon the river's surface. He reined in to hear the unmistakable tip-tap-tapping of a busy woodpecker. Then he moved downward again more slowly still to see his grandparents, hand in hand strolling in perfect amity between banks of Buddlea bushes; pink, purple, white, these were seemingly weighted down by the burden of perching Peacock butterflies which covered them.

He saw his 'two old ducks' turn towards his Great-Aunt Marguerite's rose garden, caught the drifting scent of old roses, then dismounted smiling at the thought that one day he would be so handfasted . . . with someone.

CHAPTER 17

Growing Up

Figuratively speaking, Nanny was by now reduced to rocking more than ever before. The cause of her frenzied agitation was the fact that 'her' schoolroom and 'her' nursery were being denuded at a pace which put her into a perpetual state of fury. This in turn set up a chain reaction through the nursery wing.

Miss Jones the English governess, generally speaking a tight-mouthed woman of enormous repression, took to muttering, albeit under her breath, 'Really, that woman is becoming impossible!' while Mademoiselle vented her frayed feelings by shrill declarations that *'Vraiement, elle est une monstre'*,[1] secure in the knowledge that Nanny still did not understand a word of French. Unfortunately the children did. Those within earshot passed the word on and soon 'Cave, the monster's coming!' became the new nursery warning. The nurserymaid and nursemaid, driven to a state of scuttling panic, simply exerted every nerve to become invisible lest the wrath vent itself upon them. This, of course, it did to such an extent that half their time was spent in the broom cupboard whispering and clutching one another. As there is normally a sharp demarcation between nursemaids and the nurserymaids who were mere floor polishers and emptiers of slops, it spoke for the state of crisis that they could share confidences together in a rather smelly cupboard.

When all was said and done the whole turmoil stemmed from the simple fact that the children were growing up. Already Stephanie was leaving the schoolroom to spend a 'finishing' year in France. Already Ralph had passed beyond Nanny's jurisdiction to be elevated to dining with the adults of the family. He was now in his last year at Harrow. Nevertheless, it had ever been so with Nanny. She played Canute with monotonous regularity. The older she became the more jealous she was of her authority over

---

[1] Really, she is a monster.

her charges and the more reluctance she showed towards handing them on to the next stage in their development.

On this occasion the exodus was enough to depress anyone in her position. Of the nursery complement there would only be three left to her: Christine's youngest Richard, now nearly four and a half and, according to his Papa, 'more in need of a lion tamer than a Nanny'; Henrietta's Gilbert, born within a few weeks of Richard but very much under his fat thumb, and 'that little faun' as Christine described Henrietta's Lucien, already seven and not evincing one single attribute which could, even remotely, be expected to help him through the early, dog days of any small boy's experiences when sent to his first boarding school. Nanny worked herself into a terrible state over Lucien's impending doom. 'Simply not suited,' she would snap. 'Poor little chap, it's not his fault he was born gentle! Why it would break his little heart to be taken away from his Nan, wouldn't it, my precious?' and she would gather the little figure into her arms and rock with him, crooning, 'Poor little Lucien.' Lucien merely snuggled closer and went to sleep, looking so totally defenceless and frail that this added fuel to the fire of her wrath. All of which was totally abortive since Lucien suffered from a vague 'weakness of the chest' which ensured him a tutor called Mr Sissingham to whom he became devoted.

The schoolroom brood *was* being denuded. Ninian and James —The Inseparables—both rising sixteen and at Harrow, now occupied their own rooms for the holidays and the most Nanny saw of *them* was when they leaned round the door to say 'Mornin' Nanny' and banged the door shut again without waiting for her return greeting. 'Gone!' she wailed, rocking furiously after one such brief encounter, and 'Gone!' she repeated sepulchrally, much as the despairing mother in *East Lynne*—which she had seen in Colchester Town Hall—had cried 'Dead...and never called me Mother!' at the bedside of her dying child. She had also overheard them clattering down the stairs and referring to the nursery wing as 'those old women and all those silly kids', which only went to show how depraved they had become without her influence!

The two boys were going through an awkward age, neither fish, fowl nor good red herring as John de Lorme had observed sadly. They were not old enough to come in to dinner whereas James' elder brother, Ralph, had been 'promoted', was rising eighteen and 'no end of a swell' according to the younger boys. Not that the lack of promotion worried the Inseparables. They dined in a small, rather nebulous room called by the family the 'In Transit' room. Here, when the covers were drawn they were endlessly occupied, studying horses, talking horses, poring over records, discussing form. They missed nothing, in their own opinions, and were no trouble either to themselves or anyone else. They did evince a marked tendency to wilt in the 'dog days' between the last meet in April and the first cubbing in September, but then there was cricket which cheered them up immensely, more records to study, more averages to work out and, in the last resort, W. G. Grace to talk about—a subject which was of course endless.

Thus there remained for the Schoolroom only two Lormes: Andrea, now twelve, and Anne, ten; while the Delahayes contributed only one of their children, Rosalind, who was now thirteen. Stephanie was at this moment poised for departure to France where she was going in the care of Mademoiselle who would take her annual holiday at the same time and thus be enabled to visit her country quite economically since in these circumstances of chaperonage she would not be required to meet the cost of the journey. The St Johns only contributed one girl to Nanny's indirect rule, little Lucy at thirteen still a tiny child of exquisite proportions who somehow still managed, like a deferential consort, to remain two paces behind Lucien wherever he went and from whom she could not bear to be separated for an instant. Had she fallen out, the situation would merely have been reversed. It would then have been Lucien who trotted off on his remarkably small feet crying, 'Lucy ... Lucy ... Mam'selle, have you seen Lucy for me, please?'

It may well be imagined with what enthusiasm Stephanie viewed the prospect of being 'finished' ready for her presentation and coming out and at the hands of her French cousins who occupied a grand *château* not far removed from Chartres. Indeed, Chartres was her only consolation. In the weeks between being told 'her fate', as she called it, and being 'despatched for polishing' she wept on to the *petit point* of her *prie dieu* and, in the words of her rumbustious cousin Ralph, 'flogged that rosary silly!' Chartres—the rose windows, the many little chapels where she could pray, pay for and light candles, these were her only consolation.

All Nanny could see was that *her* nursery was down to three, and *her* schoolroom reduced to five—and that to be four by the morning!

The girls' routine was in no way disrupted during Mademoiselle's absence. Immediately after breakfast there would be backboards for one hour, supervised by Nanny. All three girls were each strapped to a hated backboard and there they would sit being read to by whomever of the 'ladies' was disposed to help out in this manner during what Nanny, of course, regarded as Mademoiselle's defection. Usually it was Christine who read to them in French. Then the English governess, who had by that time prepared their papers, would take them in the three Rs, having released them from their backboards until after luncheon. At any sounds of protest she merely drew in her mouth and said sharply, 'All young ladies use backboards. No young lady should slouch!' After luncheon it was backboards again while Miss Jones read a chapter of Mrs Markham's *History of England* and questioned the girls thereafter on the subject matter contained therein.

Then, released once again from the bondage of those backboards, they all went for 'a nice bracing walk in the grounds'. During this exercise they were required to supply both the Latin and common names of such trees, shrubs, alpines and herbaceous plants as they passed. Sometimes, for a treat, they were allowed to identify in the great stove houses, but this was rare, for the atmosphere was considered 'coddling' and 'young ladies must be bracee or where would they be for glowing, rosy cheeks?' This rhetorical question always left them mumchance, for who indeed could tell an English governess where they *would* be!

On returning they toiled away at watercolours, poker-work, beaded book-markers or sticking shells on to small boxes or picture frames. After tea, Miss Jones doled out religious instruction until five-thirty when they were permitted to pursue Art again, of the needle-work variety, samplers or netting purses, tatting or knot- or crewel-work, or their favourite—poker-work which produced a horrible smell of singed velvet. Only Rosalind was allowed to work on past the hour of seven. The rest were bundled off to get into their flannel or calico nightgowns, brush their hair and teeth, say their prayers, and climb into bed.

It was curious that with all the rocking and all her percipient monologues to Rose, Nanny never saw fit to query the logic of the work entrusted to her as training for the girls' futures. Born as they were into the privileged classes at a peak period of indulgence, the pursuit of pleasure with elegance and a slavish obsession with 'fashion', the woman who was primarily responsible for preparing her charges for entry into the brittle, sophisticated world of adults, never spared a single thought for the inadequacies of the training which she supervised. The one provision that was subscribed to wholeheartedly was *languages*. Miss Jones had been selected to teach in these later years simply because long sojourns in both Germany and Italy—always with the very best families—had made her proficient in both languages. With Mademoiselle safeguarding the children's French, this was sound enough and far more so than the rest of their curriculum might lead anyone to suspect.

Indeed it was eloquent that arithmetic was taught in the Lorme schoolroom by means of household books. 'Gentlewomen always inspect their household books in order to keep a Very Firm Control on Expenditure.' This was one of Miss Jones' favourite dictums. She prided herself upon being extremely practical and, though she held the private view that Stephanie, for one, would, like herself never marry; none the less, Miss Jones handed her pupil on for France to 'finish', satisfied that the girl could add up simple columns of figures, subtract and multiply adequately to meet any demands of household and Charity causes. The times were the educational measuring rods.

A dancing master came regularly to the Castle. The footmen rolled back the rugs in the Music Room. The music master with whom the morning had been spent at piano lessons, seated himself at the Bechstein grand and prepared to play. The girls in bronze dancing shoes, criss-crossed at the ankles with brown elastic, the boys in patent leather pumps and wearing gloves, presented themselves, and at each session they were all first taken though the Court Curtsey and the 'Royal Acknowledgement', as the fussy little dancing master styled the Royal bow. Then the sounds of the waltz, the polka and finally the gallop would be heard by staff and Family alike as they passed through the corridors.

The brood were not, it is feared, a great source of pride and joy to their music master. They were not musical, as their greying tutor confided to his equally greying wife when returned from the Castle. 'But, my dear, we must not mind at all because apart from the fees, which are most generous...' They both thought about these with veneration for a few moments, and then the little music master's voice dropped steeply as he added, 'it is all worth while because of little Master Lucien. That dear little boy has a Gift. He is truly remarkable for his age.'

But Nanny knew nothing of this. So she began rocking and brooding again about her lost babies: Ralph St John, coming up to his eighteenth birthday taller than his father Eustace by half an inch, and James, the younger by two years, already giving every indication of being as tall if not taller. So did his inseparable companion both at home and at school, Ninian, the fifteen-year-old second son of Christine and Gyles. The two, who were seldom seen apart, also bore a surprising resemblance to one another and had recently had another nickname attached to them —David and Jonathan.

They were a straightforward, uncomplicated pair, of totally similar tastes. Indeed, as Lady Marguerite had commented in an unusual mood of criticism, 'When they are not fishin', ridin', talkin' about horses, soldierin', shootin' or eatin' you can be assured they are asleep.'

Having worked through their Harrow salad days, the pair were beginning to enjoy themselves. Both played in the School Corps Band. To do this together had been no mean feat as there was less than nothing of the musician about James. Ninian was all right because he blew, as he put it, 'a nifty trombone,' but James had set to work and had finally managed to convince his music master that he was a dedicated neophyte of the euphonium. Thus he marched with Ninian regardless of the fact that even on this instrument he could only blow the open notes.

They played the Corps out upon a day's exercise. They played them back. In the lengthy interim they withdrew with discretion and celerity to the local public house, which was of course out of bounds. They had already cozened the landlady. She was a comfortable soul with a ready laugh and a motherly *tendresse* towards juvenile wrong-doers. The moment she spotted them coming round to her side door she whipped them into a small room at the back where she shut them in with a terrible photographic enlargement of her late husband, a table with a crimson plush cloth upon it, two pillow-filled, broken-spring armchairs, a cabinet filled with improbable presents from Brighton, Worthing and other southern seaside resorts, and a foul-mouthed parrot whose vocabulary the boys were steadily enlarging. Here she supplied them with food and drink. They sank pints of ale, sprawled about, talked 'horse', munched huge wedges of pie and felt 'hellishly grown-up'.

Ralph, of course, was as far removed from them as a general is from the rookie. He had already achieved the Upper Sixth, become Head of his House, and in his last year a Monitor. He was also proficient at many forms of what he termed mockingly 'le bloody sport' so was able to discard his white straw hat and wear a speckled one instead. In fact, sartorially, he was most impressive—at least to his fellow Harrovians. Being a 'blood' too, and a member of 'Phil', he could wear a bow tie with his school dress, build up a collection of extremely fancy waistcoats, have the lapels of his coat recovered in silk, stroll about with his hands in his pockets and wear patent leather shoes. There was already a touch of the patronising about him. Even so, he had a capacity for detachment which enabled him to stand aside from himself and grin ironically at his own as well as everyone else's idiosyncracies.

His study was always extremely tidy, unlike his brother's and his cousin's, both of which resembled cells into which some demented dervish had flung half the Army and Navy Stores' Sports Department. Ralph hung Aubrey Beardsleys on his walls and installed a set of very handsome bookshelves. He covered them with hand-printed linen wrappers in the virulent mixture of greenery-yallery papers which came directly from Mr William Morris' emporium. He had a food cupboard which was a nice piece of oak, box-fronted and fitted neatly into one corner. The Inseparables had a Grub Corner.

In Ralph's cupboard were to be found such delicacies as Patum Peperum, Messrs Fortnum and Mason's Bloater Paste, Bath Oliver biscuits and a stone jar of Port-Fed Stilton. Such feeding would have upset his grandfather mightily.

The Inseparables stood their half-empty pots of jam on the floor, put butter, in its papers, too near to the fire, so that melting layers of it had dripped into the disreputable old rug which was their only floor covering. An opened tin of crusting Marie Elizabeth sardines was frequently seen mildewing on the mantelshelf. An opened packet of Garibaldi biscuits ('Squashed Flies') could likewise be seen all too often with its contents spilling down a bookshelf which was crammed with lurid cowboy literature. The fireplace was filled with crumbs, a bent toasting fork and a tin of cocoa. Moreover, there was absolutely nowhere to sit as all three chairs—wicker, and already most unsteady—were piled high with books and low-grade magazines, leavened only by *The Field* and *Punch*.

The pair treated their fags leniently, cuffed them rarely, and gave them little to do except roast chestnuts in winter and brew up endless pots of tea.

It would have been illuminating to any observer to note the contrasting ways in which the three boys spent the last hour of the holidays. Ralph strolled off through the topiary and down to the edge of the lake, where he took a small copy of Mr Swinburn's verse from his coat pocket and settled down to read on a stone seat. Nanny observed him from the barred nursery windows paying little heed to the colours on the far side of the lake. She merely grunted, 'Typical'. It meant nothing to her that the Coral Tree was coiled with necklaces of coral masquerading as blossoms or that a precocious *Quercus*, doubtless exhausted with the summer's intense heat, was hanging out red leaves as brilliant as the seed pods of the *Iris Foetidissama* which stood like redcoats in an unbroken phalanx against the bank edge. The great Swamp Cypress, clearly exhausted too, was flying the flag of early autumn and making itself into a pink backcloth for the rest while every leaf of *Salix* still wept clear green due primarily to the fact that it grew with its roots implanted in the water. A company of water birds were disputing on the surface of the lake. To complete the scene, two black swans sailed majestically into their midst. Ralph read on, equally oblivious and, had the truth been told, totally disinterested.

The Inseparables, on the other hand, catapulted down the staircase shouting, 'I'll beat you to it' and 'Oh no you won't, and skidding on the marble as they wrenched the front doors open. They raced towards the stables to spend their last hour with Plum and their respective mounts amid the comforting ambience of leather and brass-cleaner, hay and manure.

They were, in fact, in a state bordering upon the ecstatic. They had just been informed by their respective parents that YES they were to go on to Sandhurst. Both sat themselves down, panting, on the three-legged stools Plum extended to them. Then they looked around them with obvious approval, taking in every cherished detail, hearing their favourite sounds: the scrunching of hay, the fretting of hooves in the boxes, the rattle of harness and the hissing of a groom with a straw between his teeth as he currycombed their grandfather's black 'Star'. Then they told Plum their good news.

'Well now,' he beamed, clearly delighted, 'all I can say to you young gentlemen is that we'll be 'aving a couple of Generals in the family before we can say knife. Mrs Plum won't harf be de-lighted too, that I'll dare swear. 'Earty congrats, Mr James and Mr Ninian.'

They had receded irretrievably and above the rest from Nanny's jurisdiction.

CHAPTER 18

Henry

The next morning Henry came down when only two sleepy scullerymaids were about. He was in a thoroughly bad temper, almost snatched the reins from Plum, returned his greeting with a curt 'Mornin'', flung himself into the saddle and straightway put the mare at the white picket fence. Clearing it by a foot and more, he galloped off recklessly between the trees, crouching jockey-like in the stirrups and using his crop.

'Now what in 'tarnation's got into him this morning?' Plum muttered, scratching his grizzled poll in bewilderment and gazing after the rapidly disappearing figure. ' 'Taint like 'im,' he told himself. Then he cussed one of the luckless stable boys and stomped off into his harness room to take it out on some girths.

Henry took Morning Star up King Charles' Hill again, then gave the mare her head over the two-mile saddleback beyond. Below him spread the Lorme lands, dwarfed by the altitude to Lilliputian size. He drew rein, dismounted, turned the mare to graze and flung himself on the grass overlooking the wide valley below.

There it all was. There was the one-time forest where it had all begun with Henri de Lorme riding through the trees attended by three of his men. He, too, had felt the strong desire for solitude all those centuries ago. He had bade the men fall back awhile and leave him to his thoughts until he should call.

Thus it was that after trotting peaceably along a tranquil ride Henri had encountered a badger crouched by the bole of a pine tree. When he observed with what unruffled calm the little bright-eyed beast stared at him unwinkingly, he had marvelled, 'This must indeed be a place of peace, little beast, since you evince no fear of man!' And he had leaned down in the saddle to peer closer. 'Nay, little badger, thou art not afraid,' he laughed. As if in confirmation the badger stared back. Then, after a small pause, he rose slowly and ambled off into the greenery at a gentle, padding pace. At this performance Henri had let out a great shout of laughter. It had brought his men at a hand gallop, fearful lest some ill had befallen him, only to see him wave an imperious, gloved hand and declare, 'Here will I build my castle and here will I raise my sons!'

He had done just that. For nine hundred and twenty-one years, Henri's Castle had stood. Not without change and not without damage, admittedly, but the foundations had remained and the chapel where crusaders spent their vigils and, over the centuries, fugitives had claimed sanctuary below the altar which concealed the cavity where the Casket and the Book lay cached. They were still there, a rusted and flaking leather and iron tribute to continuance and a record of sorrows in cyphers.

The rising sunlight sparkled on a pane of glass reminding Henry of another survival ... Archers' Viaduct, the stone corridor with its slit windows through which hails of arrows had, in the distant past, rained down upon foolhardy invaders. Now it was a place in which the Maypole was stored. In it, generation after generation of Sawbridge children had played during bad weather when their mothers were driven by their uproar to take down the enormous iron key from its nail in the Sawbridge kitchen, unlock the heavy wooden door and shoo them in.

The original towers had fallen too, but they were restored. The original Guard Houses had gone; in their stead were cottages on either side of the old drawbridge, now permanently down even as the moat was now permanently dry.

There too, drowsing serenely in the morning air, were three of the home farms with their rosy roofs and outhouses, survivors of the time when all was enclosed within the outer walls even as, as the very beginning, the builders and their families and beasts were fenced in for protection against attackers in immediate proximity to the rising wooden structure which was to be the first Castle.

Loop and chain ... loop and chain ... the patterns overlocked each other. Overlooking the ancient Lorme valley Henri could also see the distant, diminished figures of smocked drovers turning beasts out to pasture. *It would all be his some day!* First his grandfather, to whom his mind automatically attached the word 'splendid', would go and with him, Henry thought sadly, a light would be extinguished which could never be lit again.

Then in the natural progression of time, his father Gyles would be called to take the Swan's Path.

Henry knew enough of Gyles de Lorme to comprehend to what degree his father played himself down in his present situation. He needed no telling as to how Gyles would grow in stature and unfold his released self when Lord Aynthorp was no longer there to throw the long shadows of his powerful personality over his son. Henry also accepted without question not only what his father was doing, but he completely understood how he was motivated. He could not be counted among the foolish who imagined that his father was crushed by the domination which the old autocrat undoubtedly imposed on lesser characters and was well aware that Gyles, who both appreciated and enjoyed his rumbustious papa, had long ago decided that the old man should never be opposed by competition from him. Gyles Henry de Lorme was well content to be blown by the totally unpredictable winds of his papa's explosive temperament. Likewise, Henry's mother was content that it should be so. Both his parents shared allegiance to each other, Lord Aynthorp and Castle Rising. His mind added a rider on that crisp dawning, that neither Dante and Beatrice, nor Pelleas and Melisand had anything for each other by comparison with the love which existed between his parents.

He then faced some totally unacceptable facts. One day Gyles would become Lord Aynthorp. Certainly that might happen at any time now, but beyond that day, stretching into who knew what decades of time lay the summons for Gyles to make that transition which men call 'death'. *Then it would be his turn.* He, Henry Gyles de Lorme, would become Lord Aynthorp.

The boy suddenly imagined, as he lay above the valley chewing on a blade of grass, that he could glimpse the years ahead. It was a false imagining, totally dissimilar from the seeing forward which had come to the Lady Mathilde on her deathbed. He would have thrown his head back and laughed aloud if anyone had quoted the lines of the late poet laureate Alfred, Lord Tennyson to him: 'The old order changeth, yielding place to new, and God fulfils Himself in many ways, lest one good custom should corrupt the world . . .'

He would have stared incredulously at any prophet who foretold that all would not always be as it was now. In fact, he had an unshakeable conviction of two things; it just lacked one to make all perfect! Through his grandfather's stewardship and his father's in turn, Henry thought he *knew*, past all fantasties and imaginings, that the years ahead would be as they had been already and that both his father and he would in turn consider it their sacred trust to ensure those years remained unchanged. They would be good ones, privileged of course, but he felt also that a sufficiency of awareness and gratitude was enough to safeguard a privilege which, after all, was his natural birthright!

He saw himself in those unformed years ahead participating in what he termed 'interestin' ploys': Master of Hounds; presiding magistrate; host to the distinguished, laying on fishing in the well-stocked river which lazed through Lorme land; standing at the foot of the great staircase to receive at balls, dinners and countless other celebrations; ordering the pattern for shoots; keeping the game book, recording the memorable bags obtained from the expertly maintained stocks of pheasant and grouse, with an occasional woodcock as well; rough-shooting with his tenant farmers for hare, rabbit, pigeon; playing polo—perhaps for England—at Ranelagh; taking the 'ribbons' when the family carriage went to Lord's; riding winners in local 'over-the-sticks' meetings; doling out gifts to his retainers at Christmastide; reading the lesson in church; presenting donations, being Lord Bountiful, for, over and above all the symbols of his pleasure— such as velvety tennis courts, fine hounds yelping in kennels, even finer horseflesh fretting in stalls, an abundant supply of foxes in his spinneys, first-rate shooting and fishing, a small yacht at anchor in the Solent, and in town, his many friends—lay the certainty of an endless supply of 'the ready' to oil the wheels unendingly.

It was not a bad picture. Yet he scowled at it. How could it be complete if the shadowy vision at his side playing hostess were not Petula Danement? This was the crux of his ill-humour, the apogee of his discontent. All this dramatised envisaging—natural enough to the manner in which he had been raised—was as nothing to him, he decided, if Petula would not share it with him.

The prime cause of all this highly-coloured inward drama lay in the fact that Petula had once again refused him. Last night, on the terrace in the moonlight, when she was looking 'positively stunnin'', he had again asked her to marry him. She had even refused to take him seriously. She kept repeating, 'Not yet, Henry ... I am not ready to make up my mind ... I have my reasons . . .' and then she had danced away like some 'demmed elusive will-o-the-wisp'. He had followed her—a fool he must have looked too, he thought gloomily, as some confounded whipper-snapper from the other side of the county wandered out (and he still at that lousy Eton!) and she had gone off with him, laughing.

She had accused him of not being sufficiently grown-up to talk to her of marriage. God's boots! but he was twenty and in under ten months would attain his majority. He thought about that, discarding the chewed grass and tugging up another from the turf on which he lay. All those celebrations! Well, if he had to have them he jolly well wanted to become engaged to Petula by then and a fat chance he stood of that happening if her present attitude continued!

That night, for the first time in his young life, Henry could not sleep. The moon, slanting through the partially drawn-back curtains which he had pulled aside when opening his windows, found him sitting upright, hands around his knees, still scowling. What possible right had that slip of a girl to tell him he was not grown-up? Then, quite suddenly, his conscience began to prick. Well, was he? he pondered; in sex . . . war . . . authority . . . administration? He could not earn a penny if he were suddenly called upon to do so. But then, he reasoned, he was not expected to be able to earn a living. He had not been raised to it any more than had his friends. His father and theirs provided each of them with ample allowances. He and his 'set' would inherit 'a packet' apiece. It was simply not expected of him, so Pet could not be referring to that.

Then sex. Did she expect him to be 'grown-up' in that sense? Surely not, since properly brought-up young gentlewomen never thought in such terms in relation to the young men they were permitted to know socially. Henry acknowledged ruefully that this was just as well, since his experience could be narrowed down to an abortive attempt to seduce a little thing he had picked up at the Empire when slightly tight. Even that ended in nothing because when it came to the point, the smell of her patchouli had revolted him so much he had just thrust some money at her and 'done a bunk'.

There remained simply Lady Pam, lovely, worldly, slightly avid, but very careful Lady Pam. Thirty-five if she was a day and married to that 'crusty old general feller who has been overseas for the past two years'. She had smoothed the primrose path for him all right . . . stayed at the Castle during a houseparty, wooed Henry out on to the terrace, permitted him to fondle her hands, patted his face and made a rendezvous with him at her house in Curzon Street. In the end he had escorted her to the Ritz to supper where he found her taken up and surrounded by her friends. She had fobbed him off with some pretty little vacuous debutante but had slipped a note into his hand which he had read under cover of his table napkin. It said, '123 Curzon Street. Come in a hansom and send it away.' He had of course taken the lure and found little to regret in so doing. He knew full well that any of his aunts—excepting his Great-Aunt Prue—indeed his grandmother, would have approved such a manner of obtaining his sexual emancipation. She had been sweet, skilled, exciting, perhaps a little frightening in her appetites, but for a few weeks he had been enthralled and then she had gone away on a cruise with their roving-eyed Monarch and he had returned to Oxford . . . to forget her until this moment.

Well then, 'command'. He could order the servants about and that was the end of the matter. He had never assumed authority in anything and as for administration, well, he had not the 'foggiest notion' of what it was about. Here he pulled up short. Was this the clue to Pet's reluctance? that he played about Lorme land and Lorme's Castle without sparing a thought as to how it all came about and how it all ran so smoothly and seemingly effortlessly. He was suddenly and alarmingly engulfed in panic. Just suppose something happened to his father? God forbid it should, but just supposing, what then would be his case?

As the moon's strength waned, so he became more and more convinced that this was what Pet was thinking about. It could be understood that she was reluctant to tie herself to anyone who did not show the slightest interest in the management of an estate which would one day be his. He made a valiant effort to put himself in the girl's place and see how it looked from there. Things would surely fall apart in the hands of an owner who had not any idea as to how his property should be run. Come to that— he reverted to his own thinking—it was a pretty shoddy state of affairs anyway and one which would have to be remedied.

He resolved there and then, staring at the paling windows, that he would, and must, become a man of purpose like his father and grandfather whose personal pleasures and indulgencies had never been allowed to come between their responsibilities. He thought how alert his grandfather was still and he decided this was because he had disciplined and educated himself throughout his long life. His memory was devilish sharp too, no doubt to the fact that he had kept it active, so that even now both mind and body, so to speak, had never been given the chance to become stiff in the joints. He probed around the evidence at his command and so stiffened his own intentions that now the vexed question remained, *whom would he consult*—his father or his grandfather? Suddenly the sleep which had so far evaded him came down like Scottish mist over his mind. He straightened his knees. He drew up the bedclothes. He turned on one side and surrendered himself to sleep, only one thought remaining through the drowsiness which now claimed him: 'Oh lor! There's such a fearful lot to learn!'

Certain as he was that he had found the clue to Petula's reluctance, his own discoveries through the night hours had so wrought upon him that somewhere in his thinking, the fearful sense of loss of her had gone. Instead, he began to envisage himself travelling hopefully towards a fulfilment of his new found purposes. Murmuring, 'just ... about ... the ... eighth ... labour ... of Sisyphus,' Henry at length slept.

Later that day he rediscovered that the sting had quite gone from 'Pet's last turn down'. Instead he was filled with eagerness to come to grips with 'the Sisyphus job'. He was conscious of a stimulation through his nocturnal discoveries, a genuine eagerness to tackle the responsibilities which both his grandfather and father had mastered so successfully. By noon he had also made his decision concerning whom he would approach. He now saw that it was only right and proper to go to his father, so then and there he hurried through the corridors and put his hand to the door of Gyles' office. Twice he ducked the issue, snatched back his hand and bolted, but finally he managed to get the door open, stick his copper head around it and ask diffidently, 'Are you very busy sir ... ? I wondered if you could possibly spare me a few moments.'

Gyles put down his pen. 'Come in, by all means,' he answered cheerfully. 'I was wanting an excuse to have a break and fill m'y pipe.' He drew an old pewter tobacco jar towards him, enquired

casually, 'Care for a fill?' and appraised his son. He saw a small
nerve twitching under the boy's left eye and registered the
thought, 'Whatever he's come for I'll lay a shade of odds it's
serious.'

Henry refused the tobacco. 'No thank you, sir, I haven't
acquired the pipe habit yet. Doubtless I shall come to it.' Then
he sat down on the edge of a chair.

'Well, there is plenty of time,' Gyles replied mildly. 'Now tell
me what I may do for you?'

'Oh lor,' said Henry so forlornly that his father laughed.

'Oh come now!' he exclaimed between puffs at the newly
tamped pipe. 'If you could see your face, m'y dear boy! It
cannot be as bad as that I am assured.'

'Bad enough, sir.' Henry eased a finger around his collar which
suddenly seemed to be choking him, then added, 'Oh well—neck
or nothing does it, so here goes . . .'

He had already made up his mind to tell everything, so now he
began with Petula, his love for her and her persistent refusals. It
made a fairly long tale. He would, of course, have been speechless
with astonishment had his father been unwise enough to tell him
that he was perfectly aware of it all. After the initial exchange
of opinions with Henry's mother after the last ball, Gyles had
made it his business to keep a sharp eye on 'the pair of them' and
he had soon seen in which direction the wind blew. Indeed the
more he saw of the two together, the more inclined he became to
welcoming such a girl as Petula into the Family, but, as the rack
would not have forced him to speak of any of this, poor Henry
blundered on, making, as he thought, 'a pretty poor job of it'
which was not at all how his father viewed these abortive
revelations.

Henry eventually concluded the first part by saying, 'You see,
sir, I wouldn't've minded being turned down in the ordinary way.
I should even less have minded bein' asked to wait. What foxed
me so completely was that Pet simply wouldn't give me any
reason, that's what's been goadin' me. Then I thought, last night
that is . . . I couldn't sleep and the idea came to me . . . Pet's got
a remarkable head on her shoulders . . . not like these silly,
giggling gels at balls and garden parties . . . and I think what has
happened is she has seen I'm nothin' but a silly loafer . . .
sponging on you and Grandfather . . . doin' nothin' to contribute.

I've been doin' some pretty hard thinkin' since then and ... well ... I hope you wont misunderstand this, sir, but ... er ... you and Grandfather won't ... can't always be here, and I fell to thinkin' what I would do if anythin' suddenly happened to you both ... I mean ... well, do you realise that I don't know a single damn thing about the administration ... will you believe me, sir, I don't even know how much you pay anyone? It's shockin'.'

'Oh no,' said Gyles, inwardly rejoicing, outwardly quite unruffled, 'it is not nearly so shockin as m'y eldest son buryin' me before my time!'

Henry looked up sharply, encountered the disarming twinkle in his father's eyes and grinned sheepishly. 'Oh all right, sir, rib me if you must,' the quick colour flooded to his face. 'I never ... you know perfectly well. ...'

'Oh do relax,' said Gyles. 'I know perfectly well what you mean, but a chap can take himself too seriously, y'know. I can assure you that I haven't the slightest intention of poppin' off in an untimely fashion. I fully expect to reach fourscore and ten, as your Grandfather is all set fair for doin' if I am any judge, and as so many of our line have done already. What *is* important however,' his voice changed, became graver, 'is that you thought all this out on your own bat. You accepted the existence of a responsibility which I had planned to let lie fallow until you were twenty-five. I had worked it out on the lines that you could play around a bit, enjoy your time at Oxford, have your colt frolics, before settlin' down to management and marriage. But ...' he held up one hand, 'just let me finish. IF you are serious about Petula, and I can tell you you will meet with absolutely no opposition from your mother or me on *that* score, then I agree it is time for you to begin examining the reins you will have to handle.'

Henry muttered, 'I never dreamcd ... oh I say, sir, that's absolutely splendid. ... Oh I'm sure if Pet knows this, she would change her mind and take me. ...'

'Hey,' Gyles cut clean across this rapture, 'rein in a bit m'lad and *think first*. If you've got any gumption you will not tell her. I recommend not a word to Petula or anyone else. I'll see to it that your grandfather knows both what's in the wind with the gel *and* the estate, but play the lass a bit, as you would play a temperamental filly. Let her think you have been severely rebuffed and have taken it to heart. Let her make the next move. There's precious little difference y'know between finely bred fillies and women of similar class. I take it that from what you have said you are offerin' me a singularly welcome helpin' hand. That is it, is it not?' He looked at his son a touch sharply, determined to press him hard.

Henry met that sharp look steadily. 'Yes, of course,' he answered.

Both were silent for a moment until Gyles resumed, 'Then I suggest that you and I rough out some sort of plan of campaign together, that we follow it through until you come down from Oxford and then we can go over the ground more fully and start puttin' you in the picture properly.' He lapsed into silence yet again and after a moment or two Henry finished for him.

'From staff wages to thatchin' run-down cottages and from general administration to Stephen and that woman's allowance, the whole boilin' lot sir, I have everythin' to learn.'

'That's about the size of it,' Gyles nodded.

Henry stood up and walked to the windows. 'It's what I want sir,' he said.

'Then come over here for a start,' Gyles rose, 'and take a look at some of these maps on this wall.' He led the boy over to a series with which the window-facing wall was covered. 'Here are the outlines to our property—marked in red. The blue ones which lie inside them show how much land Henri of Normandy had from the King and thus you see we can determine exactly how our estates have grown. Once the majority was deep forest land where wild boar rootled and deer ran free. Then decimation began and now the seeing forward in terms of forestry is a prime responsibility of ours. What we take down, what falls through age, must be replaced, for one of our most valuable assets is our timber. The inroads upon it are heavy. This is why you see so many small patches filled in with dots denoting where new plantations have been made. Here are the outlines of our property, showing also the various dwelling on our lands, farms, lodge houses, cottages, barns, the villages all marked very small on this one, but I will show you others in which they are visible in fullest detail.'

'And we own the whole village?' Henry queried, peering fascinated.

'No,' Gyles smiled. 'We own 'em both from pub to cemetery,

from cottage to church to village hall, so each and every one is
in our charge for maintenance and keeping in sound heart. Like
the land, and that applies to both Upper and Lower Aynthorp.
You will find the records of both in Morant's *History of Essex*,
and in the Doomsday Book. You know already that when William
came Henri was given the land. The ownership has come clean
down since then to us. We are an old family as families go and
I like to believe we are as lusty as ever still. Now come here and
look at this one, it is interestin' too.' He moved again to the left-
hand wall, this time to where a series of small sections were
marked out showing the fluctuations, the losses and deprivations
which came as the family's fortunes rose and fell.

'And all linked with the stories of our runts?' Henry muttered.

'Not entirely. Remember the rising periods were not solely due
to runt maraudings,' Gyles reminded him, 'nor the falls to runt
depletions. Look at it this way, we have had our runts, agreed,
but we have a pretty distinguished record through the centuries
as well, which is the root cause of all our closing up and concealing
the blots made upon our invisible escutcheons by people like
Patch, Butcher and the abominable Justin only a few years back.
Now come and look at this one. . . .'

When, a few moments later, Christine opened the office door, she
discovered her husband and eldest son rump-ended upon the
floor, poring over yet another plan. As she entered, 'Here it is!'
Henry shouted, 'right on our boundary line.'

'Here is what?' enquired Christine smilingly. 'I have come to
inform you that the luncheon gong will be sounding any moment.'

'Oh drat the luncheon gong!' Gyles looked up smilingly.

'Oh listen, Mama,' interjected Henry, 'it is so colourful and
sort of romantic. . . .' Eyebrows were raised and glances exchanged
between husband and wife. Gyles' expression reassured Christine.

'What is it, my love?' she enquired of her son.

Henry read out to her: 'Upon this spot was found and taken
up a beam of vast girth and great antiquity which had been
preserved in peat, but nevertheless was still soft with decay. It
was brought to the surface with great care. Then it was discovered
that words had been carved deep upon it. When it had been
treated by experts, the words upon the beam were found to read
'Henri de Lorme won this field off Charles Edward Danement
in fair. . . .' Henry broke off, 'This bit,' he explained, 'is in Latin,

Mama, so I'll have to slow up.' He returned to his translating. 'In fair battle, no,' he corrected himself, 'in fair combat.' He lifted his head again, 'since when it has been Lorme land, sir?'

'It still is,' Gyles told him drily.

'Gosh,' said Henry, profoundly impressed. 'Where is the beam now, sir?'

'In the custody of a friend of mine who has great repute in such matters at the British Museum. He assures me that we can put it into our small museum—you do not know about that project yet, I fancy—and keep it for a further thousand years under glass, after the very special treatment being given to it currently.'

All Henry could say was again, 'Oh gosh,' so Christine, to whom the sound of the luncheon gong did not fall upon deaf ears, begged leave to inform the enmeshed pair that Grandmama would be by this time processing towards the dining room and would they kindly put themselves in some order forthwith and without further delay.

Henry pelted ahead to wash, his father and mother followed on, giving Gyles sufficient time to murmur to her, 'The best mornin' of m'life except the day I married you, m'love. . . . I will tell you everything later.'

CHAPTER 19

Petula

The relationship between the eighty-two-year-old peer and his youngest neighbour, Petula Danement, had always been a source of wonder to the family. One day, when she was a very small child, she had clambered on to Lord Aynthorp's knee and settled there to suck her thumb. Clucking distressedly, Nanny had sought to pluck her off, ejaculating, 'There's a naughty little girl, bothering his Lordship like that! And how many times have I told you not to suck your thumb, I would like to know?' Lord Aynthorp had merely glanced down at the curly head and protested, 'Really, there is no need to worry Nanny, the old lion rather likes being bearded in this fashion. Hey!' this last addressed to Petula who started a little at the rumbustious sound, took out her thumb, and looked up, wide-eyed. Then she blandly invited him, ' 'Gain, do it 'gain, Grumpy', and prodded him in the stomach. He shouted with laughter. The nickname stuck. When he talked to her with great solemnity over the fundamental badness of little girls who sucked their thumbs and explained how truly shocking was such a habit she examined the damp little thumb as if she had never seen it before said 'Bad!' and started to tickle him, but as Nanny was never tired of recounting, 'That little Miss Petula never sucked her thumb again.'

As she grew older Petula treated the old peer more and more like an indulgent grandfather to whom she could take her small griefs and problems. When the family doctor attempted to give her an injection, she had a screaming fit which even her Nanny could not control. They sent for 'Grumpy'. Having been forewarned he merely strolled into the night nursery, raised his powerful voice over the screams and there was silence. Then he sat down beside her and grunting, 'Get on with it man while we're talking', he began by whipping out his own white linen handkerchief and mopping up the tears. Then he took her on his knee and began telling her about one of the hounds who had just whelped. Save for one little yelp and a glowering look at the unfortunate doctor, she was no further trouble.

Now aged nineteen, and still taking her own line in everything, Petula sought out 'Grumpy' once again, which explained Henry's having seen the pair of them from the windows as they crossed the Home Park side by side, walking their horses and clearly engrossed in conversation.

After a typical, appraising glance at the girl, Lord Aynthrop 'herumphed'. Petula turned her head. 'So you approve of my new habit?' she said.

'How the devil do you surmise that, Miss?'

'I can tell by your herumphs. That was a satisfied one not a Grumpy one, so I knew it had to be all right.'

This won a twinkle from him. 'You look very much to my taste,' he conceded, 'but that is not what you brought me out for this morning I'll dare swear!'

'And you would be perfectly right.' She turned in the saddle and he saw that she was looking very grave. 'Grumpy dear, this is of very great importance to me, but I must stress that you promise me, that no matter what happens in the future, you will never breathe a word to anyone.'

'Anyone?' This raised an eyebrow.

'Anyone,' she repeated. 'But most particularly anyone in the Family.'

'Meanin' my family?'

'Precisely.'

'Done,' he said suddenly. 'I'll accept. But I do not think I am goin' to be too pleased. You know, young woman, the day will come when you will cease windin' me round your little finger and runnin' me ragged as you have done all your short life so far.' To this she said nothing, being perfectly confident that she at least could and would always manage to get her own way with him, even though it might in some cases be prefaced by an outburst of the famous Lorme temper.

Then, after staring between her horse's ears, obviously thinking very hard, she began. He listened to her patiently. Apart from a few startled grunts he did not interrupt until she had done. Then, 'Are you absolutely sure, my dear?' he queried gravely.

'Absolutely sure Grumpy, word of honour, cross my heart and die.'

At the use of the childish phrase his face relaxed. He even

managed to smile at her indulgently. 'All right my dear, I'll play your little game with you, cross MY heart and die if I do not! But I must confess to a certain unease . . . do you not suppose it could be possible that you have gone too far? Have you taken our temperament sufficiently into account? We're a headstrong lot y'know. None of us respond very easily to the bridle. . . .' He tailed off, the eyes under those shaggy brows anxiously scanning her face.

'That . . . is . . . my . . . gamble,' she said very softly. 'I am prepared to take it. . . .'

'For yourself or for the common good?' He looked at her very keenly.

'For both,' she answered, 'because as I see it there cannot be one without the other.'

'Sometimes I think you should have been a boy,' he spoke a trifle crossly. 'Ridin' to hounds the way you do, thinkin' this thing through—which I have always maintained no woman can do, not from the beginnin', due to the silly mess-up Eve made of the whole business. Once or twice I've wondered if you were not capable of something demmed close to *reasoning* which in itself is illogical, you bein' female.'

'And a very feminine female at that, Grumpy,' she retorted, with some return to her usual sparkle. 'It's not reason, I think, but plain common sense which influences me now.' Her quick, disarming smile flashed. 'Trust me, Grumps. Keep my secret and we will both watch very carefully and share what we see, yes?'

He gave her a long, low stare as if he were trying to see that which a female can always conceal. Then she held out her hand. 'Come on, Grumps. Shake on it,' she pleaded for a reply. He took the extended hand and said, 'You are right, my dear, you are a very feminine woman. So be it.' Bending low in the saddle he kissed the extended hand with grave courtesy.

The routine pattern was developing along familiar lines as the year grew older. Henry was closeted with his father on several occasions but as neither made any comment upon these sessions and no one in particular had noticed them, they went unremarked and in due course Henry returned to Oxford. He had seen Petula several times. Once he came across her in the dairy, the full sleeves of her blouse rolled up. She was, she informed him very coolly, learning how to make butter under the benign eye of Mrs

Peace who had clearly come along to set the seal of suitability upon the exercise.

When Henry unwisely quipped, 'Whatever do you want to know buttermaking for, Pet?' she eyed him warily and replied, 'Well, you never know, I might marry a farmer, might I not, Mrs Peace?'

Mrs Peace looked faintly shocked. 'I trust not, Miss,' she said primly, 'I should expect you to look among the higher levels of society when the time comes for you to choose a bridegroom.' She turned away to remove a fold of her skirt which had caught on a nail so Petula was able to pull a grimace at Henry. He made no attempt to extend the meeting and after one or two further trivialities he moved off.

The Danements came to the private chapel service on the following Sunday and Henry caught the girl peering at him through her fingers while she knelt in a graceful attitude of prayer, but when he came out into the September sunshine, she was already away across the fields with her father, brother and young sister and he did not go after her as he might have done before that fateful meeting. So he went back to Oxford for the Hilary term without anything of import having passed between them.

He managed one shoot before he left but it was an anti-climax of a day. He was shooting badly, Pet who frequently acted as his loader was conspicuous by her absence, he missed a simple left and right and his loader on this occasion was too slow and failed to hand him his gun before the covey had passed. His mother, who had taken over command of the shooting luncheons, was also distinctly put out by the fact that the hay boxes had been loaded on to the last brake with the puddings and pudding plates, coffee and liqueurs so everyone sat round the hastily assembled tables and chairs with, as Henry sighed dismally, 'mountains of plates and nothin' to put on them'.

'Well, you can stave off your gnawing pangs with a bit of grouse pie or a hunk of Stilton if you like,' Charles Danement pointed out cheerfully. 'I say old chap, you do look down in the mouth.'

'I'm deuced hungry,' Henry answered shortly. 'That's all's the matter with me.'

In went Charles with both feet by saying cheerfully and with a mouthful of pie, 'Looks like you've been crossed in love or some such rot. That's what I would say if anyone asked me.' Flicked on the raw, Henry flashed back, 'Well, no one did, old boy, so why don't you stuff a pillow in your face.'

'Children, children,' remonstrated Christine, both surprised and shocked, 'anyone would think you back in the nursery. Now, Henry, apologise to Charles and you, Charles, stop baiting Henry.'

Totally deflated, the one mumbled his apology to the other and Charles relapsed into sulky silence until the brake arrived. Then Gyles wandered up, followed by a tenant farmer of the name Gurney, to whom the whole family had taken a liking. He had come out of Norfolk when his home went up in what had begun merely as a hayrick fire.

Lord Aynthorp appeared, gaitered and in a deplorable hat, talking nineteen to the dozen and looking immensely pleased with himself. 'Sawby,' he yelled, sinking into a chair, 'did you bring some Madeira? . . . Yes! . . . Well, pour me a glass, there's a good feller; I've taken an uncommon amount of exercise this mornin' and got a prodigious thirst. No, Gyles, as I was sayin' to Sir Ralph here, it isn't every day that an old octogeranium like me brings down four birds in as many seconds and, mark you, I was dependent on m'loader. Sawby!' By this time Sawby was at his master's elbow pouring his Madeira and well-nigh deafened by the shout. 'Oh there you are. DO remind me after luncheon to tell that man Perkins what a good loader he is.'

'Certainly my lord,' said Sawby, looking extremely cold.

The old man turned in his chair and scrutinised him. 'You look frozen,' he commented. 'Got anythin' warm on under that black jacket?'

'Er, no, sir.'

'Well then, more damfool you! Get back into the marquee where my man left some extra things for me. You'll find a Guernsey in there. Take yer coat off, pull on the Guernsey and then button up the coat. No one will see.'

'Really my lord,' Sawby protested, 'I am quite all right.'

'Oh no you are not,' his master cut him clean down. 'I don't want waitin' on by a man with his teeth chattering. Here, take this,' indicating the Madeira which Sawby had left at his elbow in its small salver. 'Pour y'self a glass of this at the same time. Do you a world of good. Very warmin' a drop of Madeiry. Now where's the food, Christine?'

'Just coming, father,' she said soothingly. 'By the time you have enjoyed your wine you will be served.'

'You'd better have a glass too,' the old extrovert decided. Sawby had beaten a hasty retreat, without the Madeira, and now Robert stood at his side. 'Here you, Robert. Take this to Madam and see she drinks it, and then get me something to eat.'

Sawby came back bearing a huge pudding basin swathed in a vast white napkin. Lord Aynthorp spotted it. 'God bless Mrs Parsons,' said he, eyeing it with immense approval. 'She's made us another beefsteak, kidney and oyster puddin'. Nothing like a good steak, kidney and oyster puddin' for a luncheon with the guns, don't you agree, Christine?'

'Indeed I do,' she said, smiling at him.

'Yers . . . yers . . .' he rubbed his hands together in anticipation. 'But it must be made the proper way. That suet crust should only be boiled for just so long as it takes to cook and rise like a feather bed. Crazy idea putting the meat in raw. My mother wouldn't stand for it. Went down into the kitchens herself and instructed the cook—none of our French chefs would ever touch them puddin's with the end of a barge-pole. What was I sayin'? Oh yes, well my old mother went down and taught cook the way of it, *en salmi*, cooked in a pot in the oven until almost tender in a thick, thick brown sauce with plenty of wine and onions and then allowed to go cold and put inside its suet crust. Then, when the puddin' was nearly ready to bring to table, cook would slice off the lid, stir in three or four dozen small Colchesters of Whitstable Natives, clap the lid back again and resteam for five minutes and not a moment longer!' Henry, quite restored to humour by his eccentric relative, watched him with eyes kindled by amusement. 'Didn't know you knew anythin' about cookin', grandfather, sir,' he remarked, highly diverted by the 'puddin'' disclosure.

'Well, you don't know everything yet, my young blade,' said his grandfather severely. 'My old mother used to say to her gels— your great-aunts in fact, Henry—"You must know how to cook. You must have your finger on every pulse if you are to have an orderly and not mismanaged household."' By now, probably with intent, he had the attention of the whole party, and the footmen and his butler who stood back, blank-faced but listening.

'I remember my mother askin' the gels a question. She said, when they were, oh I dunno, about fifteen or sixteen, "How can you complain about the sauces to your chef if you are totally incapable of puttin' your finger on the flaws and if needs be, of pushin' the feller out of the way and showin' him how it should be done? Otherwise," my mother said, "No servant will ever respect you." They didn't expect to do the job themselves but by knowing how it should be done they could make their complaints and criticisms constructive, as they should be.'

There was a brief respite while he ingested some of the mound of 'puddin'' upon his plate, helped himself to Jerusalem artichokes and red cabbage, tasted again and then announced, 'Capital, capital, there should always be red cabbage served with this puddin''.' He shot a wicked glance under his craggy brows at Henry. 'Must be cooked with plenty of wine vinegar and sugar eh, Sawby? Have you had that Madeira yet?'

Sawby was now back by his side and hovering: 'Yes, my lord; thank you, my lord, and indeed, my lord, I have never seen a pudding brought to your lordship's table without the meat and kidney had been cooked *ong salmee* as Chef André calls it, nor red cabbage cooked without brown sugar and wine vinegar as your lordship rightly says.'

Aynthorp shot a further triumphant glance at Henry. 'Now Petula,' he went on wickedly. 'There's a gel with the right ideas.'

'In what way, father?' Christine looked across interestedly.

'Told me she thought it was already past her time for learnin' the woman's side of country livin'. Said she was a proper town mouse when it came to runnin' houses. She did not try to fool me by claimin' she couldn't handle a rod gun or horse but otherwise—nothing.'

Inadvertently Henry let slip, 'So that's what she was doin' in the dairy the other day.'

'Learnin' to make butter. Precisely,' said the old man in triumph. 'And cheeses, I don't doubt, and the proper delivery of calves.'

'Oh, father,' this was too much for Christine, 'surely not?'

'Why not?' he snorted back. 'Half the trouble with the nineteenth century was squeamishness. From the day Queen Victoria put her heavy little foot upon the first step of the throne the whole goddamn nation of women became squeamish, all hartshorn and vapour waters and I don't know what. Well, we're in the twentieth century now and we don't want a carry over from the last one. Modesty is becomin' in a woman, provided she's a pretty one, but finicking ways . . . never. Babies get born, calves get born, what's the difference?'

Christine knew better than to put up any argument, for, as she murmured softly to Sir Ralph who sat on her right, 'We shall have the whole *histoire* of calf-accouchements if I dare to encourage him. It is not a case of "by opposing end" anything with father, as doubtless you have found out already.'

'Indeed yes,' said Sir Ralph, ruefully. 'I cut my teeth on that one many years ago.'

The beefsteak pudding came and vanished. Finally Sawby carried the empty bowl from the table into the small marquee which the footmen had erected. They were in no way put out that there was none left for them as Mrs Parsons had envisaged just such an eventuality. Even now Richard was unpacking another from its hay box and slipping knives, forks and plates on to hampers piled one above the other to do duty as a table for the staff.

'You'd better pop that one back awhile yet,' Sawby advised. 'We haven't reached coffee and I for one don't want to eat my midday meal like a jack-in-the-box, now up, now down, and don't know your tail from your nose.'

'Very well, Mr Sawby,' Richard obeyed dismally.

'And look sharp with the treacle tarts,' Sawby further commanded. 'Cut 'em up in here then carry them round. Where's the silver slice? You cannot serve the Family with treacle tart without a silver slice! Find it, man, find it and look slippy about it.' He busied himself with the cream bowl which he pronounced over-fresh and not as thick as it might be, it having come as it were straight from cow to table. Mrs Parson's Treacle Tart, as it was known among both the family and those friends who came to them for the shooting, was an institution at these luncheons. Indeed no *al fresco* meal with the guns was considered complete without it.

'Which,' as Mrs Parsons was wont to observe to anyone who would listen and every time she made some, 'it is *not* anyway. No of course not! It ain't treacle tart at all. I never know how it come to be called that in the first place, it being made with Tate & Lyle's Golden Syrup through and through plus lemon juice and the finest grated lemon zest and soft crumbs from a milk loaf. Golden Syrup, that's what it is, Tate and Lyle's superfine Golden Syrup, wot we always 'as used in this Castle.'

'Well, wot did you do when there wasn't none?' enquired one of the kitchen maids boldly.

'Made 'orrible things with 'oney,' said Mrs Parsons balefully. 'So thank your lucky stars, Miss, you wasn't born then, my girl, or narsty stuff like 'oney would 'ave been your lot and like as not raped by the 'ead of the 'ouse and the eldest son as well, it being their perquisite in them days,' she added with some relish, and a noisy sucking of her teeth.

Be these things as they may, the treacle tarts were eaten and approved. Indeed the rest of the luncheon passed without further hitch.

Christine was joining them in the afternoon's shoot. Lord Aynthorp was not. He was expecting the 'Pelicans' who were to be collected off the London train to confer with him and with Gyles over the matter of his son's inheritance. For was it not already September? Henry would come of age, with all the concomitant celebrations and ceremonies to be arranged, on February the twenty-sixth next year and there was no time to be lost in putting matters in train, especially as he had pointed out to Lady Aynthorp only last night: 'With Christmas, the Boxing Day Meet and the Fancy Dress Ball on New Year's Eve to come in-between, not to speak of the fact that cubbing had already started, there will be two if not three days a week accounted for in the hunting field, m'y dear.'

When he reached the house in the carriage which Plum had brought there was a message awaiting Lord Aynthorp that her ladyship would be happy to see him for a few minutes in her boudoir before he received the lawyers. Obediently he went along the corridor, scratched upon his wife's door and opened it extremely carefully lest she be asleep.

He found her sitting bolt upright in the big bed scribbling away at some notes with a positive avalanche of papers spread about her. 'Thought you might be asleep,' he said, explaining his stealthy entrance.

'Dear Justin, how thoughtful! Come and sit down a moment and let me tell you. I have had an absolutely brilliant idea for savin' time, savin' money and runnin' two things into one.' Her husband regarded her with the gravest suspicion but said nothing. Palliser materialised, soundless as usual. 'Knowing how your Lordship dislikes sitting on beds,' said she, reeling a bit under the weight of a large winged chair, 'I brought this for your Lordship,' and so saying brought the chair up beside the big bed and relinquished it.

'Very considerate,' he grunted. 'Thank ye. Now Emmy, what's all this farrago?' He settled himself, cast an anxious eye at the Sèvres clock on the mantelshelf. 'Got to get meself changed. Lawyers comin' at three-thirty or thereabouts. Cut it short, Alicia, I beg you.' Lady Aynthorp first quelled Palliser's curiosity with a single glance which banished the woman immediately. 'I will tell you very briefly,' she then assured him. 'Now listen,' she scratched about among the many papers, drew one out triumphantly and began to read. 'Henry's birthday is less than two months after New Year's Eve.' She turned to him, 'Well, isn't it?'

'Yes,' he grudged, 'but I don't see. . . .'

'You do not have to see yet, dear Justin, just listen. We always have a ball for the heir when he comes of age, do we not?'

'You know we do.' His irritation was rising.

'Well, there you are! Why not run the two together? Save ourselves all the pother of a fancy dress ball on New Year's Eve and make Henry's comin' of age ball into a costume ball affair. Do you not think that is a wonderful idea? Killing two horses with one brick!'

'Two birds with one stone,' he corrected her automatically. 'But, Alicia, we have never made a comin' of age ball a fancy dress one, have we, my dear?'

'That is not to say we cannot begin to do so now.' She became a trifle tart, too. 'I am sure Christine and Gyles would agree and let us remember the majority of *our* work now devolves upon *them*. Moreover, I am perfectly confident that all Henry's young friends would enjoy dressin' up far more than wearin' conventional clothes. The young always do, my dear.'

Some subterreanean rumbles indicated that her spouse was debating the matter. Eventually he managed to articulate, 'Let's see what they think, then. Personally, I don't mind havin' both, but then, as you say, there's Christine and Gyles to consider. Then again if Henry did not like the idea that would make an end of it, would it not?'

'Oh yes,' she agreed. 'but I am perfectly confident he will like it.'

'Why?' he shot her one of his suspicious glances. 'Have you been talking to him already?'

She hesitated. 'Not to say talked with him, dear. Possibly I just mentioned my idea to him.'

'Oh God almighty,' he rose to his feet a trifle stiffly. 'Then why not come right out with it as a *fait accompli*. You have obviously planned the whole thing already and now you only need to bring me in line to get the affair right off the ground. Really, Alicia, I wonder sometimes if I have ever been allowed to take a decision in the whole of our long married life.' He was off.... Lady Aynthorp just leaned back contentedly against the pillows and began debating the relative values of one period costume against another which might become her more while her Justin worked himself up with consummate artistry into the role of a downtrodden, browbeaten, nagged, compliant husband ruled over by a thoroughly unreasonable and irascible wife. Eventually, unable to restrain herself, she burst out laughing.

'If you could see yourself,' she told him gurgling. 'Red as a turkey cock, workin' yourself into a towerin' rage just because *for once* I have dared put up a suggestion. You have had your own way, as you know perfectly well, over almost everything through the years and you *always* fly into a tantrum if anyone dares suggest otherwise than your chosen way. I think this is a very good idea. Christine thinks it is a very good idea. She undertook to me that Gyles would be, to use her own words "very thankful". He is terribly busy with estate work and he has already confided in her that he would probably have to cut down his huntin' this season, and that, as we both agreed, would be unthinkable! So now then—just say yes or no!' He hesitated. The battle was won, and not by him as he well knew, but for face's sake he could not yet capitulate completely.

'Well, hum,' he prevaricated, 'we'll see. I shall have to think it all over very carefully.' He rose, kissed Lady Aynthorp's hand, and added, 'Now, my dear, I really must dress or I shall be late for those confounded lawyers. I do not know about Gyles but *I* can claim to be absolutely run off m'y feet what with one thing and another.' Saying which, he made for the door and stomped off, leaving an extremely contented wife behind him. Presently, she reached for a clean piece of paper and began making a first draft of her plan for her Grandson's Supper Menu for a Twenty-First Birthday Costume Ball....

CHAPTER 20

A Finger in Every Pie

As in many other similar establishments, the occupants of the Servants' Hall and the Steward's Room depended upon their Family for the provision of an abundant supply of gossip. They thrived upon it. It could be claimed, indeed, that they lived vicariously upon their family's activities and drew solace from the emotional stresses which were few and far between in their own lives. With one day off a month and only an occasional errand to take any of them outside the Castle grounds in between, there was little else for them to sustain themselves upon, except the very small coinage of their own gossip about each other which, at best, was poor stuff by comparison.

The literature which was available to them with which they could broaden their outlook and stimulate their limited intelligence was minimal too. True, the scullery and kitchenmaids smuggled into the Castle regular supplies of a tuppenny magazine called *Heartsease* which they spelled out laboriously whenever left to their own devices for a few moments. True, too, that Chef André had a whole shelf of enormous tomes to which he referred constantly, but these were all cookery books written in French so they remained unopened by any other members of the staff. Then there was a small bookshelf in the Steward's Room. This supported a Debrett, *Who's Who* and an *Almanach de Gotha*. All three were consulted whenever a 'foreigner' or a 'distinguished guest'—the two being sharply divided below stairs—was visiting. Then, one of the upper servants would relate tidbits to the rest, with André obligingly translating such facts about European families as would cast lustre upon any 'foreign person', more especially if he or she were French. Besides these sources of reference were Mrs Marshall's five cookery books over which Mrs Parsons pored. She could be seen with a lamp drawn close to her elbow, spectacles on nose, combing the sections devoted to cakes, biscuits, scones and breads. These were her sole reading.

True, she had ventured into the realms of Recherché Sandwiches and Breakfast Dishes and when reading out the title of the former group, had evoked such eldritch screams from André that she had put herself under his, purely temporary, tuition and could now refer to '*Ree-share-shay*' Sandwiches, which she considered tantamount to being bi-lingual. There was also one rather ravaged copy of Mr Charles Dickens' controversial *Pickwick Papers* and two bound volumes of *Punch Magazine* for 1884 and 1885. These with two up-to-date railway time tables and a copy of *Old Moore's Almanack*, completed the below-stairs library.

There was also The Scrap Book, scorned by the upper servants, destined to become a treasure and source of some rather pathetic pleasure to the under female staff. Their materials seeped down to them via the Family's waste paper baskets from whence they salvaged Christmas, Birthday and Valentine's Day cards which were neatly scissored away from their inscription pages and stuck in with glue and minute tabs so treated to secure the corners.

It was during the early evening one winter night when four afternoon-capped heads were bent over this ploy that Sawby stood at the head of the Servant's Hall dining table, recapitulating on an instruction which he doubted had penetrated the rather thick skull of 'his' footman, Richard. As he completed his small homily and turned towards the Steward's Room, Richard confided in Pearson, 'Well, there's one change here, any road. Her ladyship has quite given over the reins to Mrs Christine and doesn't seem to be bothering at all any more.'

Sawby swung back. 'That will be enough of that,' he snapped quellingly. 'Besides being unwarranted impertinence from the likes of you it has the double sin of being quite untrue.' He glowered at the offender and the remaining assembled staff were silenced. 'Let me inform you,' Sawby continued, 'since you presume to poke your noses into what is none of your business, that her ladyship is just as active as she ever was and make no mistake about that. Though it may be said she goes about it in a quieter and, sometimes, possibly a little less direct manner, but she still has her way as is only right and proper, so don't go making a statement like that again within my hearing concerning a matter about which you ... know ... absolutely ... nothing ... whatsoever. Now take in the teapot and see you bring in plenty of hot water with it.' He paused to make sure his words had sunk in sufficiently.

Richard, crimson-faced, rushed in search of the pot and hot water and Sawby stalked back into the Steward's Room.

He exchanged his coat for his old alpaca, settled himself in his accustomed chair, waited until Richard had completed his deliveries, then closed the door behind him and observed wearily, 'I just don't know what younger servants are coming to these days.' Then he told his companions what Richard had said.

'Stuff and nonsense,' exclaimed Mrs Parsons, putting down her tatting and stuffing it into her bag as if it were an errant ferret, 'and fudge and fiddlesticks! Her ladyship has a finger in every pie. Why, though I would never dream of having it dragged from me outside of these four walls, she manages his lordship, for a start, like no one else ever can except that little Miss Petula. She makes him feel as if he is having his own way and then winds 'im round 'er little finger.' In her crosspatch condition her aspirates flew in all directions.

'And that ees not all,' concurred André in an unusually benign humour, 'she rrules the rroost in more ways than one. I see so much of which I never spik; but I am sure it will do no harm to say that it was her ladyship and not Mrs Christine—nice and efficient though I will say she is—who thought of the idea of having the two balls run into one to save work and trouble for everybody including us.'

'And then,' added Sawby, *basso profundo*, 'it became a foregone conclusion, although his lordship was dead set against it.'

'It is the same with the menus,' said André, dunking a piece of bread in his coffee and making loud sucking noises as he ingested it. 'It is Mrs Christine who 'ands them to me now, but it is Milady who shapes them first. Then Mrs Christine discusses the final choice with me. I seldom have to alter anything Milady is a great expert at the making of the menus. Her *Souper de Bal*, in the first draft of course, is ...' he groped for the word and Mrs Peace came to his linguistic rescue.

'Exemplary?' she suggested.

'*Mais oui, exactement, ex-emplary. Merci, Madame.*' He stared at the crumbs floating in his coffee, raised the cup and in that sudden extraordinary mood of amity which had sprung up between them all, drank it back and rose.

'I shall show you,' he announced and forthwith scuttled off on his slippered feet.

'Well,' said Mrs Parsons, astonished, 'we are coming on, aren't we? He's never offered to show us nothink like it before. All secretive he is. I must say this is a nice change,' and she poured herself a third cup of tea.

When André returned, flourishing his papers, they all crowded round to study the first draft of what merely represented, to them, an inordinate amount of hard labour. It was written in Lady Aynthorp's spindly handwriting. It stated:

WORKING DRAFT: *MENU DE BAL* (*Six cent personnes*)
Entre'acte
6 Socles de Caviare de Sterlet.
Les Potages
Bisque d'Homard; Consommé Alexandra; Germiny; Lait d'Amandes.
Poissons Froids
10 Mousses des Soles Farcie au Beurre d'Oursins; 4 Turbots entière en sa gelée et garni; 4 Saumons entière Sce. Ravigotte.
Grosses Pièces Montées de Crustaces
3 Buissons d'Ecrevisses; 3 Buissons de Crevettes.
Grosses Pièces
3 Dindes Truffés, Sce. Perigueux; 4 Buissons de Truffés, (sur socles); 10 Filets de Boeuf Entière en sa Gelée.
Entrées
8 Brioches de Foie Gras Truffée; 8 Chaudfroids de Perdreaux; 8 Chaudfroids de Becassines en Bordeurs de Gelée; 8 Galantines de Cailles Chaudfroids.
Grosses Pièces Froid
4 Langues de Veau Garnie; 4 Jambons au Pêches en Gelée.
Legumes
80 ks. des Asperges en Branche, Sauce Blanc; 20 plats des Petits Pois Lucullus; 300 Fonds d'Artichauds André.
Les Salades
6 Salades de Crosnes; 6 Salades des Laitues à la crème; 6 Salades de Romaine à la crème; 6 Salades Méli-Mélo.
Entremets de Douceur
4 Gelées de Kirsch garnie des Cerises Maison; 4 Bavarois

*d'Avelines et Pistaches; 4 Gelées au Citron garnie de Fraises; 4
Charlottes au Chocolat Pralinée; 4 Pavé de Marrons enrobé de
Sucre Filé; 4 Macedoines de Fruits au Champagne; 4 Soufflés
Glacés aux Peches.*

Gros Pâtés Truffé

*2 Brioches de Foie Gras Truffé; 2 Brioches de Pâté des Gibier
aux Pistaches.*

Patisserie

4 Cornets d'Abondance.

Pièces de Fond

*60 Petits Brioches; 2 Biscuits de Savoie; 2 Nougats Parisienne
sur Socles; 2 grosses Babas au Noyau; 2 Gâteaux Napolitaine.*

Entremets de Patisserie

*2 Gènoese Pistaches; 2 Manqués au Petit Sucre; 20 Tartelettes
au Reine Claude; 2 Gondes Fourrés; 2 Marrons à la crème; 2
Mirlitons; 8 Corbeilles de Sucre Filé des Friandises.*

Supplementaires

*400 Sandwich Assortis; 30 Corbeilles des Petits Pains à la
Française.*

Rèserve

2 Barons de Boeuf en gelée.

Les Fruits en Pièces Montées

Boissons

*Champagne Moët et Chandon 1898; Champagne Cup; Limonade
Frais; Ponche de Lorme; Grand Fine Champagne; Grandes
Liqueurs.*

The senior servants studied avidly. At length Mrs Parsons summed up. 'A tidy bit of work for all of us,' she said approvingly.
'Nothink like it anywheres else in the county I'll be bound. Very
satisfying altogether is what I say,' and no one saw fit to disagree
with her.

While all this was occurring below stairs Henrietta was saying
to Sinclair in the privacy of their own sitting room, 'Really, I
do not know what I am to do with Stephanie when she returns
from France! How does one cope with a girl who sets her face
against the whole of one's own way of life? She is so stubborn
and so scornful. I simply do not know what is to become of her!'

But Stephanie did. From the ordered seclusion which was the
natural way of life for any extremely conventional French family
—surrounded as she was by tutors, governesses and other young

girls of her own age and background; hedged in by convention, most strictly chaperoned at all times—she had not the slightest idea how she would achieve her chosen way of life. She merely resolved to take a certain course and, in the fullness of time, she took it.

On the face of it, her mother could only be delighted by the fact that her daughter had put aside her desire for religious life. Even so it was a moot point as to whether her mother could have endured the shock of learning what she intended to do instead.

It all began harmlessly enough with a visit from her Aunt Prudence. Prudence had been ill. She had, with increasing fervour, flung herself into what her brother, Justin, spoke of irritably as 'that Pankhurst Woman's Disgraceful Exhibitionism'. Long hours, nervous strain, overwork and underfeeding had conspired with her age—she would be seventy-three on her next birthday—and a way of life which had never included any form of physical discomfort, to bring her to a state when even she realised that some form of medical attention was becoming essential.

The doctor, recommended to her by her colleagues, practised in a seedy Islington side street. After examining her, he sat himself down in a shabby chair, in his even shabbier consulting room and spoke with some frankness. Prudence faced him, straight-backed and grim-looking.

'Miss Lorme,' he began, 'I am compelled to tell you that your health does not permit you to live for very much longer the life which you are living at present. You need rest, country air, good food and tranquillity—at any rate, for several weeks, if not for some months to come. May I be permitted to enquire, therefore, if you have any personal means or are ... er ... entirely dependent upon the remuneration you receive for the work you are doing for ... er ... Women's Suffrage?'

Prudence had flushed, met look for look and then replied scornfully, 'I can assure you doctor, that I am possessed of ample means. I am merely doing what I have chosen to do as the natural outcome of deep and sincere convictions.'

A look of relief spread over the doctor's face. 'Well, that is a blessing,' he said more cheerfully. 'My prescription for a rest in the country is not an idle hope, as is the case with so many of my patients, but one which is completely practical and,' his face reassumed its normal gravity, 'I must stress, absolutely vital if you are ever to resume your chosen work.'

Prudence had fought him. He had countered stubbornly. Finally he summed up.

'Your background,' he said slowly, 'your upbringing, your whole way of life has been against you from the onset. You were gently born into a pattern of privilege. You have always lived a secluded life in what may best be described as well-cushioned circumstances. . . .'

'Too well cushioned,' Prudence exclaimed impatiently, 'a useless life. Oh, I have done what I could, work with the poor in the surrounding villages, work for the Church, but really nothing significant until, when I had quite given up hope, this wonderful opportunity arose to do something worthwhile before I die.'

The doctor had observed the significant details of his patient's exterior. The cut of her sober dress and coat, the hand-made shoes, the plain but costly handbag, the simple gold hair brooch pinned across the high collar at her neck, all of which spoke eloquently of means. Abruptly he asked, 'Are you, may I be permitted to enquire, any relation to the de Lorme family?'

'Yes,' said Prudence shortly. 'I am Lord Aynthorp's sister. How did you guess, doctor? Have you ever had any association with my Family?'

A flicker of amusement passed over his face. 'Yes, I have, but only very slight. It was when I was newly qualified, I took a post as *locum tenens* to a doctor in Upper Aynthorp. While I was working in this capacity, I was quite suddenly called upon to attend your brother. A most unusual character, as I recall.' His smile became a reminiscing one.

'A loving autocrat,' Prudence acknowledged very fairly. She continued: 'If I am to take your expert advice, doctor, I must be reassured on two points. Firstly, that in prescribing this rest you are not in any way influenced by my connections? And, secondly, that you do consider this most unwelcome rest as vital to my resuming my work for the Cause thereafter?'

He shook his head. 'I regret I cannot give you any such reassurance, Miss Lorme. You see, I am very strongly influenced by—how did you phrase it?—your connections. They constitute the prime contributory cause to your present ill-health. Had you been a working-class woman, born and raised in this area, you would have been fully accustomed to long hours of heavy work from a very early age. You would very likely have experienced the added strain of constant child-bearing and thus your system, part built by your environment and part by your parentage, would have long ago adjusted itself to malnutrition, damp, dirt, disease. Even you with your devotion to social work have very little idea of the conditions to which I refer because, at worst, they are urban ones. It would indeed pain me to have to detail to any high-born maiden lady some of the almost routine horrors to which the really poor are subjected in our cities.

'So you see, it is because you have suddenly subjected your totally unprepared system to unaccustomed rigours that you find yourself in your present condition. Miss Lorme, I beg of you, take my advice. It is at worst professional and totally unbiased—with that I am convinced you would agree. Go away, rest, fortify yourself, so that you can survive to fight again. Ignore me and I tell you in all sincerity, I cannot and will not be answerable for the consequences.'

Prudence returned to her friends. Over thick cups of strong cocoa, she told them what she had been advised to do. They all urged her to go.

Mrs Pankhurst had recently arrived in the United States for a fund-raising lecture tour arranged for her with the help of Mrs Harriot Stanton Blatch, daughter of the great American suffrage pioneer, Elizabeth Cady Stanton. Her devoted supporters in the Islington rooms were rejoicing at the reception given to their leader on her first appearance at the Carnegie Hall. In her absence, the forcible feeding of suffragettes continued. Despite this, there were still willing volunteers who protested on the occasion of every important Cabinet Ministers meeting. Only this evening the news had been brought to the little group of Emily Wilding Davidson's arrest and imprisonment in Strangeways gaol.

'So you see,' said the leading woman in their group, a pretty slip of a creature with high-piled golden hair, 'we do not lack for militants. There is no shortage in my age group of women who are prepared to endure any indignity, suffer any rigours, but such work should not be taken on except by the young and strong. Not for one moment,' she added hastily, 'does that denigrate your work with us. We need you, we need every single dedicated woman like yourself, but not to have them battered about by policemen or half-drowned by hose pipes. Dear, dear Miss Lorme, you are of inestimable value to our cause, in the background, doing the dull work, missing all the heroics.'

'Oh heroics!' interrupted Prudence. 'My dear, there are no heroics in the Movement, only inestimably brave and gallant women and it is my honour and privilege to have been included among them.'

They gathered round imploring her to withdraw from their ranks, just temporarily, so as to build up her strength and be enabled to return to the battle refreshed both in body and mind.

'While,' she said bitterly, 'you are suffering and struggling on.'

Yet even so, after a sleepless night, she gave in. On the following morning, before she left their meagre headquarters, Prudence went into the main office with its horrific, gruesomely detailed posters of forced feeding, its stacks of leaflets and its busy workers. She withdrew a piece of paper from her muff saying shyly, 'I want you to have this, to help you in my absence. I am deeply ashamed of my own frailty in leaving you, even temporarily, at a time like this. At least I hope I may be allowed to contribute something to the cause.' So saying, she handed over a cheque for one thousand pounds to her astonished colleagues.

She then returned to Castle Rising, where she kept her own counsel and vouchsafed nothing. For their part the Family had only the vaguest ideas of what was going on in the cause of Women's Suffrage. They knew, of course, that Prudence was involved. Because of this, her announcement that she was going on holiday came as a great relief to them representing, as it did, a postponement of anxiety lest she suddenly break loose and chain herself to railings and thus, most heinous offence of all according to Lorme ethics, 'get her name into the newspapers'.

Prudence explained that she was slightly fatigued, so planned a leisurely sightseeing and sketching tour among the *châteaux* of the Touraine. In the course of conversation she also mentioned that if she felt up to it, she might possibly propose herself for a short visit to Stephanie of whom she was extremely fond. As this announcement caused no flutter in the Castle dovecotes, she sat down and penned a letter to the girl's cicerone, The Viscomtesse de Launay. In this she proposed herself for 'a very brief visit' in order to bring her dear niece news from home.

A swift reply, couched in the most graceful terms, assured her of a warm welcome at any time. It then went on to urge her not to put herself to the trouble of such a journey for only a brief stay. She was informed that the *château* and all its inhabitants were hers to command for however long she could possibly be persuaded to stay. Thus was the stage set for the first act of yet another Lorme drama.

Within a week, Prudence made her departure in an aura of martyrdom and surrounded by impedimenta: luncheon basket, plaid rug, overnight case, knitting bag, strapped stack of books, umbrella and inflatable travelling cushion. Surrounded by these indispensable accompaniments, she was conveyed to the station by Plum in a Lorme carriage with Richard up beside him on the box. Richard then bestowed her and her Lares and Penates in a first-class, non-smoking railway carriage, with her back to the engine and strict instructions to the guard to 'see to Miss Lorme proper' on her arrival at the end of the first stage of her journey.

With the departure of Prudence, Henry up at Oxford, the older boys at school, Primrose and John settled into their Newmarket home where they would remain until Christmas, the worthy Bishop and his Dorothy safely inside their Palace, Christian with his regiment and his Claire camp-following, the remaining hard core of Family, plus the nursery and schoolroom brood, settled contentedly into the rhythm of autumn-into-winter Family life. As it had been, so it was again and everyone settled down to enjoy a round of engagements, the planning of entertainments and the spending of money in anticipation of yet another Christmas, plus the longer-term plans to be completed for Henry's coming-of-age ball in February. A steady round of house parties kept everyone in a state of satisfactory activity which pleased them immensely. At such times the Castle and its occupants presented the most felicitous face to the world. Departing guests carried with them tremendous reports to be disseminated at countless other dinner tables and At Homes, on how simple yet lavish, how pleasurable yet seemingly effortless were the entertainments offered at Castle Rising. All London—as any one of their friends would have described the limited circle inside which they lived, moved and spent their whole existence—was subsequently regaled with details concerning the superb table, exquisite cuisine and rare vintages offered for guests' delectation. Any who were unfortunate enough not to have experienced

Lorme hospitality were regaled with eulogies concerning the abundance of game at the shooting parties—'such gay and amusin' shootin' luncheons too'—the treasures with which the old Castle was filled and, notably, in the van of all praise was the subject of Gyles' Christine, 'takin' over the reins from her tiny mother-in-law with commendable skill and ease'.

It was a happy time. It was above all a secure time. 'As it had been, so it was and ever should be' was the implicit acceptance which tinted everyone's vision *'en couleur de rose'*, the season's most fashionable shade for both ball and tea gowns.

For such country folk as the Lormes, London had a charm deriving from infrequent visits. There they met friends, attended first nights, dinner parties and At Homes, and the women in particular stood for interminable fittings. The conspicuous figure of Lord Aynthorp was currently seen at Sotheby's and Christies. On these occasions he was often accompanied by his nephew Damien, who always enjoyed basking in the reflected glory which Lord Aynthorp invariably disseminated. Damien trailed like Sancho Panza after him, managing to abstain from spending any money himself, unlike his Uncle who bought anything which happened to catch his eye and which he deemed 'a sound investment'. Thence the older man would be borne away by his cronies for luncheons at such clubs at Whites, Brooks, Boodles or the Athenaeum. In between these expeditions, there were frequent visits to Purdy's, to his bootmaker and his tailor (Henry Poole & Co.).

In their role as Castle host and hostess, Gyles and Christine were less on the London 'silly season' scene than the other members of the family. They played host and hostess at all the shooting parties with Lady Aynthorp generally attending the *al fresco* luncheons swathed in rugs and playing a deliberately passive role. She dearly loved these occasions though she herself had not joined the parties at the butts for many years.

Gyles was extremely busy. He had always been deeply interested in estate affairs. Now that he held the reins, he had, with extreme caution, made some investments. These had turned out to be highly successful so very gradually he increased his stakes, always after some fairly strident scenes with his irascible Papa who was suspicious of all transactions which carried the merest whiff of 'trade'. Nevertheless, he had already acknowledged, albeit grudgingly, that Gyles had 'a sneakin' talent for this sort of thing', which secretly delighted him since the increases in revenue enabled him to spend even more lavishly.

Gyles, through the Monarch, with whom he was extremely popular, had met several 'wealthy tradesmen' as his father called such men as Alfred Rothschild, Ernest Cassel and Edward Lawson. Always an unexceptionable listener, Gyles had garnered the crumbs of information disseminated by these financial giants whom 'Teddy' had drawn into his circle so that although Lord Aynthorp still ranted on that 'Gyles will have us in the bankruptcy courts before he's done', he was well pleased with the outcome. Thus Gyles was able to render an account of his stewardship at the end of his first year showing only a little short of a quarter of a million's increase in capital.

Inside this same period the valuation of the pictures in the Long Gallery and the Main Reception Rooms—Mr Truslove always managed to speak of these in capitals!—had been completed. They totalled over six hundred thousand pounds, so Gyles had every reason to be thankful. His especial content arose through Henry's by no means flash-in-the-pan interest in such matters. In fact, his son on his last flying visit spent most of the time closeted with his father in his office and had actually expressed regret that he was still up at Oxford and unable to give all his time to such matters. There was one slight flaw, as Gyles confided in his Christine. 'The moment we can show an assured increase in our assets, m'father is off on another spending spree. Of course his judgment is impeccable, I only wish I had a fraction of his knowledge, but even so . . .'

Christine was sitting at her dressing table completing her toilette for dinner. She replied soothingly.

'Well, dearest, as long as you keep ahead of him, we will all, in my opinion, do very well indeed. What was it that Mr Dickens put into the mouth of Mr Micawber?'

Gyles smiled and obligingly repeated, 'Annual income, twenty pounds, annual expenditure nineteen pounds nineteen six, result happiness. Annual income twenty pounds, annual expenditure twenty pounds nought and six, result misery!'

'Exactly so,' Christine pinned a spray into her hair, 'and that is what is happening now, my love.' Then the dinner gong reverberated through the Castle and they went down together holding hands until the servants came into view.

*   *   *

All too swiftly Christmas came round again. The full complement of Family returned and the customary rituals were faithfully observed from tree and sled to Yule log, bonfires and the ceremonial dinner.

The only change in the pattern was that the three boys, Ninian, Ralph and James, were permitted to attend one or two informal 'dances' at neighbouring houses. The fortunate inheritors of these privileges, in stiff collars, dancing pumps and white gloves, were borne off in a Lorme carriage, ungratefully wishing that 'we were goin'' in Grandfather's Royce and not a stuffy old carriage'.

The mantelshelf in the day nursery was thick with invitations to children's parties at which, as everyone knew, there would be such treats as rabbits being withdrawn from top hats by gentlemen in tailcoats and stiff shirt-fronts, and Punch and Judy Shows.

The nursery folk in turn laboured over their reciprocal invitations for which 'Harlequinade' and 'Carriages at 6.00 p.m.' were inscribed in copperplate engraving. This Harlequinade, for which a troupe had been engaged, was performed in the small ballroom where fifty small gilt chairs were set for the children, their Nannies and the Castle Mamas. It was all pronounced a tremendous success. Admittedly, one small girl from The Priory at Nether Rising burst into loud sobs when intimidated beyond bearing by the Policeman. She had to be fished up and borne out by a crimson-faced and furious Nanny. Otherwise, from the jellies made by Chef André himself and sent up in shivering pyramids of vari-coloured balls, to the 'snowstorms' which were presented to each small guest, everything produced rapture.

The children were also given most marvellous indiarubber frogs which depended from narrow rubber tubes with bulbs on the opposite ends. Sawby had caused a very large crystal bowl to be installed on the main table in the Great Hall. Here Robert demonstrated the accomplishments of these frogs. On departure, clutching their gifts, the children crowded round to see Robert squeeze, causing the frog to jerk his tiny rubber legs and swim back and forth across the bowl of water.

There had never been such a wonderful party, but then there had never been quite such a felicitous Christmas altogether as both adults and children agreed unanimously.

The snow fell and settled. The toboggans were brought out

and made ready. Mufflered, fisher-capped flying figures shot down the inclines. Lord Aynthorp had never been more benign. Predictably and admittedly there was a slight contretemps over whether he should or should not toboggan with the rest. Was it not erring just a fraction upon the side of foolishness for a man of eighty-two to launch himself upon such a perilous journey? Bones became brittle as the years went by. After some fairly pithy comments about mollycoddling and some pishing and railing he allowed himself to be persuaded. Then again, fur flew briefly when Henry, skylarking with his cousins on the west lawns, inadvertently hit his grandfather's patrician left ear with a particularly hard snowball and was severely roasted for his pains.

Later that evening The Inseparables had also drawn a modicum of invective upon their luckless heads. They set fire to one of the tree's branches during a scuffle. They were banished forthwith to reflect upon their infamy, pursued by that all-too-familiar-voice roaring, 'Would you burn us all in our beds, you young rapscallions? Damme, what is the world comin' to I would very much like to know! When a man is in danger of bein' roasted alive by his own chimney piece . . . ! ' But such were merely the small change of Lorme life and, thanks to their persistent French strain, the fires flared up and then sank down again with matching rapidity in only a shade less time than it took Robert to sublimate the sizzle of flame with his damp sponge on its long cane.

The late choral service on Christmas Eve, the apple-bobbing, the Snapdragon, carol singing, and present bestowals had all gone according to Hoyle.

The Christmas dinner table was especially memorable. A friend of André's, with whom he corresponded regularly, had written to him describing two 'fantasies' created for Sir Basil Zarahoff's dinner table which he had actually seen for himself. They were the handiwork of yet another *camarade* who worked for Sir Basil. His description of these fired André with a passionate determination to produce some of them for his Family's Christmas dinner. He enlisted the help of Sawbridge who was equally fascinated by the proposition. So, Sawbridge grew and cherished in one of his stove-houses, twelve little basil trees, each controlled to one foot four inches in height. In due course these were brought into the house, plunged into the icy maw of André's largest charge cave where he proceeded to spray them with water.

Every two hours he opened the charge cave and sprayed again. In between he fabricated canapés which would be hung from the branches once these were completely frosted. At length the trees were ready to receive their edible baubles. By this time they were totally encased in frozen water with the most miniscule of icicles depending from each small branch.

André patiently hung his Lilliputian canapés in position, allowing the staff, turn and turn about, to file in and inspect his tiny masterpieces. At the moment prior to the announcement that dinner was served, all twelve trees were rushed to their appointed positions on the great table where they stood glittering down its length as though they had been carved in crystal.

When the ceremony of dining neared its end, the menservants put out the lights, removed the candelabra to the hall and André appeared carrying his Christmas pudding. It was not the traditional one but a recent creation of Georges Auguste Escoffier who was at the time *Maître Chef de Cuisine* at the Carlton Hotel. Escoffier had christened his pudding *Le Pouding des Rois Mages*.[1] He had designed and ordered a giant log-shaped mould in which the concoction was cooked. The pudding was black, as it should be, rich with fruit, as it should be, but it was light, for he had almost totally eliminated flour from his mixture and replaced this with fine white breadcrumbs.

André carried his exact copy round the table ringed by flames which did not go out. The secret lay in the fact that he had made an encircling band of cotton wool soaked in equal quantities of brandy and vodka. On the outside of this, concealing it completely, was his berried holly which was in turn protected by a second band of water-soaked cotton wool. The blue flames rose and quivered. Imperceptibly André shook the dish as he travelled, thus creating the slight draught which was all he needed to ensure his flames held. They were still burning when he completed his tour and set the dish upon the waiting hot plate. Then the footmen returned with the candelabra and replaced them. The pudding was served.

No one at that festive board ever forgot their 1909 Christmas at Castle Rising. It remained in their memories like buried treasure, unharmed by the passage of time. Every tiny incident lay recorded for them, ineradicably printed upon the retinas of memory. From preparation to fulfilment, from the first assembly

[1] The Pudding of the Three Magi.

to the last departure, it was, while it was happening, the gayest, most decorative, most exciting Christmas of them all.

Lord Aynthorp was at his most splendid, autocratic as ever yet benignant and courtly. At Christmas dinner he wore the knee breeches, silk stockings and buckled shoes below a black velvet coat set off with silver buttons and a fall of old lace, which the young irreverently and privately called 'Lorme Livery'. The men wore it only upon special Family occasions. It became the old man mightily, as it did his eldest son. Indeed, it also made both men look considerably younger than their years. Henry was slightly jealous and feeling a shade put out at not being able to assume the 'livery' himself since he was not yet come of age and thus was not entitled to it.

Nor, in particular, did any one of them forget the very special moment when Sawby drew back young Ninian's chair. As the youngest present, taking Christmas dinner with the Family for the first time, it fell upon him to give the toast. He rose, with quaking knees, slightly white around the mouth, right hand gripping the stem of his port glass very tightly.

'Grandfather,' he looked directly towards the head of the table, 'by your leave, sir, I will now propose the Loyal Toast.'

Lord Aynthorp inclined his head gravely. Ninian bowed back to him. Then in his clear boyish voice he spoke the familiar words.

'Ladies and gentlemen, may I please ask you to be upstanding . . .' he paused again. The sound of chairs being drawn back was accompanied by the singing whispers of rustling skirts. As the company came to their feet, he proclaimed, 'Sir, members of my family, I give you His Majesty the King.'

Ninian was to recall it all thirty years later for his nephew, Henry's eldest son. They were leaning against a sand-bagged command post under a winter sky, with such a galaxy of stars imbedded in the midnight blue above that they reminded Ninian of the jewels which had winked and sparkled at his Grandmother's throat all those lost years ago.

'It seemed to me,' he told the boy, pushing back the tin hat on his head, 'as if my mind took an instant photograph . . . Grandfather lookin' absolutely magnificent, standin' straight as a ramrod; Grandmama, your great grandmother, in black velvet, blazing with diamonds; Great-Aunt Marguerite lookin' quite the

prettiest old lady I ever saw in silver grey with her sapphires.'
He unconsciously slipped back into the speech of those far away
days. 'M'y mother looked simply ravishin' too in a white gauzy
affair with the emeralds yer Great-Grandmama had only handed
over to her that afternoon ... and the table ... shimmerin' with
gold plate, the white cloth draped and swagged with tightly
berried holly ... scarlet candles in their sconces ... that Puddin'
of Escoffier's which André had made for us ... every single
detail.'

He drew one deep almost shuddering sigh. 'Then I remember
so clearly when the footmen went out, Sawby closed the door
behind him and we were alone in the candlelight. That was when
Grandfather began tellin' us of how he and Grandmama had
dined with the Queen the week she went to Balmoral one December many years before; and how they had been taken into a small
drawing room to see their very first Christmas Tree. It had been
ordered from Germany and there it was, all decorated. He told
us how he had come back post haste on the followin' mornin' and
had managed to persuade *his* father to cut one down and install
it in the great hall.

'Grandfather had drunk pretty deep as I recall. As so often
happens with the old, if the balance is right, which it was, the
wines had invigorated him. I can tell you that he brought that
sixty-one-year-old scene to life for all of us. He spoke for over
twenty minutes. The port was with him again—as I recall it had
completed its second tour. He launched it for the third time. I
can see him now.

'Yer know the ladies always stayed in the dinin' room on this
night of the year. Well, Grandfather charged his own glass,
passed the decanter and then he leaned back in his huge chair
and spoke to us about the Family. It really was the first time I
had ever appreciated what it all meant. Remember, I was only just
past fifteen. He invested our past with a kind of chivalry. He
made us all feel as if we had some kind of grail. Oh I dunno, it's
hard to describe, but it all seemed very splendid then and totally
entrenched. Strong and indestructible would perhaps be a fairer
description. I know I thought, *it is all pre-ordained*. In time my
father will hand on to Henry, yer father, and Henry to ... and
so on and on with nothin' to break the splendid continuity. Then
Grandfather proposed *his* toast. He gave us The Family coupled

with the name of our illustrious forbear Count Henri de Lorme of Normandy.'

Ninian sighed again. This time it was an infinitely weary sound. Then he lapsed into a silence which lasted for a long time. When he spoke again, it was as if he were speaking to himself.

'Little did I or anyone else at table that night imagine what really lay ahead.'

CHAPTER 21

A Change of Heart

By the time the snowdrops were ringing their green-tipped heads over the turf in the Home Park and shaking their china-white buds together like a clack of gossips outside a village hall, Prudence had already been staying at the Launay *château* for over three weeks.

During that time she and Stephanie had fallen into the habit of taking a long, leisurely stroll through the formal gardens each afternoon. Prudence referred to these walks as 'my little constitutionals, and Stephanie, graciously released from more strenuous exercise with the rest of the girls, welcomed their perambulations: firstly, because she was lonely and had always found a more kindred spirit in this great-aunt of hers than in any other of the Lorme ladies, and secondly, because Prudence was the one person with whom the girl could relax.

One fateful day she questioned her great-aunt on the subject of her activities when away from Castle Rising. Prudence answered her. She was at all times scrupulously truthful, so she began by explaining to Stephanie exactly what was the opinion of her brother, the child's great uncle, and all the other elders of the family concerning these activities. When Stephanie replied, 'But that is how they feel about my religious interests. They simply do not understand anything except their own selfish and frivolous way of living,' Prudence warmed to the girl and with understandable weakness poured out her views and aims into ears that were only too willing to hear what she had to tell.

After several days of 'strolling', during which Stephanie asked all the questions which she had stored up from her interim reflections, she knew as much in theory about Women's Suffrage as did her Aunt. Then, some two and a half weeks after her Aunt's arrival, she exploded her own small bombshell over her astonished relative.

'I want to work for Women's Suffrage,' she announced. 'I have listened to you, Great-Aunt. I have read the books you have given me, very secretly of course, because Madame would have a fit if she knew what they were about, but I now know what it is that I should do with my life.' Suddenly the floodgates were open. All the repressions which the girl had imposed upon herself were loosed over her flabbergasted relative. Stephanie had at last found someone to whom she could speak with absolute freedom and also without any fear of reprisals. She admitted that it had been her intention to take the veil. She confessed that, after many hours upon her knees during which she had wrestled with the problems and, as she put it, 'taken them to God', she had seen, as it were like some miraculous and momentary vision, that this was a selfish choice which she now considered rendered her unworthy of even thinking towards the privilege of withdrawing from the world and working for the Lord.

'It is not right,' she declared with passion, 'for only now do I see things in their right perspective—that I should expect my path to be smoothed for me in order that I can give myself to God in some enclosed order, away from the world in which I have had no interest and from a way of life which I simply dread being forced into. Why,' she demanded with rhetorical vehemence, 'should I expect the ultimate in happiness to be given to me without my having done a single thing to deserve such divine compassion? What you have taught me has shown me the way I should take. It only comes through service, prayer and sacrifice. If I cannot offer these things to God, what possible right have I to expect that He should fulfil my petty wishes? You have taken the right way, Great-Aunt. You and your friends are prepared to sacrifice themselves completely and utterly to this great cause. Now I am determined that your way shall be my way and I will take it! Oh yes, my mind is made up now. I will take it, though how and when this may be brought about I have not the slightest idea—yet.'

Prudence had expostulated. She pointed out the obvious impossibility for a young girl, not yet come out, to escape from the trammels of parental control.

'In the first place,' she explained, 'you could never achieve it. *They* would find you no matter where you went. You must remember that you are nothing until you are twenty-one. You belong to your parents. Your private income is tied up securely and you must wait until you come of age before obtaining a single penny of it. Until then you are bound hand and foot, child. There is no possible way out.'

But Stephanie remained unconvinced. She persisted, 'We can find a way out, I am assured of it.'

Fairly, scrupulously, the old woman had set her face against her own convictions to reason with the young girl, but Stephanie would have none of it. For four successive afternoons she fought back until, eventually, with the greatest reluctance, still torn between her own convictions and her loyalties to the Family, Prudence let herself be driven to the admission that there just might be one way in which Stephanie's ambition might be achieved. She preached extreme caution, extracted a solemn promise from the girl that never by word or inference would she ever divulge anything to any of the Family, and at length outlined the plan which she had devised. Poor, ageing Prudence had first spent several sleepless nights over her problems. During these nocturnal agonies she wrestled valiantly between the two aspects of her conscience which in its promptings was so similar to her niece's. She was, in any case, profoundly moved both by the girl's attitude to religion and her response to what she had indiscreetly taught her concerning Women's Suffrage, but she was fighting a losing battle. The girl's concepts were echoes of her own. Stephanie's response to suffrage was identical with her own and she herself warmed the lonely old woman's heart. Even so, she continued to exhaust herself with prevarications and vacillations.

At length her host and hostess observed how exhausted she had become and how fine-drawn was her appearance. They dosed her with tisanes, inundated her with cordials and other specifics until she added flatulence to her growing discomforts. Conversely, they were very successful in persuading the windy and distraught old lady to accept the use of one of their carriages every afternoon so that great-aunt and niece could drive instead of walk. On these journeys as Prudence informed Stephanie, 'We shall speak exclusively in English lest an inkling of what we plan be made known even to the coachman.'

Stephanie was nothing loth since it really was becoming plain to everyone that she was doomed to become the one member of the Family who simply could not master the French language and manifestly found no pleasure whatsoever in her attempts.

The weeks sped by. The Launays would not hear of Prudence leaving until she had recovered in health and looks. During this extended time together Prudence's nebulous idea took shape very gradually until, by the time the snowdrops were out in the Home Park, she was able to complete and despatch a long letter to Henrietta. This missive, patiently and economically crossed and recrossed, was read by Henrietta in the seclusion of her own sitting room.

Sinclair had caught a cold. He had taken a toss out hunting, staggered angrily from a wet and muddy ditch, remounted and stubbornly insisted upon 'finishin' the day's sport'. As it had begun to rain shortly after his untimely spill and had continued to do so throughout the entire day, he had ultimately squelch-trotted home, soaked to the skin. Even a powerful mustard bath, followed by an eau-de-cologne rub down from his father-in-law's valet and a stiff whisky and soda thereafter had failed to fend off the cold.

Now he sat with streaming eyes and a thumping head while his wife slit open her envelopes and read out to him such snippets of news from her correspondence as she thought might divert him from his unlovely state.

When she came to the one with the French postmark she lapsed into total silence. There was no sound in the room save for the rustling of the pages and the crackling of the fire in the chimney piece. When she had read the letter right through she turned back to the first page and reread her Aunt Prudence's missive. After this she refolded the letter, reinserted it in its envelope and tucked it into the pocket of her morning skirt.

A few moments later, having devised a suitable excuse, she rose and left the room, first tucking a rug around her ailing spouse's knees and making sure that he had everything he required. Once she had closed the door behind her, Henrietta picked up her skirts and hurried through the corridors. For once in her life she had given herself time to pause and reflect. Now, with surprising good sense, she had decided to take Prudence's letter to her Aunt Marguerite. As she reached her door, Palliser emerged with an armful of billowing dresses. She bobbed respectfully, held back the door, closed it again with Henrietta inside, then—regrettably—she crouched down and listened at the keyhole with her left ear firmly clamped to the small cavity, her eyes swivelling rightwards in an attempt to keep watch on the head of the corridor lest anyone came round the corner and observed her in such a perilous pose.

The little Countess was sitting at her escritoire writing letters. She looked up as Henrietta spoke her name.

'Why, how delightful,' she exclaimed, rising. 'My dear Henrietta, how good of you to call upon me. Pray sit down my love and I will make you a cup of my own very special tisane. I must confess I was toying with the idea of making one for myself, but these wretched letters that I must write are long overdue. I have been most remiss. Now I shall be more so because I must confess, my dear, that I positively detest letter writing and welcome your call as a most happy excuse to postpone my boredom.'

Henrietta remained standing. She simply extended Prudence's letter.

'I have received this,' she thrust it at her aunt, 'from Prudence. It is about Stephanie. Sinclair, as you know, has a most dreadful cold and I could not bring myself to add to his discomforts, so I came to you. Will you please read it and tell me your opinion of the contents.'

Marguerite's manner changed abruptly. She took the letter, returned with it to the escritoire and Henrietta sank into a chair. Carefully, Marguerite smoothed out the pages, lifted her lorgnette and read the letter. She rose thereafter, crossed to the windows and looked out over the grounds.

'Do you wish for my opinion of the contents?' she enquired gently.

'Yes.'

Marguerite turned. 'Then I say that this is a most fortuitous letter.' She rustled it between her fingers. 'The very fact that Stephanie has of her own volition said that she no longer desires the life of a religious would be occasion enough for rejoicing, I should have thought. The suggestion that we begin to bridge the enormous gulf which exists between Stephanie and the life of a girl in her social position is a further fortuitous circumstance.' She crossed the room and sat down beside her niece. Then she laid the letter down, took one of Henrietta's hands between her own and continued, stroking the cold fingers which now lay passive between her own. 'Let us analyse the letter together before we speak of it to anyone else. Let us look at the matter in it quite dispassionately.' Henrietta lifted her drooping head and looked up, revealing an expression of complete bewilderment.

'Come now, Henrietta,' Marguerite urged, 'of course we abstained from talking about Stephanie's religious bents for we did not wish, any of us, to cause you more pain, but we were all aware of her ... er ... somewhat excessive devotions. Indeed she also left none of us in any doubt as to her opinion of her coming out and all that this entails. Now here is Prudence,' Marguerite reached for the letter and once again smoothed the pages, 'writing quite plainly on the matter.' She began to read it aloud.

' "I can assure you, my dear Henrietta, that Stephanie has quite put from her mind (I must stress, entirely of her own volition) any idea of embracing the life of a religious. Indeed she told me so herself and then she expressed a new wish and hoped that in due course I might represent it to you and obtain your sanction. By this time the child knew that I had come to a decision of my own. My friends, with whom I was living in London, have gone from their place of residence. I must confess, too, that when I came out here it was on the recommendation of my doctor. He found my state of health so poor at the time (rest assured I am very well again now) that he recommended a change of scenery and plenty of fresh air as the best aids to complete recovery. Since coming to France I have had ample time to reflect. I had already made up my mind to find some quiet rooms in London, somewhere where I could be well cared for in my absences from the Castle and not too far from the British Museum where I intend to resume my reading. (I am by way of doing some research for a book I wish to write.)

' "When I learned how little Stephanie had failed to master the French tongue (so very odd in one of us!) and how much the poor girl was ashamed by her manifest inability, I realised that I had gained her confidence and that she had found (for some curious reason) that she could speak easily to me of matters which were of extreme importance to her. Subsequently she disclosed that she had long wished to be able to express herself in song and indeed in the playing of the pianoforte.

' "It transpired that the German governess (Stephanie's German is, by the way, coming along very nicely) informed Sybilla that the girl had a very pretty but totally untrained soprano voice. So when Stephanie expressed the wish (again hers, I do assure you, and not mine) I thought how much she was improved by her French visit. She said that she did realise at last that (much as she dreads it) she must endure her coming out and all that it entails. Then she explained that if she did have a pretty singing voice and this could be developed, and if too she could study the pianoforte under a really first-class tutor, she would have something to do instead of just sitting mumchance. I thought it quite pathetic when she told me with great gravity, 'To stand up and do something even fairly well would, I think, help me to overcome my shyness and distaste for social occasions.'

' "So, my dear, here is the plan which I now put to you for your consideration. I have discovered that all the reading matter I wish to obtain can equally well be found in the London Library, which as you may know is situated in St James. I also know of a young person in straitened circumstances, the daughter of an impoverished clergyman, who is anxious to obtain a post as companion. If I found rooms somewhere between St James and the Royal Academy in the Marylebone Road and if I engaged this young person, I could ensure that Stephanie was chaperoned to and from the Academy and could pursue her desired studies with perfect propriety.

' "Stephanie herself welcomes the idea of staying with me. You and Sinclair could always visit her and see that all is well and I would have the pleasure of a young girl's company in what would otherwise be a very lonely way of life (as indeed a writer's always is). So pray, dear Henrietta, do give this matter your closest consideration and bespeak the same of Sinclair to whom as always . . ."

'Oh yes . . . well etc. . . . .' the little Countess broke off. 'We need not bother with the rest need we? But what could be better? Fancy dull old Prue coming forward with such a suitable suggestion! It seems a great waste of time for the gel to remain with the Launays. She must either go to a finishing school or have some personalised grooming between now and her presentation. I know I should jump at the opportunity if it were my gel. You can even stipulate, if you so wish, that permission is granted on the clear understanding that she attends dancing classes too. Clever Prudence, such an agreeable surprise!'

Henrietta listened intently. She must have well-nigh known the contents of that letter by heart by now but still she frowned and looked around her uncertainly.

'What about Aunt Prudence's Other Interest?' she enquired uneasily.

'That women's fiddle faddle!' the little Countess spoke scornfully. 'My dear, if you had known Prudence as long as I have, you would have been able to read between the lines of that letter. Prue has always taken up things with an almost *fierce* enthusiasm. Then, after a while, each one has fizzled out and she has taken up something else equally *fiercely*. It was the same when she was here.' She raised a beringed hand and began counting off the fingers. 'First it was Jellies and Visits to the Sick,' down went one finger, 'then a new curate came and she started Bible classes with him for the village children—that was the phase we called Religious Instruction for the Very Young,' down went a second finger. 'After that, now let me see, yes, it was the turn of Exercise. Calisthenics, I think they were called. Health through Exercise, with boxes of horrible dumb-bells arriving here by the brake-load for distribution at the Village Hall where she wore the poor little village children to shreds!' The third finger was ticked off. 'Then, as I recall, she took up with some new sect she called the rosy ... rosy ... ah, yes, Rosicrucians. I never did quite get the gist of that one but I do recall it involved the bringing here of the strangest men and women in flowing garments of unparalleled hideosity. . . .' She dismissed her fourth finger, then contemplated her thumb for a few moments, gazing at it with some intensity.

'Ah yes, and then came Prue's Vegetarian Phase. I never saw Justin so incensed in all my born days as when Prue embraced that! She tried to reform Uncle Justin. At her most vehement phase she even suggested that we dismiss André! ... André! Imagine that! It did not last any longer than the other obsessions. Finally we had this last silly nonsense about Women's Rights.' She put her exquisitely coiffed head on one side and twinkled at her niece. 'I am sure I understand *that* less than all the others! I never found myself in need of any "rights". I think we women do very well as we are and I want no such unattractive prospects dangled before *me*.

'Now you mark my words, Henrietta, for I am confident I can tell you exactly what has come about. Her "rights" business had begun to pall. That was the *real* reason why she went off to France. These people with whom she was involved moved, or went away, or found Prue more of a hindrance than a help. It will be something of that kind you may be sure. She went away to lick her sores and quite by chance found a new ploy in this book of hers, and in your Stephanie, and those two things will keep her out of any further mischief for many months to come.'

During this eloquent *sommaire* of her aunt's 'good works',

Henrietta's expression had begun to change. Gradually she began to look less and less anxious until at length she said in a relieved voice, 'Well, I am sure I am extremely happy to hear your opinion. Indeed I am immensely relieved by what you say. If you really think that Aunt Prue has given up her suffragettes I would be happy to let Stephanie stay with her. Indeed I was only saying to Sinclair recently that I was at my wit's end to know how to bring Stephanie round to some more normal behaviour. Of course she will never have the family beauty but, given a measure of compliance on her part, and some pretty clothes—we must see about getting her some just as soon as she returns—I think she could acquit herself quite well.'

'I am assured of it,' Marguerite affirmed. 'She is tall, I do admit, and her feet *are* rather large, but she carries herself well and has such a pretty, graceful neck. I am persuaded that if these projects came about,' she tapped at the letter with her now-folded lorgnette, 'provided we dress her with some skill—in which, my dear, we are not entirely lacking—she will do splendidly. Perhaps we may manage to get her a Bishop or some even more lofty non-celibate ecclesiastic!'

This made Henrietta smile reluctantly. 'Well,' she said with only a trace of reluctance, 'I am immensely indebted to you, dear Aunt Marguerite. I am encouraged to tell Sinclair and venture to obtain his sanction.' She shook out her skirts, preparatory to leaving.

Marguerite nodded with approval. 'Exactly so, you are very wise,' she agreed. 'There is nothing to fear and much to welcome in these proposals. I am only so astonished that Prue should suddenly evince such commonsense,' she smiled up at her tall niece who, after a further moment or two of vacillation, straightened her back, turned for the door and when she reached it, said over her shoulder:

'Who knows, if Sinclair is so sensible he will probably see it as you do and not be bothered from the onset with my silly misgivings,' and so saying she hurried back to her own rooms.

Sinclair was 'sensible' as his wife had hoped. Ever one to take the line of least resistance, he embraced the scheme wholeheartedly, praised Marguerite's endorsement and later in the evening even rallied sufficiently to write a long letter to Prudence expressing wholehearted approval of the scheme and offering to travel to France and escort the pair home. In this he was unfor-

tunate. Imprudently taking what he termed a 'stroll' the following morning, his cold turned to influenza and he retired to bed,
so Prudence and Stephanie were left to make the journey
untrammelled by Sinclair's presence which fact secretly delighted
the pair of them.

There was little doubt in any of their minds—once hindsight
enabled them to see Stephanie's behaviour in perspective—that
from early childhod the girl had been intent upon martyrdom.
Her attitude to religion contained more than a mere touch of
medievalism. She desired pain, more especially self-inflicted pain,
and in this respect must have been, even as a little girl, a
masochist. She wanted opposition. She sought persecution. She
inflicted pain upon herself—though only Nanny knew about the
little flail which Stephanie had abstracted from among the
souvenirs her unmentionable Uncle Justin had brought back
from his first Egyptian visit. In the privacy of that cell-bedroom,
Stephanie lashed herself with the flail. It was therefore hind-
sight-clear that tempted by the indignities and danger of force-
feeding, further titillated by pictures which her Aunt had
unwisely shown her of women being dragged through the streets
by uniformed policemen, and others of similar women chaining
themselves to railings outside the Houses of Parliament, Stephanie
thrilled to the work and seized upon the very slender opportunity
offered to her to participate.

In after years, Damien was to comment with pederastic
insight, 'People like Stephanie never care what cause they
embrace, so long as it gives them their desires. Professional politicians have much in common with such types. They never mind
to what party they belong provided it assures them speedy high
office. Masochists merely take the same line by grasping whatever
opportunity will yield the forms of masochistic ploys which to
them represent the ultimate peaks of pleasure.'

Even Damien could not attribute any such motives to 'poor,
old, good, misguided Aunt Prudence', as he described her in this
context. She had in fact laid down quite stringent rules which
governed Stephanie's behaviour under her roof. The girl would
be chaperoned by the hair-pin-moulting, spotty issue of an
impoverished clergyman called Sprout. In fact this was a most
perfect piece of casting as Primrose Sprout, zealous suffragette,
willing to immolate her unlovely person upon any altar of 'sacrifice' was herself hampered by her determination to keep such

knowledge from the Reverend Augustus Sprout. She knew that her father would, so she explained earnestly to Prudence, 'die of shame if he ever learned what I am doing'. 'Poor darling!' she exclaimed. 'He could not possibly understand. I am assured the shock would kill him. He already enjoys the worst possible health.' The Reverend Sprout was, in fact, a dedicated hypochondriac. So Miss Sprout was effectively debarred from any suffragist activities which would, even remotely, court disaster for her by making headlines in the newspapers.

Stephanie too was studiously hampered by her great-aunt. She was warned by her in no uncertain terms, 'You must realise and accept, my dear child, that the whole Movement is very much quieter at the moment. There is a lull. This will enable you to pursue your musical studies and have some tangible results to produce for Mama and Papa when, *faute de mieux*, they come to visit us'.

Thus the strange trio settled to a near-respectable routine. Off went Stephanie in the mornings to the Royal Academy of Music in the Marylebone Road with Miss Primrose Sprout in attendance. Once Stephanie had been handed to her first tutor the hard-working Sprout returned to work with Prudence on her book. This masterpiece entitled *The Freedom Martyrs* was intended to be a lasting record of the Suffragette Movement, even though it was developing as a somewhat biased version of their indisputably courageous stand. At luncheon time Sprout returned to collect Stephanie. After luncheon she conducted her to her daily class for Dancing and Deportment after which came the highlight of each day. On all except those on which Henrietta and Sinclair were expected, the leading women in the Movement converged upon Prudence's rooms for tea, sandwiches and further plotting. It was at these daily meetings that Stephanie really learned to what extremes of agony the militant suffragettes had been submitted.

By January 24th she was obediently recording for Prudence, 'The elections are going against the Liberals and their sins will come home to them one after another,' and on the following evening, 'People returning home congregated outside our rooms and shouted "good old suffragettes". They even cheered three times!'

A day or so later the Conciliation Bill was drafted at the instigation of Lord Lytton whose sister Lady Constance was gravely ill. She had become a militant suffragette. She had been arrested, sentenced to imprisonment and force-fed without any medical examination. It was now apparent that had she been examined heart trouble would have been discovered. As it was she was released from prison in a state of collapse and was still in a serious condition.

Even such slight relaxations and supports so encouraged them that Mrs Pankhurst and the Women's Freedom League formally declared a truce to militancy a week before Parliament re-assembled. Thus Prudence was proved to have spoken no more than the truth to her niece. There was a brief respite at this time. While it lasted—for far longer than had at first been ex-pected—Members rested and devoted themselves to more peace-ful forms of campaigning. This, as it turned out, was the eventual cause of Stephanie's downfall.

The Members worked ceaselessly at the sale of such suffrage literature as *Votes for Women*. They held drawing-room meetings throughout the provinces. They spoke in small halls and some even went to the extremes of holding outdoor meetings wherever and whenever they could draw crowds. At these meetings, ex-prisoners with hideous experiences to recount became the princi-pal speakers, while fervent organisers whipped up support for the printing and distribution of hand bills, working up the meetings and securing full halls by all-out efforts to arouse local interest in the cause. Some rode along country lanes, singing the Women's *Marsellaise*. Stephanie chafed so much at being debarred from even these mild participations that eventually Prudence gave in under the girl's avalanche of bewailings and reproaches. Between them she and the Sprout devised a costume which created an effective disguise for the girl. Great was her excitement when, at long last, she too mounted a bicycle and pedalled in a parade placarded like a sandwich man with the details of forthcoming meetings.

It was the thin edge of the wedge which was now to be driven deeper and deeper by the fervent acolyte in ensuing weeks. Stephanie was having, for the first time in her life, 'a wonderful time'. She was radiantly happy and asked for nothing better out of life than this. Then came the bombshell in the form of a long and tactful letter from Marguerite to her sister. In it she disclosed that the family had decided upon an eighteenth century ball to be the climax of Henry's coming of age celebrations.

'Doubtless,' the little Countess wrote, 'Henrietta will be communicating with you herself. There is no time to be lost now in deciding upon your costumes and in having them made. I just thought you would like to know that at long last everything is settled and Justin is highly delighted after having resisted the idea somewhat powerfully until now.'

Stephanie was appalled. Prudence accepted the news with the resignation of one who has endured such tribulations throughout a long lifetime. When she had heard her niece's tirade from beginning to end she said calmly, 'What cannot be cured must be endured, my dear. I suggest we anticipate your Mama and bespeak a couple of suitable gowns before she can involve you in interminable fittings which I know you find very disagreeable. We shall have to appear. We must appear for our own sakes lest we antagonise them and thust cause them to probe too deeply into our affairs. I have an idea whereby we may come by suitable garments without any fuss.' She explained to the now sullen Stephanie how she had met, while staying with the Launays, a very distinguished member of the *Comédie Française*.

'An actress!' ejaculated Stephanie in sepulchral tones.

'An actress,' nodded Prudence, 'who, if *persona grata* with the Launays is suitable enough for our purposes. She happened to take very kindly to me while staying in the *château*. She even invited me to witness one of her performances as her guest—you remember we had intended to stay in Paris for a short while on our return?—well it only remains now for me to write to her and tell her what is toward. We will send her your measures and my own, and request of her the loan of two elegant gowns of the period which we may wear with confidence. She spent a very long time telling me all about the remarkable wardrobes of the *Comédie Française* and the infinite care which is expended upon them. Thus we can continue working until the last possible moment, go down to the Castle for this tiresome ball and return as speedily as possible thereafter.'

At first Stephanie refused point blank to go but Prudence reasoned with her, pointing out how any resistance at this stage might result in the girl's being taken away altogether and this so terrified her that in the end she gave in grudgingly and consented to stand for her 'measures' which were taken by the indefatigable Sprout.

CHAPTER 22

Organised Chaos

Meanwhile, at the Castle, all was in train for Henry's coming of age. It had always been his secret dream to become engaged to Petula Danement on this night. Now, his conviction that this represented the outside edge of impossibility did much to diminish his enthusiasm for the elaborate festivities which had been arranged. The climax was, of course, the Ball. This, after much reasonable and some unreasonable debate—the majority of the latter stemming of course from Lord Aynthorp—had been agreed should be as Marguerite had explained to Prudence. Invitations were dispatched. House parties were made up all over the country. An astonishing order was given to the shop in Piccadilly which Lady Aynthorp still persisted in calling 'Mister Fortnum and Mister Mason'. This was for a thousand candles with which to fill the sconces and the chandeliers in the Ballroom and reception rooms. As the little Countess Marguerite had pointed out, 'Anything else, with eighteenth century dress, would be unthinkable!'

Once Lord Aynthorp had been persuaded that it was a 'capital thought' and had indeed managed to ascribe majority credit for the idea to himself, he let himself go in the matter of detail. Sawby, who was much liked by his employer, and therefore enjoyed special privileges, ventured to remind his lordship that the four chandeliers in the Ballroom had by this time been converted to what was still thought of below stairs as 'that new fangled electricity'.

'Then convert them back again,' snapped the titular head of the Family. 'Damme, it's not every day m'grandson comes of age, is it?' this last delivered somewhat fiercely with the white head thrust forward and the old eyes flashing.

'Indeed, no, my lord,' Sawby replied urbanely, 'I only wished to ascertain your lordship's wishes. Have I your lordship's permission therefore to send for the electrical expert to set matters in train?'

'Yes, yes get the feller here and let him begin immediately—
oh Sawby, see to it that he stands by to put the whole contrap-
tion back again thereafter, otherwise her ladyship will roast us!'

'There is just one small point which remains to be settled,'
Sawby continued unruffled. 'With, as is estimated, my lord, a
thousand candles being used, not to speak of any replenishments
we might be requiring, I would venture to submit to your lordship that the risk of fire is such that we shall need to engage the
services of an extra ... er ... roster of men to be on the alert for
any misadventure and prepared to deal with it immediately.'

'Then get 'em,' said Justin Aynthorp, 'and now get me some
Madeira, all this talkin' is unconscionable thirsty work!'

Sawby did as he was bid. He took himself to the Aynthorp
Arms where his old friend Joseph Stapley was by now very
successfully entrenched, and there, over a pint of ale, he put out
the fact that he was looking for 'half a dozen likely lads with
good legs and reasonable appearance to do candle duty on the
night of the ball'. 'But mind you,' he warned, 'they must be
upstanding young ones with a proper sense of occasion and I
shall need to choose them very soon now, for they will have to
be measured and fitted for their footmens' livery *and* of course
they must wear powder.'

One more visit four days later yielded a score of likely lads
lined up for Sawby's inspection. From them he finally selected
six of reasonably matching heights, arranged for them to come
up to the Castle and be decked out in their finery so that they
might, 'accustom themselves to wearing livery with some semblance of ease', and then further present themselves for drilling
in the niceties of backing instantly against whichever wall was
nearest in the event of Royalty entering any rooms in which they
were situate. Rumour had it that Henry was to be honoured by
the presence of his Monarch, quite apart from a sprinkling of
European royalties.

Other rumours, less pleasing, were in current circulation. The
King, it seemed, was unwell. Sawby, who managed by means
only known to himself to be perpetually advised of all events
which even remotely concerned the Castle and its occupants, was
indulging in some grave head-shaking on this score and had
actually relaxed so far as to say to Mrs Parsons, in the privacy
of the Steward's Room that *he* had grave doubts as to whether
the Ultimate Seal of Distinction would in fact be bestowed upon

Mr Henry. By this he meant that he feared the King's health would debar him from participating in this glorious and excessive piece of junketing. Indeed there were grounds for such rumours. Nevertheless, arrangements went on apace. Much attention was given to the planning of the card room with a special private buffet for his delectation should the King come. There were, too, some high level discussions on the subject of whom to invite for his amusement. Mrs Keppel had been sounded discreetly and had expressed her immense pleasure at the prospect. A cousin who was lady-in-waiting to the Queen then relayed the information that her Majesty was at present 'too tired' which, as Lord Aynthorp stated baldly, 'merely indicates she prefers to give in gracefully and let the King enjoy himself'. This heartless *sommaire* stemmed from his detestation of deafness in anyone even his Queen.

'Besides,' added Lady Aynthorp drily, 'we have a very carefully timed schedule and though it may be *lèse majesté* it would be a trifle difficult to time *anything* if we were to be so honoured!' Aynthorp snorted amusedly and went off to play billiards with his eldest son.

In the meantime Pierre, Chef André's cousin, arrived on loan from M. Voisin's famous restaurant in the Rue Royale, armed with his knives, mandoline and some templates from which he would create some of his *chef d'oeuvres* for the ball supper. In his train he brought his eldest son, a stripling of some seventeen summers who was already making a name for himself in the centre of the gastronomic world as a coming master of sugar and confectionery work. On this trio devolved the whole responsibility and from them the lesser labours were disseminated among a small brigade which André had assembled from among his *camarades* working in London.

With only three weeks before the Ball the Castle presented all the appearance of an overturned ant's nest and only the Family's private rooms were sacrosant. The ant heap swayed and spread on the ground floor from Ballroom to sitting-out alcoves, from Card Rooms to Supper Rooms, Drawing Rooms and ante-rooms, and there were constant comings and goings, incessant shiftings and liftings, succinctly described by the titular head as 'makin' it impossible for a man to move a flamin' inch on his own property without stumblin' over some confounded men measurin', takin' down, erectin' or hammerin''. He rampaged on: 'If I'm not bein'

rammed by pole-carryin' fellers or deafened by noise I'm bein'
butted by flamin' pot plants. It's not just a matter of Burnham
Beeches comin' to Dunsinane but the whole dam' place bein'
turned into a perishin' flower show and a bear garden to boot!
If it goes on much longer I shall go to m' club until the whole
pox-stricken army of them is cleared out!'

All this was of course punctuated by roars for 'Sawby' and
'Madeira' until even his spouse lost patience with him and gave
him a severe dressing down. After this he calmed a little but
remained perilously close to eruption point.

The only person in the entire Castle who took part in the
proceedings with undiminished enthusiasm and undisguised
enjoyment, was the tiny *châtelaine* who could be found from dawn
to dusk conferring with Mrs Peace over the programmes—which
were exact replicas of those used for the first Royal Ball of King
George II's reign—supervising the fittings of gowns which were
brought down from London in huge hampers and taken back
again thereafter; interviewing two men from the Bank of England
who came down with Lorme Jewels which had lain in the vaults
for many years and arranging for a detective to be added to the vast
army of persons who now slept on the premises. Lady Aynthorp
then spent happy hours opening the boxes with the detective
stationed at the door of the gun room, in which unlikely situation
the jewels were taken from their boxes and matched to silks,
satins, laces and furbelows. The vast display cabinets were then
plundered for fans ranging from chicken skins to fine laces, and,
finally, a hairdresser with his two assistants was installed in a
small bedroom adjacent to Mrs Peace's stock room where they
set out, curled and powdered a vast array of wigs in the styles
worn by the Lorme ancestors and also laid out an assortment of
patches from which the family would make their choice.

Then the tailors arrived and Lord Aynthorp was persuaded
to assume the costume in which he would appear on the night.
When, after the usual expostulations, criticsms, grumblings and
complainings, he was finally decked out in the black and silver
which he had elected to wear and had actually submitted to a trial
powdering of his hair, the whole family assembled to inspect him.
Then he suddenly turned benign and seized this opportunity to
instruct them all in the manner of walking, bowing, taking snuff
and tossing back a ruffle at the wrist until he had all his descendants engaged upon a similar ploy and Lady Aynthorp clutched

the little Countess Marguerite in helpless laughter at their popinjay performances.

During such ploys the worthy Bishop and his lady arrived and reinstalled themselves. Then Damien and his brother descended upon them briefly from a nearby house party with huge hampers containing their clothes for the great occasion. No sooner had these members of the family become settled in their respective quarters than the St Johns were swept up the drive in the Rolls. The Castle was filling up. The rumour went around that Damien was wearing white satin, had scarlet heels to his buckled shoes and would carry a small muff. This last 'on dit' caused Justin Aynthorp to snort derisively but he later relented sufficiently to invite Damien to participate in some sword selection.

The Armoury included a special annexe in which dress swords had been housed for several centuries. With Lord Aynthorp leading and the rest of the menfolk following, a foray was made upon the hoard, swords were buckled on over jodhpurs, breeches, knickerbockers and drain-pipe trousers with immense gravity until the little Countess appeared and again laughed them out of court for their antics.

'We really are rather ridiculous,' Gyles agreed as he unfastened a splendid jewel-hilted dress sword which had been worn by Rupert de Lorme at the court of George II, 'but I never could resist dressing up even when I was small.'

'We all love it,' agreed Sinclair, recovered from his influenza and now frowning deeply as he debated the relative suitability of an emerald-hilted sword and one studded with rubies. 'I shall have to ask Henrietta which I should wear, she has such splendid taste in such matters,' he decided. Then turning to Bishop Alaric he asked, 'Which one have you chosen, sir?'

'I am not wearing one,' replied Alaric, 'as I recall, Cardinal Orsini's accoutrements did not include a sword.'

'Orsini, eh?' Justin Aynthorp looked up sharply. 'So that's your choice, is it? Very suitable I declare! The religious who as Pope Benedict the Thirteenth became unsparing in his efforts to abolish luxury and undue pomp among his Cardinals!' After which Parthian shot he turned to his sister, 'Meg, my dear, did you come to admire, chide or summons, I wonder?'

Marguerite regarded her brother amusedly. 'Now don't pretend, Justin, that you are not enjoying yourself hugely. If you must know I came to summons you to the Blue Drawing Room.

Alicia has the snuff boxes out. Her detective is with her. You are to make your choice. Then the boxes will go into the man's safe-keeping to be redistributed upon the night.'

'Well at least Uncle Gyles will not find their manipulation difficult,' Damlen observed sheathing the simple light dress sword he had selected. 'I have never taken to the snuff habit, but I must beg you, sir, to instruct me now for I simply must carry one.'

'With white satin?' Gyles twinkled.

'Precisely.'

'Then,' said Gyles, unbuckling his sword, 'I *had* better instruct you.' He withdrew his small gold snuff box and took snuff. 'So,' he said, sniffing from the back of his hand with the ease of long practice, 'now pray take some yourself.'

Damien extended one plump white hand and rather gingerly complied. The others watched amusedly. Damien choked, sput-tered and was enmeshed in a gale of coughing. . . . When he could speak he gasped out, 'Damme, what a barbarous habit! I declare it is not for me. Really cousin, this is beyond the outside edge of endurance!' and he buried his face in his pocket handkerchief.

'It is an acquired taste,' Gyles agreed sympathetically. 'I dare say if you flourish the box, take snuff, as you do quite elegantly, but practise twisting your wrist so that the snuff is then discarded and merely direct your sniff very slightly to one side of the snuff, you will deceive the majority and avoid being enmeshed in a choking fit. Let me perform for you as I suggest.' He took another pinch, laid it upon his hand, gave a swift twist of his wrist and then sniffed just beyond the area where the snuff had lain. 'You see?'

'Really most kind,' Damien regarded him with streaming eyes. 'When I have recovered from that excruciating experience, I will endeavour . . . most obliged . . . really.'

All this was accompanied by some fairly stentorian nose blow-ing over which the sound of the luncheon gong bestirred them all and effectively put an end to their capers. They hastily removed the swords and handed them to George who had been a blank-faced but highly entertained witness throughout. While he affixed the labels which Christine had prepared and then replaced the swords in their cabinets, the men hurried towards the small dining room.

There were five days left. Already the bonfires were hugely stacked. Already the marquees had been erected at a safe distance from them so that the villagers would be assured of adequate sustenance when they streamed up the long drive to take their share of Henry's coming of age celebrations. An unceasing rattle of carts on the gravel betokened the arrival of more and more ale barrels, more and more potted plants, while an antlike procession of farm hands could be seen through the hours of daylight wending their way in the direction of the marquees with trestle tables and regiment of chairs and small tables, some from storage in Archers' Causeway, some from the new Village Hall which had been donated by the family and opened for the first time only eighteen months ago.

To this ant-procession was added another from the kitchen gardens and stove houses as Sawby supervised the transportation of kitchen fruits and vegetables to Mrs Parsons. Then tumbril-like, horse-drawn vans began to draw up at the main entrance. Out of them poured men in green baize aprons carrying multitudes of small golden chairs and small tables with gilded legs destined to fill the supper rooms on the great occasion. In these rooms, under Mrs Peace's jurisdiction, a team of sewing women attached the frills and flounces, the bows and tiny flower springs with which the base coverings of these tables were to be swagged and draped. Their luncheon time break was taken *in situ* with Pearson in charge of this operation at a trio of side tables from which she dispensed sandwiches, plain fruit cake and tea from a great copper urn. All over the Castle similar buffet services were in operation as the ants toiled and moiled about. Wherever they worked Sawby—who seemed almost capable of manifesting himself in several places at once—was sure to be seen, lynx-eyed and quick to pounce upon the smallest action which found disfavour in his sight.

He would 'materialise' in the doorway, dip into his vest-pocket, withdraw and affix his steel-rimmed spectacles and survey whatever team of beavers he had chosen for security. Then his commands would be issued. As the family streamed towards luncheon with Robert and Edward already awaiting their arrival in the dining room, Sawby made just such a descent upon the sewing army in the main supper room. His survey completed, 'Mrs Peace, will someone please remove that sewing machine from our parquet on to a really thick drugget?' he requested coldly.

This raised startled heads and Mrs Peace, biting her lip at her own omission, despatched two girls for the aforesaid drugget instantly. Then Sawby bent himself into a croquet hoop shape to retrieve two pins as if they were dead mice and, brushing his finger-tips together ostentatiously, said 'See to it from now on that whomever is in charge of the needlework activities in here . . . Mrs Primble, if I am not mistaken . . . ?'—Mrs Primble looked up from her work and ripped the elastic banded pincushion from the back of her left hand and Sawby fixed her with an intimidating glare—'delegates one of your workers to maintain this activity at short and regular intervals and,' Sawby stepped three paces into the room along the wall to ease out a chair which had slid back until it actually touched the wall, 'kindly see to it that no chair is allowed to come into contact with these historic and valuable wall decorations.' So saying he returned his spectacles to their pocket, turned and moved towards the dining room with as much speed as was concomitant with his dignity, arriving just in time to draw out Lady Aynthorp's chair at the precise moment her tiny personage approached the table.

Below stairs, with Sawby currently aloft, Mrs Parsons was practising that art in which above all others she excelled—that of Making Herself Felt! As the days fell away and the pace increased, so her convenient rheumatism asserted itself proportionately as did her shortness of temper and fluency of tongue until the Servants' Hall and 'her' kitchen resounded to her complaints, exhortations, strictures and criticisms.

The customary one hour break at this time of day was now shortened to forty-five minutes and a stern dictum was issued by Mrs Parsons who was responsible with her maids for all staff meals, that this would be further truncated to thirty minutes for the last three days of preparations, with what she called 'a running buff-ett' on the day itself.

Very applicable to the seething which all this engendered in the servants' quarters was a phrase which the precocious Lucien, in holiday collaboration with Lucy, had written out in laborious ink copperplate inside an exercise book which contained the growing story of a family of eels and elvers which Lucien was illustrating in his own fashion. Lucy had suggested, Lucien had approved and illustrated the happy phrase—emanating from Mrs Eel who in turn was very busy in her own undersea kitchen—the performance of her son, Sammy Elver, who was fraying her nerves with his capers. 'Sammy, will you please stop swimming yourself into swirls, you are getting on my scales,' she was made to exclaim.

The entire staff one way and another were 'swimming themselves into swirls' and the thump, bang, thud of incessant feet travelling up and down the stairs at speed had, as Mrs Parsons informed them all with stentorian relish 'made my pore head split', which was untrue but nevertheless eloquent of a bad headache.

'Gawd!' ejaculated George coming down at speed and on his heels, 'the old girl's a right termigant today! I wish I wos invisible.' And so saying, he dashed past a weeping girl for whom Mrs Parsons' rebukes had proved too much, but, kindly young man that he was, he managed a not wholly respectable twitch at the girl's skirts as he flashed by and an encouraging murmur, 'Chirp up chicken. The old girl's bark's far wors'n 'er bite and you've no call to let 'er make you cry.' Having retrieved the object of his descent, he dashed back and was rewarded by a spate of sniffs and a watery smile, plus a slightly choked, 'Thank you kindly, Mr George, but honest, she's bin somethink orful this morning!'

On the morning before the Day, Henry arrived. As soon as he had supervised the laying out of his costume and stuck his head round the door of the 'wig room', to settle the time when M. Léon would affix his powdered curls, he fled to his father's office. They were deep in discussion about tithe barns, while Henry was also busy pinning some charts to the office boards which he had prepared at Oxford for his father, when to his carefully suppressed delight Petula stuck her curly head around the door and enquired, using the purely honorary title, 'Uncle Gyles, may I come in?'

Gyles rose instantly. 'With the greatest possible pleasure, my dear,' he smiled, 'Henry has kept my nose so close to the grindstone for the past two hours that your visit is doubly welcome.'

He drew out a chair for her and busied himself with a tray on which stood a decanter and some schooners.

Petula gave Henry a light greeting and asked curiously, '*You* keeping your father's nose to the grindstone? Since when and what about, am I allowed to ask?'

Henry looked at his father significantly, but Gyles had clearly decided upon his own course of action. He replied smoothly: 'Oh Henry is quite my severest taskmaster these days. May I offer you some sherry?"

She accepted and looked uncertainly from father to son. 'And what has Henry to do with your affairs?'

'My son's affairs, Miss, are my affairs and *vice versa*. He long ago assumed the first of his future responsibilities.'

Petula contemplated the contents of her schooner with somewhat excessive intentness, 'Did he now,' she said, her voice expressionless, 'In what way may I ask?'

'Well you see...' Gyles began.

'I thought, you see...' said Henry simultaneously. Then they both broke off, looked at each other again and Petula gave a gurgle of laughter.

'Oh you do look funny! You sound funny too, both talking at once and ... er ... both saying absolutely nothing!'

Gyles handed a filled schooner to his son and reseated himself. 'It is only some business affairs concerning the estate. I believe we should not run the risk of boring you with such matters.'

Petula's eyes were dancing. 'Oh no, Uncle Gyles, you cannot brush me off like that. After all I have practically grown up with that young flibberty-gibbet over there.' She lifted her lashes at Henry who went scarlet and then lost colour alarmingly. Two little lines crept to the corners of his mouth and the famous Lorme temper sparked in his eyes but before he could speak his father resumed with the same unruffled serenity.

'Oh, my dear, you are so very much in the wrong, if you will permit me to contradict you. Young Henry here has literally saved my reason in the past months and made it possible for me to get some huntin' this season. Y'see, estate management becomes increasingly complicated these days. *Droit de seigneur* is beginning to be outmoded and one's responsibilities grow apace.'

'Really.' Petula's eyes still maintained that sparkle but behind it Gyles, who was watching her intently, screened by his own urbane exterior, perceived a flicker of some other emotion as well. 'Do you mean to say,' she spoke more slowly now, considering her words, 'that Henry, although he is still up at Oxford has involved himself practically in estate management in collaboration with you?'

'Of course.'

'Henry,' she then switched her focus, 'we've been lifelong friends yet you never said a single word to me about it. Oh false friend!'

Henry by this time had regained control of himself and his

nonchalance now matched theirs. He said quickly, 'Not false, Pet, but thoughtful. I have seen so little of you in the past few months that I hesitated before runnin' the risk of wearyin' you off the place altogether by talkin' to you of rents and things, replacements of pheasants, raisin' of wages, maintenance of stables and a thousand other similar routine duties.'

The girl continued twirling her schooner between small slim fingers. 'I see,' she spoke even more slowly now. 'Well perhaps you will make amends by riding with me for a short while this afternoon and then *you* can tell me all about it while *I* make myself understood to you on certain aspects of *my* interests of which you in turn seem extraordinarily unaware.'

Henry replied shortly. The 'flibberty-gibbet' label was still rankling. 'If my father can spare me I assure you nothin' would give me more pleasure, but we really are heavily pressed at the moment.' He then addressed his father. 'You know, sir, I had promised to give you those harness stock lists today and to settle that matter of Carver's Barn.' He crossed to a long table piled with papers, riffled through them and produced a pink-taped document. 'I have all the necessary facts in here and if you are in a hurry for it I shall have to deny myself the pleasure Pet proposes.'

Gyles, who was enjoying the small scene hugely, and, to boot, finding himself hard-pressed not to laugh at the stateliness of the exchange between these two 'silly infants' as he inwardly summarised them, now hastened into the breach with his assurance, 'But of course not. You have helped me so much, dear boy, that I am actually ahead on some matters. We've got the sheep to discuss, the new plantations to study and pass together and there is also that business over Parr's brassica field, but in the main I can easily spare you. After all,' he smiled benignly at Petula, who was now glancing from one to the other in acute surprise, 'you are here for a week and after the meet tomorrow we can hope to settle down to three or four days of uninterrupted work, so do pray take Pet ridin'. And now you must permit me to leave you. I am promised to yer mother, Henry, for a final dress rehearsal and a dozen other things besides.'

'If you are thinkin', sir, that you have to deal with those electricians, I have already done it,' said Henry quickly. 'I saw the foreman this mornin'. I arranged for him to take his men off tonight and I have arranged with Cousins to fix them up with accommodation in Lower Aynthorp. Then I further suggested he go with the Cousins to the bonfire celebrations and only show up here again the day after tomorrow. I thought,' he looked hopefully at his parent, 'that with the removal men swarmin' about, the staff cleanin' and all the rest of the aftermath, they'd only be a dam' nuisance millin' about with wires and scaffoldin' until things were cleared up a bit.'

'Excellent,' Gyles exclaimed. 'That takes another ploy off my shoulders. I'm extremely grateful. It was an admirable idea and I shall be obliged if you will confirm it. Meanwhile, you two children can cut off after this scratch luncheon . . .' he broke off. 'You're staying to luncheon of course, Pet?'

'Well,' said that well-nigh speechless young lady, 'Aunt Christine did ask me and Lady Aynthorp was there and she did say "yes, pray stay child, we are sure we shall think of somethin' we shall want to ask you to arrange at the last moment".'

'Then that's settled,' said Gyles briskly, his stomach muscles inwardly cramping with laughter as he saw clean through the 'young puss's manoeuvres' and the way in which she had now managed to turn the tables so that Henry knew she must have grown as close to the leading Lorme women in the past few months as his son had to him.

When they took themselves off, he did not set out to keep his 'urgent appointments', but sat in his old swivel chair, threw back his head and laughed until the tears rolled down his cheeks. Then he mopped himself off and went in search of his Christine to tell her the good news.

Lord Aynthorp and the residing detective, the latter now re-inforced by two assistants, spent a final hour touring the rooms and corridors which would be used that night by upwards of a thousand guests. During the course of these perambulations the detective took the plunge, saying, 'If I may respectfully submit, my lord, the current arrangements do err ever so slightly on the casual side. I trust your lordship will not take this comment amiss.' This broadside was delivered athwart the central library table, the two assistants standing watchfully two paces to the speaker's rear.

Justin Aynthorp said, 'Herrumph,' which neither discouraged nor inspired but the dogged detective plodded on.

'You see, my lord, these swords, snuff boxes, fans and indeed all these valuable period costumes which are lying around in hampers, rightly belong in cabinets in a properly protected, display museum. Would it not be advisable, after this ball is over, for your lordship to give consideration to the assembling of such a museum? Every year such items become increasingly valuable. Doubtless your lordship is very fully insured but even so I cannot believe that any insurance company, in the event of losses by theft, would take kindly to the ... er ... somewhat slight protection given to a great number of your treasures. The main Armoury alone has items in it of very great value dating ...' he hesitated 'dating back to how far back would your lordship estimate?'

'The Norman Conquest,' replied his lordship thoughtfully.

The man pressed home his advantage. 'I am fully aware, from the specified lists sent to me by your insurance company, that what your lordship would probably term the main treasures are protected; but the ... er ... lesser items are, it seems, wholly unlisted and do represent even at the present time, very considerable value.'

Half of this Justin Aynthorp heard vaguely. What had produced the profound effect and caused his current reflective mood was to him the great potential in the phrase 'properly protected museum'. His agile old mind was already assessing potential areas where such a museum could be housed and seeing in such an enterprise a project calculated to amuse and interest him. Indeed he was likewise reflecting on how much he could do for future generations, setting aside his own content in such ploys, by further investments in such items as would enhance both the value and interest of such a museum.

He said as much, if somewhat briefly, to his wife when, in the tranquillity of her boudoir, he was installed by Palliser in his favourite chair and supplied by his man Cuff with a tray at his elbow supporting his Madeira.

'You see, Emmy,' he enlarged, 'there are really three aspects to consider: our duty to the Family and in particular to future generations; the protection of our property and the care which would surely result in added longevity for these items; plus the remote possibility, with all these confounded rumours of increased taxes which are causing me some disquiet at this time, of our opening the Museum to the public at a fixed entrance fee which would more than cover its maintenance and custodianship. At the same time we must accept absolutely from the onset that it must be so housed as to give access to such persons as might wish to visit it without their ever impinging on family privacy. This must be regarded as sacrosant at all times.'

His 'Emmy' sipped her tisane slowly and reflected awhile upon her husband's words. Characteristically, she took the salient point first.

'Are you serious about these taxation rumours?'

'Yes I am,' he assured her. 'I have it from the most unimpeachable sources.' He frowned at her portentously, thereby indicating that Palliser's presence in the room made a more detailed report impossible.

'What are you doing, Palliser?' enquired her mistress without turning her head. The woman replied, 'Laying out milady's costume for tonight. Setting milady's jewels upon her *toilette*, and airing milady's fan which still has a faint but distasteful aroma of moth balls.'

'Ah yes, well no matter,' her mistress grimaced back at her spouse. ' 'Tis of no consequence now, Justin, but if you think so then, my dear, I am all enthusiasm for the project.' She lifted one hand and ticked off the points as she saw them. 'A. you are absolutely right in what you say. I agree with you on all counts;' one finger went down, 'B. my dear Justin, the augmentation of these collections, the choice of a suitable venue according to the points you have made;' down went a second finger, 'and, most felicitous of all, C. the finding of suitable display cabinets *of the right periods*—some of which I admit we may have already within the Castle but others of which will have to be purchased will give you a restful and rewarding labour which I feel sure you will enjoy once you have embarked upon it.' A third finger descended. 'D. constitutes the only possible problem—have you consulted Gyles and Christine and if so, what is *their* opinion; for you do recall that we have made it a *point of honour* between us not to implement any schemes before acquainting them and obtaining their approval?' Thus she reminded him of his bounden duty in unassailable terms since they included the lynch-pin 'a point of honour'.

'I have not had the time,' he replied. 'This only occurred an hour or so ago. Christine has half a hundred things to settle before we all need to dress for dinner. Gyles is likewise heavily involved and he asked me to be mumchance on another matter which absolutely precludes my consulting him until after this Ball is over.' Palliser appeared beside them. 'Ah Palliser, *encore de Madère, s'i vous plaît*. Emmy, more tisane? *Bon, et encore de tisane pour milady*.' Palliser obeyed and then returned to her labours.

'And what is this "other matter"?' Lady Aynthorp enquired softly.

He dropped his voice. 'Henry and Petula have gone ridin'. It seems the gel surprised them this mornin' in Gyles' office and found Henry thick in estate matters with his father.'

A slight chuckle escaped. 'Oh, Justin dear, would it not be fortuitous if they . . . er . . .' she glanced over her shoulder, then added, 'if they did you-know tonight.'

'That,' her outrageous spouse whispered back, 'has been my intention since Pet honoured me with her confidence some months back, under the seal of absolute secrecy. In this instance I have not even spoke of it to you for,' he twinkled back at her, 'I had, shall we say, a sufficiently strong conviction that you were well acquainted with what was in the wind and how Henry's parents were tackling it. You will recall I asked you a long time ago what would be your reaction should . . . er . . . should such a thing come about.'

'Absolute and unqualified acceptance and approval.' Lady Aynthorp spoke the words so loudly that Palliser glanced up in surprise. 'Palliser,' she continued, '*priez demander à Madame La Comtesse si elle porte les sapphires ce soir. Allez vite, Palliser, mais, au debut, demandez à sa femme personelle si La Comtesse se repose encore, ou non. Surement elle sait à cette dernière heure.*'

'*Immediatement, milady*,' Palliser put down her work reluctantly and withdrew on this wholly fictitious errand.

Lord Aynthorp opened his cigar case. 'Mind if I smoke a cigar, Emmy?'

'You know I love the aroma, Justin, so pray do. Now, with these things clear between us I would just like to run over the timings with you for tonight. At six twenty-five precisely the carriage takes you and Gyles and Henry to the Marquee. You make your short speech acknowledging Gyles' seigneury. Gyles makes his even briefer speech and then Henry addresses them. You all take a drink with our people. They sing *For he's a jolly good fellow*. At a signal from Plum—who will have stationed himself at the marquee entrance—there will be a fanfare. Sawby will enter and make the "presentation". Henry will thank everyone, you will withdraw. Then the bonfires will be lit.

'All this has been estimated to take five minutes each way in the carriage, fifteen minutes for the speeches, five minutes for the presentation and acknowledgement, and a further five minutes for all three of you to circulate among the most senior of our employees. You should be back here by 7.00 p.m. You then have forty-five minutes in which to change into your costumes and rest a little, if you can, as I pray you will do. At 7.45 p.m. we shall all assemble in the Chinese Room where Henry's gifts have been laid out. We will present him with the family ones. The detective will then take over.

'We shall return to the Great Hall by 8.00 p.m. to receive Her Royal Highness and escort her to the White Drawing Room to present the rest of our guests and go in to dinner at 8.30 p.m. You will be allowed as much time as remains after dinner for your port. We, meanwhile, shall touch up our toilettes and generally refresh ourselves in readiness for the ball and be back under the receiving arch which will have been installed at the foot of the staircase while we are dining. We must be in readiness to receive the first of our guests by 10.15 p.m. precisely. We shall receive for thirty minutes, and then move to the second floral arch at the entrance to the ballroom and there receive again until approximately 11.00 p.m. On the hour the orchestra will tune up and begin to play and Henry will open the ball with Her Royal Highness. We will remain where we are until Sawby tells us that the last guest has arrived. In the meantime Gyles will then lead out H.R.H. for the second dance and by that time, my dear Justin, it will be your turn to dance with the Princess.' Lord Aynthorp made no reply. 'Justin,' she chided, 'are you listening?'

'Yes m'y dear, I am. But you set off a chain reaction of memory. I fear I was deep in my own twenty-first ball—May the third, 1835 it was. I led out Her Royal Highness, by no means a beauty I can tell you, but later in the evening I had my reward, for Phillipa Wentworth had come and she was a ravin' beauty.'

'The naughty Duchess,' said his wife sharply, 'a Duchess who was well-known to be very generous with her favours. She was as I remember also famous for her penchant for very young men.'

'She was,' the reply was laconic.

'And you were no exception?'

'I was no exception.' He suddenly sat bolt upright in the big chair. 'Why Emmy, I do believe, after all these years, you are jealous!'

They were both in the mood for admissions. 'Indeed, Justin,' she told him, 'though we are old and grey, I choose to tell you at this moment that there has never been but one man in my life, and you are he.'

He picked up her left hand as it lay in her lap and bent his head over it. 'Then,' said he, putting one hand under her still pointed little chin, 'let me make fair exchange. There has never been any woman but you, my dear, from the first time I clapped eyes upon you.'

She gave him her hand and he clasped his own around it.

'We have had a good life,' she said gently, seeing the sadness in his eyes for emotions long spent and fires burned down.

Then they were both silent for a while. He spoke first, saying: '*Cherie, je t'aime, et je ne regrette rien!*'

'*N'y moi non plus.*' There were tears in her eyes now. Through them she smiled. 'We have been . . . extremely blessed, my love, and we have had—what is that vulgar phrase of yours?'

'I have so many.'

'I remember: "We have had an unconscionably good run for our money." '

That made him laugh too. He stood up.

'I shall go to my room now and collect our gift to Henry. When I have handed it over to those detectives I shall take a short rest before tea.'

'Thank you, my dear.' She lifted her face to his and he bent and kissed her. 'And thank you for—everything.'

'No,' he said, his lips against her hair, 'it is I who thank you for so much my love. As we agree, we have done nothing to each other for which we have regrets.' Then, as if ashamed of such an emotional exchange, he turned and marched resolutely from the room.

His wife remained unmoving. She too was remembering. When she finally dried her eyes every word, every movement, every inflection of her husband's voice was ineradicably etched upon her memory.

After they left Gyles' office, Henry and Petula walked slowly through the Castle towards the stables to bespeak their mounts from Plum, whom they ran to earth in the saddle room, a straw between his teeth and little hissing sounds emerging therefrom as his knotted old fingers worked with astonishing deftness at a straw dolly in the shape of a fleur-de-lys. Hearing their approach, Plum put down this work somewhat furtively. Then he flung a saddle leather over it as the two figures cut across the bright sunlight in the doorway. He stood up hurriedly, pulled two stools forward, dusted them with his elbow and invited his visitors to be seated. Petula accepted but Henry remained lounging against the open stable door.

'What was that you were doing?' he asked Plum casually.

'Nothing important, Mister Henry, just something for the missis,' the old man lied quickly. 'Now what can I do for you, sir?'

'We want a little exercise after luncheon, if you could manage a couple of mounts by 2.30. Say, Mornin' Star for me and Indian Star for Miss Petula.'

'Well now,' Plum put his head on one side like a Robin and debated. 'We're huntin' termorrer. You'll have to promise me no larkin' and no hellferleather stuff, for Miss Christine's bespoke Indian Star and you, Mr Henry, will want to ride Mornin' Star—what you won't do no way if you ride 'er 'ard s'afternoon.'

'We'll be good, Plum,' Henry promised. 'We only want a pocketful of air in our lungs before the shindig tonight.'

'Wot a way to speak of yer comin' of age ball I must say,' Plum observed disapprovingly. 'I'd like to 'ear wot yer Nanny would say ter callin' it a shindig and you twenty-one an all, a man, and come of age! If I 'adnt wished yer well this mornin', and shall do it again ternight, blow me if I would now!'

'Never mind him, Plum, he's just self-conscious,' Petula excused Henry. 'I can assure you he's looking forward to it enormously.'

'Wot's he wearing?' Plum then enquired slightly mollified. 'All fanciful I 'ear.'

Henry grinned. 'If you must know, Plum, I'm wearing powder blue, embroidered with silver, a silver weskit picked out in silver thread and fastened with diamond buttons.'

'Real diamonds?' Plum enquired disbelievingly.

'Real diamonds,' Petula promised.

'Well, wot else?'

Henry ruffled his head, a habit he had never lost from childhood. It had the effect of capturing the February sun in sparks of smouldering copper.

'Pale blue and copper?' Plum debated in the interim.

'I'm wearing powder,' Henry explained, 'a powdered wig. I am also carrying a blue and silver cane and wearing high-heeled buckled shoes with diamonds in the heels. I shall buckle on a small dress sword which was carried by one of my ancestors.'

'Lawks,' ejaculated Plum. 'Can I see yer . . . with Miss Pet?' he hastily added.

'What about it, Pet?' Plum had dispelled the constraint between them and made them feel like children engaged upon some escapade.

'Why not?' Pet turned to him. 'We could slip down after changing and before dinner.'

'Where?' Plum wanted to know.

'Here.'

'Not enough light,' Plum shook his head gloomily.

'Well, we'll meet you at the garden door at five minutes to eight. We shan't be able to stay long because we have to receive the dinner guests at eight and before that I have to meet the family in the Chinese Room to receive my presents.'

'Ar,' said Plum knowingly, 'I know a thing or two about that, too.'

'What?' Petula wheedled him. 'Come on, Plum, tell.'

'More'n my life's worth. That's all I'll tell you and not even you, Miss Pet, can wheedle no more out of me. Right though, I'll get my Missis and we'll meet secret-like by the garden door, West Terrace, five to eight sharp, and I'll 'ave them osses ready for you 2.30 but mind you—no larkin' . . . or I'll 'ave yer lights and livers!'

They retraced their steps slowly. 'I think he's a dear old man,' said Petula happily. 'He lives and breathes for the "fambly" as he calls it, have you noticed?'

'Yes, my dearest Pet, and you must surely know what I think of the old chap! He lifted me on to my first pony and put the reins into my hands. He showed me how to hold 'em. He taught me the saw: "Your head held high, your hands held low, your knees kept close to the horse's side, your elbows close to your own." '

'Bless him,' said Pet. 'I think he and Sawbridge are two of the nicest men I know. Now tell me what have you been doing with Uncle Gyles?'

Their pacing slowed still further. Henry looked round at her rather sharply, scarcely crediting his luck, and countered question with question. 'Why do you want to know?'

It was her turn to hesitate. Then, taking a deep breath she plunged in. 'Because I am interested. Because whatever else has happened we have been "best friends" ever since we were tiny, like you and Plum who, by the way, was the first to lift me into the saddle when I was three-and-a-half and there was a terrible scene with our Pat when he found out.'

'Then why on earth did you call me a flibberty-gibbet to my father?'

Petula pulled hard at a sprig of precocious forsythia which had burst into flower. 'If you must know, because I wanted to draw you. You said something some time ago which made we wonder and I thought it might at worst provoke one of the two of you to tell me more.'

Henry stopped in his tracks. He put out his hands, took the girl's shoulders and turned her to face him. She dropped her eyes, and then, as if deciding this was cowardly, lifted them and met his look.

'Why?' he reiterated.

She twitched those shoulders, but he held on. 'I've told you because . . . oh, Henry, don't force issues, please, please don't be too intense! Just talk to me. Tell me what you have been doing. Tell me how it started. I want to know everything.'

'Do you have the right?' he shot out the question, with a touch of sternness in his young face.

'Nnno, but I would like to know.' Now her expression was pleading, which defeated him, so, crushing down the impulse to take her in his arms, he loosed his hold on her and resumed pacing.

'You started it,' he said curtly.

'Me?'

'You told me I was nothing but a boy . . .' He reminded her word for word of what she had said. He spoke of his fears, his sleepless nights, his eventual resolve to tackle someone. He recounted his uncertainty at first as to whom it should be and his final decision to go to his father. He told her everything, including how he eventually summoned enough courage to open that office door and spill out his dilemma to his father. He ended rather lamely: 'And then we started in, right away. The guv'nor told me some bits of back history. He offered to teach me more . . .

everythin' in fact, so I accepted. That's all there is to it. You can say if you like that I *am* a flibberty-gibbet, but grant me that I was one who has seen what a fool he had been.'

Petula said nothing. They climbed the steps to the West Terrace, and as they did so the sound of the luncheon gong floated out, warning them that on this day above all others punctuality was essential.

'Heavens,' she exclaimed. 'I must wash and tidy my hair. Now let us agree, we ride this afternoon. Then we go our separate ways until we meet again, right here,' Henry was holding open the garden door for her to pass through, 'at 7.55 precisely—in all our finery.'

'Yes,' said Henry meekly, exercising almost superhuman restraint. Petula was not unaware of this, but she ran off ahead. As she turned the corner, she looked back and blew him a kiss, thereby sending him into luncheon with the curious sensation that instead of being in the small dining room, he had suddenly been transported to heaven and was more than willing to display his state of rapture.

Christine saw them go that afternoon. She watched them pacing sedately across the Home Park deep in conversation. So reassuring did she find this sight that she called Gyles and, tucking one arm inside his, drew him to the window.

'There, I think,' she said, 'we see a most promising picture of . . .'

'Don't say it, my love,' Gyles laid a finger across his lips. 'I too had my hopes raised this morning. Indeed I did further the cause a little I fancy, but the young are so extraordinarily sensitive. Until we know something, it is incumbent upon us to remain *bouche fermé*. While we are on the subject of lips, however, may I remind you my love that yours fill me with as much desire as they did the first time I kissed you . . .' and so saying he drew her close to him. The next time he spoke, it was lip to lip. He murmured, 'I can only wish for them that they are as happy as we are.'

There was a brief final exchange between Henry and Petula. They dismounted after their ride and handed the mares to a groom, with strict instructions as to their rubbing down, nose bags and blankets. Then they hurried off, feeling distinctly guilty.

Henry, realising the time, promptly commandeered Plum's

bicycle. He left word with the groom that he would be back in half an hour, then he pedalled off with Petula riding undignified pillion behind him. He took her to the steps of the Danement home, mist-shrouded now in the descending dusk. The old façade had assumed a wraith-like appearance in the dying light. Through it, like some fantastical mirage, lights rayed out into the mist in similarly wraith-like radiance. For Henry it was all part of this now magical day. As Petula jumped off and began running up the steps, he called after her, 'Pet, you haven't told me what you are wearing tonight?'

She turned, waved and called back: 'You'll find out at the garden door tonight. Don't be late!' By the time she spoke the last word she was almost out of earshot. Henry wondered, as he rode off, whether he had imagined it, but he thought that she had called, 'Don't be late, love.' He pedalled back furiously, yelled for the groom who came running, gave him the bicycle and pelted up to the Castle just as the 'tactless young cousin' as she was known to various members of the family, descended from her carriage, assisted by Robert. The two of them went in together while Robert began carrying in the girl's portmanteaux.

CHAPTER 23

The Twenty-first Birthday

And now it was all happening. Quite suddenly there was no more time. Below stairs such phrases as 'well, it will have to do as it is'... 'there's no time to do any more to that'... and 'now you *will* have to stop'... were being bandied about as the last tray-loads for the buffet were being scurried up to the supper rooms and the last sugar baskets on which André had worked for so long were being hurriedly piled high with petits fours and carried towards the supper tables.

Outside the main entrance Sawby was supervising the lighting of the flambeaux to be held aloft by the fourteen stalwart young men from London who had arrived on the afternoon train and were now hurriedly taking up their positions on either side of the seven steps. They had all been forced into the primrose and gold liveries! They all endured the discomfort of padded calves and thick wigs with primrose and black bows. Sawby surveyed them, then issued them with their last instructions.

'No fidgeting, mind you,' he commanded. 'Has everyone been to the toilet?' There was a ripple of laughter, then one delinquent stepped out.

'I forgot,' he said sheepishly.

'Then hurry,' Sawby snapped. 'You've been told, that I do know.' The luckless one scuttled away while the rest were apostrophised and exhorted.

'Now remember, eyes on each other to see those flames are held in descending line on either side. You can fall out for the first time when one of my footmen comes to tell you that the household is seated at table. There will be hot soup and sandwiches for you in the Servants' Hall. Does everyone know the way?' he paused for any dissenting voice. None came so he continued, 'Unless any lady or gentleman is seen to be in difficulties with their clothing or drops something *none of you move*. If you have to assist any guest, see that the man above you puts out his free hand immediately to take the helper's flambeau. Then whoever of you steps out of line, *get back to your station with all possible speed.*'

There was a general murmur of assent. The absentee on 'toilet' duty edged himself into place. The flambeaux were handed out.

'One more timing to remember,' Sawby told them. 'You resume your stations at 10.30 and you remain at them until 11.30. Then you return to the Servants' Hall and await my summons. When it comes you resume stations once more and remain until the last guest has departed *and that you will be told by me.* You are not required to make decisions, or have opinions either,' he added as a salutary afterthought.

By this time the Castle seemed new-come from Camelot and dropped down upon these English acres by Merlin's magic. Like a fragment of history in stone, it rose and soared above its original foundations laid down by Henri de Lorme of Normandy —an illusion heightened by the low-lying mist which swirled in from the river. It hazed the grass. It lapped the trees about, leaving only their upper trunks and still bare branches clear of it and free to filter the starlight through. It seemed, too, as though those old trees were transformed back in time to tree men and women of the forgotten days now come to pay tribute to yet another heir apparent upon his birthday. They created the misted illusion of having come to congregate and contemplate the Castle which was so very young, as they knew time. From their vantage positions they could see how every lower window and, above, how every window embrasure of the Picture Gallery was starred by slender points of candlelight. This flowed out so very softly from those old windows, adding again to the image of a faerie Castle with faerie inhabitants who ever and anon flitted past those windows, pausing as they did so, to peep out before they followed their pursuit of some enchanted dance through the almost endless loop and chain of rooms.

It engendered such thoughts in Plum as he closed his cottage door, having cheered himself hoarse during the marquee presentation ceremony. Not that Plum knew of Camelot, or Merlin either, though it might well be that his knowledge of tree men and women came closer to the truth than was the case with any speculations of his 'betters'.

'Come along of me, Mum,' he said now, taking his wife's hand and setting out yet again on the long plod through the park. 'We've plenty of time afore our Mr Henry comes, so we can go slow like and look at the Castle as we go.'

'I should've thort you saw enough of the Castle,' commented his wife indulgently. 'Seeing it as you 'ave every day of yer life since you was born here and raised here and never did no work for no one else.'

Plum ignored this. His slow mind was assessing what he saw in intermittent glimpses through the tree trunks.

'Tonight, love,' he said softly, ' 'tis kind of like a tale told to a nipper. A tale about fairyland.' He held a small lantern in his other hand so that, as the couple went unerringly through the darkness and those trees, he seemed—at least to Christine and the little Countess who were both looking out of their upper windows—to resemble a will-o-the-wisp now darting behind an ancient bole. Now vanishing into the mist, now reappearing, Plum took a devious path through the trees and the impression of flitting along was further engendered.

'It's floating,' Plum stated, helping his wife over a fallen bough. 'Look what that mist has done to it!'

'Very pretty, I'm sure,' agreed his spouse, a soothing note in her voice. She had already been married to him for a long time and she knew well enough that this mild and gentle old creature could turn termagant if ever a word of criticism was breathed in his presence by anyone—his own wedded wife included—against either *his* Castle or *his* 'fambly'. On this night above all nights she had no desire to wound or even lightly to offend him.

Unspoken, impossible images raced across Plum's mind. At the most ordinary of times the Castle had that effect upon him and now, only dimly appreciated and indefinably experienced, nevertheless atavistic instincts were at work within him. He tried to put some of this into his lumbering speech and eventually managed, 'Tell you what, Mum, I wouldn't be one whit surprised if Puck was to float up out of 'is 'ill and pass before my eyes with a regiment of hob-goblins dancing behind 'im.'

'Such fancies,' the woman exclaimed and then as the fourteen flambeaux pierced the darkness with their flames,

'Oh, look, there go the flambows!' They stopped in their tracks as the smoke from the flames rose vertically in the still air and the bright fire plumes lit up the still figures. They were like men frozen in widening lines of descent on either side of the steps up which a thousand guests would walk . . . very soon now.

Behind the motionless figures, behind the candle-lit windows, the Great Hall had been stripped of almost all its furniture. Only a few of the eighteenth century carved and gilded 'arms' remained together with the long central table at which Doges had dined in the Venetian Palazzo from whence it had been brought to Castle Rising. On it stood an enormous épergne cascading with spring flowers. Under the huge marble chimney-piece the crackling of logs sent up little firework displays, the heat drawing out the scent from the massed flowers. Down the wide staircase— carpeted for this night in soft dark green—were clustered banks of yellow orchids from the stove houses, forced white and yellow iris, interspersed with the white and yellow of freesias and the feathery plumes of mimosas. It was these intoxicating scents which mingled with the burning cherry and apple wood in the chimney piece.

Henry came down those stairs very carefully in his finery. He was the first to do so. The Hall was empty. Twin silver gilt candelabra wore crowns of white candles pointing their tiny plumes of light towards the ceiling designed by Inigo Jones.

The setting gave so much credence to Henry's appearance that he seemed quite naturally costumed for such surroundings. As he stepped on to the polished floor the wide skirts of his blue satin coat, draped over his dress sword, brushed against a lintel and on that instant the bell pealed. Footmen came running, saw him and slowed to stately pace. They folded back the doors to reveal Petula, wearing powdered curls, a white rose tucked against one side and a single curl lying against one even whiter shoulder. Deliberately, she stepped in, permitted a man to take her cloak and extending one small hand sank down into a deep curtsey, her white and silver brocades billowing about her and one diamond-buckled slipper just peeping out from beneath the foamy flounces of her under-dress.

Henry took the extended fingers, bent to kiss them. The instant magic of the moment wrought formally upon them both. Behind her stood Petula's father and her brother smiling, conscious of the currents which were flowing, watchful. Petula held her curtsey a moment longer than was customary, then she permitted Henry to raise her and, as she came up, she lifted her eyes and enquired, 'How do I look, sir? Do I meet with your approval?'

'You dazzle me,' he retorted, pressing those fingers to his lips.

Plum and his wife reached the rim of the drive.

'We're early, mother,' Plum observed after scratching about inside his outer garments until he reached his moleskin waistcoat and from it produced a gunmetal watch which he had carried since the day his father handed it to him on his death bed. 'Seven forty-five. Let's have a closer look at them hired flambow men.'

They stood before the motionless figures like two old children examining the guards outside Buckingham Palace until Plum decided, 'Not bad for amatoors. Let's get on to the terrace now.' Thus, as they rounded the south wall and came to the West Terrace, with Plum holding the old lantern high for them to climb the steps, they saw Petula and Henry and stopped in their tracks, standing mute and staring.

Henry had picked up a candelabrum from a table as he hurried away from the Chinese Room. So the couple's first sight of him was with one ringed hand holding the sparkling hilt of his sword and the other, just as Plum had done with the lantern, holding the candelabrum high to illuminate his lady.

She was wrapped in her ermine cloak again. In the still cold air the candle flames barely flickered. As she saw the old couple she swept them just such a curtsey as she had made to Henry on her arrival.

'Hello,' she greeted them, 'do you think we look nice?' this last delivered with head tilted and with that one white curl falling across her bare shoulder as the cloak fell back.

'Like a princess in a fairy tale,' said Plum hoarsely.

More practically, Mrs Plum trotted forward. 'You'll catch your death, Miss Pet,' she fussed. 'Never mind showing us, cover up now please.'

'Why not come inside?' Henry suggested, having played amused spectator to this little scene. 'Then we can display ourselves in all our party finery and none of us need get cold.' He turned as he spoke, leaving them no option and held back the old garden door for them to pass through. Henry went a few paces down the corridor, opened the door of the garden room, switched on the electric light which had not been disconnected at all in this wing, put down the candelabrum on a white, cast-iron garden table and took his lady's hand. Suddenly, as he touched Petula's fingers, fear and uncertainty left him. Something emanating from the warmth and simplicity of the old couple who had trudged across the Park for a glimpse of them illuminated him more brightly than any man-made light.

Without pause, without even thought—or so it seemed to him in retrospect—he said simply, 'Now you can look at us. Dear Mr and Mrs Plum, permit me to have the honour of presenting you to my future wife.' For an instant Petula's fingers tightened over his, then she half turned to face him as he bowed low with all the ceremony concomitant with his dress.

'And my future husband,' she told him proudly, her eyes on him.

Mrs Plum burst into tears. 'Oh, my little love,' she wept, forgetting her place, forgetting everything except this most poignant news. Then she clasped Petula to her. 'Oh, Miss Pet, this is the day I dreamed on, *we've* dreamed on. It's wot we've all wanted and hoped and prayed for....' She broke off, became aware of what she had said and done and stepped back, hand to mouth. 'Oh I never...' she stammered, 'I beg your pardon Miss, but I was that overcome....' The tears were still on her cheeks but her eyes were suddenly full of embarrassment at the enormity of what she had done.

Petula just leaned forward to kiss the old tear-spattered cheek. 'Whatever happens, dear Mrs Plum,' she said, a trifle unsteadily, 'no congratulations from anyone else can ever be as sweet as yours. Thank you for a beautiful compliment.'

Plum had managed to get hold of Henry's right hand and was wringing it as if it were a piece of his wife's Monday wash. 'Oh Mr 'enery, oh, sir ..., Mother, ain't it wunnerful ...?'

'And may God bless you, my pretty pair,' she interjected.

Plum had managed to excavate a large bandana handkerchief from his stratified garments. This he now flourished, blew his nose loudly and handed on the handkerchief to his wife to mop herself off. The pair were now burbling incoherently.

'I 'ad an 'orrible feeling for some time...' Plum babbled, pausing for another trumpeting blow. 'It seemed summat had gorn wrong as I tole the Missis.'

'I knew better!' Mrs Plum triumphed. 'I said to Plum, "Leave 'em be. The young is always contrariwise and 'as their ups and downs. It'll all come right in the end, you mark my words." And so it 'as, my lovely pair, and so it 'as.'

'Has it?' Henry bent his head to Petula's. 'Has it, my little love?'

For answer, standing in the dusty room, she lifted her face to his.

'Indeed it has, my darling,' she told him, oblivious of even the Plums now. As their lips touched, she murmured, 'It's been so lonely, Henry, but now it really is like a fairy tale and all my dreams have really come true.'

Suddenly, Mrs Plum regained her self-possession. She looked at her husband. She jerked her head behind her. Plum nodded, then very softly the pair of them moved. When at length, rather dimly, the sound of the great gong reached them, Petula drew back with a little gasp.

'Henry... the time!' she exclaimed, guilt-stricken and, 'Oh, Henry, the Plums have gone!'

Late as they were, Henry startled Petula by his breathless request as they ran towards the Great Hall: 'Wait for me when you get there. Grandmama will never go in until we have arrived. Hide in the angle where the Crown Derby is, in that big cabinet. I've got to get to my room and back in twenty seconds flat.' So saying he swerved leftwards, paused to whip off his encumbering shoes, then, with them in hand, he went hell-for-leather up the back stairs, round and down the corridor to his room. Once there he dashed across to his dressing room, wrenched open a drawer, seized a small box—characteristically tucked under a pile of handkerchiefs—and raced back again until he had gained the last step of the angle in the main staircase. Then he stepped into his shoes again, concealing the box inside the hand, which now lay negligently against his sword hilt, and so descended, panting, but outwardly serene.

Heads turned... the hall seemed full of people, full of up-tilted questioning eyes. Henry smiled down vaguely but went directly to his grandmother to make his excuses. As he did so he caught a horrified whisper from his Mama—'Where on earth have you been you naughty boy?'—and, as he edged his way forward to be with Petula and armed her in to dinner, proceeded to make dutiful small talk while the procession moved forward with what seemed exasperating slowness.

'Was it not a happy thought after all, my dear Petula, making this a Costume Ball?' Then, dropping his voice, 'I adore you.'

She played the game with him. 'Indeed it is. Everyone looks so glamorous . . .' and whispered, 'I thought you would never say it.'

Henry was so shocked at this he forgot to whisper and quite clearly exclaimed, 'You hypocrite, you know you wouldn't let me!'

Again heads turned and a warning voice came from behind him—Gyles's—as 'Henry!' he said reprovingly.

Henry turned for a moment, rewarding his father with a smile of such radiance that it told him all he needed to know.

He leaned forward and spoke into his son's ear: 'Ah yes, I *quite* understand.'

Henry replied, 'I feel so funny, sir, going in ahead of you.'

'Then pray remember,' came the voice behind him, 'this is strictly for one occasion only and as soon as is at all possible on this night I shall welcome your presence in the library—alone.'

The procession had reached the dining-room doors.

'Not with Pet, sir?'

Softly came the reply to this as they moved to their places. 'Very well, with Pet. Is . . . that official, may I enquire?'

As he passed Henry flung back. 'Yes, sir. I take it your sanction is, too?'

As everyone sat down Christine's eyes were on Gyles. He made an infinitesimal nod which gratified her so much that she turned to the worthy Bishop with such a ravishing smile on her face that he was driven to remarking, 'May I be permitted, my dear niece, to compliment you on your appearance. I am bound to admit I have never seen you look quite so beautiful.'

'I have reason,' Christine nodded, 'and in due course you will know why, my dear Uncle Alaric . . . and now pray oblige me by turning your observant eyes to Petula. Does she not look exceedingly lovely?'

The Bishop diverted his portentous gaze to the head of the table, vacated for this occasion by Lord Aynthorp and occupied instead by Henry for this, his twenty-first birthday dinner. Petula sat upon his right.

'Radiant, I think is the word I would choose,' the Bishop replied thoughtfully. 'Is . . . er . . . is there anything . . . er . . . special toward?'

'Yes, there is. But I think we must still wait awhile before making any further observations.'

'Quite so . . . quite so,' he agreed benignly. 'I shall only remark what a fortuitous occasion this would be for . . . er . . . any conjectures I might be making inwardly.'

Christine chuckled, 'Exactly so,' and she bent her whole attention upon the *blinis* on her plate.

Dinner progressed according to Hoyle, at least it did until the termination of the fish course. Then Justine Aynthorp, seated in his unaccustomed place at the foot of the table, with his Alicia on his right, leaned back in his chair as the entrée plates were withdrawn, came up straightening his back abruptly, stared fixedly ahead of him and made a slight movement which brought the vigilant Sawby to his side. Sawby bent, his lordship raised his table napkin and under its cover said very quietly, 'Sawby, pray present my compliments to Mr Henry when a suitable opportunity presents itself for you to do so unobtrusively. Just ask him if the ring upon Miss Petula Danement's engagement finger is his?' Then he replaced the table napkin on his black satin-covered knees and resumed conversation with his sister Prudence whom he thought looked shockingly drawn and tired in a ponderous gown of brown brocade re-embroidered with black jet and passementerie.

Sawby's moment came, or possibly Sawby made the moment by assuming the duty of a footman for a moment in handing the salver of *Marcassin, Sauce St Hubert* himself to 'Mr Henry'. Down the table Justin Aynthorp kept gimlet watch upon his grandson. He watched Sawby bend and murmur. He watched the slow flush rise to the boy's powdered curls. He lip-read rather than heard the reply, 'But of course, Sawby. Tell my grandfather so with my compliments and add that I hope to have read him aright in imaginin' that I had his full approval so to do,' and he watched Henry raise his glass, look down the table and deliberately toast him.

'Young jackanapes!' he snorted inwardly, highly delighted.

Gyles had also observed the single solitaire diamond on Petula's hand as had Christine so, when at length the covers were drawn and by mutual agreement Lady Aynthorp abstained from her customary collecting of eyes, the whole family remained in their chairs as the port made its first circuit in what could possibly be described as telling quietude.

Then Lord Aynthorp rose and stood for a moment fingering the laces on his cravat and looking up the long table ... at the Danements, the Pulteneys and the Fulmers—lifelong friends whose own forbears had for many generations formed the vine of friendship with the Lormes—and at his own family. Then he spoke: 'My old friends and family, I had thought to ask you to join me in drinking a toast to my grandson on this, his twenty-first birthday but now it seems that with infinite pleasure,' his old eyes blazed with warmth and affection as he looked down the table, 'quite unexpectedly but wholly delightfully, I must now couple Henry's name with the name of my future grand-daughter-in-law Petula for I have the honour to announce the engagement of my grandson to my favourite gel', excludin' only my beloved wife. Ladies and gentlemen, I give you Henry and Petula. I only add that never have I proposed any toast in my long life with greater pleasure and love. May you two children upon the threshold of your life together enjoy as long and as lusty a one as I have done with my wife who has been my strength and inspiration throughout the fifty-three years we have spent together. So may God bless both in your union even as ours has been blessed.'

The room rippled with the two names as everyone rose: 'Henry' ... 'Petula' ... 'Henry' ... 'Petula' ... and, as the glasses went down, Sawby made his way down the stairs to the Servants' Hall.

He was already exhausted. The long night stretched ahead of him, as it did for all of them, yet his eyes were shining as he halted on the last step and shouted, 'May I please have everyone's attention.' He, who had never been heard to shout in all his years of Castle service, shouted now and in alarm the staff came running in from all directions. Mrs Parsons waddled forward exclaiming, 'Lawks, Mr Sawby, you give me quite a turn!' The wide-eyed kitchen maids and little Boots came thronging and even Chef André, startled by the unaccustomed sound, joined them wiping his hands on the cloth which dangled as usual from his waist tapes.

'Now,' said Sawby, surveying them, 'we are pressed for time so pray do not allow the information I shall give you disturb the tenor of the work assigned to you.'

'Whatever can it be?' speculated Pearson, rising from her seat at the long table with her mouth still full of the food she was hurriedly cramming in.

'I have an announcement to make. Just now in the dining room, his lordship give ... gave,' he hastily corrected himself, 'a toast, but *not the one we have all been expecting*. He asked everyone present to drink to his grandson and his future granddaughter-in-law—in fact, Mr Henry is engaged to Miss Petula.'

Strictly on cue, Mrs Parsons burst into tears and had to be led to a chair where she wept and mopped in a positive orgy of emotion.

On forged Sawby. 'I cannot waste any more time now giving you details but it will not come amiss for any of the upper staff when waiting or serving to offer their congratulations to Mr Henry or their respectful good wishes to Miss Petula. Now all of you, back to work and look sharp about it. This is a joyous night for us all but there are jobs to be done and responsibilities to fulfill so never lose sight of that fact for an instant,' on which final note he forced his way through the goggling press and closed the door of the Steward's Room behind him. Once safely inside he took a quick nip from the brandy bottle in the staff cupboard, poured another into a glass for Mrs Parsons, did a tiny little jig of exultation then straightened his coat, composed himself and marched out, glass in hand, to administer to Mrs Parsons.

The ball was nearly over. Supper had come and gone. Tactful as ever the Royal Lady had taken her departure while the night was still comparatively young. Servants poured from the Castle, hastily flinging coats over uniforms and liveries, tucking themselves behind trees, taking cover in the shrubberies, seizing every scrap of opportunity for concealment in order to watch Her Royal Highness leave. She descended the steps between the two lines of rigid footmen. Lord and Lady Aynthorp had insisted that Christine and Gyles wait with them upon the royal departure. In powder and patches, stiff brocade skirts making a frou-frou on the stone, the royal descent was made leaning upon Justin Aynthorp's arm. Closely following were her ladies. Her shy, rather large, angular person was duly handed into her carriage and bowed to ... very low. Lady Aynthorp swept a magnificent curtsey, the plumes in her white hair nodding as she went down. Christine sank into her graceful duty too. The footmen riding postillion, the cockaded coachman on his box, all caught the spirit of the occasion. The coachman cracked his whip, the postillions leapt up and the carriage began to move over the gravel, crunching it under the turning wheels. A white-gloved hand flashed for a moment at the carriage window in a last gracious movement, another shadowy figure leaned forward to close out the night air, and carriage, lady, coachman, postillions and all disappeared down the curve of the drive and into the night.

'Charmin',' pronounced Lady Aynthorp. 'Agonisin'ly shy poor soul. . . . Justin, your arm if you please, I am now hungry!'

The tempo quickened. From the ballroom sounded the strains of a Strauss waltz. Henry standing atop the steps with his Petula suddenly caught her around the waist and waltzed her, protesting . . . but not very strongly, across the Great Hall, down the long corridor into the ballroom where he began reversing, his lips almost but not quite touching her hair.

'Oh, Pet,' he whispered artlessly, 'I do love you so . . .'

CHAPTER 24

An Invitation Meet

Hounds met at Castle Rising on the morning of February 28th, by which time every trace of what was to go down in county history as 'the greatest ball ever' had vanished save only for the restoration of electricity supplies. An army of cleaners invaded the reception rooms. Mrs Peace spent the busiest day of her life seeking out spots of candle grease and supervising operations with blotting paper and warm irons. The forest of trees and shrubs were borne away. George and Richard, exempt from normal duties, played running footmen about the county in the yellow Rolls Royce, returning lost fans, reticules, swords, brooches and other precious impedimenta whose ownership Sawby had traced by way of using the speaking tube to various houses.

For the family it had been a day of quiet rejoicing. Henry and Petula had busied themselves with presents. These were removed from the Chinese Room to what had become known as the Present Room. This lay opposite the garden room and was the venue for the annual wrapping and tying, sealing and labelling of Christmas gifts. Henry's were still pouring in as were the messages of congratulations to him and the bouquets of flowers to Petula. They had decided that since they were, in Henry's words, 'working on two fronts' all these should be sorted from the Castle so a further despatch service was initiated from the Danements' Priory and a delighted kitchen maid loaned from below stairs to fill the great funnel-shaped 'steeping' vases with fresh rain water and to unwrap and install the blooms as the bouquets arrived.

Christine, doing her 'rounds', put her head round the door to enquire 'How are you two getting on?' at which Henry straightened his back from delving in an enormous box and said: 'Well mama, we really do not know where we are.' He sighed. 'I dunno, but I think I feel like a chameleon on a plaid pillow! Lord, what a shockin' mess,' and as usual when bayed, he ruffled his head into matching total disorder.

'What about the "Mrs Collinses"?'[1] wailed Petula, surfacing from a froth of tissue paper with a smudge on one cheek.

Christine laughed, commented, 'Ungrateful puss', and went on her way rejoicing. At her next port of call she discovered Sir Charles Danement closeted with her husband in his 'office', an ice bucket between them and half the bottle of Krug Reserve, which was buried therein, already vanished as they revived themselves with the hair of the dog. She consented to take a thimbleful with them and sat down thankfully, glass in hand.

'Oh, what a fortuitous circumstance that the Meet is not until tomorrow!' she exclaimed after settling herself in one of the worn leather chairs. 'I have just looked in on those two children, hock-deep in gifts and bouquets. Really, Charles, this is the happiest event since my own marriage—the joining of our two families!'

'Y'know,' Gyles produced his snuff box and proffered it to his friend who waved it away saying: 'I took enough snuff last night, thank you, to fill my head for some time to come!'

'Y'know,' Gyles repeated, 'it is a remarkable circumstance since you and we have been neighbours for more than seven hundred years, that there has never before been a marriage between our two families. I suppose we must put our heads together over a suitable commemorative entertainment?'

Christine chuckled again—she seemed as gay as a girl after only a few hours of sleep. 'And the onus falls on Charles,' she reminded them naughtily. 'The biter bit, in fact.'

'Lord yes,' Gyles agreed, 'I hadn't thought of that. Too much champagne last night.' He reached for the bottle, emptied it, pulled the bell, and sat down again. 'What do you propose, Charles?'

Sir Charles gazed reflectively at the bubbles in his glass. 'The usual announcement in *The Times* and the country papers, then —if you agree—I have a feeling for a series of small dinners rather than another ball. Anything of the same nature will inevitably be an anti-climax comin' on top of yours last night, but,' he went on, still watching the bubbles intently and clearly embarrassed at touching on his own situation, 'I do not think you can *both* get out of it quite so easily. I shall need to take your

---

[1] Bread and butter letters.

counsel as to who will play hostess for me in my circumstances—
widowers do not entertain solo!'

'Ah,' Christine caught her breath, 'dear Charles, should it not
be your sister? Sara would do it beautifully.'

'If she would stay in one place for long enough to see the
matter through,' he reminded them. 'Sara won't like it. She calls
me a country bumpkin and only really enjoys following the court,
especially when the King goes to Cannes or Baden Baden.'

So he revealed to them his doubt that anything so implicit of
dowager status should be found acceptable by his lovely and
somewhat wayward sister whose name, as he could not possibly
infer even to his closest friends, was not perhaps the one calculated to set the seal upon anything so parochial as a series of
country dinner parties.

Christine instinctively assessed his meaning and, equally instinctively, stepped into the possible breach. 'Then why not let
me travel to London for a few days so that I can quite naturally
arrange a luncheon party for Sara, make the approaches myself
and see if it would be more acceptable to her for me to play her
part. No one ever does anything to the best of their ability when
their heart is not in it and at least I can assure you that mine
would be!'

'Then that is settled,' Gyles replied.

Edward appeared in the doorway. 'You rang, sir?'

'Ah yes, Edward, ask Sawby to bring us another bottle if you
please and tell chef that Sir Charles and Miss Petula will be
stayin' to luncheon. And that,' Gyles added as the door closed,
'will enable us to make our plans in depth and to indulge in all
those delightful aftermath exchanges which I am comin' to think
are the very best and most amusin' part of any celebration such
as last night's.'

'You really thought it went well?' Christine looked at Sir
Charles.

'It was magnificent, m'dear. The mind boggles at the organisation! How could you have coped and then turn up the next
mornin' lookin' as fresh as the proverbial daisy beats me.'

'Papa enjoyed it, I think,' Christine reflected, at which the two
men smiled at her indulgently.

'The remarkable thing to me was that m'father drank so very
little last night,' Gyles mused. 'He was extraordinarily abstemious.
After the thing got goin' and he had done his duty dances, he

retired to the card room with his old cronies. I kept lookin' in
on them—the play was pretty deep—and exactly as at dinner he
seemed not to be in a drinkin' mood.'

'And Lady Aynthorp?'

'Tangled with the dowagers. I saw her lookin' like a tiny barque
enmeshed by a flotilla of warships, fannin' and chattin' half the
night away. What I want to know is who's huntin' tomorrow.
Are you?'

'Of course.'

'Christine?'

'Certainly, and I can account for Papa and of course the boys.
I think it'll be as full a turn-out as usual from here. I can tell you
who will not be with us.' The men waited so she gave them the
tally.

'Uncle Alaric and Aunt Dorothy never hunt as we know.
Robert and Damien are leavin' this mornin', so is Aunt Prue
she is anxious to get back to Stephanie though the nurse who is
looking after her reported last night that her influenza was not
serious. We all know Mama will follow in her dog-cart and Aunt
Marguerite will probably still be in bed as there is little she can do
to her roses in February. She never even starts her prunin' until
March. You can count in everyone else includin' George,
Priscilla, Rosemary, Claire and Clarissa.'

Gyles nodded approvingly. 'Then we should have quite a good
turn-out with Ralph, James and Ninian. I just hope we find at
first covert. I did not have an opportunity last night to discover
what coverts Philip has his eye upon.'

At this point George returned with a fresh bottle of champagne
which he duly sank into the ice bucket. 'About fifteen minutes I
would suggest, sir,' he said, giving the bottle a dexterous twirl.

Again Gyles nodded. 'Very well George, thank you. That will
be all.'

Christine rose, concealing a tiny yawn. 'He's probably head
down now workin' it all out today,' she said. 'Philip has proved
himself to be a splendid Master since he took over from Papa, so
we can leave all that to him with perfect confidence. And now I
must leave you.' She moved towards the door, paused and looked
round. 'Oh, there is just one other thing if you will forgive me,
Charles?' They exchanged smiles, Gyles closed the door again
and Christine continued, 'This idea of Papa's about a museum.
He has already spoken about it to me and wishes to consult you.

Please, Gyles, let him have his way. He seems very excited about it and I think it could be quite a good thing for the future.'

'I agree.' Gyles looked surprised. 'Did you think I might not, and do you want me to broach it?'

'Well, you see,' she hesitated, 'Mama told me and said that she and Papa would not dream of proposing it unless they both had our consent!'

'Then,' said Gyles reopening the door, 'I will do the necessary. Never fear, my love!'

When Christine had gone, 'May I ask what all that was about?' enquired Sir Charles. So Gyles settled back in his old chair and explained.

As was the custom for an Invitation Meet within the grounds, Lady Aynthorp made her appearance bright and early on the morning of the 28th. She entered her receiving post—a spanking little trap—settled herself and permitted Palliser to swathe her in furs. She then dutifully tucked her gloved hands into a muff which Palliser had supplied with a hot water bottle. The woman also tucked another fur rug around her knees. Thus ensconced, her charge was able to look about her, bright-eyed and spry as a linnet after a good night's sleep and despite the fact that the Castle clocks were chiming 5.00 a.m. when she had mounted the staircase upon her husband's arm on the night of the Ball. Lord Aynthorp was out, too, already mounted on his much-loved Star and declaring roundly that he was 'rarin' to go'!

All the Lorme hunters were called Star. Their prefixes and suffixes ranged from White, Silver and Gold Star, through Dainty, Eastern and Shining Star and on—for house guests— through Star Quality, Blue, Arab, Persian, Northern and Southern Stars.

Gyles then appeared walking his favourite mare Starlight around the eastern corner, immaculate, as were they all, in hunting tops, buckskin breeches, pink coats and silk hats; all cravatted, gloved and further equipped with a flask and sandwich box apiece. In each of these boxes were some of the Lorme Foxhunters' Sandwiches.[2]

Then Christine came in sight from the same direction, riding side-saddle on Indian Star, holding the reins feather-handed and looking, as Gyles had just told her, 'demmed elegant, m'y love', in

[2] The recipe for the Lorme Foxhunter Sandwich is in the Appendix.

her dark blue habit and veiled bowler. The next to appear was young Ninian in full fig for the first time, wildly excited but endeavouring to look slightly bored. In this he was failing dismally having, if the truth were known, a tricky time with Starry Night and being filled with envy of his cousins Ralph and James who were mounted on Twinkling Star and Evening Star and, as Ninian admitted grudgingly to his mother, 'lookin' as if they had been welded into their saddles'.

Then came Henry on Morning Star, by Stargazer out of Eastern Star. The bay was so named for her seemingly incurable habit of looking skywards when mounted and fretting for hounds to make the first music.

'Tell you something,' James called across to Henry, at the same time dealing firmly with a slight tendency on his roan's part to start curvetting, 'it's goin' to be a welterin' full turn-out! '

Henry grinned. 'Lay you a fiver I finish up in the van ahead of you,' he offered obligingly.

'Done,' said James. 'It'll make a dent in my allowance but I'll pay up. I won't have to though. Tell you what, I'll lay you your fiver and five more I'll show you a clean pair of heels from "gone away" to kill.'

'Done,' Henry called back. 'A fool and his money are soon parted.' His warm smile anaesthetised the sting. 'Anyway,' he added equably, 'I'll give yer the father and mother of a run for yer money. See if I don't.'

During this cousinly exchange the drive had filled up. Pink coats were everywhere, glossy toppers flashed on and off, the dark habits of the side-saddle hunting ladies formed a trim contrast to the men's coats.

Footmen and hunt servants were emerging from the Castle carrying the Lorme Stirrup Cup[3] from which the steam rose sharply in the crisp air. Pink coats leaned down over greys, roans and chestnuts to take their quenchers, then moved slowly out of the growing press to make way for latecomers who were still coming slowly up the last drive curve into the massed company below the main steps.

Some still unmounted hunters were being led about by their gaitered and bowler-hatted grooms. More late arrivals came spanking up in pony traps, dog carts, while one Rolls Royce crept slowly towards the gathering. Gyles saw this mechanical *faux pas*,

[3] Recipe for Lorme Stirrup Cup is in the Appendix,

frowned, shrugged his shoulders and went forward to do the honours. He had felt constrained to ask the occupants since they had but recently leased some Lorme property from him ... but ...

'A Royce at a meet!' Lord Aynthorp came alongside his eldest son as the car eased up between the horses. 'Damme what are we comin' to? Shockin' bad taste—who the devil are they?'

Gyles explained, very softly, after which his father muttered, 'Someone should tell 'em. I love my Royce but I hope I have the good taste to keep it hid on an occasion like this.' He turned quickly in the saddle to tip his topper to the offending pair.

As soon as he could conveniently escape, he bent his shaggy gaze upon a brace of shining-eyed schoolgirls mounted upon a pair of wise-looking geldings. Then he paused a little farther on for a word with a bandy-legged little farmer in ratcatcher. By this time Sawby and the rest had replenished goblets and were now making their way around collecting them.

The Master was chatting with the Mayor, always a guest on such occasions, and greetings were being exchanged on all sides as the press thickened more and more.

Henry was acting mentor to a cousin from overseas, George Landaye, who stayed close beside him so that Henry could introduce him to all the 'big-wigs' as he termed Gyles' guests with some inelegance.

'That old shocker over there,' George tipped his crop towards a rather disorderly old man mounted on a markedly inferior piece of horseflesh, 'who is he, Henry?'

Henry's eyes followed the crop flick. 'The old codger with the seat like a sack of potatoes?'

George nodded, grinning.

'That old shocker is his Grace the Duke of Barton and Sale,' said Henry, grinning back. 'If you can manoeuvre to get to windward of him, you'll find out that he's the foulest-mouthed old boy in the county. I tell you something though: on that unlikely mount he'll still be up at the kill though to see him ride you'd suppose he'd take a toss at his first bit of cut and laid.'

George examined the Duke with some interest. 'Well,' he drawled, 'you must admit he sits that cob as if she were a rockin' horse!'

Henry shouted with laughter and turned to find Petula at his side. He greeted her gravely. She smiled upon him, gave him leave to 'present m'y cousin'...and moved off again almost immediately.

'Phew!' exclaimed George when she was out of earshot. 'What a corker, what an absolutely slap-up gel! Tell you what, Henry, you've picked the prettiest girl in England for my money.'

'And for mine,' Henry agreed. 'Come on, we're movin'.'

Suddenly everyone was ready. The driveway was emptied of new arrivals. The Master drained his goblet and handed it down.

'We must be close on two hundred, muttered Henry. 'Now mark my words well, George. When we "find" it'll be hell-for-leather and the devil take the hindermost so keep up, dear boy, keep up!'

Even as he spoke, the Master moved to the van while the whippers-in busied themselves with the sixteen couples of hounds.

Gyles looked down at them with pride; at Lurcher and Frolic, at a bow-legged, badger-pied hound called Daring, who ran in concert with their great Rover III, at Dainty, Develish, Badger, Bouncer, Winsome and Watchful. Then came a deviation from the name level into the odd couple, Brutus and Caesar, and again back to the hum-drum Badger and Bouncer who were likewise closing in with Gallop and Canter close behind their feathering sterns.

In moments the whole assembly was jog-trotting over the gravel and down and around on to the road, heading for Lorme Pasture through Little Aynthorp lane where the villagers were congregated to see the Castle folk go by. They packed the road-sides, farmers in breeches, farm hands in smocks, women holding fast to restless youngsters, a smattering of what Lord Aynthorp called 'miscellany dogs' tethered close, mostly by bits of rope, all utterly ignored by the hounds. There were, too, a few rangy colts tightly reined in, a few modern would-be 'followers', leaning over the saddles of bicycles, all watching intently, forming an assembly of knowing, critical country folk, interlarded with a smattering of horsecopers all hopeful of a 'turn up' in the shape of a gullible foxhunter.

The press was thickest at the crossroads. Here farm gates made convenient spectator grandstands. Here, too, were a cluster of gigs, and here, too, the 'field' took shape with the hopeful followers tagging behind at discreet and respectful distance. The last to make her departure down the long drive was Lady Aynthorp, who would follow for a couple of hours, but was under the strictest instructions from her daughter-in-law to return home for luncheon and take a good nap in the afternoon. She, who knew every foot of the country over which hounds would presently be running, was privately determined to be in at the first 'kill' wherever it happened, so for her daughter-in-law's peace of mind she hoped they would be lucky enough to 'find' at the first or at worst the second covert.

The boy who held the reins now relinquished them to Plum who presented himself, spoke a warm 'Good morning my lady,' and enquired, 'Is your ladyship quite comfortable? Then by your leave we'll be moving off.' Saying which he settled himself, gathered up the reins and the pony moved forward, with the trap tagging the field by a respectful twenty yards. As they moved forward, Plum carefully keeping his distance between field and pony's head, Lady Aynthorp noted with pleasure that 'everyone' who was anyone to the Family had turned out for the occasion. She could see the Tilney contingent from Nether Hall already in the van with her Justin, Gyles and—riding in trio at this stage —Ralph and Ninian with George their cousin from overseas. There were, too, Sir Edward Alleyn from Birdbrook Place and, close by, his wife, the Lady Daphne; the great house 'Flambards' was well represented by Lawleys, father and sons and the lovely, rumoured-to-be-very-naughty, Dionysia Montchesney from Plechenden. As they trotted forward she noted a cluster of Kyghleys from Stetchall Abbey led by Sir John and his wife and presently there came into view more and more . . . Crawleys and Cavendishes, both of whom had hacked ten miles to join them . . . Devenhues and Calvers. . . . The little old lady's eyes sparkled with pleasure. It was all such fun!

It was 'outstanding good fun' for her three grandsons too, who were unquestionably 'larking' as she could see from her first vantage point where Plum had reined in, halted the pony and settled himself to watch with matching absorption.

It was a little more than outstanding good fun for Henry. Deliriously happy as he was over his engagement to Petula, the sharp contrast between his present and his future, allied to his previous resignation to and acceptance of the fact that he would in the course of time take over the estate, inherit the title and end the ancient line, since he would marry no one but Petula and she had refused him three times, acted on him so powerfully that his temperament sought outlet for the unbounded relief which flooded him. He was after all only just twenty-one. His blood ran high, his colouring provoked it, the challenge to Ralph merely set seal upon it, and now, waiting still, chafing at the waiting, in a state somewhat in excess of 'rarin' to go', as his grandfather had stated was his case, only a lifetime of training kept him in check, but the hold was tenuous and loosening every minute.

Ironically, the Master had chosen a first covert lying on the other side of the ride which Henry had taken on that never to be forgotten morning when he had lain chewing grass, in the foulest of tempers and reviewing a future which, in the mood of despair which only youth experiences, he accepted as inevitable since Petula had again refused his proposal of marriage. The field began to stream out along this self-same ride towards the spinney which lay to leftward.

Plum halted the dog cart atop Brandon Hill where he and his passenger could see the hunt well spread out by now and nearing the rim of the spinney. In went the hounds, whimpering, the hunt moving like a small restless sea of pink coats, blue habits and white buckskin, weaved and swayed... then suddenly the hounds gave tongue. In a moment they were out of the spinney as a brown streak shot into view through the trees with hounds towling and rowling, and the great cry rising: 'Gone away!' The dog fox cut a line to leftwards of the spinney's far side and stretched it down the hill, clearly bound for Abbot's Spinney with a couple of miles to go. Henry stretched it, too, only just behind the Master and the whippers-in, galloping like a jockey with James on his heels, hooves thudding and Ralph pulling up to level with them. Then Lord Aynthorp and young Charles Danement came thundering up with Christine, and the old Duke, just as Henry had predicted, bucketing along as if he were riding a roundabout but with Gyles only leading him by a short head. The pace was now terrific as horses and riders swept in pursuit up and over the hill crest, down to the valley beyond.

Plum so far forgot himself as to rise on his box and shout to the wind as hooves' thunder broke and rolled over the grazing on Lorme land. This and hounds' music went to his head like home-brewed barley wine. With the wind sailed the cries: 'Yooi, Caesar, forrard, forrard, holloo... yoiks, yoooho!' Then, as the stragglers hove into view and the main field poured away, Plum grabbed the reins, touched the cob lightly with his whip and was away again.

On streaked the dog fox ... Master ... field, now down to a mere one hundred and sixty souls all with their hearts in their mouths and the blood pounding in their ears, while Lady Aynthorp obeyed Plum's enjoinder to 'hold on milady, we'll be in at the kill, I promised yer'. Plum knew his passenger. He was fully aware he would hear on the instant the going got out of hand for her and was equally conscious of his responsibilities towards her. Was she not the apple of his eye? giving place in his unswerving devotions to only one person: her husband to whom Plum's allegiance lay just this side of idolatry. They rounded a bend in the lane. They saw hounds check at this second spinney fringe. They saw how after that almost infinitesimal check, they plunged boiling and seething in a welter and froth and they heard the towling and rowling once again. Plum drew rein, turned round and made his apologies. 'Beggin' your pardon, my lady,' he said a trifle shamefaced, 'I so far over-stepped myself I got that carried away ... wot with seein' Master, I mean Mr Henry ridin' like ...' he drew himself up on the brink of a further indiscretion and substituted, 'like wot his Lordship did when he was younger.'

Lady Aynthorp chuckled. 'And still does, Plum,' she reminded him calmly, a calm which was at total variance with the two bright spots on her cheeks.

As the field closed in at that check she enquired very gently, 'Pray tell me Plum, did you not mean to say Hell-for-Leather Harry? If I am not very much mistaken that was what you all called his Lordship in the past!'

Plum opened his mouth like a cod on a fishmonger's slab and gazed at her dumbfounded. He was unable to emit more than a startled croak.

The soft voice came again. 'Plum,' it chided, 'when will you all learn that throughout the years his Lordship and I have been together I have usually known what is said and done concerning every aspect of the Castle's life.'

She bowled him over. All he could manage, after opening and shutting his mouth again several times, was a subdued, 'Yes milady, I'm sure I'm very sorry milady ... it's jest that I never expected ...' then he broke off.

On the far side of the second spinney after snaking and turning, streaking and doubling, the dog fox broke cover and stretched it again at a killing pace over Six Mile Saddle. As they watched so they saw the wily Reynard veer, hounds pelting after him, their music piercing the air and then away they all went again, hounds, huntsman, Master and field with Henry and his father now galloping neck and neck and both Ralph and James hammering away to draw level. Even as the dog cart whisked around another bend and the whole scene came back into view Lady Aynthorp and her remarkable old coachman saw the press thundering towards her menfolk, saw it thicken, widen, separate, as the pace took its toll somewhat, showing them the riders strung out as they galloped towards a tricky bit of double fencing. Henry soared up and was over. Then his father rose and landed, then his grandfather, his mother, and cousins, taking the fence like birds. It then became clear that Henry had lost his topper.

'Now we can see my eldest grandson very clearly,' laughed Lady Aynthorp. 'It's the hair, Plum, it's the hair!'

'Aye, milady,' Plum responded, his eyes on the cob and the road down which they swung and jolted. 'The Lorme thatch was ever wunnerful 'andy for pickin' 'em out in a tangle.'

The thought flashed through the grandmother's mind . . . 'And so it was at Hastings . . . Agincourt . . . Oxford .. . Oudenarde . . . the Transvaal.' They went rattling on. They glimpsed hounds gaining slightly, or was it, both wondered in that short glimpse, that the fox was tiring?

'May we budge along a mite faster?' Plum asked eagerly as the next hedge gap revealed the field diminishing in size and spreading out of vision.

'Oh yes, Plum, please. I will hold on, I promise you.' She was up to her neck in the thrill of it now. 'Take the Abbot's Road by Whiteways, cut through the lane and that should bring you levelling with them. I promise I will hold on or let you know if I am feeling the pace.'

'Then mind you do hold on, milady,' he muttered under his breath, 'or 'is Lordship will string me by my neck from a topmost tree.' Saying which he tickled up the pony who by this time seemed also to have entered into the spirit of this chase.

Aloud Plum commented, 'It should bring us abreast of 'em provided that Brer Fox don't go to ground.'

But Brer Fox did not. True to his breed he was playing hounds. He had ample in hand yet as he showed now, for as hounds did gain ground on him, and the hunt pelted after them, so he spurted, running so low that he seemed like a red-brown arrow sped from an archer's bow and skimming along just above the turf. He was really stretching to his limit, with hounds running mute in his wake. That flaming coppery head lay fourth, both Gyles and Ralph were leading him in pursuit of their grandfather with Ninian, almost too close for clean riding, delirious with excitement and pride at 'keepin'' up with the old man'. He was whooping like a child with croup.

Plum drew the gig to a standstill just in time to see the fox make one huge swerve, for all the world like a swathe cut by a scimitar and then go tongue-hanging to the gates of a farm.

'The wily varmint,' Plum cried out, almost beside himself by now, 't'other side of that there Petty's farm goes railway and that's what the crafty devil is making for . . . if so be he knows there's a train coming we're done for . . . which is wot un's reckkernin' on . . . hark milady . . . how he hears it even now . . . look at that durned spurt him be making. . .!'

Even as he tumbled out the words so a distant toot sounded and a long plume of grey and white smoke betokened the coming of 'that there dratted train'. But the fox was through, pelting now across poor Petty's cabbage patch and flinging himself like a serpent through a gap in the farther fencing. Hounds overran that cabbage patch too, pouring through a gap widened by a falling horseman. Thunder and lightening, hell and tempest could never have flailed that patch harder than the hounds which flung across and the hunt which drummed and thundered in their wake. The train came on. Every horseman and every hound knew full well that on the farther side of that railway track lay the river Umble—in which 'that there durned fox' could disseminate his scent—and beyond the fence and the river a sharp steep rise which spread itself into a cat's cradle of old disused rabbit warrens.

On, on came the juggernaut and on and on flung the hunt.

'Ahhhhh, he's done it. Who says they don't think and work as they run? Why, Plum, foxes devise their own campaign, play the very dickens with hounds.' Lady Aynthorp rose chattering in her excitement, holding the fur rug about her hips, the better to see this marvellous drama unfolding. Then she sat down again with a half-relieved, half-regretful sigh as a long, lumbering goods train crossed the track *with the fox on the farther side.*

'And that,' said Plum's passenger to herself, 'will be that, we shall find!'

The field had reined in, panting. The train thundered on moving with what seemed like deliberate slowness, truck after truck passing their line of vision until at long last, or so it seemed to every man and hound fretting and fuming in concert, the final truck peeled away at infuriating snail's pace and hounds shot over the track. Hounds then flung into the river, churning up the water, hauling themselves up the farther side. But it was to no avail. As Henry remarked, sweat streaming, hands aching, thighs aching, face flushed and hair a tousled chaos, 'Old brer's down among the dead men so far as we are concerned and I'm sure and certain the Master won't even suggest puttin' in the terriers or tryin' to dig him out.' And so it proved to be.

Henry sidled alongside his cousin Ralph. 'First blood to me I fancy,' he drawled, unfastening his flask and taking a healthy pull. Ralph's reply was somewhat muffled and his speech a trifle incommoded by a vast mouthful of Lorme Sandwich, but it sounded to Henry like 'The day's young yet, old sport, and there's a long road ahead to hoe before we count our chickens. Lord, what a mixed metaphor!'

'Stinkin' English, I'd say,' said Gyles coming up to them and eyeing the pair with marked suspicion. 'Might I enquire if you two rapscallions were skylarkin' because you know what a roasting you'll get from the Master if you go too far?'

'Oh no, really sir,' Ralph contrived to look astonished. 'Just enjoying a crackin' good run.' Gyles mouth quivered then he turned away.

'Accompanied, if I am any judge by the feet of Ananias thunderin' in yer ears,' he commented drily. 'Just remember you have been warned.'

'Fair enough, sir,' Henry acknowledged, his face creased with laughter, 'but you must admit it was a crackin' good run before that wily son of Satan went to ground.'

Hounds, Master, huntsmen and whippers-in were on the farther side by now but the field elected to wait, using the breather to quench thirsts and 'take a bite at our excellent Lorme Sandwiches'. True enough, after a short conclave with hounds whimpering and weaving and never a whiff of scent to give them joy, everyone made way and the Master came back to lead them towards another distant covert. Before they moved off, Ralph whispered wickedly to Henry, 'Now let's see yer mettle young fellermelad, let's see some ridin' and jumpin' from the carrot-headed heir apparent!'

The Master had a word with Justin Aynthorp as he came back through the water and began to climb the slope. 'Take our cut all of us on the damage to old Petty's cabbage patch, Justin,' he said cheerfully. 'We'll take it easy now to give everyone a breather. Then I suggest we work our way towards a bit of your rougher country, if so be you've a mind for some hard ridin'.'

'That's just what I was hopin', Gerald,' said Henry's octogenarian. 'I'd like to stretch me old muscles a bit, this doesn't do much more than, what's that song of Marie Lloyd's?—*Tickle one's Fancy*—yes, that's it,' and he grinned at his younger crony.

'Then through Shepherd's Field,' the crony nodded. 'We'll cut across to skirt Puck's Hill takin' the lower land to bring us into that rougher stuff of yours where I think we might "find" again without much trouble,' saying which he tipped his cap, trotted off, gathered his 'brood' together and they were off at a jog trot, hounds looking dejected and registering immense frustration. 'You and we will have to do better than that before the day's out,' they seemed to say.

Gerald Dewhurst nodded down at them as if he heard the unspoken words, settled his cap to his satisfaction and moved off. Soon they were all away, levelling off to a gentle canter which they maintained to the lip of Lord Aynthorp's 'rougher country'.

Plum had anticipated them and was now taking the pony at a mild jog trot down the lanes having been informed by his passenger of exactly where the field was heading. She told him: 'Lord Dewhurst will certainly want to make the day a memorable one. I think he will head off around Puck's Hill so if you take me quite quietly towards the farther side we'll come to roost on the summit of the lane by Parker's barn and can then see everything.'

Plum obeyed, to be rewarded as they came into field view once again, their objective made and the pony halted, by the sight of a vixen tearing across the open space which was separated by some very tricky thorn from the gorse-spattered meadows beyond.

'Goooone Awaaaaaay!' the cry rose again and with it came more music, as hounds erupted from the wood in a churning black and tan explosion of speed. Like a salvo they spurted in pursuit with the red-gold streak of vixen arrowing it along the dark brown soil, newly turned by the plough.

Now they saw hounds fleeing mute, sterns straight as gun

barrels, hackles risen, eyes blazing, the fox in view, the scent
acting like a flail on every taut nerve and the fox, sighting the
canal, smelling the scent of water, running with her life in her
eyes, her only hope that distant canal Mecca. After her pelted
the hunt, and Lady Aynthorp could see her husband's white locks
in the van, for *his* topper had now disappeared. He was riding the
ride of his eighty-three lusty years, defying time, hands sure,
thighs sure, eyes steady though the breath whistled now through
his nostrils and a thin line of blue was developing in time's creases
on either side of his mouth. Henry flung himself in his grandfather's wake with Ralph pounding doggedly at his heels.
Thrusters ahead was the order of the day now, second flighters
holding back, the wise heading off to skirt the abundant gorse, the
timid making clean for the roads and the bridle paths, intent
upon steering clear of the thorn.

Now the eager music poured from hounds' throats and Henry,
seeing ahead of him a great stone wall looming, set his mare to it
with a whoop. The jagged top seemed to tear towards him, to
fling itself at him, then he glimpsed away below him and knew it
was over . . . and rocketing on to face a bullfinch as impenetrable
as dreaded barbed wire. Somehow, silent now as he rode, one
pink sleeve with whip hand held high to protect his face, there
came the sensation of a thousand million needles being driven into
every particle of his limbs, a sound of rending cloth as the bullfinch ripped at his coat and then he was through, admittedly
rapscallion in appearance by this time, but he *was* through and
in sight of the pack who were running stern to stern so close they
seemed like one gigantic many-limbed beast out of Fantasy by
Delusion. . . . There they went! Only a field away with huntsman,
whippers-in, thudding on after them half a field behind. Henry's
rapture was intense, then ahead of him loomed a double post and
rails. . . . Out of the corner of his eye he saw Ralph's mount peck;
saw Ralph describe a dishevelled parabola; hollered 'You all
right?' heard the reassuring shout back and slammed on across
a stretch of ridge and furrow to face a thorn ditch; heard
an outraged imprecation from a far too close and justifiably blas-
phemous huntsman; took another post and rails and whooping
all the time joyously, raucously, he closed in along a blessed
stretch of flat, winning a God-sent breather for a moment with
fox out of vision . . . then fox back into vision . . . then, 'The
damned rorty vixen,' he shouted, 'she's headin' for the canal,'

and he dug in his heels so that the mare seemed to take wings.

And that was when it happened; at the end of this stupendous, pluperfect, rapscallion run. Plum saw it all from his place on the box ... *and she,* she above all saw it too, standing again in the little dog cart, cheering and not knowing she cheered, exhorting and unconscious of her words, knowing only that her Justin, very blue around the mouth by now, but still erect, still clear of every fence was sweeping forward, coming in still in the van as the vixen took to the water.

Lady Aynthorp never saw hounds follow. None of the Lormes had any idea at what point they dived, nor when they gained ... nor when the vixen faltered and went down, submerged in a churning, heaving tan and black sea. They were upon her with no Master, no huntsman, no whippers-in. All eyes were upon Justin Aynthorp. He reached the canal slope at a licketty-spit-hell-for-leather-Harry pace as if he was still a young sprig like his grandson. Then the mare slipped and as she slipped, so unaccountably hound music stilled so that only the awful 'Ahhhhh ...' which rose from over a hundred constricted throats and the panting of men's breath broke the unnatural silence. As the mare went down, so her rider attempted to check and hold her, but on the instant, this unthinkable instant, his left stirrup leather snapped throwing him sideways, tipped him out of the saddle to topple ... struggle ... fail ... and then he went down hitting his head against a jagged piece of stone protruding at the canal rim.

Plum and Henry reached him first. Henry turned his head away for a second to see Gyles dismounting at the top of the slope and then racing towards his father. In that instant Plum's hands stretched out to Justin Aynthorp who lay with a rent in his head from that broken stone piercing his brain, draining the life away from him. Plum's hands, working with infinite gentleness, reached for that blood-spattered head and lifted it into the curve of his arms, crooning despairingly over it as he did so, unconscious of the futile sounds he made ... by now half-crazed with grief and shock.

'Don't,' said Justin Aynthorp thickly ... and again, 'Don't,' then the mouth went slack and breathing seemed imperceptible as Plum leaned closer.

Philip Philpot thrust through, to kneel beside the old man whom he had first attended when he was new-come from walking the wards; when he, as had happened to others before him, took his baptism of fire from the old autocrat while strapping up a cracked rib for him after an earlier toss in the hunting field. The figure in the dog cart sat rigid. She saw the doctor's movements, interpreted each one all too clearly, saw him lift her husband's head, rise to relinquish it to Henry, to Gyles, saw his lips move as he spoke reluctantly. 'I'm sorry,' he muttered, 'I'm damned, desperately sorry.'

Even so the figure moved again. 'Open the Box,' the words came somehow from the blue lips. 'Open the Box.' And so saying, Justin Henry Aynthorp died.

Still that figure on the box remained motionless. The head bent for an instant, then lifted. Slowly, very slowly, she rose to her feet, her eyes once more on the terrible mime being played out below her. She saw the doctor rise and shake his head. She saw the awful ripple of movement as her son and her grandson ripped off their coats and held them out mutely. She saw the doctor take those coats, bend once more, then straighten his back as he laid those coats over the body.

Only then did the watcher move forward to the rim of her cart. She began pulling herself over on to the box. Somehow she managed it. Somehow she gathered up the pony's reins. She turned him, brought the cart round and quite deliberately she set the pony on the long way back over the lanes through which she had come so gaily from her home. On that dreadful moment, on a nod from the Master, the huntsman, already on his feet, lifted up his horn, put it to his lips, and over the silent, bare-headed, mud-spattered assembly, he blew the 'Home'.

Despite the shock, her mind was clear enough for the lines of a poem to recall themselves from memory's storehouse: '*In a dream untroubled by hope!*' thought acknowledged, '*and that is my state now.*' And that was how she drove, taking horror by the throat, doggedly determined upon her objective, forcing herself to set grief aside with the rueful, quickly suppressed sob of acknowledgement that there would be ample time for that . . . presently. First she must reach home. Then she must withdraw into herself for long enough to assemble her forces. With these she must hold herself together in the days ahead, if she only did so by setting an example to those whom she knew would be even deeper concerned in the horror which would come down upon them like Scotch mist . . . poor Gyles and Christine.

In the meantime she . . . remembered. In memory, super-imposed upon the familiar lanes, Alicia Aynthorp saw herself as a girl again, a bride coming to the Castle in an open carriage with her husband . . . saw the servants, lined up to greet her, saw them make their bows and curtseys . . . felt herself being carried up those white steps and over the threshold in her husband's arms . . . being set down with infinite gentleness . . . ahhh, but it was pain-ful. She choked on those thoughts then struggled again for com-posure. The cob trotted on without need of any direction. A drover cleared a way for her between his cattle to stare dumb-founded as she went by, head set, eyes narrow under the tight-drawn veil in an attempt to stay the tears which would well up, only to be beaten back by the indomitable spirit which still held on. . . . No one whom she passed that day in those quiet lanes ever forgot their sight of her, nor failed to tell their children the tale of the little figure driving herself home, her dead husband left to her menfolk on the hunting field, fleeing the scene lest they suffer further embarrassment and pain through her presence.

Even as the last echo from the huntsman's horn diminished and faded into the rising wind, the women left the field. Christine was the first to go. The moment she saw her mother-in-law gathering up the reins, she guessed her intent. She flung herself into the saddle, wheeled and galloped off with only one thought, one driving persistent thought—that that old darling, that proud and bereft old love, was at this moment trotting through the lanes alone with her thoughts of her dead husband and there would be no one except the servants to meet her when at last she came to that home, unless she, Christine, reached there in time. She dug in her spurs, knowing full well that she *must* be there to receive her mother-in-law when, eventually, she drew up at the steps in that dog cart. Christine spared no thought for failure on either side to keep this tryst. In certainty, she settled down in the saddle, prepared for the ride of her life. Field after field sped past. Furrowed ploughland took over from gorse and that perilous thorn over which Indian Star sailed unscathed, merely casting up over her rider's habit great gouts of foam in what she also knew must be her greatest effort. The mare understood. That was as plain as a pikestaff. Indian Star had taken the scent of death into her nostrils, and knew it was up to her as, with nostrils blow-ing, lips curled back over her teeth, she seemed ready to take on the hounds of hell and deny even them the right to cause her let or hindrance. She never checked her pace. She never faulted a foot. She just lengthened her stride, stretching herself as she had never done before, bearing her light burden home to receive the new-made Dowager.

Christine hung on, thigh, knee and calf to the smooth hide, her knees cold as marble under her habit, thighs aching, sweat running down between her breasts. She could feel it coursing between her shoulders too; her arms were throbbing as if they were already part torn from their sockets; but still she hung on while hooves thundered and smacked, fences surged up and then fell away behind, until at last, at long and weary last, she saw the blessedly familiar Home Park looming ahead and heard the mare's desperate panting as she, too, recognised home territory and put on one last gallant spurt. Christine could see the drive now—miraculously empty—blessedly marvellously empty! A moment more and she was dismounting. She went straight to the mare's wet head, she gentled her, making small consoling sounds to her, as she quivered and shook, gentling her tenderly as both of them struggled to diminish their panting and quiet the thudding of their hearts.

It was at this moment that Sawby from an upper window saw horse and rider below. He was down the staircase faster than he had ever moved before, out of the doors and down those steps stunned with horror by Christine's disarray. Her veil was torn. One single strand of hair made a travesty of a curl across one foam-flecked, mud-flecked shoulder. She was visibly sagging, clearly using the mare for support, while her slim figure still heaved as she fought to control her breath.

'Sawby,' she panted, 'spare no courtesies for me. *I am all right.* Try to forgive me for the shock I must give you now.' Somehow out of her inmost self she essayed a piteous smile. 'I must tell you, you see, that his Lordship has been killed while hunting. Her Ladyship saw it all and I have raced back so as to be here to receive her. Her Ladyship is somewhere in the lanes, unattended.'

She saw the man whiten, step back, saw *his* desperate fight for control saw the battle won as training asserted itself in him, and finally heard him ask, 'What is it that *your ladyship* wishes me to do first?' She turned her head away again, but not before she had looked at him uncomprehendingly for one horrible moment. Then she realised and realising played her part.

'Tell the rest of the servants, please. Then draw down the blinds, close the curtains, and send Pearson to me. Somehow you must also get Palliser into the Servants' Hall *and keep her there.* The...' she was stammering badly now, '...the Dowager will have no place for hysterics from Palliser at such a time...can you do all that, Sawby?'

Sawby replied, 'Of course, my lady....' He turned to go, paused, turned back again. 'My lady,' he faltered, '...I have no words...'

'And nor have I,' she replied, 'but thank you just the same,' and at that moment they both heard the sound of horse's hooves. Again he wavered, but Christine's urgent 'Hurry, Sawby, hurry,' put an end to hesitancy; he took the steps two at a time and disappeared into the Great Hall.

They laid her love upon a hurdle hurriedly wrenched from its foothold. They drew the pink coats around him in a pathetic gesture towards one who could not feel the cold, while she trotted on through the lanes, being taken home by the pony. Plum stood by, head bent, tears dropping upon his tortured hands. All the while his fingers worked away crazily, knotting and unknotting, curling and plaiting under the falling rain of tears as if they were performing some uncontrollable fandango of their own.

Plum stepped back one pace as the hurdle went down. As he did so he flung a glance of such mute, stricken appeal at Gyles that 'Plum, take your nearside end,' he commanded curtly, 'Sir Charles will take the other. Henry, take this end with me and you, Ninian, stand by to follow us with Ralph and George lest anyone find the goin' too exhaustin'. We have close on ten miles to cover.'

Ninian, in his middle years, was wont to say to his sons when he recalled that day for them, that he saw on this instant one quick glance from the white face of Sir Charles Danement, from under brows tight drawn in the rigid control he was exerting on himself and as Sir Charles bent to pick up his share of that burden, he distinctly heard him say from just under his breath a long drawn-out, 'Soooooo...' and then, 'the mantle of Elijah *has* fallen upon my friend's son after all.'

Gyles spoke again. He stood there in the hoof-churned canal, fringing mud-spattered, coatless and hatless. He looked around him slowly. 'As for you, gentlemen,' he said, without inkling of his own stature in this moment, 'if any of you wish to go home, now is the moment, I would suggest. I would only add, thank you for what you have done. Should any of you wish to accompany us, we should be deeply honoured.' Then he bent to his hurdle and they all began to move.

CHAPTER 25

The End of an Era

In moments the Rolls Royce was slipping down the drive. The
Countess Marguerite had been told—by Christine whom she dealt
with with unaccustomed firmness. She was extremely composed.
Only a small muscle in her cheek escaped control and twitched.

'Where is Alicia?' she asked when she had been told of her
brother's death. 'And whom, pray, is with her?'

'No one,' Christine told her wearily. 'She begged—insisted
perhaps would be more accurate—that she had total privacy for
a while. When we reached her rooms she patted my cheek as if
I were a child, then she said very quietly, "I need time, my dear
. . . alone . . . please. Now I beg of you, go to Marguerite," so I
came.'

'Well now you can go again,' Marguerite spoke almost briskly.
'Let Pearson draw you a bath and help you to change. I will send
you some brandy. Please take it.' Christine made a small movement of rejection so she added, 'You have great responsibilities
now, my dear. We shall all have cause to call upon you during
whatever lies ahead. Do as I ask, my dear, and leave everything
else to me for a little while. Just tell me where I shall find you
when you are changed.'

'Chapel,' Christine said limply. 'Will you bring flowers?'

'Yes, and everything else which will be needed.'

When she was once again alone she went to her armoire and
took out a plain black gown. Then she unfastened her peignoir
with unsteady fingers prior to performing the unaccustomed
office of dressing herself.

Having done so with commendable speed she pulled her bell
and gave her orders in a voice which brooked no questions. She
bade the chauffeur go in the motor immediately to find the returning cortège. When found, she stressed, he must try to estimate
as closely as possible how long it would take to complete the
journey. She added, 'Come to me. I shall either be in the stove

houses with Sawbridge or in the Chapel. Hurry, man. Waste not
a single moment.' So the man flew while she sat down for a
moment reviewing what she must do. Then she rose. She hurried
to collect Mrs Peace, passing little clusters of weeping servants
as she went by unseeingly. She stated her requirements to Mrs
Peace, waited at the door of her room while the woman found
what was needed and when Mrs Peace reappeared with a very
large cardboard box, Marguerite led the way by devious empty
corridors through the Castle and out along the path which led to
the Chapel.

She halted at the closed door, took down the heavy iron key,
inserted it in the lock and pushed. The door went back, creaking
as it did so. The two women crossed the flagstones, turned left
up the aisle and were beginning to drag out the sections of the
catafalque which had been used for many bygone Lormes when
Sawbridge appeared.

'Oh my lady,' he exclaimed, 'pray let me assist. Mrs Peace, you
should never . . .'

Marguerite silenced him. 'At such a time, Sawbridge, it matters
naught. We all do what we must.' She turned. 'Mrs Peace, pray
lay out that pall along those choir stalls to let some of the creases
fall away. Sawbridge, send one of your men to request the key
of the cellar which houses the altar furniture, and,' she added,
'meet me with two pairs of sécateurs at the first stove house where
I shall be waiting for you.'

She glanced around. 'Now, Mrs Peace, when the key comes,
use it to unlock the cellar. Go in. There you will find four altar
candlesticks—the silver gilt ones—place them at the four corners
of the catafalque. Be sure to retain whomever comes with the
key so that he can be despatched to appraise me the instant there
is any sound denoting the arrival . . . of . . . his . . . late . . . lordship. When I go, as I do now, through the kitchen gardens I will
send two more runners so that you may be adequately supplied.'
She paused. 'It is better,' she said more softly, looking at the
woman's red-rimmed eyes, 'that we should all busy ourselves as
much as can be contrived, so stay your weeping pray. In the
meantime, get me sconces for the flowers. Fill water into their
containers and set four of them in line across the head of the
catafalque.' With a swish of skirts she was gone, leaving the
woman to move like an automaton about her appointed tasks.

The chauffeur was the first to return. He reported that the

cortège was taking the line the hunt had taken that morning; that it was moving very slowly indeed with all the foxhunters leading their horses behind.

'The ole field, milady, comes walkin' slow, Master, huntsman, whippers-in and all the gennelmen riders. Mr Gyles, 'is lordship, is carrying 'is late lordship with Mr 'Enery, Plum and Sir Charles Danement. The lanes is full of folk. I could scarce get the motor by in places. I expec' that's why *they* 'ave taken to the fields to be more private like.' Marguerite received this report at the entrance to the stove house.

Then, 'Back to the Chapel with you,' she said, and thrust an armful of flowers at the shaken man, 'we have no time to lose.' She went on ahead, hurrying him. 'What is your estimate of the time we have left at our disposal?'

'Best part of an hour I should say, my lady. They're walkin' powerful slow and they have not come to the summit of the rise that leads to the Saddle Back.'

Marguerite nodded. 'Now, when you have given those flowers to Mrs Peace—Sawbridge is coming with the rest—stand guard at the end of the graveyard and shout if you see a glimpse of them through the Home Park trees.' Saying which she hurried into the Chapel, leaving the man standing sentinel mid-way between nave and porch. Seeing him still there she urged, 'Well, go on man, what is keeping you?'

'Beggin' your pardon, milady, but my son is coming right now. I thought as how it might be better for you if my boy acted as runner between the post you chose and me here. Then I can turn and tell you with scarce a moment's delay and no further fraying of your nerves, milady.'

Her face softened. 'Thank you, it is well thought; but where is your son?'

'Coming along of the path right now with Dick to stand at the farther end. I'll tell him now.'

Somehow the news had spread, somehow the lanes, empty save for that solitary drover when Lady Aynthorp had gone by in her trap, were now thick with villagers, with farmers and their womenfolk and children, all craning over hedge-tops, peering through bushes, standing on tip-toe. Every moment the crowd thickened until all passage was halted by men on horseback, men in traps and men on bicycles who poured in from the villages as the word spread, just to stand in a silence which was broken only by the sound of women weeping. With bared heads they watched the man they had loved and respected being carried back to his home.

Plum might be close to dropping in his tracks but no money on earth could have persuaded him to relinquish his proud post. Son and grandson were in their shirt sleeves. Neither were aware that it was cold. Two of the foxhunters had come abreast at one stage, leading their mounts, and had urged them to take *their* coats, but both shook their heads unwilling to relinquish their burden even for a moment.

Behind them came the rest of the field, for not a single one had chosen the alternative which Gyles had offered. They likewise considered it a privilege to slow-march close on ten miles across the way they had all ridden so joyously just a few hours before. They were unaware of the villagers, unaware of that silent company who paid homage as they went by; but faintly on the rising wind, like the sad keening of curlews in the distance, that wind carried to them the sound of weeping.

Outside the Castle, Sawby stood below the steps, hatless and without a coat over his sombre black. He, too, had received his instructions from the little Countess. 'When you see them, go down the steps,' she had instructed. 'Lead them to me here. Tell ...' here she did falter, 'tell your new Master,' she compromised, 'that all is in readiness and, Sawby, if there are any accompanying riders, let them come too. No one must be kept out of the Chapel unless it becomes too full to hold any more. Even then you must let whomever wishes wait and then come in as soon as others leave.'

So now Sawby waited, his face once again impassive. He saw the first of the Lorme ladies walking their horses up the drive. He issued sharp orders to the concealed, waiting footmen who hurried to do his bidding. By the time the first rider had come level with the steps, grooms were there to help the riders dismount and to lead the horses away to the stables.

Sawby then repeated Marguerite's message saying, 'The Countess and her ladyship left word that they were in the chapel should you wish to join them, ladies.'

'Which ladyship?' choked Clarissa, surrendering to tears. But no one answered her so she too followed, stumbling as she went and feeling Primrose's arm about her on the instant. 'Oh Prim,' she wailed, 'it is all so unimaginably dreadful!' Primrose hushed her and they went on together.

Christine had reached the Chapel a moment before the Bishop arrived. Then came the organist, an old Swiss friend and fine musician who lived nearby. He jumped from his gig, hurried in and went immediately to the organ loft. There he began to play. The clear, almost mathematical precision of Bach calmed and inspired the women below.

Massed white flowers were now falling like tears from the sconces, their china whiteness making stark contrast to the black velvet which now lay over Mrs Peace's outstretched arms as she stood motionless and waiting. At the altar Christine and Marguerite were placing the last blooms in their vases. Then the Chauffeur appeared, saying very quietly, 'They are coming ladies, your Grace,' then he disappeared once more.

Christine turned. She caught up a pile of black lace from a choir stall and hurrying down the aisle reached the porch in time to meet the women of her family. As they came in, so she flung a scrap of black lace over each head, then put up her hands to draw her own lace down across her face. Marguerite followed her, performing the same act for herself. They all filed into the foremost stalls.

The watchers in the porch saw Sawby, whiter now than any of those flowers, pacing very slowly ahead of that dreadful hurdle. When he came to the porch he stood aside as Gyles, Henry, Plum and Sir Charles passed him and made their slow, leftwards turn. Then followed the foxhunters, their booted feet sounding very loudly on the stones. When the last of the hunt had passed, Sawby fell in behind to halt at the back and watch intently. He saw the black velvet with the gold-embroidered edges lifted high by Christine. He saw Gyles take those corners from her, saying as he did so, 'No, my dear. Turn away now that you may always remember him as he was this morning.' Then Henry and Ninian took away the blood-stained coats, Charles and Plum reached for the opposite corners and all four laid the pall in place.

The little chapel was full by now. Family and foxhunters filled every stall. As Sawby watched, looking down the short aisle to where the body lay under its heavy folds, so Christine and Marguerite came in again with long wax tapers between their fingers. With these they kindled the candles' wicks and stood back as the points of flame wavered and then steadied. Then it was that Sawby dropped to his knees on the flagstones. He did his best to pray; but after a little while he sighed heavily, rose and went out, where a shaft of sunlight met him. He lifted his face to the sky and as he did so he saw what proved to be his undoing. Very slowly the flag above the Castle was being lowered to half mast. Equally slowly the tears came.

George cannoned into him as he walked through the kitchen entrance, which in itself was an unheard-of thing for Sawby to do. George apologised—saw the butler's face—then turned and ran back along the way he had come. He helped himself to the things he needed. Helpless in the face of such profound emotion as he had just seen, he then did the best he could. He made Sawby a 'nice strong, hot cup of tea', and carried it himself to the closed door of the Steward's Room, knocked, and without a word, as the door opened a little, he pushed the tray round the door and closed it again. 'And none of you go in there for next 'arf hour,' he muttered, setting himself with arms folded to deny ingress. 'Even,' he told himself quietly, 'to that 'ole cat herself if needs must. 'E *must* 'ave 'is cry out undisturbed.'

And now it was done. The avalanche of flowers had come and gone, to the Cottage Hospital, the Infirmary, the Orphanage and the Workhouse. The bells had tolled and stilled. Quietly, very quietly, Justin Henry had been laid among his forbears under a slab of stone in the Chapel. The funeral service was conducted by the dead peer's brother, Bishop Alaric. He was assisted by the local Vicar. None of the Lorme women attended, but all save the widow were waiting in the library when the commitment was over to serve tea there to the waiting Truslove before the will was read.

When the Chapel was at last emptied, Sawby brought a message to his new lordship requesting that he go as soon as was convenient to his mother's room. He had not seen her since his father's death. No one had except Palliser and Christine. She had kept to her rooms throughout the whole three days and Palliser, quite unexpectedly behaving in a way which no one could possibly fault, seemed to dare anyone by her tight-lipped demeanour to ask *any* impertinent questions.

The lowered blinds and the closed drapes across the windows were being drawn back again, letting in the ironically gay spring sunshine. In the Home Park the first daffodils were shaking their heads at a sweet, lilting wind which denied the truth of the old adage that March 'came in like a lion'. There were new-born lambs on the grazing. There were piglets protesting in the styes. Even as Justin Henry's body was committed to the cold stone lining of the tomb into which his coffin was lowered, a mare foaled in the stables and the foal, new-licked, struggled unsteadily to its fragile legs. Doves and pigeons cooed in the roof tops, perched on the buttresses, cut swathes in the air with their wings.

Lord Aynthorp had died. That was the only incident which cast a long shadow over the spring afternoon. But even so, there was another Lord Aynthorp now—Gyles Henry—and another Lady Aynthorp in the person of Christine de Lorme. The old Lady Aynthorp now bore the prefix to her title, 'Dowager', and Henry had become next in line.

He had broken away after the interment. He had gone wandering off alone and now was walking along that long Saddle Back of land again thinking . . . remembering . . . deciding. For he had a decision to make. There was no thought in his head now of a quick marriage to his Petula. The proprieties forbade that anyway, but more than that he was concerned for his future in terms of what he now saw to be his duty. He did not deceive himself. He acknowledged that he was having a 'hell of a good time' at Oxford, he likewise built up for himself a picture of what the ensuing months would hold for his father, the son who had always walked in the shadow of his rumbustious sire, now forced to do . . . what. . . .? Henry wondered . . . broodingly. He tried to stand back and examine his father—the attributes of the reserved meticulous, punctilious, sometimes home, Gyles. Then he recalled the scene beside the canal . . . Sir Charles' muttered comment and again Henry wondered. . . . How would his father stand now that he stood clear of *his* father's shadow? That was the question.

With this thought his intentions crystallised. He put all further irresolutions to one side. He would leave Oxford, he would take up his future duties as he had begun to take them up already. He would be, in his turn, as well equipped in terms of experience and knowledge *when his turn came* and he would go straightway to his father and tell him so. Henry turned in his tracks and began to run back the way he had come, his young blood wakening at the exercise, his head clearing. He settled to a steady trot and, trotting home, he swerved suddenly so that when he dropped down into the Home Park he was taking a direct way, not to his father's Castle, but to Petula's home. He would ask Petula first.

She was coming down the steps as he reached the house somewhat breathlessly. She too wore black against which her little pointed face was made smaller and more ethereal.

'Henry!' she exclaimed. 'My darling, whatever is the matter?'

'Nothing,' Henry panted, 'except that I wanted to tell you somethin'. Wait, love, until I get m'y breath back.'

'Then I'll talk while you do,' she replied a trifle tartly, heading him back towards the Castle. 'You may have overlooked the fact that after tea, which I can safely assume is being served now, you are expected in the library for the reading of Grumpy's will.'

Henry's crestfallen, guilty expression set up a faint tremulous smile as, 'Lor,' he said weakly, 'I'd clean forgotten. We'll have to hurry. Are you comin' too?'

'I was so invited.'

'Well then, listen while we go.' He then proceeded to expound his thoughts and his intentions to her as they hurried along the path, ending, 'What do you say to that?'

Petula smiled sagely. 'I think that by all means you should tell your father and propose yourself as his aide, but do not be surprised if he turns you down. I have a distinct feeling that Grumpy will come again *in many of his aspects* to my future father-in-law.'

'Father have bouts of flamin' temper!' Henry exclaimed. 'Father go rollickin' up to London on reckless spendin' sprees!... Father?' He looked at her incredulously. 'Oh no, I can't believe that, it's not in his nature!'

'Maybe,' Petula agreed. 'I am only putting the point to you as a *possible* one to consider. Anyway,' she concluded, 'we shall soon know—but, darling, just remember what I said and we can discuss it all again later.'

While the family were assembling in the Library, Gyles slipped away to his mother, whom he found standing in her boudoir in her widow's weeds, veil drawn over her face, hands gloved and folded over a prayer book. 'Oh my darling,' she greeted him. He stepped forward, then took her in his arms, experiencing a shock as he did so at how fragile she felt and how much, much smaller she had become. So they stood, enfolded for quite a long time, then she put up her hands and unknowingly echoed the words which Charles Danement had muttered.

'The mantle of Elijah has fallen upon you, my son. You will

wear it exceedingly well and will do honour to our line. No, do not interrupt,' as Gyles attempted to speak, 'let me finish. You are very like your father in many ways. Oh I have watched you over the years. You must not think I have no eyes with which to see! So many people make that mistake with me. I have seen you stand back for your father over and over again. I have seen you rein yourself in to let him go by, but I have always known that under that rigid control which you have always imposed upon yourself, there lay just as much fire, just as much temperament. These things are all in the future, of course, and now is not the time for us to talk. I merely wished to tell you what I knew and explain to you what will eventually happen. For the moment I wish you to do something for me.'

'What may I do for you?' he asked simply.

She instructed him. 'Go ahead of me now. Clear me a way—the old way—through the picture gallery and down those little-used stairs to the door which leads to the Chapel. See no one is about. In five minutes' time I wish to take that way to the Chapel and when I get there I would like to be left undisturbed. I will find my own way back again. That is what I wish, so will you please arrange it for me?' He nodded, unable to speak. 'Then,' she said, flicking invisible specks of dust from his black coat, 'go now and rest assured I will send for you again just as soon as I am ready.'

Gyles went. He startled a little maid who was dusting in the Long Gallery, sent her scuttling off with the injunction 'to see everyone is gathered below stairs and take my instructions to Mr Sawby that there you all stay until I give you word to return to your upstairs duties.' The girl fled, and he glanced down at his watch. Three minutes to go! He walked on. He opened the requisite side door, set it wide with an old lion door stop, walked round the outer walls thereafter until he came to the Library windows. Then he reached and pushed one up, stepped over the sill, dusted his hands and crossed to the tea equippage where he accepted a cup of tea from the hands of his Aunt Dorothy. He vouchsafed nothing concerning his unorthodox entry among them. He simply made painstaking small talk, drawing in the Trusloves who more than ever before resembled two attenuated crows hesitant but hungry for the tid-bit, in the shape of the Will reading which was to come within reach of their beaks in a very few moments now.

The Will was duly read. It contained no great surprises except perhaps the extent of the dead peer's personal estate and the news that he had bequeathed one hundred thousand pounds to Petula Annabelle Danement or that he had caused to be written, 'whom I loved like a daughter, in the hope that it may prove to be a welcome gift to her from her "Grumpy" '.

The Trusloves took their leave of the family, promising to return in a week to begin the complex matters which would need to be settled thereafter. They were driven to the station in the Royce motor. The rest of the family went to their rooms to dress for dinner leaving only Gyles and Henry in the Library. Henry stood staring through one of the big windows on to the terrace outside. Gyles sank thankfully into an armchair, reached out and pulled the bell.

Sawby appeared. 'Ah, Sawby, do you know anything of my mother's movements?'

'Yes, my lord. Her ladyship is back in her room. Palliser was so good as to advise us of the fact so that the other servants could return to their duties.' He said nothing concerning his dinner instructions.

'Then please bring me a large brandy and soda. Henry, d'you want anythin'?' Gyles looked at his son.

'The same, sir, if you please,' he answered promptly.

They waited in silence. Sawby returned with the two drinks, ascertained his presence was no longer required and went out closing the doors behind him.

'Is your problem urgent?' Gyles inquired abruptly.

'In one sense, yes. In another no. It *can* wait if you wish.'

Gyles debated silently. 'No,' he decided, 'I prefer you to tell me now.'

Henry looked around the room thinking how it always seemed to be his lot to have to take the plunge one way or the other in this 'confounded Library'. He took a long pull at his brandy, set the glass down and plunged in. 'I want to leave Oxford.'

'Think I can't cope adequately without your assistance?'

'Not at all. Thought I might help, that's all.'

'Well oblige me by stayin' where you are,' Gyles sipped reflectively then resumed. 'Let me put it like this. You need Oxford, it's part of your trainin'. When you come down we can have another talk. Do not think I am failin' to appreciate your offer. In short, I believe you have borne yourself exceedin' well over the past three days, given me immense support too if you did but know, but I will not have your young life interfered with in any way because of what has happened. *I* think you should go back and *I* shall be obliged if you could bring yourself to agree with me without any wearisome arguments as to why you should not.'

'I see, sir.' It was Henry's turn to reflect once more but prudence did not come easily and suddenly he blurted out. 'That's exactly what Pet said you would say. I think that girl knows a sight more about my family than I do myself!'

'Your grandfather held that opinion,' said Gyles evenly.

'Do you, sir?' the question flashed out.

'Yes, I do. I think Petula has a demmed fine head on her shoulders. In many ways—if indisputably not in her appearance—she is old for her years. You have chosen well, Henry. Shall we leave it at that?' Gyles sipped again, then abruptly shot out a question of his own. 'What was the other matter?'

Henry stalled. 'How did you guess . . . I mean . . . oh lor . . .' his hand flew to his hair and he rumpled it distractedly.

'Well why in the world don't you sit down and stop prowlin' about like a damned leopard in a cage? Come on now, lay it on the line, there's a good chap, the dressin' bell will be goin' any minute."

'Oh hell,' said Henry, 'it's so difficult!'

Gyles raised an eyebrow at his son. 'Would you like me to tell you then?' he enquired more gently.

'How do you know, sir?'

'I think I know the workin's of your mind by now. It's about your grandfather's words, isn't it? . . . after he had taken his last toss.' Then Gyles repeated them, ' "Open the Box" '.

'Yessir,' Henry stammered, 'that was it. He knew what I had always felt about it. It seemed fantastic but . . . well . . . he did say it. . . . A number of us heard him.'

'I among them,' Gyles agreed, reaching for a pipe and drawing a tobacco jar towards him.

'I must admit it surprised me,' he continued. 'No, it did more than that, it startled me. Why, when the sands were runnin' out for him, did he even think about the Box? It doesn't make sense on the face of it.'

Henry could only repeat lamely, 'But he said it, didn't he, sir?'

'Yes,' Gyles replied, 'he said it.' It seemed now that his whole attention was upon the successful tamping of his pipe. 'I know full well he did and there's the rub. . . .'

Henry ventured, 'You think there's more to it than meets the eye?'

'Yes, I do,' Gyles met his son's eyes. 'I am uneasy and yet I have no reason for feelin' as I do. I expect I am feelin' the strain a bit, as all of us must be in fact. There's nothin' to influence me against openin' the Box anyway. Nothin' in the old records against it, more than ever nothin' in view of what m'father said. They were his last words, "*Open the Box*", just like that.'

'Then will you?'

Father and son looked at each other. Henry's eyes were eager, Gyles' were shadowed with sadness and . . . a suspicion of sternness was there too. 'Why do you want me to open the Box?' he enquired, 'I want to know more of your motive.'

'I don't think I know rightly m'self, sir.'

'Well try to find out, look inwards. Nine hundred years, remember, is a deuce of a long time.'

'I know that too.' Again Henry's hand flew to his head.

'And stop makin' your head look like Strewelpeter for heaven's sake,' his father exclaimed irritably.

Henry's disarming grin flashed out. 'You said that exactly like the old octogenarian!' he exclaimed. 'Pet said you would grow to be like him!'

'Herrumph!' said Gyles, frowning mightily. 'I repeat my question, Henry. Why *should* we suddenly break with tradition after centuries. . .?'

Henry stared into the fire. He seemed to find there something to help him. 'I think . . .' he began, 'it is probably because I don't give a tuppenny for tradition . . . by itself. It has to have meaning . . . and this does not . . . for me, anyway. Yes, that *is* what I am drivin' at. It just happened that no one opened the Box after Henri died. Then it became a useless habit instead of a tradition worth upholding. Father, can you possibly remember what the Lady Mathilde said when she sent her eldest son to England to give the Box to Henri?'

'I could never forget,' Gyles said evenly. He took out his monocle and began to polish it assiduously before beginning to quote the words which had been spoken in the eleventh century. He repeated what had been said by the Lady Mathilde's eldest son to his younger brother in the Kent castle. . . . 'But first,' he

said, 'let me set the scene for you. . . .' He then told of how
Edouard had crossed to England after the Lady Mathilde's death
and how he came upon Henri with the King. How he hurried
Henri away from the court into his private quarters and there
told him of their mother's death, how she announced to Edouard
that she was dying, despatched a messenger to him while he was
out hunting. Then she was shriven. Stage by stage, Gyles recounted the drama saying, 'When Edouard came she was abed.
On seeing him she withdrew a great casket from beneath the furs
which covered her saying, "Bear this to Henri, for I do tell you,
my eldest son, that I have the gift of seeing forward at this time",
then she said, "the thing within this casket is of no value so I
take nothing from your inheritance!" Then she prophesied that
the line would die out in France, as indeed it did, save for some
distant connections. She bade Edouard, "Charge Henri that he
treat the contents of this casket as an heirloom to his descendants"
and bid him pass the word on thus to *his* firstborn and so on down
the line. She commanded, "Charge Henri thus, for while he does
as I have said there will be Lormes who will seed themselves, put
down good roots and bear fruits even beyond my vision." She
foretold that all would weave themselves into the English pattern,
hold fast, gain stature and flourish . . . then she died . . . but
before she died she rallied again from the apparent coma into
which she had sunk . . . and suddenly she laughed . . . and,
laughing, died.'

'But she said nothing about any embargo on opening the Box
nor did she prophesy any ill from so doing?'

'Not according to the records.'

'Well then, sir?' Henry rose abruptly and stood looking down
at his father, making of his words a question, but as he spoke so
the dressing bell sounded.

'Go and dress,' said Gyles sharply, 'we will continue this after
dinner.' And with that Henry had to be content.

CHAPTER 26

The Casket

No one went into the small drawing room when they were dressed. The sherries and the Madeiras remained untouched. Sawby sounded the dinner gong. His footmen took up their accustomed places. The family filed in slowly. Gyles, frowning deeply, walked to his father's place; Christine went to her mother-in-law's at the opposite end of the table. Then, as everyone was gathering around the table, the doors opened once more to reveal the little Dowager. The half-seated rose, Gyles started forward.

'Good evening, everyone,' said she with great composure, moving very stately despite her lack of inches towards her eldest son's right hand. They all watched in silence as she permitted Sawby to draw out her chair. She sat down. She made a slight motion with one hand, then spoke again: 'Henry, will you please regard this as your place at family occasions from now onwards,' and she gestured him to the chair upon her left. 'Now,' she said clearly, 'will you say Grace for us, Alaric dear, if you please?'

The Bishop obeyed. They all rallied to her fortitude and with the last words whispering away the servants proffered the first course. The little figure shook out her table napkin and quite deliberately examined the menu through her lorgnette. 'How kind of you, dear Christine, to order my favourite soufflé,' she commented, 'I do believe that I have quite an appetite. It must be the glorious spring weather.'

Inevitably they all began talking at once, but after a little, under the dominance of her iron control, they all achieved a measure of calm as the meal proceeded. Little was eaten but a steady flow of conversation was maintained—somehow—for had she not, by every calculated move she had made since those doors reopened to admit her, the *châtelaine*, made it as clear as if she had issued an edict upon the matter that life was to be resumed without further let or hindrance. Had she not stated without any need for word that for her part she could be relied upon to impose no mask of tragedy upon any of them, nor assume, other than in her apparel, that overnight her 'whole life's love had gone down in a day.' The word's of Swinburne's poem flashed into Gyles mind: 'I will say no word that a man might say whose whole life's love goes down in a day....' He gripped his hands together under the tablecloth, experiencing more pain in his mother's demeanour than in anything else he had endured since the moment of his father's passing.

When dessert had been served and with the port decanter at Gyles' elbow, the Dowager addressed her son. 'Gyles, I think we would all prefer to be together tonight. May we have your permission to stay, instead of making our customary withdrawal?'

'Lor, she is splendid!' Henry muttered under his breath to his Aunt Marguerite. He felt one hand moving involuntarily towards his head. Marguerite caught the movement, laid her own over it and whispered back.

'Good boy, steady now, one really cannot rumple one's head at the dinner table!' Henry looked at her helplessly and suddenly experienced an almost unbearable desire to laugh. Gyles was dismissing the servants. As the door closed behind them the Dowager put down her napkin and looked around the table.

'Thank you for your support,' she said, suddenly forthright. 'I must now try to make you understand something which I must make clear to you in order to ease you all in respect of myself.' She clasped her hands together on the tablecloth, pushing the dessert plate aside to do so. 'I wish you to appreciate the fact that I am not a bereaved widow at all, nor do I in any case find such a role acceptable. I am a separated person under the will of God, for I cannot stress too strongly to you all that I have no shadow of doubt that in His time, *we* shall be together again. I have always held the belief that this is so. Alaric,' she turned her head slightly to her brother-in-law, 'you must forgive me if my words shock you, or cause you any pain, for that I am extremely reluctant to do in any circumstance, more especially after you have been so nonpareil to us all over your brother's death.' Bishop Alaric simply bent his head and made no attempt to reply, so the little figure continued.

'What I must tell you, my family, is very simple. It is very rare indeed for the final great mercy to be granted to any two people who have lived and loved together for many years. I mean, of course, a simultaneous passing which is the hope of all whose lives are inseparably entwined. It has not happened to *us*. Therefore I consider it a sacred charge upon me, in the absolute conviction which I now hold, that I contain myself in patience, live my life as my other half ... would have wished and bear myself with fortitude and gratitude too for the infinite happiness which was ours for so many years. In this I hope for and most humbly ask your support and understanding.'

She let the ensuing silence lie. She seemed, in fact, looking at her clasped hands, to be listening into it; to be hearing sounds which were beyond the hearing of the rest. Then, after what seemed a very long time, she sighed once more as if putting all that mattered most behind her. Eventually she managed a smile, looked at her son and said quite briskly, 'And now, my dear, I feel that I would very much enjoy a small glass of that port wine if so be I can persuade you to circulate it.'

Gyles started, hurriedly did as he was requested, so by the time the port had completed its circuit he had made *his* decision.

'Then, mother,' he said, 'may I do what I have always done through my life and ask that you decide for me and indeed for Henry what we should do over a matter which is seemingly of great import to Henry. I should add here that I have no feelings about the matter either way.' Christine, eyes brimming, was watching intently from the opposite end of the long table. Now those eyes registered surprise. Henry's head came up with a jerk.

'The Box?' queried the Dowager, with muted voice.

'Yes mother, the Box. We had not thought ... after the matter was raised by m'father three years ago that it would become a further matter for debate so soon ...' his voice trailed off. 'But ... it ... has.... Would you consent, Mama, to our opening the Box?'

All eyes were upon the little figure who was once more examining her hands as if she had never seen them before and now found them objects of extreme interest to her. Then she lifted her eyes to her eldest son and, with a deep sigh, spoke. 'Yes, my dear,' she replied tonelessly, 'I can see no possible reason why not. Did not your father say at the last, "Open the Box"?' So saying she rose. 'Shall we therefore await you in the library, my dear?'

Below stairs, a scullery maid, busy with the dinner washing-up, was startled by a knock at the outer door. Hurriedly wiping her hands upon her apron, she scurried to the Steward's Room and poked her mob-capped head around the door. 'Begging your pardon, Mr Sawby, but there is someone knocking at our outer door.'

'Then answer it, girl!' said Sawby sharply. 'Answer it, and I will follow. Hurry along now don't dawdle!'

He followed her out into the Servants' Hall, pausing first to struggle out of his alpaca coat and into his black one. By the time he was half-way across the big room, he could see that the visitor was Plum who came hesitantly into the Servants' Hall. He stood there twisting his cap into a mangled rag. He was the epitome of distress and indecision.

'Good evening, Mr Plumstead.' In the presence of the female servants gathered at their sewing around the big table Sawby spoke formally, but inwardly he was shocked by the man's appearance. 'Please to follow me,' he continued, turning about. Plum trailed after him. The door closed upon the pair and then the whispering began around the sewing table.

'The rest of the senior servants have retired, somewhat over-exhausted by the events of the past few days,' Sawby explained, busying himself with a bottle and two glasses. 'Take off your coat and sit down in Mrs Parsons' chair by that nice warm fire. She won't be seen again so we can be nice and private.'

'Ar,' said Plum blankly. He obeyed Sawby but he only perched on the extreme edge of the old chair. Then he began staring into the coals.

Sawby extended a filled glass. 'Drink that down,' he urged, 'you look exhausted. The world will seem a better place after you set that coursing through your veins.'

'I'll be surprised,' Plum muttered. He sipped obediently, however, and instantly resumed his staring into the coals. This continued for a full five minutes. Sawby waited patiently. His old friend and colleague rather frightened him.

'You're in a state of shock, that's what you are,' he said at last, not meaning to speak aloud.

'Yes,' said Plum lifting his head, 'and so would you be, Arthur, if you wos to find yourself in my di-lemma. It's not knowing which is right nor which is wrong, not nohow and yet them words wos said and how'm I to interpret them, I should wish to know, when 'im as said them is lying cold in his grave?' He choked and relapsed once more into his coal-gazing.

'Tell them to me,' Sawby urged. 'Two heads is always better than one. You can try, anyway. After all, that is why you came, isn't it?'

Plum turned his head again. 'Yes,' he said, 'that is why I come.' He struggled within himself. He fished for a bandana handkerchief, blew his nose, stuffed the bright cotton back into his jacket pocket and spoke. 'When 'is lordship fell I lef' 'er ladyship. I 'ad no option. It was done without no thought. Some'ow I went down that bank as the leather broke . . . I think I slid the bank, then I was through the water. I saw the 'ole thing of course. Then I took 'is lordship's 'ead in me arms and he said, "*Don't.*" Ee said it twice, Arthur, and after that I thort 'eed gorn. By then Mr Gyles was there and Mr 'Enery and, oh, there was a milling crown around, and then 'is lordship spoke agin. Ee said, "*Open the Box.*" He said it loud and clear and then,' tears were now pouring down the piteous face, 'and then,' Plum repeated, ' 'ee died!'

Sawby asked gently, 'Did Mr Gyles, 'is lordship I should say, did he hear, and Mr Henry?'

'Yes . . . but don't you see, Arthur, they didn't 'ear the '*don't*'. At the time it didn't seem to be of no importance, but then I got to thinkin'. I 'aven't slept much since it 'appened. I thort and I thort and suddenly it come to me it might 'ave bin summink *of* importance. He could 'ave said "*Don't open the Box.*" 'O course, it don't mean nothink to me nowise! But I went on thinkin' and worryin' and the words ran round in my 'ead. I come to the point where it seemed as if it might be that 'e tried to say all them words at once, which give 'em a contradickory meanin' . . . "*don't open the Box*"; but 'is strength was failin' fast and first time 'e only mannidged the one word "*don't*" and then maybe 'e was jus' ramblin' in 'is . . . in 'is larst moments. Wot do you think, Arthur?'

Sawby repeated the words. First he said thoughtfully, adding ' "*Don't*"—you know, Plum, that might have been because you moved his poor head.'

'Ezzakerly,' Plum nodded woefully.

'Then again,' Sawby debated, 'wot would the box bit mean? "*Don't open the Box*" would seem to have more meaning but as I know nothing whatsoever about any box it seems unlikely.'

'Wot should we do?' Instinctively Plum counted on his friends.

'Tell 'is lordship Mr Gyles,' said Sawby decisively, 'and let him make sense of it, but look here,' Sawby leaned forward, 'it's more than my life is worth to disturb them now. They decided to stay in the dining room for port. There was something afoot, though believe me I do not know what it could be. They dismissed me. I'll go upstairs if you like in a minute and see if those dining room doors are still fast-closed, but if they are you will simply have to wait.'

Plum looked up, suddenly eager. 'But you think I should tell?'

Now it was the butler's turn to stare into those glowing coals. His mind was turning over those words, seeking a logical solution, accepting that, in *his* knowledge there was none. At length he spoke, saying, 'Yes, I think you should,' on which he rose with a sigh, put down his emptied glass and added reassuringly, 'Now just you sit here quietly and I will go upstairs and see what is happening.'

He hurried up the stairs. As he reached the green baize door he almost cannoned into George who was coming through with a tray.

'Begging your pardon, Mr Sawby,' the footman apologised, stepping back.

'Never mind that, George. *Where* did you get that trayload?'

'From the dining room,' stammered George. 'I came down the front stairs, the doors was open, so I went in. But the library doors are tightly closed and as I went in so 'is lordship put his 'ead round the dining room door and said, ever so stern, "ah, George, we are all in the library and we do not wish to be disturbed until we ring." '

'Thank you, George.' Sawby inclined his head. 'Pray continue to clear away. I am going to the Steward's Room and I do not wish to be disturbed either until I call, is that clearly understood?'

'Yes, Mr Sawby, said George meekly. Sawby turned away. When he re-entered the Steward's Room he saw that Plum had not moved. The little man looked up eagerly, however.

'Well?' he asked.

Sawby told Plum what had passed, ending, 'So we have no alternative but to wait. Now, do you understand?' He spoke as to a child. Indeed Plum resembled nothing more than a shocked, bewildered, very aged child. 'That bell system up there,' Sawby pointed over the mantelpiece, 'will tell me when the library bell rings. Then I will go up myself and ask his lordship if he will see you. In the meantime we can only wait,' and, so saying, he reached for the brandy bottle and poured more into Plum's glass.

As Plum sat, so did the Dowager, bolt upright in one of the great leather chairs drawn near to the leaping log flames under the chimneypiece. She simply waited, staring at those flames, even as Plum did likewise in the room below stairs. The family had repeated her late husband's last words to her. Oddly, she reflected, they did not seem to be the confirmation they were considered to be by the rest of the family. They made no sense! She knew that her Justin had reverenced and respected the Box, or Casket as he had always preferred to call it, but that so far as she knew—who knew him so very well—the object had never loomed very large upon his horizon save as part of the heritage, part of the link with the coming to England of Henri de Lorme of Normandy. 'Why then?' the question remained in her mind. 'Why should he in his moment of death see fit to speak of it at all?'

The family were scattered around the big old library. Petula on a large black leather sofa with Henry holding her hand... Primrose and Christine side by side on another sofa... Bishop Alaric in an armchair drawn close to the great circular table which centred the room... Gabrielle and Eustace... Marguerite and Dorothy... John in the shadow, drawn farther back than the rest... Rosemary with her Charles who had hurried home from France in time for the funeral... Priscilla... Christian... Claire. Only Gyles was missing and even now he was summoning George to open the doors for him as his hands were holding something bulky which the footman could not see.

Gyles, having withdrawn the Casket from its niche in the Chapel, had taken a choirboy's surplice, which was hanging in the vestry and with it carefully wrapped the heirloom to conceal it from prying eyes. Now he carried it to the table. The click of the opening doors aroused his mother who looked round immediately, an expression of extreme bewilderment upon her face.

The rest of them rose and came towards the table. Very carefully, Gyles spread the white material out over its surface. As he did so little red-brown flakes fell away upon it. Some fell upon the floor, too, disclosing an immeasurably rusted iron box measuring some twelve inches by ten by eleven. Gyles lifted the lid which made a groaning sound in protestation and sent up another little shower of those flakes as he laid it back. Then he put his hands inside and withdrew the Casket. For a moment he stood there in silence looking down at what Edouard had brought from Normandy. The leather was dreadfully fragile. It scarcely seemed able to contain whatever it was that lay inside. Great cracks and splits had broken between the struts. As Gyles attempted to insert the key the whole lock came away in a little cloud of those red-brown rusty flakes.

He paused. 'So old!' he marvelled, 'so very old. I do believe, Mama, that had we left it for another century it must have fallen away altogether!' He laid the lock down on the surplice. Bishop Alaric's lips were moving as if in prayer, one hand was lifted to embrace his dangling cross. Abruptly he rose and moved towards the rest.

He took two further steps which brought him face to face with his nephew across the table. Then he lifted one hand to sketch the sign of the cross over the Casket. Slowly, very carefully, Gyles raised the old lid which likewise gave at the rotten hinge-holds and came away into his hands. The Bishop looked down. They all looked down, but as he saw what lay within the Bishop snatched his hand back as if he had burned it in a fire. Gyles' long thin fingers delved. There was a rattling, clinking sound, and then he held up the object which had lain there undisturbed throughout the centuries.

It, too, was irretrievably rusted, but its hinges held. The tiny padlock dangled secure upon it and in the interstices of the fore-piece all could see the *fleur de lys* which had been cut from the metal. It, too, showed very clearly as, white to the lips, Gyles Aynthorp lifted the thing for everyone to see.

He held it for that circle of frozen faces. They might indeed have so looked had it been the Gorgon's head which he was holding up aloft for all to see. Then the Dowager spoke from her chair, entirely without emotion in her voice.

'*That*,' she said very clearly, '*must be the Lady Mathilde's Chastity Belt.*'

Henry was staring as if hypnotised. Then he spoke the *vale* to that little scene. Hand to mouth he shouted the words into the quiet room. 'It is, Grandmama, it is ... no wonder the Lady Mathilde ... died ... laughing!'

Des Cotils, Jersey, April 14th, 1974

Appendix

DINER

le 2ieme Septembre 1907

Le Menu

Colchester Natives
Caviar aux Blinis à la Muscovite

Crème aux Amandes Normande
Consommé Royale
Les Amuses Gueules du Chef

Les Soufflés d'Ecrivisses Guillaume Le Conquerant
Angelets à la Coigny
Marceline de Cailles Chantilly

Ponche à la Romaine

Selle de Chevreuil à la Crème à la Normande
Mousse de Foie Gras du Château

Coeur de Romaine
Fonds d'Artichauds Lucullus

Bombe Alexandre
Les Friandises

Dessert

Les Vins

Champagne Moët et Chandon 1898
Vodka Cuvée Privé de S.A. Prince Dimitiri Kandaourow

Grand Montrachet 1889
Johannisberg de Prince de Metternich Cachet bleu et or 1893
Château Margaux 1875

Romanée Conti 1870

Champagne Veuve Cliquot Riche 1898

Terrantez 1790

Oporto Croft 1870

Delamain Extra Fine Vieille Grande Champagne 1830

The Lormes' Foxhunter Sandwich
(filched from the Lorme Family 'Receipt' book)

Ingredients
　1 tin loaf (made by Mrs Parsons, now called a 'sandwich' loaf)
　1 6 oz. thick fillet steak
　Freshly milled black peppercorns
　Gros Sel (use Malden Sea Salt *faute de mieux*)
　Grated horse-radish (must be fresh)
　English made mustard

Method
Grill steak 'rare to medium-rare'. Cut the two end crusts from the loaf with a ⅓rd of an inch crust. Season cooked steak with salt and pepper; spread both crusts lightly with mustard. Clap above and below steak. Wrap thickly in blotting paper (use waxed paper today). Tie securely with fine trussing string. Place under a letterpress, tighten the screw gently and steadily. Leave for half an hour. By this time, due to pressure, the steak's juices will have impregnated all the crust's inner crumb while the crust itself prevents these from escaping. Pack in a sandwich box lined with white paper (use aluminium kitchen foil today).

The Lormes' Stirrup Cup

We use it at our traditional Christmas Party when the drive is spattered with glowing braziers, all is lit by old Victorian street lamps, the entrance is dressed overall with bay, laurel and scarlet ribbons. Guests on arrival are served with this heartening beverage while being serenaded by Carol Singers carrying swinging lanterns. A lit Christmas tree stands in the central drive bed and welcoming candles are set in all the front windows of our Queen Anne house. We adore this.

Ingredients
  2 bottles white rum from Jamaica
  2 bottles brandy
  4 pints water
  4 lemons
  4 oranges
  1 flat teaspoon mixed spices
  3 torn bay leaves
  4½ oz. green tea (obtainable still from Mr Laity, The Tea Shop, St Ives, Cornwall, or substitute the best only Orange Pekoe tea)
  ¾ lb. unrefined (beige) loaf sugar (substitute soft, brown dark pieces sugar)
  1 small stick cinnamon, 1 split vanilla pod, generous eggspoon of nutmeg from the nut

Method
Make, rest for 30 minutes, then strain the tea. Sweeten to taste, add cinnamon, nutmeg and leave until quite cold. Then place in a very thick pan to heat to, but not reach, boiling point. At the moment of service rub loaf sugar pieces on oranges and lemons until these crumble and turn yellow/orange. Do this into a large silver punch bowl or make in two half batches in smaller punch bowls. Strain in the juice of both citrus fruits. Heat rum and brandy together *without* boiling. Set alight to mixture, ladle up and down high to cause spirits to burn well for one minute. Douse flames with very hot infused tea, stir and serve into heated glass or silver goblets. If the former add a silver spoon to each glass one to avoid any risk of cracking.